DEADSTOCK
AN ANT & BEA MYSTERY

RACHEL WARD

SANDSTONE PRESS

First published in Great Britain by
Sandstone Press Ltd
Dochcarty Road
Dingwall
Ross-shire
IV15 9UG
Scotland

www.sandstonepress.com

The publisher acknowledges subsidy from
Creative Scotland towards publication of this volume.

ISBN: 978-1-912240-42-5
ISBNe: 978-1-912240-43-2

Cover design by David Wardle at Bold and Noble
Typeset by Iolaire Typography Ltd, Newtonmore
Printed and bound by Totem, Poland

This book is dedicated to my dad, David Neish (1932-2018) and to my mum, Shirley, who looked after him with kindness and compassion until the end.

Prologue

Nobody was around to see the car draw to a halt on the road bridge. There was hardly any traffic on the Kingsleigh bypass and the occupants waited, engine off, until there were no headlights carving a path through the darkness below them.

'Now?'

'Now.'

They got out of the front seats and helped their passenger from the back. He was unhelpfully heavy but they managed to prop him up. His head and torso flopped onto the parapet.

'Are you sure he's dead?'

'Yeah. I'm sure. But if he isn't, he soon will be.'

They heaved his legs up, so he was lying along the top.

'One, two, three . . .'

It didn't take much force to tip him over and off.

There was an eerie silence for a second or two, then a sickening noise – a thud, a crack – as he hit the tarmac of the hard shoulder, the sort of noise you'd never forget.

'That's it. All done. Let's get out of here.'

1

'All staff to the staffroom, please. Morning huddle starts in three minutes.'

The voice was female, but it wasn't Anna or Kirsty or any of the other staff Bea recognised. She sighed and checked her make-up again in the mirror. The megalashes were in place. Her eyebrows were pencilled to perfection. Her lippy was just the right shade of pillar box. But she got no satisfaction from her reflection. First day back after three days off over a disappointing New Year, and she wasn't feeling it.

'Morning huddle?' she said to Eileen, who was running a brush through her hair at the mirror next to her.

Eileen still wasn't officially talking to her, blaming Bea for her son, Dean, getting the sack from Costsave, but she managed a grunt, and, 'It'll be something to do with the new manager.'

'Oh yeah. He starts today, doesn't he? George Prentice, Anna said. From Swindon.'

'Swindon.' Eileen said the word like it was something particularly unsavoury she'd found in the gutter. She put her hairbrush in her bag and slouched out of the room.

Bea sighed again. She wished Dot was there. They could have had a proper gossip. Things hadn't been the same at work since Dot had been on sick leave with a broken hip. She was well on the way to recovery and was likely to be back, at least part-time, soon. But not today. Bea would have to deal with the new regime on her own.

She put her make-up bag away and walked along to the staffroom. All the usual faces were there: Bob-on-Meat – Dot's not-so-secret admirer – Eileen, Kirsty, Joe, Anna. Bea couldn't help thinking about those who weren't there: Dot, of course, but also Ginny, murdered on her way home from Costsave's get-together in the pub, as well as the man who had murdered her.

She was wondering whether to fight her way into the room or stand on the edge, when someone tapped her on the shoulder. She turned round to see Ant grinning down at her.

'All right, Bea?' he said. 'Have a good New Year?'

'Yes, thanks, Ant. You know, quiet.'

'Night in with Queenie?'

'No, I went to the pub with my friends. They're all at uni. It was . . .I dunno . . .it was all right.' She couldn't face telling him that they didn't have much to talk about these days, that the squad they'd called the Four Musketeers at school seemed to be the Three Musketeers and Bea nowadays.

Ant pulled a face.

'At least my night was better than that guy they found on the bypass,' said Bea. 'Awful.'

'Yeah, I heard about that. Do you know who it was?'

'No, no one does. Such a sad thing. Anyway, how about you? How was your New Year?'

'Had a great time. Got wrecked, snogged the face off a girl,' he said.

'Yeah? Who's the lucky lady?'

He looked a bit shamefaced. 'I don't actually know.' Bea's elegant eyebrows shot up. 'The details are a bit hazy. I'd had an absolute skinful.'

'Did you get a number?'

'Nah, and I've lost my phone and all. Woke up on my bedroom floor about teatime on New Year's Day with empty pockets and big gaps in my memory. Must've been a good night. Still feeling a bit rough, though. Should be off sick really.'

Bea sniffed. 'Self-inflicted wound. No sympathy here.'

'Ha, you're just jealous. Wonder what the new bloke's like.'

They'd shuffled into the room and found a place by the back wall. It was getting quite crowded now. Bea stood on tiptoe and looked towards the front, where Neville, the deputy manager was standing, clutching his clipboard to his chest. There was a woman beside him, thirty-something, in a rather expensive-looking jacket. Her make-up was immaculate and her shoulder-length blonde hair was cut in a sharp, smooth bob. She was looking round, scanning the faces in front of her. She was smiling, but the smile didn't quite reach her slate grey eyes.

'Reckon the new bloke's a woman, Ant,' Bea said.

'Really?' said Ant, just as Neville tucked his clipboard under his arm and clapped his hands vigorously together.

'Okay, everybody, a bit of quiet please,' he said. He waited for the noise to die down, then, 'Welcome to the start of a new year at Costsave. And welcome to our first –' he looked nervously at the woman standing beside him, who nodded encouragement, '– our first huddle.' He ignored the ripple of tittering. 'I'd like to introduce our interim manager, Mrs Prentice, who would like to say a few words. Mrs Prentice.'

'Thank you, Neville. It's George Prentice, actually. I'm not a great believer in titles. We're all equal here. I'm very happy to be managing the Kingsleigh store. I know that last year was a difficult time for you, but I don't want to dwell on the past. It's a new year. This is a new start for me and for you. I've had a very clear brief from HQ. This store has the potential to be the top performer in the region, if not the whole country, and I'm going to make sure we fulfil that potential. I want every customer to be a happy customer. Every conversation is an opportunity to sell. You'll find I'm very hands on –'

'Steady,' said Ant, under his breath.

'Shut up,' Bea hissed.

'I'll be there with you on the shop floor, in the stores, in the delivery yard, morning, noon and night. I want to see you smiling and I want to see you selling. I'll be reporting today's sales figures at tomorrow morning's huddle.' She checked her watch. 'Okay, the store opens in five minutes. To your stations. Let's make today a good day.'

She swept out of the room, closely followed by Neville and Anna, leaving the staff agog at what they'd just seen and heard.

'What do you reckon?' said Ant.

'Pretty impressive,' said Bea. 'I don't think she'll stand any nonsense.'

'Yeah, that's what I'm worried about.'

'Come on, Ant. You'll be all right. What are you on today?'

'Paracetamol and Red Bull.'

'No, what job are you on?'

'Outdoors. Trolleys, bins and recycling. Do you know how cold it is out there?'

'Fresh air'll do you good.' She looked at Ant's dull, spotty skin and bloodshot eyes. 'Well, kill or cure.'

Ant put on his Costsave-issue thick, padded fluorescent jacket. He added a beanie hat and some gloves before following Bea out of the room. They parted company at the bottom of the stairs – Ant using the staff door to get out into the back yard, and Bea heading for the shop floor and checkout number six.

She went through her warm-up routine: check and adjust

the chair, switch on the terminal and log in, inspect the conveyor belt and keyboard and give them a wipe down, moisturise hands. She was ready for business at the precise moment that Neville reached the front door with his big bunch of keys. First through the door was, of course, Costsave's most reliable customer. Smelly Reg, there for his cigarettes and today's *Racing Post*. Bea watched him shuffle towards her checkout. She wasn't fond of his musty uncared-for aroma, but, after a few days away from the store, she was strangely pleased to see him. Things were getting back to normal.

'Morning, Reg,' she said, as he placed his two items on the belt. 'Happy New Year!'

'Don't know about that,' Reg mumbled back.

Bea beeped his shopping through. 'Well, the way I look at it, this year can't be as bad as last year, can it? So perhaps it is a happy one.'

'Hmph,' said Reg. He dropped his receipt on the floor and shuffled off towards the front door.

Bea sighed. She could have had a good laugh with Dot about Reg being a ray of sunshine, but checkout five was empty. Come back soon, Dot, she thought. I need you.

There were only three of them on checkouts to start with, and a steady stream of early birds kept them busy. Her regular customers were glad to see her back, and Bea was glad to see them. There was Norma, with her tartan trolley. And Charles, whose golden retriever always waited outside the front door for him, tied to one of the special D-rings for dogs, with a complimentary bowl of water nearby.

At lunchtime, Ant wasn't in the staffroom and, finding no one else to gossip with, Bea put on her coat and went looking for him. She found him by the cardboard cage, where boxes were broken up and stored before being taken for recycling. He had his back to her, and Bea thought he might be having a crafty cigarette, although she couldn't see any smoke. She was about to give him a serious bollocking for causing a fire hazard, when he spun round.

'Don't come any closer,' he said. He stepped towards her and spread out his arms a little, like he was trying to block the view.

'What? Why not?'

'There's something...I found something in there. It's not very nice.'

'Don't be silly, Ant. I'm a big girl. I can cope.' She bustled past him and then stopped. The 'something' was crumpled up in the corner on top of the cardboard. An old grey painty rag, Bea thought. The paint had smeared on the boxes in front of it. She moved a step closer and realised that it wasn't paint. It was blood. And the rag wasn't a rag. It was fur and skin and bone. 'Oh Jesus.' She put her hand up to her mouth and turned away, blundering out past Ant.

'I told you, didn't I?'

Bea leaned against the rough brick wall, sucking in some clean air, trying not to be sick. Ant joined her, reaching into his pocket for a cigarette and lighting up.

'What is it, Ant? Is it a rat?'

'Think it's a cat. Was a cat. Used to be.'

'What's happened to it?'

'I dunno. Thought it might have been hit by a car and crawled in here, but not in that state.'

'It looks ...' Bea swallowed hard to fight the bile that was rising up towards her throat, 'it looks...shredded.'

'Mm. Poor little bugger.' He tipped his head up and blew a long stream of smoke into the cold air.

'What are you gonna do?' said Bea.

'Do? Stick it in the general waste, I suppose.'

'You should report it.'

'Who to? The RSPCA? Bit late for that, innit?'

'Someone in management?'

'George? I don't think so. Hello, welcome to your first day here, you don't know me, but I'm Ant and this is a shredded cat. First impressions count, Bea. I wanna keep this job.' He stamped out the cigarette stub on the ground.

'It's just that someone should know about this. For a start, the owner's going to come looking for that cat.'

'Unless it's a stray. I'm just going to get rid, Bea. Easiest way.' Bea looked at him doubtfully. 'Honestly, Bea, if it was your pet moggy would you want to see it like this?'

Bea sighed. 'Okay, then,' she conceded, 'but let me do this first.' She whipped out her phone and started taking pictures.

'Jesus, Bea, what are you doing?'

'I just want to have a proper record, before you destroy the evidence.'

Ant held up a warning finger. 'Evidence? This isn't a crime scene, Bea.'

Bea started checking the images on her screen. 'Looks like this cat's been tortured and then murdered. If that's not a crime, what is?'

'It was probably a fox, Bea. Are you going to track it down and charge it?'

'Did a fox throw it in here?' Bea asked.

'Maybe. I've seen a cat chuck a mouse about. And there were those killer whales on the telly, weren't there, flinging seals about? Perhaps it's the same.'

'No,' said Bea. 'Someone's done this. It was dumped here.'

'And you're going to find out who.'

'If I can. They shouldn't get away with it.' She checked the time on her phone. 'Damn. Lunch break's nearly over.'

'Have you had anything to eat?' said Ant.

'No. Don't think I could now.'

'Mm, me neither. Jeez, there are some sick people about, aren't there?'

Bea went back to the locker room to hang up her coat, glad to make herself scarce before Ant disposed of the body. As she went back to the checkouts, she tried not to think about it too much, but she couldn't help remembering the images on her phone and wondering if there was someone in Kingsleigh knocking on their neighbours' doors at that very moment, asking if they'd seen a grey cat.

At four o'clock, Bea spotted Neville walking towards checkout six with a young man by his side. The guy was shorter than him. He had his hair drawn back into a bun, and a rough beard clinging to his jawline. He should have looked a mess, but he didn't. He looked as cool as fuck, and Bea's stomach gave a little flutter as they got nearer and then stopped by her checkout.

'Bea, this is Jay,' said Neville. 'He's going to do some late afternoon and evening shifts. He's worked in Costsave before, but not this branch, so he knows the ropes, but give him a hand if he needs one.'

'Yes, of course,' Bea said. 'Hi.'

Jay looked at Bea and smiled. 'Hiya.' His voice was lower than she expected, but soft-toned and warm, like he'd just gargled with honey. He reached forward and held his hand out. Bea shook it and it felt rough to her carefully moisturised touch. She looked up at him and noticed his eyes – one blue and one green.

'Wow, your eyes,' she said, cursing how much she sounded like a fangirl. 'Like David Bowie. Bet no one's ever said that before.'

'No,' he said, his voice deadpan this time. 'You're the first.' Then he winked his green eye, and Bea liked him even more.

Bea was clocking off at five and during the next hour there was a frustratingly busy flow of customers. She kept hoping for a lull so she could find out a bit more about Jay, but just as she thought there was a gap opening up another bunch of schoolkids with fizzy drinks and crisps, or a desperate parent on a nappy run would make a beeline for her till.

When five o'clock rolled round, Bea processed her final customer and logged out of her till. Jay was dealing with a rather harassed-looking early commuter, obviously heading home to cook tea for her family – bag of baking potatoes, ready-grated cheddar and a couple of tins of beans. She and Jay were chatting about the body on the bypass and what a shock it had been to see it on the news. It would have been rude to interrupt, but Bea didn't want to go without saying something. She waited until the baked-spuds-and-beans woman was putting her purse away and picking up her shopping bag, and swooped in.

'Coming back tomorrow, then?' she said.

'Yeah, I reckon.' He stretched his arms up above his head and cracked his knuckles. At that moment Ant sauntered along the checkouts and stopped casually near Bea.

'Walking home?' he said, and then, as if he was noticing Jay for the first time, 'Oh, all right?'

Jay nodded to him.

'This is Jay, Ant,' said Bea. 'Jay, this is Ant. If you ignore him long enough, he normally goes away.'

'Oi!' said Ant.

Jay pulled a face. 'Harsh.'

'Firm but fair,' said Bea, and noticed another little ripple of excitement in her stomach as Jay grinned at her.

Ant had noticed something too. 'Ha! David Bowie eyes.'

Bea and Jay exchanged a quick glance.

'No way,' said Jay. 'Did he have this too?'

'Yeah, man. He's famous for it. Look it up. Oh.' Realising he was being teased, Ant looked down at the floor and kicked at a pile of wire baskets. 'Yeah, right.'

'Come on, Ant,' said Bea. 'Time to go. Are you doing the same shift tomorrow, Jay?'

'Yup, four till ten.'

Bea's stomach gave a little flip. 'I'm on that one too,' she said. 'See you then!'

'What's up with you flirting with that numpty?' said Ant, as they walked across the car park.

'One: I wasn't flirting. And two: he's not a numpty. He seems okay.'

'Bea, I don't know if you noticed,' Ant explained carefully, 'but he's got a man bun.'

'So?'

'A *man bun*. That's all you need to know.'

'I think it's kind of cute.'

Ant rolled his eyes. 'Gah! Students. It's 'cos of people like him that people like me can't afford to live anywhere.'

'How do you work that out?'

'Landlords buying up all the houses to rent them out. Pushing the prices up. The only way I'm going to get a place is if I knock someone up and we go on the council list.'

'Charming,' said Bea. 'With an attitude like that, I'm surprised you haven't got a little family already. You must have girls queuing up.'

'Fighting them off, Bea. You know me. Still, there's always room for one more.' He put his arm round her shoulders.

Bea chose not to take him seriously. The only person that she knew for certain had dated Ant was her friend Dot, who was thirty years his senior, and that hadn't ended well. 'It's all right, Ant. I think I'll stick in the friend zone.'

Was that fleeting look on Ant's face relief or disappointment? Bea couldn't tell, and she didn't mind either way. She'd been sworn off relationships since she'd slept with Tom, the rather hot police constable, who had turned out not to be single.

Ant took his arm away from her shoulders and they walked

along towards the High Street. Bea heard the distinctive clip-clop sound of heels trotting behind them, as if someone was trying to catch them up. She turned around and saw Anna running in their direction.

'Hey, Anna,' Bea greeted her.

Anna acknowledged her but kept running. 'Can't stop. One of my girls didn't come home last night. I need to get back, check that she turned up.'

They stood aside and let her clatter past. 'Hope everything's okay,' Bea called out to her receding back. She knew that the 'girls' that Anna doted on were, in fact, rather fat, rather lovely pedigree cats called Bette and Joan, after the Hollywood screen sirens. They featured in the only photo Anna kept on her desk. Bea felt her stomach lurch.

She grabbed Ant's arm. 'Ant?'

'Yeah?'

'Anna's cats, the ones in the picture on her desk, they're grey, aren't they? They're Persian greys.'

2

It took a fraction of a second for the point she was making to register. Bea could actually see the moment when Ant put two and two together, because his jaw dropped a fraction and his eyes went wide.

'Oh, shit,' he said. 'You don't think?'

'I dunno. Maybe. Oh my God, Ant, what if it is? Can you catch her up?'

'And say what?'

'Just tell her I want to talk to her. Say it's urgent.'

'No, Bea. Her cat could be sitting at home, licking its bum, for all we know. It's not fair to frighten her. Have you got her number on your phone?'

'Yes.'

'Leave it for ten minutes, then. Let her get home, then give her a ring.'

'Yeah, you're right. Will you wait with me?'

'Okay. Can we go somewhere, though?' He rubbed his hands together. 'It's too chuffing freezing to hang around outside.'

Bea nodded her agreement. 'Corner caff?'

'Sounds good. Bea, what if it *is* her cat?'

'At least she'll know.'

'She can have the body, if she wants it.'

Bea frowned. 'I thought you threw it away.'

'Not exactly. It's in the freezer,' he said.

Bea screwed up her face. 'What?'

'I put the cat in the freezer, at work. I thought about what you said and I couldn't just bin it.'

'In with the *food*?'

'I wrapped it up in three plastic bags.'

'Jesus, Ant. *You'll* get binned if anyone finds out.'

'Shit, do you think so? I'll go and fetch it now, sneak in without anyone noticing. If it's Anna's we can give it back to her. If it's not, we can chuck it away.'

They scurried back across the car park and round to the staff entrance. The door opened from inside just as Ant was pushing against it and he stumbled forward, more or less on top of Neville. Taken by surprise, Neville was pushed back against the wall with Ant's face a couple of inches from his.

'Anthony!' he spluttered.

'I'm sorry. So sorry.' Ant regained his balance and put both hands on Neville's shoulders, helping to right him.

'You should look where you're going.'

'I didn't know you were there. Sorry, mate, Neville, Mister—'

Neville brushed Ant's hands away. 'I thought you'd clocked off.'

'Yes, I did. I just—'

Bea stepped forward. 'I forgot some shopping I'd left in the cold room. Ant was just fetching it for me.'

Neville sniffed. 'Well, you know you're not really supposed to put personal shopping in there.'

Bea caught Ant's eye and tipped her head towards the stores. Ant took the hint and scarpered.

'Yes, I know. It was just that the fish finger offer was too good to miss, so I nabbed a couple of packets at lunchtime. I won't do it again.'

'Well, it *is* a very good offer. I'm prepared to overlook it this time.'

'That's kind of you. Oh, I think you've got a bit of dust on you from the wall. Here,' Bea started brushing Neville's jacket with her hands.

Alarmed at the physical contact, Neville tried to sidle out of the door. 'Okay. Ah, thank you. I can deal with that.' And he was off, out into the cold evening, and making a beeline for his car in the staff car park.

Bea waited by the doorway. She checked her watch. It was at least ten minutes since they'd seen Anna. Ant reappeared, carrying the plastic bag.

'Come on,' said Bea. 'Let's go somewhere quieter and ring.'

They walked to a corner of the car park and leaned against the metal railing of one of the trolley parks. Bea dialled Anna's number.

'Hey, Anna. Just wondering if your cat got home safely.'

Anna's voice was tense and quiet. 'No, Bea. Joan's not here.' Anna's voice was tense and quiet. 'She's never done this before. She's never been out all night. Bette's beside herself.'

That explained the pitiful miaowing in the background. Bea took a deep breath. 'I'm so sorry, Anna. The thing is ...' She stopped, not knowing what to say next.

'What, Bea?'

'Anna, I don't want you to panic, but we—' Bea checked with Ant, who nodded his encouragement '—that is, Ant and me, we found a body, a cat's body, this afternoon. It probably isn't your Joan, but ...but it could be her. I'm so sorry.'

'You found her? Where?'

'It could be her. It was, she was, in the cardboard recycling, at the back of the shop.'

'The shop? What would she be doing at Costsave?'

'I don't know.'

'It can't be her. She never goes far from home.'

'Well, then. Sorry to alarm you. Hope she turns up soon.'

Bea was about to ring off when Anna said, 'Bea? You still there?'

'Yeah.'

'What colour is the . . .the cat you found?'

'Grey.'

'Short or long hair?'

'I'm not an expert, Anna. I guess, longish?'

She heard a gasp at the other end of line. 'Have you still got her?'

'Yeah, but—'

'I'd better come and have a look. Where are you?'

'We're still at the store. We could meet you halfway. We'll start walking.'

They met in the High Street, near the newsagents.

'Not here,' said Bea. 'Let's go outside the Leisure Centre.'

They walked along together, in a silent knot. Glancing sideways, Bea could see the tension in Anna's jaw. Near the entrance to the swimming pool there was a sort of colonnade over a wide stretch of pavement, well-lit, but with hardly anyone around. They stood near the wall, away from the road.

'Is that her?' Anna said, looking at the plastic bag in Ant's hand. He pressed his lips together and nodded. 'Okay. Let's do it.' Her words were businesslike, but there was a slight wobble in her voice. Cold air seemed to funnel between the concrete pillars, but Bea found herself becoming hot and sticky under the arms and across her chest.

Ant fumbled with the bags. He'd tied the handles up and there were several layers. Eventually, he peeled the plastic open and held it towards Anna.

She peered in. 'I can't see.'

Ant crouched down and put the bundle in front of him. He folded the sides of the bags over and over until the cat was revealed. Then he shuffled back, so that he wasn't casting a shadow onto it, and Anna stepped forward and knelt on the ground. She put a hand out and touched the animal's head, then gently stroked the length of its spine. The little body was stiff. Bea wondered if it was from the afternoon spent in the freezer or the effects of rigor mortis. Anna felt around the neck. The fur there was dark and bloody.

'I can't find a collar,' she said, her voice a dull monotone. 'Her throat's been cut.' The last word came out as a sort of yelp, as she started sobbing.

Bea crouched down now and put her arm round Anna's shoulders. 'Is it her?'

Anna squeaked her confirmation. 'It's Joan. It's my baby.'

Bea put the other arm round her and drew her close. 'I'm so, so sorry.'

They stayed together for a minute or more, then Anna drew away and started wiping her eyes and blowing her nose.

'Someone's done this,' she said, when she was able to talk again. 'Someone killed my cat.' She unfolded the sides of the bag and gathered the handles together.

'Do you want us to get rid of her?' said Bea.

Anna picked up the bag and cradled it like a baby. 'No,' she said. 'No, I can do that for her, at least. One last thing.'

Bea helped her to her feet. 'We'll walk you home.'

It wasn't far to Anna's flat. She had the ground floor of a small house in a terrace which faced onto a sort of square made from some old people's bungalows, a row of modern two-up two-downs and a couple of blocks of low-rise maisonettes.

'Are you going to be okay?' said Bea.

'Yes. I'll be fine.' It was one of those times, thought Bea, when 'I'll be fine' meant exactly the opposite, but she couldn't think of anything to do to help – except perhaps one thing.

'Anna,' she said.

'Yes?' Anna's look was sad, defeated.

'We'll get them. Whoever did this. We'll get them for you.'

Anna tipped her head sideways and looked as if she was about to say something, but then she just turned sadly away and let herself into her front door.

'Jeez, poor Anna,' said Ant.

'I know,' said Bea. She shivered.

'Do you want me to walk you home too? 'S not far. I don't mind.'

The Kingsleigh Stalker was behind bars, of course, waiting for his trial date, having been released from hospital, but the town still didn't feel like the safe place it used to be. Before all that, Bea hadn't given a second thought to walking home on her own. These days, she had to steel her nerve to do so.

'Actually, I think I'll call in on Dot. Wanna come?'

Ant looked down at the pavement. 'Nah. Don't think so. I'd only be in the way.'

'She misses you, you know,' said Bea. 'Not in that way, just to talk to. She told me.'

'Yeah, well, another time. I got a call from Mum earlier. She's cooking a chilli and she wants us all home for six. Sounded more like a threat than a promise.'

'Oh, okay. Good luck with that. See you tomorrow, then. We can talk about the cat killer then. I meant what I said to Anna. We've got to find who did that. They can't get away with it.'

Bea texted home to tell her own mum, Queenie, that she'd be late and walked on to Dot's little house. It was in the older part of town, a series of Victorian terraces near the river. When Dot answered the door, Bea was surprised to see she wasn't using a walking stick, even though it was only eight weeks since she'd broken her hip in a night-time misadventure.

They embraced in the doorway.

'Wow, Dot, you're looking great! No sticks!'

'I don't need them round the house any more. Still use one when I'm out and about.'

'That's brilliant.'

'Yes, I'm coming along nicely. Got a meeting with occupational health soon to talk about going back to work. Come on in and tell me all about it. First day back today – how was it? Wanna cup of tea or a drink drink?'

They settled in Dot's cosy living room with a couple of glasses of white wine. The coal-effect gas fire was on, the curtains were drawn and Bea sank happily back into Dot's comfy sofa and told her all about George and Jay and the grim discovery in the cardboard.

'It's all happening, babe,' said Dot. 'Weird thing about that cat, though. I bet it was foxes. There are loads of them round here. There are some living under the garden shed a couple of doors down. The neighbours feed them as well.'

'Do they? I'd love to see that.'

'They're not fluffy pets, Bea. They used to get into my dad's chickens when we were little. They'd kill every last one. Horrible it was.'

'It's just their nature, though, Dot. I love foxes, I do.'

'Hmm. They could easily do that to a cat, though.'

'It wasn't foxes, Dot. The damage was done with a knife. Throat cut. Belly shredded.'

Dot hunched her shoulders and shivered. 'Ugh. Poor Anna. She must be devastated.'

'Yeah. She was. Doubt we'll see her at work tomorrow. How about you, Dot? When do you think you'll be back?'

'Well, I could try straight away if it was only for a few hours. My leg gets sore sitting still or standing for very long, but I reckon I could do two hours on the till. If they needed me to be back full-time, that's a different story. Mind you, do you want me back now you've got, whatshisname, Jay?'

"Course I want you back.' She took a sip of wine. 'Just not in the evenings.'

'Ha! I knew it. You prefer a student hipster to me.'

'I didn't say that. Okay, he's interesting, but I don't really know anything about him yet. He might be a massive knob for all I know.'

'Or have one?'

About to take a slurp of wine, Bea lowered her glass and started laughing. 'You see *this* is what I miss,' she said. 'There's no one like you, Dot. Never will be.'

"Course not,' Dot said, with a smile of satisfaction. 'And the new boss? What's she like?'

'Well, she's interesting in a different way. Bit scary, if you ask me. Do you know anyone who works in Swindon? Would be nice to find out the goss on her.'

'Anna's the one for that, isn't she? She knows everyone. Oh, I'm itching to come back now. I miss everyone so much.'

'Especially Bob?' Bea winked at Dot. It was well known that Bob-on-Meat had the hots for Dot, but so far she had kept him at arm's length, apart from the odd lapse now and again.

'I don't get the chance to miss him, babe, he's round here every other day. He's been fixing my taps and changing my light bulbs, bless him.'

'Ooh er,' said Bea, with a wink. 'That's a new name for it.'

Dot only just managed to keep hold of her mouthful of wine. She swallowed rapidly. 'You're terrible, you are. Worse than me.'

'You love it,' said Bea. They raised their glasses and chinked them together.

Queenie was in the lounge watching the TV news when Bea got home. From the cups on the coffee table and the book next to the chair, it looked like she'd been there all day.

Bea sighed. Before Christmas, it seemed as if her mum was starting to get over the agoraphobia that had held her back for years. Now it felt like nothing had changed.

She roused herself with Bea there, though, and made dinner for them both, and they ate it on their laps as usual. Bea told her the story of her day, pretty much as she'd told Dot.

'That cat,' said Queenie, sometime afterwards, when they'd cleared away the dishes and were watching the soaps. 'You did a good thing there.'

'Mm,' said Bea.

'You've reunited it with its owner. Job done.'

'What do you mean?'

'It's a horrible story, but it's over now. You've done your bit.'

'Yeah. It's odd, though. I mean, why would it turn up at Costsave, nearly half a mile from home? And why would anyone kill a cat in the first place?'

'I knew you were dwelling on it! Not your cat, Bea. Not your problem. Look what happened last time you played detective.'

'What happened was we caught the bloke that did it. He's in jail now.'

'And he nearly killed you.'

Bea tutted. 'It wasn't that bad, Mum. I had it all under control.'

She hadn't told Queenie she still had nightmares about being trapped in the Costsave offices with a killer's hands round her throat.

Queenie looked at her and narrowed her eyes. 'It *was* that bad. It's a wicked world out there. Just leave things be now, darlin'.' The *Emmerdale* signature tune filled the room signalling the end of the programme. 'You got the remote? Flick over to *EastEnders* now. Don't want to miss the beginning.'

3

Neville was at the staff door ushering people inside like a headmaster in a school playground.

'Come on, come on, everyone. Two minutes until the, hem, huddle.' The unfamiliar cosy word seemed to stick in his throat. Ant, the last of the stragglers, grinned.

'Morning, Neville.'

'It's Mr Fellows to you, Anthony.'

'Don't think so, Neville. First names only, according to George. What do you prefer, Neville or Nev?' He squeezed past in the doorway and was about to head for the stairs, when Neville called him back.

'Not so fast, Anthony. I need a word with you.'

Ant pretended to look at his watch. 'Not now, Nev, don't wanna be late.'

'I saw you last night as I was driving out. It didn't look like fish fingers to me.'

Ant stopped. Now they were uncomfortably close, face to face in the confined space of the stairwell. 'Sorry, you've lost me.'

'The bag you handed over to Beatrice,' said Neville. 'It didn't look like there were packets of fish fingers inside. It was something larger.'

'No, mate, I'm telling you,' said Ant, setting off up the stairs.

'There's something fishy going on, Ant, and I don't think it's fingers. I don't know what you're up to, but I'm onto you.'

Ant stopped and turned around. Neville's eyes seemed to be glittering in the dim light.

Neville had never liked him, and now it was clear he thought he'd found a reason to get rid of him. But Ant could hear George's voice drifting down from the staffroom. 'Ah man, we're missing it. I'll tell you later, okay?'

'I'll look forward to that. I won't forget, Anthony. I've marked your card.'

Ant and Neville took their places at the back of the crowd.

'Good morning, gentlemen,' George said, and everyone turned around to see who she was referring to. 'Better late than never.' Little pink mottles of embarrassment appeared in Neville's skin under his eyes.

George resumed her briefing. Her words washed through Ant's brain without registering. He was busy panicking about the dead cat, Neville's threats and the bad impression he'd just made. The temptation to sneak out and just go home to bed was almost too strong, but then he remembered last night's chilli and the news that had come with it. His mum's voice echoed in his head: 'We'll deal with this how we always have. We need to stick together.' Now wasn't a good time to lose this job.

George's voice swam back into focus. '—for personal reasons, Anna's had to drop out so there's a space on the one-day First Aid course taking place tomorrow. I know quite a few of you are trained up already, but those of you who aren't, any volunteers?'

The room fell silent. Feet were shuffled. Gazes were aimed at the floor.

'This is incredibly worthwhile as a personal skill and important for the store. Anyone?'

Bob-on-Meat coughed and everyone looked at him expectantly, waiting for him to speak up. Instead he took out his hanky and proceeded to blow his nose loudly.

Beside Ant, Neville drew air in through his teeth. He was tapping his foot on the old, stained carpet, impatient to get on with the day and the business of putting Ant in a tight corner. Ant raised his hand.

'Me,' he said. His voice was rather quiet and only those nearest to him heard. They turned around, and Ant cleared his throat and said it again. 'Me. I'll do it.'

George made eye contact and beamed. 'Excellent,' she said. 'I'm sorry, your name is?'

'Ant,' said Ant. Somebody at the other side of the room sniggered.

'Great, that's the spirit,' said George. 'A positive contribution from Ant. Well done. See me after the meeting for the joining details.'

Bea's late shift meant that she had most of the day to spend with Queenie and she was determined to encourage her to move from the sofa. To be fair, her mum kept herself busy pottering about the house, doing a load of washing, dusting and hoovering. Bea joined in to show willing, giving the bathroom a good going-over, even though it was pretty spotless to start with. Queenie liked a clean and tidy house.

'Shall we go to the shops in a bit? We're nearly out of milk.'

Queenie looked towards the window, and the cold, grey afternoon outside. 'No, we're not that desperate, are we? You can pick some up later.'

'A walk, then?'

'Have you seen the weather? I'm cold just sitting here. I'm not going out in that.' Queenie made a show of wrapping her cardigan more firmly round her middle. Bea clamped her lips together, trying not to say the wrong thing, but, of course, Queenie noticed. 'What?'

'Nothing.'

'No, what? Come on, spit it out.'

'It's just, just that I thought that you were, that we could . . .'

'What?'

' . . .get out a bit more. You were doing so well before Christmas.'

'It's cold, Bea. It's dark about twenty-three hours a day. I don't like it.'

'So, basically, you're hibernating. Like a hedgehog. Or a bear.'

'They've got the right idea, haven't they?'

'Yeah, but not everyone can do that. I can't, can I? I have to go out to work.' Bea bit her tongue as soon as she said it, but she couldn't take the words back. Queenie's benefits had been stopped at the end of the year. Now Bea's wage from Costsave was the only money coming into the house.

'I know I'm not pulling my weight, Bea. No need to rub it in. I'm well aware of how hard you work . . .' Queenie got up from the sofa and headed upstairs.

'Mum, don't. Mum—' But she was gone.

Bea knew it was better to leave her to stew for a bit. Going after her now might escalate the row. Arguing didn't do any good, did it? She wondered what it would take to get Queenie to take the next big step.

On her walk into work, Bea tried not to think about the row. Instead she texted Anna to see how she was doing.

'Taking a couple of days' leave. Have told George you can fill in. xxx'

Bea had had a spell in the office when Anna had been on

secondment. She'd found the work interesting and she'd surprised herself that she was able to tackle it without too much trouble, but the thought of the management suite made her feel a bit sick having been attacked there, and so nearly come a cropper.

Now she tried to blot out bad memories by thinking about Anna and her cats. She'd made a promise to Anna and she was determined to keep it, but how best to start? Perhaps the office held the key, after all. If she was able to use Anna's computer, she could access the store's CCTV and if she scrolled back she might be able to see who had dumped the body.

She was deep in thought when she saw Jay walking a few metres ahead of her on the High Street. Her stomach gave a little flip and she couldn't help smiling. Four till ten. Six whole hours to get to know him.

She pursed her lips, about to wolf-whistle him, then stopped herself. He might not appreciate her sense of humour. She started to break into an ungainly trot and then slowed back down to a walk. Silly to look too keen, she thought. Keep it cool, girl. She followed behind until they got to the store. Opening the staff door, he spotted her and held it open.

'After you,' he said, with a gallant sweep of his arm.

'Ta very much,' Bea said, trying and failing not to colour up. 'Decided to come back, then?'

'Yeah,' said Jay. 'Gotta pay the rent.'

'Tell me about it,' said Bea. 'My student mates are still home from Christmas. Did you stay here all the time?'

'Went home for a couple of days. About all I could stand. I had things to get on with here anyway.'

They parted into their respective locker rooms.

When she'd got her uniform on, Bea steeled her nerve and walked along the corridor to George's office. The door was open, and Bea knocked on the frame. George looked up.

'Hello,' she said. 'Come in. It's Bea, isn't it?'

'Um, yes,' Bea said, wondering how George knew her name.

'Do sit down.' George indicated the chair in front of her desk. Bea noticed a couple of framed photographs by her computer with their backs towards her, and a calendar on the wall with January's page featuring a large photograph of a white baby seal on an iceberg. Apart from that, the office wasn't any different from how it had been before.

'So, Bea. I was going to come and find you today anyway. You may not know, but Anna's suffered a family bereavement and is going to be off work for a couple of days – I've given her compassionate leave – and she mentioned to me that you've worked in the office before. Neville and I have managed today, but might you be able to cover the office for a few hours tomorrow, say, nine until twelve here and the rest of your shift on the checkout?'

'Um, yes,' Bea said again, aware that she was starting to sound like the village idiot. She sat up a bit straighter in the chair and smoothed her skirt. 'Yes, I'd love to help, if I can.'

George smiled. 'Great. Was there anything else?'

'No, that was what I was coming to ask about, actually.'

'Great minds,' said George.

Down on the shop floor, the store was nicely buzzy. Ant was indoors today, supposedly shelf-stacking. Bea noticed him making regular detours past the checkouts, wandering along with the same empty cardboard box in his hands.

'Busy?' Bea called out to him.

He grinned. 'Oh yeah. Always busy.' He came nearer and bent down to whisper in her ear. 'I'm trying to keep out of Neville's way. He made me tell him about the cat. He's not happy about me putting it in the freezer, but he doesn't want word getting out to the customers, so we might have got away with it.'

'You reckon?'

27

'Yeah. I tried not to drop Anna in it. She's not in today and I don't know if she's told them why. Anyway, I'm not in tomorrow, going to First Aid training, so you'll have to deal with it if there's any flak.'

'Oh, cheers for that. First Aid training?'

'I volunteered. Tactics,' he said, tapping the side of his nose and looking pleased with himself. 'That's tomorrow, though. Still got another half hour of this to do. You just started?'

'Yeah.'

The flow of customers had ebbed a little. Bea twiddled her chair round away from Ant, so she could see Jay.

'So, student is it?' said Ant, walking over to Jay's till.

'Yeah,' said Jay. 'Is it that obvious?'

'What are you reading?' said Bea.

'Environmental studies. Birds and the bees.' He smiled and she could feel something birdlike fluttering in her stomach again.

'Is that a book?' said Ant, resting his cardboard box on Jay's conveyor belt.

'What are you on about?' said Bea, glancing up at him.

'You asked him what he's reading.'

'That's what you say, isn't it? Another way of asking what they're studying.'

Ant's expression darkened and he busied himself peeling a label off the side of the cardboard box.

The tannoy crackled into life. 'All staff on the shop floor, it's time for a ten-minute rumble.'

Ant started singing under his breath, 'Let's get, let's get, let's get ready to rumble.'

'What's a rumble?' said Jay.

'Just a clear-up,' said Bea. 'Tidying up cardboard on the shelves, empty packing, that sort of thing. Putting the fuck-its back in place.'

28

'The what-its?'

'When people change their mind and leave things just anywhere. They're the fuck-its.'

'Ha! Love it.'

'I'd better get on it,' said Ant. 'See you tomorrow, yeah?'

'Yeah, all right, Ant. See ya,' said Bea. She watched as he took his cardboard box along the row of checkouts and then into the soups and tinned vegetable aisle. 'Sorry about him,' she said. 'He's all right really.'

'It's cool,' said Jay, reaching for the divider on his conveyor belt and greeting his next customer, a man in his forties, wearing typical country gear – flat cap, Barbour jacket and the sort of jeans that look more like workwear than fashion. The skin on his face had a weathered quality, as if he spent a lot of time outdoors. He had six bottles of beer, a half-bottle of whisky, a couple of steaks and some frozen peas on the belt. 'Good afternoon, sir, do you need a box for the bottles?'

Bea watched as Jay assembled one of the cardboard bottle carriers. Neville was right, he knew the ropes all right. Good with the customers too.

They passed the rest of the afternoon companionably. It wasn't the same as having Dot working next to her, but he was easy on the eye and easy to get along with. She felt comfortable in his company and was enjoying thinking of little remarks and quips to amuse him. He responded gratifyingly and they were soon more than halfway through their shift.

Charles was approaching her checkout. He seemed to be walking even more slowly than usual.

'Bit late for you, isn't it?'

'I ran out of this,' he said, patting a bag of dry dog food.

'Ooh, that'll never do. Poor old Goldie. She outside?'

'Yes, she's a good girl waiting for me.'

Bea took his money. 'You're not carrying that, are you?'

'No, I've got my trolley. I'll be fine.' He heaved the sack into the tartan bag on wheels and pulled the lid shut.

'Okay, you take care now.'

He tipped the brim of his tweed trilby at her. 'Will do. Goodnight, Bea.'

'Do you know all your customers?' Jay asked from over her shoulder.

'Ha! Not all of them, but quite a lot. He's a good 'un, Charles. Bit lonely, I think. Like a lot of them. Sometimes wonder if I'm the only person he talks to all day. Apart from Goldie.'

'Man's best friend. Gotta love a dog.'

'Hmm, I've never been a pet person. You got any?'

'No, not here. Wouldn't go down too well with my landlord. Always had dogs growing up, though. Talking about customers, did you recognise the bloke I had earlier – flat cap and Barbour jacket?'

'Beer and steak?'

Jay's eyes grew temporarily wide. 'Wow, yeah. How'd you do that?'

Bea smiled. 'It's just my thing. Noticing stuff about the customers. Sussing them out. Makes the job more interesting.'

Jay mimed running his finger along the edge of a blade and shook his hand vigorously, 'Owww. Sharp as.'

'Nah, just been here long enough,' she said, hoping her skin wouldn't betray her this time with a beetroot blush.

'Did you know that bloke, Mr Barbour Jacket?'

'Don't think so. Why?'

'Ah, it's nothing. I thought I'd seen him somewhere before. Maybe just around town.' Jay shrugged, then stretched his arms out and cracked his knuckles. 'How much longer have we got, Bea?'

Bea checked her watch. 'Another two and a half hours.'

'Jeez.' He rolled his chair back a little and stood up, then, keeping his back straight, he folded forward and hung there for a while before standing up again.

'Whoa, you're very bendy,' said Bea.

'Yoga,' said Jay. 'You should try it.'

'Not sure it's my thing.'

'Maybe it should be. Useful being bendy.'

There was no stopping the blush now. Bea's face was on fire.

4

It was a cold, crisp night as Bea and Jay left Costsave. A dusting of frost was already forming on the tarmac, sparkling and golden in the sodium glow from the tall lights that studded the car park.

Jay pulled his hood up. 'Brr,' he said. 'Cold enough, innit?'

'Yeah. Where do you live?'

'Off Jubilee Avenue.'

It was one of the streets in the estate near the former chocolate factory, where Bea's dad used to work, which was now being redeveloped as flats, in the opposite direction to where she was heading.

'Ah, there's quite a lot of student houses there.'

'Yeah.'

'So,' she said, unable to think of any way to prolong their conversation, 'see you tomorrow.'

'Yeah, see ya, Bea.'

Bea turned her collar up, hunched her shoulders a little and headed into the High Street. As she turned the corner a dark figure stepped out of the first doorway. She gasped, and her heart felt as if it had been jump-started, suddenly beating like the clappers.

'All right?' said Ant.

'Jesus, you numpty. You frightened the life out of me.'

'Oh, sorry. I didn't think. I was going to wait on the corner, but it's freezing. Thought it might be warmer in the shelter of that door.' She reached up and swatted the back of his head. 'Sorry, Bea, hey, hey, I've said sorry!'

'Just use your head next time. I don't want to have to do you more serious damage.'

'Got it. Point taken.'

'Let's get walking. It's too cold to stand around. What are you even doing here, Ant?'

'I needed to talk to you. I've got a bit of a situation.' His voice was so serious that it instantly calmed Bea down. Ant wasn't the most communicative bloke in the world. Something was really wrong.

'Go on.'

'I need some time off work, but I don't think I've been there long enough to apply for leave, not officially like.'

'Well, you need to check your contract ...oh.' Too late, Bea remembered Ant's problem with reading. 'I mean, I could check your contract, but if it's something important I would just ask. They can give compassionate leave – they've given some to Anna. What's it for, mate?'

'It's just a family thing. No one's died or anything.'

'Hmm, family stuff. It never stops, does it? Queenie's lost her benefits, you know. It's starting to bite.'

'That sucks, man.'

'Yeah.'

'She's going out a bit more, though, isn't she?' said Ant.

'Not really. She was doing quite well for a couple of weeks, but it feels as though she's gone backwards. Most days, she hasn't seen anyone, hasn't been out of the house. It doesn't feel like we're getting anywhere.'

'I'm sorry, Bea. I didn't know. I just thought everything was going great.'

Bea pinched her lips together and shook her head. 'When

33

people ask it seems, I don't know, disloyal to say how it really is. It's not what people want to hear anyway.'

'I'll come round, shall I? See if I can help?'

'Yeah, maybe. Not tonight, though. I'm ready for a soak in the bath then bed. Anyway, what were you going to tell me earlier?'

They were nearly across the rec now. A late-night dog walker was heading towards them. The dog was a thickset terrier type, wearing a studded harness and a collar with spikes on it. It was trotting along quite calmly until it spotted them on the path ahead, then it leapt forward, straining against its harness. As they got closer, Bea noticed that there were strings of drool at either side of its mouth and it was making little grunting noises. She stepped off the path onto the grass, pulling Ant with her. She glanced at the dog's owner and her heart sank. Peering out under the hood of his coat was the familiar weasely face of Dean, Eileen's son, formerly employed in the stores at Costsave.

'Tyson, leave,' Dean said. His dog's front legs were off the ground now as it lunged towards Ant and Bea. 'Leave!' He yanked on the lead, jerking the dog backwards. Bea started to feel sorry for it.

'You don't have to do that,' said Ant.

'Would you like me to let him off?' Dean sneered. 'He's vicious, he is. Needs a firm hand.'

'We all know you've got strong wrists, don't know about your hands, mate,' said Ant.

It took a while for the insult to sink in, then Dean's face darkened. 'I'm not the wanker here, am I? I'm not the snitch.'

'Leave it, Ant,' said Bea. 'He's not worth it.'

'Leave it, Ant,' Dean mimicked in a sing-song voice. 'Cosy, aren't you? Always thought you were made for each other. No one else'd touch you. Even that granny you shagged dumped you.'

34

'Right, that's it,' said Ant. He let go of Bea's arm and took a step towards Dean. The dog lurched forward again, with a barrage of frenzied barking.

'Ant!' Bea screamed. 'Let's go. Let's just go.'

She wasn't really expecting him to listen, but he did. He turned away from Dean, grabbed her arm again and started walking away. They could both hear Dean's grating laughter as they left the rec and crossed the road.

'Thinks he's the big man strutting around with a dog like that. It's pathetic,' said Ant.

'Everyone knows what he's like. A dog doesn't change anything, even a nasty one.' She shivered. They'd rounded the corner of the shops and were at her front gate now. 'Thanks for walking me back, Ant.'

'That's okay.'

'You're not going to go after him now, are you?'

'Nah, you were right the first time. He's not worth it. I'll duck down the other side of the rec. You go in now, it's cold.'

Bea headed inside. It was only when she was taking her coat off that she realised that Ant hadn't told her why he needed the day off. *Family stuff*. Hmm.

'That you, love?' Queenie shouted from the lounge.

'Yeah, Mum. Who else?' she replied. 'Want a cuppa?'

'Yes, please.' Her mum appeared in the doorway. 'Is it cold out?'

You'd know if you went out, thought Bea. If you tried. Family stuff. She took a deep breath. 'Hang on,' she said. 'I'll just chip the icicle off my nose, then I'll tell you.'

5

Bea tried not to think about ghosts as she walked into Anna's office the next morning, but it was difficult. She hung her coat on the hook behind the door and sat at Anna's desk. Facing her was a framed photograph of Anna's two cats, staring at the camera with cool amber eyes. Bette and Joan, or was it Joan and Bette? One of them was a little bit thinner than the other, but she didn't know which was which. The body that she'd found could have been either of them.

She turned in her chair a fraction and reached forward to switch on the computer. Two pairs of eyes seemed to follow her. She looked back at the photograph. 'Sorry, ladies. Just for today,' she said, and turned it face down on the desk.

While the computer fired up, Bea riffled through Anna's stack of post trays. There were a few papers in the one labelled 'Filing', so Bea picked them up and headed for the grey cabinets behind her.

As she searched the staff records to put away some training requests, she realised her fingers were resting on the file for Ginny, her fellow cashier, who had been murdered a couple of months before. Someone had written 'Closed' under her name label, and this made Bea feel sadder than ever. Was that it? Was that all Costsave did when one of their staff members died?

She finished the filing, settled back at the desk and looked at the email inbox. She made some notes and soon had a list of things that needed actioning. She took it through to George and put it in her in-tray.

'Do you need anything, George?' she said. 'Cup of tea?'

George looked up from her screen. 'Oh, bless you. No, I'm fine. Just working through the sales figures, doing a departmental analysis, looking for where we can do better.'

'I'll leave you to it, then,' said Bea. 'I'm just updating the leave request folder for Neville to look at.'

'Good, good.' George wasn't really listening. She was already looking back at the screen.

Right, thought Bea, back in Anna's office. Unless Neville comes bothering me, the coast's clear. In fact, she could call up the current screens, including those for the shop floor, to keep an eye out for Neville. Bea kept that window open in a corner of the screen, then started to search the stored footage for the night before poor Joan was found in the cardboard bay.

She quickly identified the camera that covered the cardboard storage cage. Working backwards, she soon discovered that the body was dumped between twenty to and ten to six in the morning. There it was, the body quite literally thrown onto the heap of broken down boxes at 5.46, flying through the air and landing unceremoniously where Ant had found it.

Frustratingly, although the cage itself was in full view, the area around it wasn't, so all Bea could see was two gloved hands sticking out of dark coat sleeves flinging the body out of a plastic bag, which clearly had the Costsave logo on the side. It was impossible to tell if the hands were male or female, but several things occurred to Bea. Why empty the body out of the bag? Why not leave it in there? Why deliberately come into the yard to dispose of the body? Why use a branded Costsave bag? Was it a deliberate choice or just what was to hand?

She thought about the time. A quarter to six. Had the culprit broken into the yard somehow, or were the gates open that early? Easy to find out, and the other cameras may give a better view of the suspect. She picked her way through the footage on various cameras. The main gate into the yard was opened at half past five. So the cat killer didn't need to break in, but did have to be careful not to be seen.

Bea couldn't find footage of the killer coming through the gate. She scrolled back and looked again. 'Come on, come on,' she said to herself.

There! A figure coming through the gates at 5.43. Bea froze the film, then went back a few seconds and played it again.

It was hopeless. While the first CCTV image had been pretty clear, this was too distant and terribly grainy. Whoever it was kept their hood up and their head down. All she could tell was that it was someone carrying a bag. She tried enlarging the image, but that didn't help.

She let the video play and saw her suspect leaving the yard at 5.47, but all she got was the impression of someone's back – a thigh-length coat with a hood, dark trousers and possibly boots of some sort, although they could be heavy shoes. She scrolled back to the best image she could find and stared at it. She was still staring when Neville walked into the room. She'd been so wrapped up in what she was doing she hadn't noticed him leaving his post on the shop floor.

'I'd better have a look at the leave requests,' he said. 'Then I'll start on the next period's rotas.'

Bea hastily exited the CCTV system. 'I'm just working on them,' she said. 'I'll be two ticks. Do you want to make yourself a cuppa, then they'll be ready.'

'It's not my break period yet, Beatrice,' he said, settling down at the other desk in the room. 'I'll just work here while I'm waiting.'

Bea tried to collate the requests as quickly as she could,

hoping it wasn't too obvious that she was only just starting them. She handed them over to Neville after eight agonising minutes.

'Thank you, Beatrice,' he said, sniffing loudly.

'What shall I do next?'

He looked towards the door, then beckoned to her to come closer. Bea hesitated. Close proximity to Neville was not something that she actively sought.

'What?' she said.

'Come here,' he hissed.

She edged a little closer but kept the desk between them.

'You could look at the CCTV screens,' he said in a loud whisper. 'See if you can spot whoever dumped the you-know-what in the you-know-where.'

Bea felt herself colouring up and tried to suppress a smile. 'Really? Is it okay to do that?'

Neville tapped the side of his nose. 'Only between you and me,' he said. 'George doesn't know anything about it. Anna told her it was her aunt that died. I wouldn't normally approve of a white lie like that, but in this case . . .'

'Okay,' said Bea, retreating back to Anna's desk. 'I'll have a go. I'll let you know if I find anything.'

She took her time before calling him over to see the blurry figure freeze-framed walking in through the gate. He studied the screen, sucking air in through his teeth.

'I don't like it,' said Neville. 'I don't like it at all. Let's keep it under our hats.'

At lunchtime, her stint in the office over, Bea settled on the sofa in the staffroom. She got out her cheese and pickle sandwich and packet of crisps, and reached for the current copy of the *Kingsleigh Bugle*. It was nearly five days old but, in the absence of any of her favourites to chat to, it would give her something to flip through.

**UNHAPPY NEW YEAR, TRAGEDY
OF THE BODY ON THE BYPASS**

Mystery surrounds the identity of a body found at the side of the main Bristol to Bath road in the early hours of New Year's Day. Police have confirmed that it was a man in his twenties but have not yet released any further details. The road bridge over the bypass is a well-known local suicide spot, and nearby residents voiced fears this week that the bridge had claimed another victim.

Suicide is the biggest cause of death for young men aged under 45. If you've been affected by this article, the Samaritans are available 24 hours a day …

The news had been on Bea's Twitter feed first thing on New Year's Day. She'd seen that the bypass was closed and read eyewitness reports of a body being found as she'd sat up in bed and scrolled through her phone. Her own New Year celebrations had left her feeling a bit down, but this was something else. It had seemed such a grim start to the year.

She put the paper down for a moment and opened her crisps and took a big one from the top. The salt and vinegar flavouring stung the inside of her mouth. She probed the offending area with her tongue and found an ulcer lurking there. She'd had to cover up a rash of spots on her forehead this morning with extra thick concealer. Good grief, her whole body was erupting. Maybe it was a winter thing, or perhaps she was run-down. She noticed one of the adverts on the front page of the *Bugle*: 'New Year, New You. Reveal your inner glow with a chemical peel at the Kingsleigh Beauty Bar. 10% off with this advert.' Peel it all off and start again, she thought.

Out of the corner of her eye she saw Neville coming into the room and heading in her direction. 'Mind if I—?'

Bea smiled wanly and moved her handbag onto the floor, allowing Neville to sit down.

'Interesting morning,' Neville said, as he opened the lid of his Tupperware box. Bea glanced across. It contained a brown sandwich and some brown apple slices and a little heap of brown raisins. She was reminded of watching *Gardeners' World* with Queenie a few weeks before and discussing why anyone would bother to build their own compost heap.

She realised Neville was looking at her looking at his lunch. 'Pardon?'

'Interesting morning in the office. Not too taxing for you?'

'Oh, yes and, um, no. I enjoyed it.'

They sat in silence.

'Anything in this week's paper?' said Neville.

'I haven't got very far yet.' She was still reading the lead story on the front page. 'So sad.'

Neville leaned sideways slightly, making Bea acutely aware of his shoulder pressing into hers, and read the article. 'It's a modern curse, Beatrice,' he said. 'Despair among the young. It's something we're trying to tackle in our church. We have a couple of very good outreach workers.' He sat upright again, much to Bea's relief, and took a bite from his sandwich.

Bea turned the page, letting her eyes skim over the other news stories. She was somewhat distracted by an odd clicking sound coming from Neville's jaw. The more she tried to tune it out, the louder it sounded. How his wife hadn't killed him long ago, she'd never know.

She carried on flipping through the pages until she got to page six. Then she stopped.

The headline read, 'Mystery of the Missing Cats' and the sub-heading underneath, 'As three cats go AWOL in a week, people are urged to check their garden sheds for missing moggies.'

'Neville,' she said, her throat suddenly dry. 'Have you seen this?'

She moved the paper towards him so that it bridged the gap between them. They read the whole article in silence. The three cats that were missing were all in the eastern side of town – two tabbies and a ginger one. Two had gone missing on the same night, the third a couple of days later. Their owners had appealed on Twitter and put up notices.

'And Anna's makes four,' said Bea. 'We should tell the police.'

Neville looked horror-struck. 'We can't, Bea. No one must know about the biosecurity breach.'

Bea worked out that this meant Ant storing the body in the freezer. 'Well, we could tell them without mentioning that bit. But they do need to know. Anna's cat was killed with a knife. That was bad enough, but if it's not a one-off, we're talking about a very sick individual indeed. They need catching.'

Neville sighed. 'You're right, of course. Do you think we can keep this out of the papers?'

'I don't see why not. It won't come from us, will it? So, it would have to come from the police, and they should understand the commercial—' she searched for the right word. '—sensitivities.'

Neville swallowed hard, and his Adam's apple bobbed up and down. 'Someone's going to have to tell George.'

6

The next morning Bea called into the office to see Anna, who was back at her desk.

'Neville had to tell George about Joan yesterday,' Bea told her.

'Yes,' said Anna. 'He rang me. It's okay. I'm not in trouble. George was really nice about it. About me lying. The police are coming in later to interview me. They'll want to talk to you too.'

The police. The Kingsleigh branch of the local constabulary wasn't exactly massive, so that probably meant talking to community bobby Tom again. The last time Bea had seen him, she'd been upset about his lack of honesty with her. She winced as she remembered calling him something rude. Shitgibbon, to be precise.

'Right-oh,' she said. 'Call me up when they're here. I'd better get back to good old checkout six. I tried to keep everything in order here yesterday, but if I made a mess of anything, you know where to find me.'

Anna smiled wanly. 'I'm sure you didn't make a mess. Everything looks fine today. We should make this formal – that you'll do office cover when I'm away sick or on leave. Do you want me to talk to George about it?'

'Why not? I like doing it.'

'Once it's on your CV, it'll help when you look for jobs elsewhere. Office jobs.'

Bea wondered if she'd misheard. 'Elsewhere? Like, leave Costsave?'

'It's a big old world out there.'

'I like this bit of the world, though. Anyway, it's good to see you back. Sorry about the—' She tailed off, not knowing quite what to say, but it was all right. Anna nodded to show that she appreciated the sentiment. Her face was set firm as she reached for the post and her letter opener, but there was a little twitch by the side of her mouth that betrayed the stress she was feeling.

'Don't be nice to me today,' she said. 'I'll be all right as long as people aren't nice.'

Bea understood. She'd felt the same after her dad died. She'd kept things together at school as long as people pretty much ignored what had happened to her. The dam only burst when they said something kind, or tried to give her a hug.

'See you later, babe.'

As Bea made her way to her checkout, she looked around the store. This was her world, had been for some years now. She loved it here. Didn't she?

First up at the checkout, Bea had a visit from one of the Four Musketeers. Beth was there with her mum, who paid the bill.

'Stocking up on tins and stuff to take back with me,' said Beth. 'Got exams coming up, so there's a bit of revision fodder too.' She patted a tidy little pile of chocolate bars and smiled self-consciously.'

'Ha! I flippin' hated exams,' said Bea.

'They don't get any better.'

'I always think it's cruel having exams straight after Christmas,' said Beth's mum. 'I wonder if – no, it doesn't matter.'

'What?' said Beth.

'I just wondered if that lad who killed himself at New Year was stressed about exams or something like that.'

'Mum, we don't even know if he was a student,' said Beth.

'There could be lots of reasons, anyway, couldn't there?' said Bea.

'Yes, you're right,' said Beth's mum. 'We don't know. Nobody seems to know about him.'

Bea tried to scan the shopping as quickly and efficiently as she could, grouping the goods in the packing area to make it easier – fresh veg, things for the fridge, things for the freezer. It was how she worked anyway, but somehow she wanted to show Beth that she was good at her job. It felt like it mattered. 'I had a spell in the office yesterday,' she said.

'Yeah?'

Bea cringed inside. Was she really doing this? Trying to impress? 'Yeah. It was all right.'

She'd cleared the shopping now, and fancied she could see a ball of tumbleweed rolling along her conveyor belt. She added Beth's mum's points onto her Costsave Saver Card and processed her payment. There were smiles all round as they heaved the bags into the trolley, but Bea felt nothing but relief when they started making their way towards the exit.

Damn, she thought, Beth used to be my *friend*. What happened?

She was glad to see someone else heading towards her, another of her regulars: a young mum called Julie, who had two under-fives. Julie was one of the ones Bea worried about, because sometimes her dark glasses didn't completely hide her bruises. Today, though, she wasn't wearing the glasses and she was looking good – hair shiny and pulled back into a neat ponytail, new winter coat in a very flattering shade of green, only one child in tow and, even better, a smile on her face when she spotted Bea.

'Like the coat. What a fab colour.'

Julie beamed. 'Yes, it's new. Dave got it for me. Wasn't even in the sale.'

Bea tried not to react at the mention of Julie's husband. She'd filed him under 'sleazeball' after he'd propositioned her in the pub one evening, and that was before she knew he hit his wife. 'How are things?'

'Actually, things are good. Really good at the moment.'

'Yeah?'

'Yes. Better than they've been for a long time.'

'That's great. No Mason today?'

'He's at a friend's house, someone from nursery. This one misses him, though.' Julie ruffled the hair of her daughter, Tiffany, who was facing her in the trolley seat, dangling her legs in front and clutching the pink plastic duck that never seemed to leave her sticky hands.

'Nothing wrong with a bit of girl time,' said Bea, 'you and Mum together?'

Tiffany ducked her head and gave Bea a shy little smile.

'We're on our way to pick him up now anyway, aren't we?' Tiffany nodded. Julie paid for her shopping in cash as usual and pushed the trolley towards the door. Bea felt relieved that she was happier, but she still had a niggle of anxiety about that little family.

She turned to her next customer, 'Hello there, would you like some help packing?'

The police didn't make an appearance until just before lunchtime. Bea clocked their car driving round to the back of the store and a little later there was an announcement on the tannoy: 'Bea Jordan to the management suite.'

She put the 'checkout closing' sign at the end of her station and signed out of her terminal. Upstairs there was quite a gathering in George's office: George herself, Anna, Neville and the two community police officers Shaz, and, yes, Tom.

There was a flicker in Tom's eyes as he saw her come into the room. Not quite a wink, but not far off. There weren't enough chairs, so Bea stood just inside the door next to Anna.

'Bea,' said Tom. 'I understand that you found the cat in the cardboard.'

'Not me,' Bea said. 'It was Ant. But he's not here today. He showed the, er, body to me soon after he found it, though.' Out of the corner of her eye she could see Anna tense her jaw when she mentioned the word 'body'.

'And where is it now? Can we see it?'

'I'm sorry,' said Anna. 'I've already taken her to the vet. She's going to be cremated. They said I'll get the ashes back in about a week.'

'But there are images on CCTV,' said Neville. 'I can show you those. They're not particularly good quality, but they do show the, um, item being dumped.'

'And I've got photos,' said Bea. They all looked at her, with varying levels of shock and disgust. 'What? I took photos. Just in case.'

'In case of what?' said Neville.

Anna looked stricken.

'I'm sorry, Anna,' said Bea. 'I took them in case they'd be useful. Exactly like now. Evidence.'

Tom smiled his approval. 'Let's have a look, then.'

Bea found the photos and handed her phone over. Tom and Shaz scrolled through them.

'You know,' said Tom, 'I can't officially endorse investigations by private individuals, but in this case, well done, Bea. Can you email these to us?'

'Yes. Sure.'

Tom handed her a business card, and she sent the email there and then.

'So we'd better have a look at the CCTV video. Let's hope it will help us ID the suspect,' said Shaz.

'Unfortunately, I don't think it will,' said Neville. 'We can identify the exact time it happened, but you can't tell much about the person who did this.'

'Monster,' Anna muttered.

'I'm sorry?' said Neville.

'The monster who did this. It was a deliberate act. It was butchery. And then her . . .body . . .was dumped quite deliberately here.'

'Yes,' said Shaz. 'It does look premeditated. It's a disturbing case.'

'But one we'll be able to keep out of the papers?' said George, quickly.

'If there's a serial cat killer on the loose in Kingsleigh,' said Shaz, 'then it's our public duty to warn people, and to ask for their help in catching them.'

'Is there any way of leaving the store out of it?'

'I'll talk to the boss and the press office, but public and, um, feline safety must come first.'

Bea stayed upstairs and had a subdued lunch with Anna in the staffroom. She was just throwing her sandwich cling film in the bin when someone tapped her on the shoulder. She spun round to find Dot standing behind her with her arms spread wide. 'Ta-dah! I'm back!'

Bea gave her a big hug. 'Are you really?'

'Just had my occupational health interview. Phased return to work starting next week. A few hours to be getting on with, then building up.'

'That's the best news ever.'

'It is, isn't it?' said Bob-on-Meat, who was standing next to Dot, beaming. 'The place hasn't been the same without you.'

''Course it hasn't,' said Dot. 'Are we having a cuppa?'

Bea checked her watch. 'I've only got ten minutes.'

'Make it a quickie, then,' said Dot, with a wink. 'You'll make it for us, won't you, Bob? I just need a sit-down.'

Bob swung into action without a murmur, while Dot and Bea squeezed in next to Anna on the sofa.

'So where is everyone?' said Dot, looking round the room. 'Where's the new one, Jay, is it? Where's Ant?'

'Shh,' said Bea, with a warning look in her eye. 'Ant's off sick.'

'Really?'

'Lightweight,' said Bob, manoeuvring his substantial bulk round the end of the sofa and putting two mugs of tea down on the coffee table. 'Been here eighteen years and I've never had a day off sick. Mind you, it wouldn't be any surprise if it was that Jay. Measly little fellow. Someone told me he was—' he leaned down towards the women and lowered his voice to a whisper '—*vegan*.'

Dot clapped her hand to her mouth in mock horror, then started laughing. 'A lot of people are these days, Bob. It's not illegal any more.'

'Well, it should be. At least, they shouldn't be allowed to work in a food shop like this. It's just wrong, isn't it?'

'Live and let live, Bob. Takes all sorts.'

He snorted his disagreement and went to fetch his own mug from the draining board.

'Anyway,' said Bea. 'Jay's not ill, he doesn't come in until four.'

'Shame. I'll have to meet him another time, then. Nice to have some fresh blood around here . . .' She stopped as Anna gathered up her things and stood up. 'Sorry, Anna. I didn't mean – I was very sorry to hear about—'

'It's okay.' Anna just about got the words out before rushing for the door.

'Oh Gawd,' said Dot, looking mortified. 'Me and my big mouth.'

''S all right, Dot. It's a difficult day. We just had the police in asking about it.'

'Grim.'

'Yeah.' There was silence for a moment or two. 'Anyway, I've missed you and your big gob.' Bea caught Dot's eye and, in spite of the sober circumstances, or maybe because of them, they both dissolved into giggles.

7

The TV news was on as usual as Bea and Queenie ate their dinner – fish, oven chips and frozen peas, because it was Friday. Queenie was lapping up Bea's news about the visit from the police and Dot's return.

'Do you think she and Bob are back on?' she asked, shaking a bit more ketchup onto her plate.

'They weren't ever a thing, not really,' said Bea, 'but he's obviously keen. And he's been spending a lot of time round at hers, helping her out.'

'I reckon he's nearly got his feet under her table.'

'Not his feet you were thinking about, though, was it?'

'Less of that. You can keep your mucky talk for Dot,' said Queenie haughtily.

'Hmm, got to admit, she is the queen of banter. I'll be glad when she's back. Oh. Oh no—'

'What?'

'Where's the whizzer? Give it here quick!'

Bea grabbed the remote control and rewound the news. Then she shushed Queenie, pressed play, and watched in horror as she realised she hadn't been mistaken. The news footage clearly showed Ant, in the ill-fitting jacket that he'd last worn at Ginny's funeral, walking along a city street and up the steps of the local crown court.

'Is that Ant?' Queenie spluttered.

'Yes. Shh!' Bea tweaked up the volume.

'Prolific offender, Colin Thompson, was in court again today to learn that he'd been sentenced to three years in prison for a string of burglary convictions. Thompson pleaded guilty to three counts of burglary in December and was branded "heartless" by prosecutors for targeting families over the festive period. Thompson who lives in Kingsleigh near Bristol, seen here on the way into court supported by his family, will serve at least eighteen months.'

'Colin, Bea. That's his dad, isn't it?'

Bea felt a surge of relief – it wasn't Ant in the dock – but if anyone else at Costsave was watching this, he was in a different kind of trouble. She reached for her phone and dialled Ant's number. After half a dozen rings, it went to voicemail.

'Ant, mate,' Bea said, trying to quickly gather her thoughts and assemble them into a message that would strike the right chord. 'I've just seen you on the sodding telly! I'm so sorry. I didn't know. Call me?'

An hour later, she remembered he'd told her he'd lost his mobile, so she tried his home phone and was pleased that he picked up.

'I'm so sorry about your dad,' she said. She could almost hear him shrugging at the other end of the line.

'It's normal, innit? Normal for us anyway. My dad's a burglar. It's his job. Sometimes he's at home. Sometimes he's away. It's always been like that, my whole life.'

'Jeez, Ant. I didn't know.'

'It's just how it is. We've all got to look after Mum now, like we've always done.'

'What if you lose your job? Calling in sick like that.'

'I'll find another one, or do whatever I need to do.'

Like your dad? Bea didn't say it out loud. 'Ant, we've got to find a way of you staying at Costsave. Throw yourself at

George's mercy. Get in there first thing – talk to her before she calls you in. Just be honest. It's the only way to salvage this.'

'Nah, reckon I'll just fly under the radar, keep a low profile.'

'Ant, you were on the telly. You'd only have a higher profile if you stuck a revolving neon sign on the top of your head.'

'They shouldn't shove cameras in your face when you're going to court. Bastards.'

'If Neville's seen it, he's bound to tell George.'

'Look, Bea, I'm pretty knackered now. I'll see you tomorrow, okay?'

'Do you want me to meet you at Costsave early on? Go in with you? I don't mind.'

'Nah, it's okay.' She could hear a stifled yawn. 'Night.'

'Goodnight, Ant.'

The next time Bea saw him, she was already twenty minutes into her shift and had processed her first handful of customers. He came slouching towards her from the back of the shop, head down, hands in pockets.

'What's happening?' she said, when he reached her checkout.

Ant slouched more deeply. 'Suspended, aren't I? I did what you said, Bea. Completely honest. Cards on the table. But it was no good.'

'Did you go in early?'

He shook his head.

'You were meant to do that before you got called out on it. Oh, Ant, I wish I'd been there with you. You're entitled to have a rep with you.'

'Yeah, well. Too late now. She was pretty harsh.'

'But you're suspended, not sacked?'

'Yeah. Suspended for a week with no pay. I mean, can you even do that? Is it a thing?'

'I wouldn't argue, mate. At least you've still – oh, here we go. Incoming.'

Neville was strutting towards them with a gleam in his eye. 'Anthony, I'll have to ask you to leave the shop floor.'

Ant straightened up a little. 'I'm suspended, Nev, haven't you heard? So, I'm a customer now.'

'What are you buying?'

'I'm thinking about it,' said Ant. 'I'm trying to remember what we need.'

'If you are not actually buying anything, you must stop distracting my staff.'

Bea had almost been enjoying Ant's spirited display, but now her hackles were up. 'Your staff?' She clutched at the Costsave logo embroidered on her tabard and pushed it forward towards Neville. 'I think it says Costsave here, not Neville.'

Neville visibly bridled. 'While you are on the shop floor, Beatrice, you are well aware that I am your manager. You work for me.'

Their voices, initially kept at the level of furious hissing, had now risen, but even so, they all heard the sound of a woman's screams coming from one of the aisles behind them, wordless to start with and then, 'Oh my God! Somebody help! We need a doctor!'

Bea looked up. There was a flicker of panicky hesitation in Neville's face, but Ant had already gone, sprinting along the end of the aisles. He swung round a display of food supplements and vitamins – 'New Year, New You' – and disappeared into 'Bread and rolls, Jam and Spreads'.

Bea and Neville followed in his wake. When they found him, he was kneeling on the floor next to someone who was flat out on the tiles. Bea saw the man's feet move as Ant leaned onto his chest and made quick rhythmic compressions. It only took a few seconds for Bea to realise that the shoes belonged to Charles.

Ant was counting out loud as he worked. When he got to thirty, he stopped, shouted, 'Has someone rung for an ambulance?' and tipped Charles' head back a little and breathed into his mouth. He repeated it three times and then was back to the chest compressions and the counting.

Bea helped Eileen and Neville to clear the aisle of customers and cone it off at both ends.

It took twelve long minutes for the paramedics to arrive. Ant was sweating furiously, still going, still counting.

'Okay, mate. We'll take it from here.'

Exhausted, Ant moved away a little and sat with his back against the marmalades, legs sprawled out in front. Bea crouched down next to him and put her arm round his shoulders.

'Well done, Ant, you were brilliant.'

But Ant wasn't listening. He was staring past her towards Charles. 'Is he going to be okay?'

The paramedics were preparing to use a defibrillator now. 'I don't know, Ant. I don't know.'

The defibrillator fired, jerking Charles' body.

'We've got a pulse.'

Ant looked at Bea and started to cry.

'It's okay. Come here. It's okay.' Bea hugged him close, while he shook in her arms and her own tears ran down her face.

When he had recovered a little, Bea helped Ant to his feet. By now, Charles was on a stretcher being carried to the ambulance and staff were clearing up the floor and reopening the aisle.

'Come on,' said Bea. 'Let's get you a cup of tea.'

As they walked to the end of the aisle, Bob stopped picking up cones and slapped Ant on the back. 'Well done, son.'

A gaggle of customers had gathered nearby. One of them started clapping. Then two or three more joined in and the sound spread and grew until it seemed like the whole of Costsave was applauding with cheers and wolf whistles thrown in for good measure.

As Bea led Ant to towards the staff door, staff and customers formed a sort of guard of honour. Ant was still sniffing.

Bea gave him a squeeze. 'Listen to that. That's for you,' she said. 'You're a hero.' She expected him to break into his trademark grin, but instead Ant's bottom lip wobbled and he looked quite lost.

'Tea,' said Bea, firmly.

George herself held the staff door open for them. 'I saw what you did. You should be very proud of yourself, Ant.'

'I think he's a bit shocked,' Bea said, steering him through the door and propelling him up the stairs. George followed them.

'Sit down, both of you,' she said. 'I'll make the tea.'

Ant sat on the sofa with his head between his knees. He sat up when George brought two mugs over to them.

'Sugar for shock,' she said.

Ant and Bea sipped at the hot, sweet tea. Bea's hand was shaking now.

Anna popped her head round the doorway. 'Got the press on the phone – they'd like to interview Ant.'

'I don't want that,' said Ant. 'I just did what anyone would. I don't want any fuss.'

George perched on the arm of the chair opposite. 'Can you think about it?' she said. 'I mean, it would help get the word out about the importance of First Aid training.'

And it wouldn't do Costsave any harm, thought Bea, sensing a source of leverage. 'I agree it would help to reassure customers to know that our staff here are trained,' she said. 'But really, given his suspension and what he's been through, I think Ant should go home.'

George leaned forward and put her hand lightly on Ant's

arm. 'Given the exceptional circumstances, I think we can overlook the suspension. I'd be very grateful if you were up to doing an interview, as a public service.'

They both looked at Ant.

'What?' he said.

'If George forgets your suspension, perhaps you could manage a short interview?'

Bea watched understanding spread through Ant's expression like the first light of dawn breaking through a fine layer of mist.

'Well. Okay,' he said. 'I could try.'

'Good man,' said George. 'Anna, can you make the arrangements, please?'

In the end both the *Bugle* and the *Evening Post* sent reporters to Costsave. Kevin McKey, the local photographer, who supplied pictures to both newspapers, turned up too. By the time they'd got there, word had reached the staffroom that Charles had been admitted to Accident and Emergency and was receiving treatment. This news, together with two mugs of tea and a couple of jam doughnuts meant that Ant had perked up considerably and was starting to enjoy being the centre of attention.

Bea went back to her checkout, from where she was able to see some of the excitement as Ant had his picture taken in aisle ten and then outside the store. He winked at her as he breezed past with a journalist and Kevin in tow. On his way back inside, he stopped at Bea's checkout.

'All right?' Bea asked.

'Yeah,' he said. 'I'm all right but we've got a bit of a problem.'

'What's that?'

'Charles' dog is still tied up outside. What are we going to do about Goldie?'

8

'What's this?' Queenie's face was a picture. If Bea wasn't feeling so stressed out by her new responsibility, she would have taken a photo and Facebooked it.

'This is Goldie, Mum,' she said.

Goldie had walked twice as far as she was used to. Now she plonked her bottom down on the path by the back step. She was panting hard, but to Bea it seemed as if she was grinning as she looked up at Queenie.

'And?' said Queenie, apparently not won over by Goldie's doggy charms.

'She belongs to one of my customers. He was taken ill at the store today.'

'Bea, you can't just take on people's pets—'

'Mum, he's in hospital. There isn't anyone else. Can we talk about this inside, please? I need a cup of tea.'

Queenie reluctantly retreated inside and Bea led Goldie into the warmth. The dog padded in and stood near the sink, huffing and puffing. Bea caught a whiff of her breath or maybe it was her rather damp fur; it had been drizzling on their walk home. Either way, there was definitely essence de dog rising up in the warm, fuggy air.

They all stood looking at each other, before Queenie

started wrinkling her nose. She looked around and then focused on Goldie. 'It smells. Honestly, Bea.'

'*She*, Mum. She smells. It's just wet outside. She'll be fine when she's dried off.'

Now Queenie launched into another tirade. 'Really, Bea, we don't know about dogs. They need things, don't they, bowls and food and beds and that? We haven't got any of that.'

'George agreed to donate a load of stuff when she heard about Goldie – food, a couple of bowls,' said Bea. 'Bob's bringing it all round in about half an hour.'

'Bob's coming here?' Queenie started scratching at her wrist.

'Just to drop off the stuff, Mum. He doesn't have to come in. Anyway, you know Bob from the old days. You could have a chat. Why not?'

Queenie looked around rapidly. 'The house is a state.'

'It really isn't. It never is.'

'I'm not ready. I need to . . .'

'You don't need to do anything. It's fine. Just put the kettle on. I'm gasping.'

Queenie scowled, but turned round to fill the kettle. While it was boiling, Bea said, 'Why don't you say hello to her properly? She won't bite. She's the softest dog in the world.'

'I don't think so. I'm not a dog person.'

'Just stroke her a little bit, like this.' Bea stroked the top of Goldie's head and then ruffled the thick wavy fur where her neck met her shoulders.

'Then I'd have to wash my hands. I've got the sausages to cook, you know.'

Bea sighed. 'Okay. Shall I take her in the lounge, then, out of your way?'

'Not in the lounge,' Queenie said. 'I don't want hairs all over the place.'

'Okay, we'll stay here.'

'But I don't want hair in the food. It's not hygienic.'

'I'll just take her up to your bedroom, then, shall I?' said Bea.

'No, Bea! We can't have her upstairs!' Queenie was practically screeching now.

'I was joking, Mum. Winding you up. It's too easy.' Bea was laughing now.

'Can't she go outside?'

'No, she can't, it's freezing out there.'

While they were talking, Goldie had quietly snuck under the kitchen table and was lying with her head between her front paws. Bea nudged her mum and pointed to the floor. Goldie was starting to fall asleep, her eyelids flickering open, then closing again. Queenie's mouth formed a taut, straight line, but she stopped protesting and turned her attention to filling up the teapot, lighting their rather temperamental grill and setting out the sausages on the grill pan.

Bea sat down and found that there was nowhere for her feet to go. A retriever is not a small dog. Eventually, she kicked off her boots and put her stockinged feet on Goldie's side. She was lovely and warm, although still damp.

They'd almost finished eating their sausage sandwiches when the doorbell rang. Goldie raised her head and gave a low, throaty growl and then a sharp bark which made both Bea and Queenie jump.

'That'll be Bob,' said Bea.

'You go, Bea. I'll just stay here.'

Bea got up and Goldie came with her, wagging her tail. A second ring of the bell set off a volley of barking this time. Bea didn't know quite what to do.

'All right,' she said to Goldie. 'It's only Bob.'

She grabbed hold of Goldie's collar and opened the door. Sure enough, Bob-on-Meat was there with a plastic bag full of goodies and an enormous sack of dry dog food.

'Ah, thanks, Bob,' said Bea. 'I can't really let go of this one.'

'That's all right, love. It's a bit heavy, anyway. Let me bring it in.' He heaved the sack of food over the threshold and started lumbering down the hallway towards the kitchen doorway. 'In here?'

'Yes, please.' Bea and Goldie followed behind. Bea could hear Queenie scraping her chair back and an awkward, 'Oh.'

'Hello, Maggie.'

It felt strange to Bea's ears hearing Bob use her mum's real name. It brought back memories of her dad, giving her mum a kiss before he went to work: *See you later, Maggie.*

'Bob, I, um, I . . .' Queenie was standing up at the table, looking distinctly uncomfortable.

'Where shall I put this lot?'

'That's a good question. We haven't really got room for—'

'Just by the door for now, Bob,' said Bea.

Bob dumped the sack down. 'If I had my way I'd have brought you some proper meat for the dog. Real dog food. But if she's not used to it, it might upset her tum.'

He handed the bag to Bea, who peered in. 'Do you know about dogs, Bob?'

'Yeah. A bit. We always had dogs when I was growing up. And we had a couple when Fiona was little. What do you want to know?'

Bea held her hands out, palms upwards. 'Everything. What to feed her. How often. How many walks. Where she should sleep.'

'Ah,' said Bob. 'That reminds me, I've got a dog bed in the car. Word got around and Kirsty brought one in when she started her shift. First things first, put some water in one of those bowls. You always need a full water bowl, if you don't want her drinking out of your toilet—'

'Toilet? Oh my God!' said Queenie.

'I'll fetch the bed in. Then we'll run through what you need to do. She's not going to give you any trouble, though, is she? I mean, look at her. She's as good as gold. Ha! Good as Goldie. Right, you do the water, and put the kettle on.'

'Kettle? What do we need the kettle for?' Queenie's voice was almost a squawk.

Bob smiled. 'It's been a long day, Maggie. You wouldn't begrudge me a cuppa, would you?'

9

There was a noise. It forced its way into Bea's dreams, dragging her up to the surface. She opened her eyes. Sometimes her mum had nightmares and shouted out in her sleep, but this wasn't the same. It was a more of a whine. It took a while then, with sickening clarity, the thought came to her that there was a dog in the house. An unhappy dog, whining in the kitchen.

Bea rolled over and squinted at her alarm clock. Eight thirty-five. Still early for her day off. She'd been looking forward to a nice Sunday morning lie-in.

The volume of the whine increased. It couldn't be tuned out.

With a groan, Bea sat up and then lumbered out of bed, grabbed her dressing gown and shambled along the landing and down the stairs. When she opened the kitchen door, the smell seemed to rush out to greet her and wrap itself round her.

Goldie was standing just inside the doorway, grinning up at Bea as though she'd discovered a long-lost friend. Bea couldn't manage to grin back. Maybe she'd start feeling the love after a mug of good strong tea.

Bea walked around Goldie, picked up the kettle and went over to the sink. The floor was wet. It happened sometimes when she or Queenie were overenthusiastic with the washing-up. But that would have dried up overnight. And this was warm.

Bea looked down. There was a huge lake on the lino and her naked feet were slap bang in the middle of it. She looked over at Goldie who was standing pretty much in the same place, except that she had turned so she could see Bea. There she was. Grinning.

Bea didn't know whether to laugh or cry, but she didn't have time for either, because she could hear Queenie's footsteps on the landing above.

'If she sees this, that'll be the end of it. She'll turn you out,' Bea hissed at Goldie. 'Stay there. Don't move.' She waded across the kitchen to the doorway and yelled, 'Mum! What are you doing? I'll bring you a cuppa!'

'There's no need. I'll come down.'

'No!' Bea's voice was almost a squeak. She cleared her throat and tried again, lower this time. 'No! I want to treat you. Stay up there. I won't be two minutes.'

'All right. I'll just go to the bathroom.'

Bea ducked back into the kitchen. She frantically squirted some Flash into a bucket and swished some hot water in, then set about mopping the floor. Goldie watched with benign interest, moving obligingly when Bea asked her to wait in the hall.

'What are you doing?' Queenie called down as she emerged from the bathroom.

'Just a bit of cleaning while the tea's brewing. I'm coming up now.' She quickly dunked a tea bag in a mug of hot water and added some milk. She padded past Goldie, realising as she did so that she hadn't washed her feet, or the dog's. 'Wait there. I'll deal with you in a minute.'

'You all right, love? You look a bit flustered.' Queenie was back in bed, propped up against a pillow and with her puzzle magazine to hand.

'I'm fine. Need to take the dog out for a walk. Shall I bring you some toast up first?'

'No, I'll get up in a minute.'

'Okay, I'll just go out for five minutes with the dog.'

Bea flung on some clothes and then headed back downstairs. Goldie was standing at the bottom of the stairs, grinning up at her.

'Okay, you,' Bea said. 'Morning walky. What do I need?' She found her warmest coat, her mittens and a woolly hat. She put her keys and phone in the pocket and clipped the lead onto Goldie's collar. 'See you later,' she called out to her mum, and stepped out through the kitchen door.

The cold air pinched at her face. The temperature had dropped overnight and the path round the side of the house was slippery with ice. Goldie padded by her side. At least she didn't pull on her lead.

'Let's make this quick,' said Bea.

They walked past the little row of shops and crossed the road to the park. Goldie walked at Bea's side, keeping pace. They completed a circuit of the rec without incident. No stopping. No sniffing. No 'business' from Goldie. When they got back to the place they started at, Bea stopped and looked at Goldie, who instantly sat down and looked back up at her, smiling politely.

'What's your game?' Bea said to her. 'One more circuit, missy, and I want to see some action.'

They set off again. This time they got halfway round when Goldie fell behind. Bea stopped and looked back. The dog was crouching with a look of concentration on her face. Their eyes met, and the contact felt very, very wrong. Bea quickly looked away. When the dog padded up to her, she inspected the results of her efforts.

'Christ Almighty! How much have you *eaten*?' said Bea, then, 'Nooo! I forgot a bag!'

Bea searched her pockets on the off-chance of finding something suitable, but there was nothing. An old, chewed-up tissue wouldn't do the job, and apart from that she only had her keys and phone. Goldie, having finished, moved away from the mess, but Bea stayed where she was. She couldn't leave it, could she? She hated people who did that, didn't want to be that person.

She heard footsteps behind her and turned round. More dog-walkers – two lads in hoodies with a Staffie-type dog pulling enthusiastically on its lead. Perhaps they'd give Bea one of their bags. As they got closer, the dog began really straining on the lead, making excited grunting noises, and Bea recognised it as Tyson, pulling Dean along. Goldie seemed unconcerned. She wagged her tail gently and smiled at the trio, but Bea stepped off the path, out of harm's way, pulling Goldie with her.

'Hey, Dean,' she called out. 'You got a bag I could have?'

The boys had drawn level now. Tyson was lunging towards Goldie and Dean was struggling to keep hold of him. 'Made a mess, have you?'

'Well, not me, but – can I have one of your bags, please?'

'I don't carry them. Only losers pick up other people's shit.'

Bea looked from Dean's sneering face to his companion. He was a lot taller and much more solid than Dean, but equally unappetising. He had two slits shaved in his right eyebrow, and really bad skin. She raised her eyebrows at him, asking him the same question, but he wouldn't look her in the eye. He was carrying a large blue plastic box with a grill at one end. Bea bent slightly forward to look inside and caught a glimpse of some white fur. Dean's friend turned the box round so she couldn't see any more.

'Come on, mate,' he said to Dean. 'Let's get going.'

'Is that your cat?' said Bea.

'No. Yeah.'

She narrowed her eyes. 'Which one is it? Yes or no? What are you doing with it?'

Dean's friend clammed up. He shuffled a couple of steps further away from Bea.

'It's none of your business, is it?' said Dean.

'It is if it's stolen,' said Bea. 'Have you seen the paper this week?'

'Who are you, the cat police?' Dean sneered. 'Oh no, I was forgetting. You're not a copper, you just shag them. You're a grass.'

'So where are you taking it?'

'The vet. It's poorly.' Dean stuck his bottom lip out and dragged his fingers down his face from under his eyes. 'Come on.' He and his friend started walking away, leaving Bea with her original problem and a growing sense of suspicion.

She watched as they followed the path and then left the park by a side alley. 'They're not going to the piggin' vet,' she said to Goldie. 'Come on.'

They walked to the entrance of the alley. The two lads were silhouetted at the far end, then turned right and disappeared. Bea and Goldie followed. When they got to the end, Bea paused and peeked around the corner. Her quarry was about a hundred metres ahead of her, following a residential road that ran between some semi-detached houses and the allotments. Keeping at a distance, Bea carried on after them. At the far end of the allotments, they joined a path that led along the perimeter, with hedges and fields the other side.

By the time Bea had reached the start of that path, they had gone. Her heart was thumping in her chest from a combination of the exercise, the cold air and the thrill of the chase. She set off down the path, with Goldie at her side. Not far along, there was a gap in the hedge and a stile. The field on the other side of the stile was flat to start with and then dipped away into a river valley. There were clearly three sets of footprints in the frost leading away from the stile across the middle of the field – two people and a dog. There was no cover at all here. If she and Goldie carried on following, they were bound to be spotted. She didn't fancy another confrontation with Dean and his mate.

A shiver ran through her. Although the sun was coming up, making the frost sparkle on the surface of the field, the path was in shade, and Bea could see her own and Goldie's breath forming clouds in the air.

While she had been looking across the field, Goldie had lain down on the path. 'Home?' she said. Goldie wagged her tail in agreement.

They set off down the path. Before they reached the end, a figure appeared ahead of them, heading their way. Bea gasped. Although it was light now, the path felt closed in and she had a sudden flashback to a dark November night and the feeling of being followed. This isn't the same, she told herself. He's gone now. He's behind bars. Even so, her heart was thudding in her chest. She shortened Goldie's lead to bring the dog closer to her. As the figure got closer, she could see them do a double take as they spotted her and Goldie.

It was a middle-aged guy, in a sort of camouflage jacket with lots of pockets, and binoculars slung round his neck. He didn't want to look Bea in the eye, but muttered, 'Morning,' as he squeezed past.

Back on the rec, and breathing easier now, Bea remembered the unhappy pile that still needed her attention. She'd go back later with a bag. Right now, she needed to get home and have a large mug of tea, to calm her nerves. And maybe a bacon sandwich.

10

'She'll need another walk, you know.' Bob-on-Meat was in the back yard, tidying up his tools, having fixed a gate to the side of the house.

'I took her out this morning, Bob,' said Bea.

'Two walks a day and let her out in the garden when she asks. Keep her fit and keep your kitchen floor clean.'

'The floor? How do you know about that?'

'Your mum told me.'

'But I . . .but she . . .'

' . . .wasn't born yesterday,' said Queenie, standing by the corner in her slippers. 'When's the last time you mopped the kitchen floor before breakfast? Never, that's when.'

'Okay. Busted,' said Bea, pleased to see her mum out in the open air, even if it was only two metres from the kitchen door. 'I guess I'll have to get up a bit earlier.'

'You can just let her out now that this gate's in place,' said Bob. 'Let her potter about out here while you have a cuppa. Then take her out for a proper walk.'

'Yeah, the gate will make a big difference. Thanks, Bob. I'll take her out now.'

'That's the girl. Talking about cuppas . . .'

'That's what I came to tell you,' said Queenie. 'The kettle's on and I've just got some flapjack out of the oven. It'll be cool enough to cut in a minute.'

Bea didn't bother with the park but walked the path up to the allotments, heading for the field. There was a bus shelter near the allotment gate. Someone was sitting there, a hooded figure, bent over. She found herself thinking about the fuzzy image on the CCTV. Dean and his friend both had jackets with hoods on. This fella did too. Practically everyone did. How was she going to draw up a list of suspects, never mind narrow it down?

There was no danger of a bus coming, not on a Sunday, and it looked like whoever it was wasn't waiting anyway, but was wrapped up in their own world. As she got closer, she saw it was Ant. There was something sad, closed up, about him. She wondered whether to stay on the other side of the road and walk past without disturbing him, but if he was sad it was better to help, wasn't it?

She and Goldie crossed the road. She scuffed her trainers on the tarmac to give him some warning. He didn't react, just stayed there with his head resting on his knees.

'Hey, Ant. Whatcha up to?'

He raised his head a little and squinted at her. 'Nothing.'

'It's a bit cold to be sitting out here.'

'Mmm.' He put his head down again.

Bea perched next to him, Goldie in front of them, her muzzle close to Ant's face. 'What's going on, mate?'

'Nthng.' Then, 'Jesus, what's that smell?' He raised his head again and came eye to nose with Goldie. Her breath plumed out, engulfing his face. 'Wow, your dog has seriously bad breath,' he said, sitting upright and fanning the air around him.

'Not my dog,' said Bea, 'as you know. But, yes. She's pretty smelly all round actually. She pissed all over the floor this morning as well.'

Ant snorted, then held his hands in front of his mouth and blew into them and rubbed his palms vigorously together.

'It is cold, isn't it?' said Bea. 'What are you doing here?'

'I just needed to …get out for a bit. Home's just … I dunno…intense right now.'

'You could've come to mine. You know that, don't you? You're always welcome. Even Queenie likes you and she doesn't normally let anyone in the house. Except now Bob's in favour.'

'Bob-on-Meat?'

'Yeah. He's round there now. Put a gate up for us, and has stayed on for some of Mum's flapjack. Do you wanna come with us on our walk?' she said. 'It's too cold to sit here.'

'Yeah. Yeah, all right,' he said, getting to his feet. 'Where are we going? Round the park?'

'No,' said Bea. 'Down here. Bit of cross-country.'

'Okay.'

She led the way along the path by the allotments. When they got to the stile she saw that there was a dog-sized gap at the side, so she got Ant to hold Goldie's lead while she climbed over and then he passed it through to her with Goldie padding under to join her.

It was actually beautiful in the field. The path stretched out in front of them, curving down and away through close cropped grass. The sun had melted this morning's frosty footprints from the part of the field nearest the hedge, but that didn't matter. Dean and his mate had been following the path, so it should be easy to find out where they'd been heading.

'You could let her off the lead,' said Ant.

'Do you reckon? I don't want to lose her.'

'I don't think she's that sort of dog.'

Bea bent down and unclipped the lead from Goldie's collar. She expected her to take off running, kicking her

71

heels up with the joy of her new-found freedom, but Goldie smiled at her politely and continued padding alongside them, matching their pace and line.

'So, do you want to tell me about it?' said Bea.

'What?'

'Whatever it is had you sitting in a bus stop.'

'I dunno, Bea. I just feel as if we've been here before. My dad going away. But this time, he's been painted as public enemy number one – we were on TV, for fuck's sake – and my mum's really upset, and she's worried about the bills and, I dunno.'

'That sounds like enough to me. Sounds like a lot.'

'Yeah, and I couldn't sleep last night. It wasn't home stuff, it was that old bloke, Charles. I kept seeing his face, his eyes rolling back. I could feel his chest under my hands. I could . . . Jesus.'

Bea looked across at Ant and was dismayed to see him crying again. 'It's all right,' she said. 'He's all right. You saved him.'

He wiped his face on his sleeve. 'I know. I don't know what's wrong with me.'

'You've got a lot going on.'

'Yeah.'

They were walking downhill now, the path leading towards a kissing gate in the corner of the field. They reached the gate and threaded their way through it, facing a choice on the other side. One path went into the belt of trees and seemed to hug the riverbank. The other went diagonally across the next field, but the undulation of the land meant it disappeared over the brow of the hill. It had been so long since Bea had walked here (had she ever walked here?), that she didn't know which one was more likely as a route for Dean and his friend.

'River or field?' said Ant.

'I'm not sure.'

'Well, it's not as if it actually matters.'

Bea bent forward and studied the ground where the paths diverged.

'What are you doing?'

'Looking for footprints, but the ground's too hard.'

Ant screwed up his face. 'What are you now? Some sort of wild woman of the woods?'

'I'm trying to do a thing,' she said, straightening up and looking across the field.

A broad grin spread over Ant's face, the first time she'd seen him smile today. 'You're investigating again. Is it the cat thing?'

'Yes! At least it could be.' And Bea told him what she'd seen that morning.

'Deano. That figures. Trying to think who the other one was. Tell me again.'

'Tall. Built like a brick . . .outhouse. Shaved eyebrow.'

'Sounds like Tank.'

'Tank?'

'Yeah, can't remember his real name. He hangs around with Dean and some other losers in the Prospect sometimes.'

'What else do you know about him?'

Ant shrugged. 'Think he did a bit of dealing. Not sure. Sorry.' He looked over the field. 'I reckon that way. Come on.'

They set off again. The sun was getting lower in the sky, sending long shadows across the surface of the grass. There was hardly any sound – no traffic noise, just a few birds shouting at each other as they flapped about in the top of the trees at the field's margins.

Through the sparse hedge on the river side, Bea could see the dark shape of a bulky figure. They were standing still. She got the eerie feeling that she and Ant were being watched, but by the time she had got further and was able to see through a bigger gap, whoever it was had their back to them and was looking across the river.

Ant and Bea walked easily together, in silence, and Bea found herself enjoying the rhythm of it. One foot in front of the other, heading up towards the sun. She was slightly breathless, but she didn't mind. It felt good. This was the sort of exercise she could deal with.

At the top of the hill they paused. Ant turned around. 'Look at that, Bea. K-town in all its glory.'

She turned too. It was a good view – the little town spread out before them, houses, the odd low-rise industrial unit and small blocks of flats and the tower of St Swithin's church in the middle. Behind that there was a gaggle of cranes where the old factory was being redeveloped, and further still gentle layers of hills and woods and the promise of Bristol beyond.

'Been thinking about that bloke on the bypass at New Year's Eve?' said Ant.

'The jumper? Yeah, it was in the *Bugle*. Terrible, isn't it?'

'What a way to go, jumping off a bridge. Not the first one there either, is it?

'It's so sad,' said Bea. 'But New Year's like that, isn't it? Thinking about the last year, looking forward to another one. It can all seem a bit bleak. Too much.'

'Hmm. Still can't remember much about my New Year's Eve, not even the girl I snogged. Must have been a good night, eh?' He tried smiling, but it was a watery effort and Bea couldn't help thinking about how sad he had looked, sitting on his own at the bus stop just now. Impulsively, she put her arms round his waist and gave him a squeeze. Caught off guard, he staggered backwards a little, taking Bea with him. When they regained their balance, Bea let go, wishing she'd left well alone and saved them both the embarrassment.

'What was that all about?' said Ant.

'Nothing,' said Bea. 'Just want you to know ...I dunno, that I'm here for you. If you need to talk or whatever.' She couldn't quite look him in the eye.

'Daft cow,' said Ant, mildly, but Bea could tell he was pleased.

'Right,' she said, turning around again. 'What's down there?'

There was another hedgerow ahead of them. Beyond it there was a group of buildings in amongst a clump of trees. They stumped down the slope and climbed over the next stile, then followed the path to the trees. As they approached, the hill behind them cut off the afternoon sun and the temperature dropped instantly. Bea's shoulders hunched as a shiver ran through her.

'I don't know about this, Ant,' she said.

'Don't be soft. We might as well look now we're here.'

The path didn't go right up to the buildings. Instead it veered off and skirted the edge of the field, but there was a five-bar gate in the corner of the field leading to the compound. There was a sign fixed to the gate: 'PRIVATE LAND. KEEP OUT'.

Ant shinned over the gate quickly and stood looking back at Bea and Goldie.

'I'm still not sure,' said Bea.

'There's no one here. We're not doing any harm,' said Ant. 'Come on.' He held out his hand to help her up.

'What about the dog?' said Bea.

There was no purpose-made gap by this gate. A smaller dog could easily have got through, but Goldie was a little too statuesque to squirm round or even under.

'We could lift her over,' said Ant, doubtfully.

Bea breathed out, puffing her lips forward. 'I don't think so. Not unless there's a winch in one of those buildings.'

Casting her own vote, Goldie lay down on the stubbly grass.

'Tie her up, then,' said Ant. 'We're only going to be two minutes.'

Bea tied the free end of the lead to one of the horizontal bars of the gate, then clambered over the gate and she and Ant approached the buildings.

There were three structures nestling among the trees; a tall open-sided barn with a corrugated iron roof, a large brick building, and a long, low brick-built shed. They enclosed a yard on three sides, with a track leading out of the fourth side. Ant and Bea made their way into the yard. It was a grey, dark space which felt closed in, even airless.

Bea stood in the middle and turned all the way round, taking pictures on her phone. There was nothing out of the ordinary here and yet it was giving her the creeps, big time.

Ant went up to the low shed. There were a couple of windows in the side, but they were either filthy or were blocked by something. 'I can't see anything,' he called out to Bea.

'Shh,' she hissed. It felt wrong to be making a noise.

She walked over to the open barn. Some bales of hay were stacked up at one end and some machinery and old tyres and bales of barbed wire were littering the other. Nothing you wouldn't expect on a farm. She made her way over to the big brick building. There were huge doors at one end, secured with a padlock. 'There's nothing to see really, is there?' she whispered.

'Nah,' said Ant. 'I'll go round the back, though.' He nipped quickly down the side of the barn and disappeared from view.

Bea walked towards the track. The yard was a rough patchwork of concrete, but the track was unmade, just frozen mud. She walked along it for a few metres and noticed how cut up it was, set into a mass of peaks and troughs, like a solid, stormy sea. It might be quiet here now, but at some point, before the temperature had dropped, there had been a lot of vehicles in and out of this yard.

She shivered again and walked back into the yard to find Ant. There was only a small square of sky visible in here and the light was starting to leach from it. She didn't want to be walking back in the dark. She didn't want to be here at all.

Ant appeared around the corner of the shed. 'I reckon I can hear something in there. Something shuffling around,' he said.

'Or someone,' said Bea, and immediately wished she hadn't. That was it. Her nerve was gone. 'Come on, Ant, we've got to get out of here.'

'Yeah, it's getting dark. We'll come back another day, shall we?'

'Maybe.'

As they approached the gate, they could hear Goldie whining.

Ant vaulted over and untied her. 'What's up with you?' he said, ruffling the fur round her neck. She stopped whining and got to her feet and started wagging, even though there were spasms of shivering running up and down her legs.

'Aw, she's cold,' said Ant. 'Me too. It's freezing now.'

'Look how bloody dark it is as well!' said Bea.

The sky had clouded over, and the fields and hedges were reduced to solid shapes in shades of grey. They set off up the hill. When they got to the stile at the top, they heard a noise. Turning round, they saw headlights coming up the track towards the buildings they had just left.

'Shall we go back?' said Bea. 'See who it is?'

'Shall we buggery,' said Ant. 'I'm freezing cold, the dog's fed up and I think it's going to snow. Plus, I don't want to get shot in the head by a farmer.'

'All very good points,' said Bea.

'Come on, then,' said Ant. 'Do you think there's any of Queenie's flapjack left?'

11

Bea woke early, listening for the sound of the dog. It was still dark, but there was a strange quality to the streetlight seeping in through the gap in her curtains. She checked her watch and groaned: 5.45. Her bedroom was cold so she pulled the duvet up around her ears and snuggled down.

She was hoping to get at least another hour's snooze in, but instead her mind kept ranging over the events of the day before – Dean and Tank, the cat in the box, and the creepy farm buildings. Was it the cat that Ant had heard in the shed? Should they have stayed and tried to get into the building? But there was that car, and then she remembered the mangled cat in Costsave's cardboard, and the missing cats in the *Bugle*, and she felt a stab of anxiety mixed up with something else.

Ant had smiled when he'd said, 'You're investigating, aren't you?' and she had to admit there was something thrilling about having another 'case' to work on.

She sat up and checked her watch again. 5.57. She groaned. It was just plain wrong to get up before six o'clock. Goldie would need a good walk this morning, because Queenie wasn't likely to do anything more than let her out into the garden while Bea was at work, but there was still time for that if she went out at 6.30. She pulled the duvet up to her chin and reached for her phone, scrolling through the photos that so far made up the evidence for this 'case'.

There were the shots of Joan's body that she had shown to Tom and Shaz, some 'screenshots' of the CCTV that she'd managed to sneak at work, and finally, the farm buildings. Next, she pulled up a map of Kingsleigh and zoomed in on the area where the four cats had lived. The street names for the missing cats had been in the *Bugle*. They were all within the same small residential area – the square where Anna's flat was and the few streets around.

She needed to write it down. She threw back the duvet and swung her legs out of bed. She went over to the bookshelves above her desk and reached down a soft-backed notebook. After Ginny's murderer was arrested and charged, Bea had stuck her printout of suspects into this book along with a couple of *Bugle* articles. It was a way of coming to terms with what had happened, keeping it because it was important, but also closing the cover, putting it on the shelf, moving on. She felt the sharp pang of grief as she opened the cover. It was almost a physical pain, the stab of knowledge that the events before Christmas had been real, that Ginny was never coming back. But it was mixed with something else, another feeling – a frisson of excitement.

She found a fresh page and wrote a heading, below which she listed four strands of enquiry as bullet points.

- Missing Cats
- the 'Square'
- the Costsave connection
- Dean and Tank

She checked her phone. Only six twenty-five. Pleased with her progress, she headed for the bathroom.

The house was in a sort of half-light as she padded

79

downstairs. She was starting to get used to the doggy fug that greeted her. There were no extra acrid notes this morning, so that, at least, was a win.

Goldie, still in her basket, looked up politely as Bea came in and scrambled to her feet, wagging benignly. Bea drew the bolt back on the kitchen door and turned the key in the lock. When she opened the door, she couldn't help smiling – there was a thick layer of snow outside, nearly two inches. That explained the weird light; the snow was reflecting the streetlight.

Goldie peered out of the door and retreated to her bed.

'Ha!' said Bea. 'We're going out in a minute, whether you like it or not.' She pulled on her coat and moon boots, checked for dog bags, keys and phone, then clipped Goldie onto her lead. They both hesitated for a moment on the threshold and then stepped out into the snow.

The houses and streets and the park were breathtakingly different this morning – a better version of themselves. Bea briefly thought about heading into the field again, but after yesterday, she didn't want to go on her own. She wasn't sure Goldie was up to the role of fierce defender. Besides, she had a plan for this morning's walk.

Bea was the first person to cross the rec, but there were animal footprints leading from one side to the other. Goldie had a bit of a sniff at them before hunching over and conducting the morning's business. Bea was just closing the lid on the nearest dog bin when she saw a shape moving on the other side of the rec. Goldie had seen it too. She was staring intently and then she gave a deep bark.

The shape stopped moving and Bea could see the fox staring back at them, before it started running. Bea grabbed hold of Goldie's collar, but she didn't need to; Goldie wasn't interested in the chase. Once the fox had disappeared from view, she just gave a little grumble and turned away.

'Good girl,' said Bea. They'd only been out for a few minutes but her feet were starting to get cold, even inside her moon boots. She bent down, formed a snowball with her mittens and threw it in front of Goldie. It landed with a soft thud a few metres in front of her. Goldie watched with polite interest, then walked slowly up to the place where it had landed, gave it a cursory sniff and looked back at Bea. Bea could almost swear she shrugged.

'All right, brisk walk to warm up,' she said and she started marching towards the far side of the rec. As they approached the square which seemed to be the focus of the cat mystery, Goldie started walking faster, going ahead of Bea, and Bea remembered that Charles lived in one of the bungalows. Goldie was heading home. She walked right up to the door and stood there wagging with her front paws on the step.

'Not today,' Bea said softly, clipped Goldie on her lead and gently started to walk her away. She heard a gentle whirring noise and looked round. A CCTV camera on the house next to Charles' was swivelling on its bracket, pointing at her. Extra security was probably a good thing, Bea thought. Old people were so vulnerable. The front garden looked strangely prison-like, a forest of short bamboo sticks poking up out of the snow with string criss-crossing between them. Something to keep the birds off, Bea supposed. As she watched the front door opened and a man shuffled out of the front door, dragging a trolley on wheels behind him. It was fluorescent yellow with '*Kingsleigh Bugle*' emblazoned on the side.

The man nodded to her. He had obviously been quite tall when younger, but was now bent over, with a permanent curve in his spine. He saw her watching and waved.

'Morning,' Bea called out. He nodded to her and Bea moved on.

There was a light on in the next house, and Bea thought she saw the curtain moving. She hoped she and Goldie hadn't worried the pensioner living there. At its worst, Queenie's anxiety made her jump at every noise outside and peer out at the side of the curtain, trying to see the source but not be seen. She wouldn't want to have sparked similar anxiety in anyone else.

'Come on,' she said. They walked around the edge of the square, past the flats where Anna lived. There was a whining sound in the background, getting louder as they walked. Despite the snow, an electric milk float turned into the square and made stop-start progress along the rows of houses, as the milkman delivered milk and cartons of juice. As he got closer, Bea could see that he wasn't in the traditional uniform of white coat and peaked hat (had that ever actually been a thing?), but was wearing a thick padded coat with a hood, and fingerless gloves.

'All right?' he said to Bea as she walked past him.

'Morning,' she replied.

She and Goldie had completed their tour of the square. They mooched back across the rec and were overtaken by two women, heads down, walking solidly.

'Don't see how the two of us can cover the whole office with our hours cut like that. It's ridiculous.'

'We'll just have to skimp a bit. Do the bogs and the kitchen, but only do the desks once a month or something. Lazy beggars can clean their own keyboards and screens.'

'Ha! And wash their own mucky cups!'

Bea checked her phone. Ten past seven. She guessed these two were coming *back* from cleaning, their early morning shifts already done.

There was a slight lightening in the eastern edge of the sky, a suggestion of the start of the day. As they left the rec, nearly home now, Bea felt the cogs in her brain turning slowly. The cat killer must work at night. After all, they'd dumped Joan's body at the very start of the day. If she kept walking Goldie around Kingsleigh's streets in the early hours, would she see them in the end? Perhaps she already had. It was a sobering thought.

She took a deep breath, filling her lungs with cold, crisp air. Time for a cuppa, some Coco Pops and maybe a bonus slice of toast. These early walks were all very good, but they didn't half make you work up an appetite.

As Bea sat at the table eating her cereal and making notes in her book about the sorts of people who might be out and about early in the morning, she could hear Goldie crunching the biscuits in her bowl. It only took the dog a few seconds to polish off the lot and then she was lying at Bea's feet. Queenie appeared as Bea was making the toast. She looked at Goldie warily.

'No accidents?'

'No, Mum, not today. We don't do that any more, do we?' Bea said, addressing Goldie, who was now sitting to attention next to her, watching her every move as she buttered the toast. 'Oh, you like toast, do you?' A string of drool formed at one saggy corner of Goldie's mouth. 'Here.' Bea broke off a bit of crust and Goldie took it delicately from her fingers.

'Oh no, Bea, don't do that! Don't feed the dog titbits.'

Bea winked at Goldie and ate the rest herself, leaning against the cupboards.

'What's that?' said Queenie, looking at Bea's notebook on the kitchen table.

'Oh, nothing,' Bea said, gathering it up. 'Are you going to be all right with the doggy today?' she asked, quickly changing the subject.

Queenie pulled a face. 'I'll have to be, won't I? Don't see that I've got much choice.'

Bea picked her way carefully across the Costsave car park. Staff driving their cars in had compacted the snow and it was starting to make rutted ice. She was nearly at the door when Ant caught her up.

'I know what I'm going to be doing today,' he said.

'Shovelling snow?' said Bea.

'Got it in one.'

A car drew up right by the door. Bob-on-Meat got out of the driver's door and jogged round to the passenger side. Then he held his arm out for Dot to hold onto as she picked her way the few metres towards Ant and Bea.

'Jeez,' said Ant, and made to go inside.

'Hang on, Ant,' said Bea, not wanting him to disappear. 'Aren't you going to hold the door open, like a gentleman?'

He puffed out his cheeks. 'Yeah. Okay. Whatever.' He punched in the access code and then stood back and held the door.

Dot smiled at him. 'Thank you, Ant. Nice to see you.'

Ant winced a little, but managed, 'You too, Dot. Welcome back.'

'I'll hug you in a minute, Dot,' said Bea, squeezing her arm as she went past. 'Don't want to risk skating across the car park.'

Bob got back in his car and went to find a space. Bea started to follow Dot up the stairs to the locker room, leaving Ant skulking in the lobby, but she went back down.

'Ant, mate, you need to get over it. Dot's fine with you. There's no embarrassment, no bad feelings. Just be normal with her.'

He scuffed his toes on the wall, looking down. 'Yeah, I know. It's just—'

'Just nothing. I can't have two of my best mates here not talking. I'll have to cut myself in half. Let's all have lunch together, iron things out.'

'Dunno what time Nev's going let me have my break today.'

84

'Well, Dot's only doing till twelve, so if you've got your lunch break then, find Dot, won't you? I'll try and have my break then too.'

'Yeah, all right.'

They headed up the stairs together.

'Here,' said Ant, 'I've been thinking.'

'Steady. You'll give yourself a nosebleed.'

'Ha, ha. No, listen, I went down the pub last night. Stevo and I took Mum, trying to cheer her up.'

'That's nice. Did it?'

'Nah, not really. She just sat in a corner, didn't say much. And I think – nah, it doesn't matter.'

'What?'

'I think people are avoiding us. Well, her. They were talking to me because of Charles and me being on the telly, but Mum was sort of left on her own. Some of the neighbours too. They usually rally round when Dad's gone away, but this time nothing.'

Bea sighed. 'Maybe it's what your dad did, nicking people's presents. It was pretty low, Ant.'

'Yeah, but it wasn't Mum's fault. She didn't do it.'

'Guilt by association, I suppose. People can be cruel. Things'll settle down.'

'Hope so. Anyway, what I was going to tell you was just before last orders Deano and Tank came in. Tank was looking as white as a sheet. Proper agitated.'

They were at the top of the stairs now. Bea checked her watch. They only had a couple of minutes before George's morning huddle and she needed to change out of her boots.

'Can you tell me later, Ant? Can't be late, can we?'

'Okay. Catch you at dinner.'

'First of all, well done for getting into work on time. The weather may put some customers off, but past experience has shown that there may also be a rush on bread and milk. I'm expecting our normal supplies to get through, so any low stock levels should be short-lived, but be prepared for some moans and groans. Meet them with your usual smiles and positive attitude.

'Talking of positive, I've got some very good news. We're up one and a half per cent on the same week last year. I want to thank you all for knuckling down and rallying round. But we can do better still. We need to be leaner and meaner. Well, maybe not meaner.' George flashed a reassuring smile around the room. 'We need to trim waste. I've been reviewing the stock with Mila – there's stuff in the stockroom from years ago. Dead stock that we will never sell – Three Lions garden gnomes from 2014, *Kung Fu Panda* bubble bath, superhero pencil toppers...'

'I've got one of those gnomes,' muttered Bob. 'Only six fifty with my staff discount. Bloody good value.'

'It's all got to go,' said George. Ant had raised his hand. 'Yes, Ant?'

'I could sell it for you. Keep it till the summer and I'll car boot it. Give the proceeds to Kayleigh's Wish.'

'Kayleigh's what?'

Anna stepped in. 'It's the store's adopted charity, George. Kayleigh's the daughter of one of our colleagues. She's got leukaemia.'

George nodded as she took in the information. 'I like your thinking, Ant, that's very generous of you. But I can't wait for the summer. This store needs sorting out now. There's no time to lose in retail. We have to be responsive, flexible, current.'

'What about selling it in store, then?' said Bea. 'Make a thing of it. We could use the bay in aisle fifteen where we sell damaged stock. Put all the dead stock in there, mixed up, like a sort of bargain basement. Call it something fun, I don't know. Call it the Crazy Aisle.'

There were some murmurs among the crowd, but it was difficult to tell if they were for or against.

George frowned. 'Well, we don't want it to look like a jumble sale. We've got standards to maintain.'

'I could make it look nice,' said Eileen. 'I like visual merchandising.'

'What?' said Ant. 'Standing all the gnomes up straight, making them point the same way?'

Eileen turned a rather nasty shade of beetroot. Ant grinned and held his hands up in defence.

'Wouldn't that conflict with our Valentine's display?' said Neville. 'That will be going in on Thursday, taking up half of the other side of aisle fifteen.'

'Nah, it's spot on, mate,' said Ant. 'We can still call it the Crazy Aisle.' He started singing and jigging about on the spot. Bea eventually realised it was his version of 'Crazy in Love'.

George held her hand up. 'All right, all right,' she said, raising her voice above the hubbub. 'Let's work on that. We can't call it the Crazy Aisle, though. Costsave as a company takes mental health issues very seriously. We don't want to cause offence to our . . .' she struggled to find the right words ' . . .to our customers. We'll think of something else and I'll ask Regional HQ if we can donate a proportion to our charity. Okay, everyone. It's nearly time. I'm expecting a busy day today – let's make it a good one.'

As Dot took her place at checkout five, Bea felt that after six weeks of things being slightly off-kilter, everything was back to normal. Or as normal as it could be, when one of your colleagues has been murdered and there are dead cats turning up in the recycling.

'Ready for this?' she asked Dot, as they watched George walk towards the front door with the master keys in her hand.

Dot stretched her arms out and wiggled her fingers like a concert pianist limbering up. 'I was born ready, babe. I'm so glad to be back. If I had to watch one more morning of daytime TV I think I would have gone mad. Mind you, if there's anything you want to know about cooking, DIY, property developing or antiques, just ask. I'm a bloody expert on all that. Don't ask me to shift my arse and actually *do* any of it, though.'

'You've got Bob for that, haven't you? The DIY and stuff. He's pretty handy.' Bea caught Dot's eye, and there was a twinkle there and a suggestion of a smile playing round the corner of her mouth.

'I know what you're thinking. Not that sort of handy,' said Dot, then the smile got broader. 'Not yet. Not much, anyway.'

'Ooh,' said Bea. 'You're a one, aren't you? He was round at ours yesterday, putting up a gate.'

'Was he?'

'Hmm, he and Mum had a nice chat. Took the heat off me a bit.'

'That's nice.'

The doors were open now and Smelly Reg was shuffling in and heading for the paper rack and his *Racing Post*. He was followed by the usual gaggle of early morning shoppers. While they waited for them to grab their goods and make their way to the checkouts, Bea and Dot watched Ant through the window. Just as he'd thought, he was on car park clearing duty, shovelling snow off the paths and sprinkling grit. He'd done all of a couple of minutes' work when he stopped to lean on one of the pillars at the back of the trolley park and light up a cigarette, thinking he was tucked away out of sight.

'Uh-oh,' said Dot, as they saw Neville, on the customer service desk, clock him. 'Quick, Bea, do something.'

Neville left the desk, but instead of going out to deal with

Ant, he found George, who was inspecting aisle fifteen. Bea got out of her chair and went and banged on the window near Ant. He looked up, startled, then grinned when he saw her. She wagged her index finger at him, but he just took a long drag, tipped his head up and blew the smoke out, then gave her the thumbs up.

When he saw George approaching he dropped the cigarette and ground it under his foot, but it was too late. He'd been caught red-handed. Bea retreated to her checkout.

'That boy,' said Dot. 'He'll never learn, will he?'

'Doubt it. He's a good 'un really,' said Bea. 'The stuff with his dad is hitting him hard.'

'Poor lad. Getting fired from here won't help, though.'

'She won't sack him, will she?'

'I don't know. Looks like it might just be a standard bollocking.'

Someone cleared their throat nearby. Bea's nose wrinkled and she fought the urge to sneeze. She didn't need to turn round to know who it was.

'Morning, Reg,' she said, not expecting a reply.

'Filthy,' he said.

Bea wondered if she'd misheard and carried on bleeping his shopping.

'Filthy weather,' Reg said, handing over the cash.

'I don't know,' said Bea. 'I quite like the snow, but keep safe, walking home.'

He gathered up his things and shuffled out.

'Blimey,' said Dot. 'Things have changed around here. Reg has started making small talk!'

12

George was right – Costsave had been much busier than usual. The bread aisle was picked clean, and there were only a few litres of full-fat milk left. Just before twelve, Dot checked her watch and then put the 'checkout closing' sign onto her conveyor belt.

'That's me done,' she said. 'I'm absolutely knackered. Glad I'm only doing a couple of stints this week. I don't think I could cope with any more. People have gone mad, haven't they? Talk about Snowmageddon. Ooh.' She winced as she held the side of her desk and got to her feet. 'I've stiffened up. Ooh, that hurts.'

'Do you need a hand, babe?' said Bea.

'No, I'll be all right when I get going.'

'I should be due a break any time now. Shall we grab some lunch?'

Dot's face was creased with pain. 'I think I'll have to go straight home. I'll get a taxi. Next time, lovely, okay? I'm in again on Thursday.'

She hobbled slowly towards the back of the store. Bea watched her go, then realised her customer was drumming her fingers on the side of the counter. She'd stopped halfway through processing the woman's shopping.

'Sorry,' she said. 'It's her first day back at work.'

The woman, in her thirties, with a smart black coat on and sleek shiny hair in a pixie cut, looked at her blankly.

'Sorry,' Bea said again and quickly beeped the rest of her shopping, which was a joyless collection of quinoa, vegetable juice, rice cakes and healthy snacks. When she'd done, she hit the call button to summon Neville and ask if she could go for her break.

'Another half an hour, Beatrice,' Neville said, with a sniff. 'You can see it's building up for another rush now.'

With a sigh, Bea started on the next load of shopping – four two-litre bottles of Coke, four of lemonade, several multipacks of crisps and snacks, little fairy cakes, frozen sausage rolls.

'Going to be quite the party,' Bea said, as she heaved the lemonade into the packing area.

'No,' said her customer, a younger woman with a thick Puffa jacket slung over a tracksuit, 'it's just for me.' There was a hint of ice in her voice.

Bea looked at her. For a moment, they held each other's gaze, then the woman smiled and shook her head. 'Only kidding, I've got twelve nine-year-olds coming after school. It's going to be the longest two hours of my life, if they all come. Otherwise, I won't have to cook for a week.'

'Ha! Got me going there,' said Bea. 'Serve me right for commenting on your shopping. I should know better. You won't need party games anyway, they can just have a snow-ball fight.'

'Mm, after about twenty minutes I'll have twelve cold, tired, wet kids, with at least three of them in tears. Oh joy.'

'Do you remember being that age and going to parties, though? Wondering if you'll win any games and what'll be in the party bag.' Bea carried on processing the shopping, but she was thinking about her nine-year-old self, happy in the years before her dad died.

'Don't get me started on party bags. It's like a crazy competition with the parents. Kids expect an Oscars-style goodie bag these days. Not at my house. It's a slice of cake, a balloon, a Kit-Kat and a fancy pen.'

'Just as it should be. Shame we all have to grow up, isn't it?'

The woman stopped and looked at her. 'That's a bit deep for a Monday, isn't it?'

'Sorry. I was just thinking about—'

'About that chap that jumped off the bridge?' Bea hadn't been, but she supposed it was on everyone's mind. 'Mm, that was a shocker, wasn't it? Odd that they haven't named him yet.'

'Yeah, isn't it?' She handed the woman her change. 'Oh well. Good luck with the party anyway!'

'Cheers. I'll need it.'

A little while later Ant slouched along the exit side of the checkouts. He stopped next to Bea. 'I've just seen Dot getting in a cab. Do you fancy some chips?'

Bea thought for about a millisecond before logging off her till. 'Yeah, go on. You can tell me all about the pub. I'll just fetch my purse and phone.'

Neville appeared out of nowhere, blocking her way. 'I said another half an hour, Beatrice,' he said, knuckles white where he was gripping his clipboard.

'It's been twenty-three minutes, Neville, and I'm dying for the loo. Not much point coming back after that, is there, so I'll take my break now, if that's all right.'

He sniffed loudly but gave way.

In the Costsave café, the hot, floury chips just out of the fryer were going down a treat, with lashings of salt and vinegar and a good dollop of ketchup. Ant got stuck in, drawing air into a full, open mouth to cope with their heat, in a rather unedifying spectacle.

'How are you getting on with the doggo?' he asked. 'No more accidents?'

'No, we're getting used to each other.' Bea was taking things more sedately, cutting the bigger chips in half to let them cool down. 'I had a nice walk with her this morning. Up before everyone else, beautiful fresh snow. We saw a fox too. Lovely things, aren't they?'

'Yeah, but vicious.' Ant wiped a blob of ketchup away from the side of his mouth.

'We walked down to the square, you know where the bungalows are and Anna's flat. All the missing cats are from round there.'

'Yeah?'

'Yeah. I had a look round but didn't see anything. There was hardly anyone about, but I was thinking there are a few people up that early. What if our cat killer is someone no one would take any notice of? Like the milkman or a shift worker.'

'Or a street cleaner or something.'

'Exactly. Someone like that.' Bea whipped out her phone and opened up the Notes section.

'So even if people saw them they wouldn't think anything of it,' said Ant. 'Yeah, you might be onto something. You're bloody clever, you are, Bea. Too clever for this place.'

'Shut up. I just like thinking about stuff. Anyway, it's just a theory. Might be way off the mark. The other thing is to think about the Costsave connection. Why did he, or possibly she, dump the body here?'

'Hmm, that's another good point. Then there's Deano and Tank.'

'Yes. We need to find out if either of them actually has a cat. If not, it could be one of them, taking the cats, killing them. Or both of them. They looked incredibly shifty.'

Ant shovelled some more chips in. 'Well, that's normal for

Deano. I know he's a nasty little fucker, but I doubt he's sick enough to kill a cat.'

'What about Tank?'

'Don't know so much about him, but I know someone who does. I'll get my special agent onto it.'

Bea looked up from her phone. 'Who is your special agent, just out of interest?'

He tapped the side of his nose. 'Need-to-know basis, Bea.' Ant had finished his chips and was smearing a piece of white bread around his plate, picking up any left-behind grease or sauce. 'We'll find out about Tank, Bea, and then maybe we should leave it. After all, Inspector Morse is on the case now. Maybe you should leave it to him.'

'But I promised Anna.'

'And she wouldn't want you getting knifed by a crazy cat killer, would she? Neither would I. Don't get mixed up in stuff if you don't have to. Life's complicated enough.' He looked at the unfinished food on Bea's plate. 'Aren't you going to eat that?'

'No,' she said, pushing the plate towards him. 'You have it.'

Bea was logging off for the evening as Jay arrived at checkout number five. Her stomach gave a little flip when she saw him.

'Hi, you,' she said, and then winced inside thinking it was a little too familiar, too fond. Had she given away how she felt?

Happily, he seemed oblivious. 'Hi Bea. All right?'

The facial hair, the man bun, it was all wrong and yet somehow so, so right. Bea tried to act normally, but found herself staring at his face. She didn't even notice Ant come shambling along.

'Hey, bro,' Jay said. He stood up and extended his balled-up hand to Ant. Ant, somewhat surprised, touched knuckles and grinned. Jay grinned back and Bea noticed how the skin at the side of his mouth creased, emphasising the smile. 'Heard all about you saving that guy's life. You're the man, Ant.'

'Yeah, well . . .I dunno about that.'

'You guys just clocking off?'

'Yeah.' Bea was making sure her station was neat and tidy and giving her conveyor belt a final wipe down.

Jay sat down, then yawned and stretched his arms above his head. 'Wish I was. Only got up an hour ago. I'm knackered.'

'Busy weekend?' said Bea.

'Yeah, you could say that.'

'What did you get up to?'

Jay leaned back in his chair. 'This and that. Out with my mates.'

'Where did you go? Somewhere nice?'

'What is this? Twenty questions?'

Ant laughed. 'You'll have to get used to that if you sit there, mate. She won't stop digging until she knows your favourite colour M&M, your credit card number and your inside leg measurement.'

'Oi? Shut up!' Bea leaned forward to take a swipe at Ant. 'I'm not that bad. I'm just curious. I like finding stuff out.'

Neville came bustling along, clipboard at the ready. 'There's a youth club on Thursday evenings at my church, if you want to have a chat. Not at Costsave. Not on my shop floor.'

'Ouch, stinger,' said Ant, flapping his hand in appreciation.

Neville looked puzzled, while Bea and Jay tried to stifle their smirks.

'Time we weren't here anyway,' said Bea, pushing her seat into place. 'Bye, Jay.'

'See ya.'

Ant and Bea walked to the staff door together.

'That new guy, reckon he might be all right. For a student,' said Ant.

'He didn't say what he was up to at the weekend, though, did he?'

'No, he didn't. Man of mystery.'

They parted company to take off their uniforms and met up again at the top of the stairs. Bea had her duvet coat on, her mittens and a pink woolly hat with a pompom on the top and ear flaps.

'That hat,' said Ant, smiling and shaking his head. He didn't have a coat, just a thick hoodie.

'What?'

'Nothing.'

Eileen followed them down the stairs. 'Dark already,' she said as they walked round the side of the building.

'Yeah,' said Bea, pleased Eileen had actually said something, rather than freezing her out. 'Not quite as cold, though.'

'When I win the lottery,' Eileen said, 'I'm going to spend the winter on a cruise ship in the Caribbean.'

'You and me both,' said Bea, who was in the same staff lottery syndicate. 'Wish we'd hurry up and win.'

'Tell me about it.'

'Who'd feed the cat, though, while you were away?'

Eileen looked sideways at her. 'What are you talking about? My Dean's got the dog, dotes on it, but we haven't got a cat.'

'Oh, sorry, I was mixing you up with someone else.'

Eileen gave her a quizzical look, then hitched her shoulder bag closer to her body and peeled away from them, heading for the opposite corner of the car park.

'About as subtle as a ten-pound sledgehammer,' said Ant.

'But we know now, don't we? No cat. So now we need to know about Tank.'

'Yeah, all right. I'm on it.'

On the High Street gritting and the general warmth from the buildings had melted the snow. There was just a bit of grubby slush in the gutters and at the side of the pavement.

'Do you know how Charles is doing?' Ant said.

'Someone said he's out of intensive care. He's been moved to one of the wards.'

'I couldn't sleep last night. Kept seeing him on the floor.'

He ran his hand over the top of his head, and Bea remembered him sitting at the bus stop, head on knees, lost in his own dark thoughts.

'You should go and see him. It might help, plus I'm sure he'd be pleased to see you.'

'Yeah, maybe. Would you come with me?'

''Course. Not today, though, I need to walk his dog.'

'Tomorrow?'

'Straight from work at five? I'll try and get one of the neighbours to walk Goldie.'

'Yeah. Yeah, that'd be good.'

They parted at the end of the High Street. Bea walked by the old people's bungalows again. There was an elderly woman walking towards her. She had a tweed coat, but it was flapping open, and she had neither hat nor gloves. Her white hair looked unbrushed and a little wild. She wasn't walking purposefully, but slowly. She seemed to be looking for something.

Bea walked past, but after a few yards, she doubled back. 'Are you all right? Can I help?'

Startled, the woman turned round, and her face was familiar. She didn't seem to have heard Bea's questions, so she repeated them.

'I've lost my friend,' she said.

'Oh, I'm so sorry,' said Bea, looking right and left, and then behind. There was no one else around. The distress was so obvious on the woman's face, she wondered whether by 'lost' she actually meant bereavement. 'Do you live near here?'

'Yes. I'm number four.' She was actually standing right outside her bungalow.

'Perhaps you should wait inside for your friend. It's a bit cold out here.'

The woman looked down at her hands, which, even in the streetlight had a bluish tinge to them. 'Yes,' she said. 'I'll wait inside. He'll be back soon. It's dinner time. He likes his dinner.'

Bea watched her walk up to her front door, which she now saw was ajar. As she closed it behind her, Bea remembered who she was – the mother of Kevin, the *Bugle* photographer. He didn't live there, but he ran a photography studio in the shed in his mother's back yard, where he liked to photograph his favourite subject – girls, the younger the better. Bea shivered, and pressed on across the rec. It was dark, but the ground was still pale here, a mixture of snow and ice after two days of being compressed by people's feet, and the reflected light gave Bea some comfort as she crossed the space towards home. The sky had clouded over and it wasn't so bitingly cold. She wondered if it would snow again or maybe it would all melt overnight. When she got to the local shops on the other side there was a police car parked in the road. What now?

Tom came out of the corner shop as she started to cross the road. Bea was trying to decide whether to keep her head down and give him a wide berth or tough it out when the decision was taken for her.

'Hey! Bea!' He started walking towards her and they met on the pavement, next to his car.

'Oh, hi,' she said. 'What are you doing here?'

'Just doing the rounds of the local shops. I've got some

fliers about the missing cats. Not the most exciting job I've ever worked on.'

There was a twinkle in his eye. He was inviting her to agree with him about the banality of being a community bobby. Bea wasn't playing. She consciously set her expression to 'bitch face' and took a deep breath.

'It's important, though. Anna's really upset. People's pets are like family, aren't they?'

'Yeah, I suppose. One good thing is it's brought us back in contact.' He leaned over so his mouth was near to her ear. 'I've missed you. I'm single now. Nothing to hold me back.'

Bea tried not to look up, but couldn't help herself. He really was very close. She could see his pale eyelashes, the texture of the skin on his face, smell his aftershave, lingering even at the end of the day. She held her expression, giving no sign that there were pesky butterflies beating their traitorous little wings against the inside of her stomach. And she held his gaze. 'What, not even your son?'

A tiny movement in the muscles beneath his left eye told her that she'd hit her target. Bullseye.

Tom straightened up and tugged at the hem of his jacket. 'Don't be like that. Let's talk about it. About us.' He put his hand on her shoulder.

Although she knew she should shrug him off, another force stirred within her – a biological urge to feel his hands under her clothes, feel his mouth on hers. Damn it, he was a tosser. He would always be a tosser. And yet...and yet...

'I can't now,' she said. 'I've got to get home. You could walk with me, round the corner?'

He smiled. 'Okay.'

Tom checked that the car was locked and they started walking. He held the crook of his arm up a little, clearly wanting her to put her arm through his, but she ignored it.

'Bea,' he said, 'I know it went wrong before, but I reckon it was right people, wrong time. We were good together.'

'You were living with someone, Tom. You were cheating on them. You've got a little kid. What is there to talk about?'

'I know I was wrong. But I couldn't help myself. My feelings for you.'

'Hmph.'

'Those feelings haven't gone away. You're gorgeous, Bea, and you know it.'

Bea could feel her resistance ebbing away. It had been a bleak Christmas and New Year. No one had called her gorgeous. No one had given her a second glance. But even so . . .

'I can't trust you, Tom. I could never trust you after that.'

They were by Bea's front gate now.

'Meet me in the pub at eight. The Jubilee. Just for an hour.'

Just for an hour. It would give her a chance to quiz him about the cat investigation. And he clearly had the hots for her. An hour's flattery would be good for her ego. She could enjoy it for what it was. It didn't need to go any further than that, did it?

'All right,' she said. 'But not the Jubilee. Somewhere outside town, where no one will see us.'

'I'll pick you up at eight,' he said, and winked.

She let herself through the gate and walked up the path. Tosser, she thought, but there were those treacherous butterflies again. Eight o'clock. She'd just have time to walk the dog, have some pasta parcels and sauce for tea (it was Monday) and get changed into something a bit slinkier.

13

Bea was all ready when Tom rang, and she opened the door while he was still pressing the doorbell.

Queenie was not happy. She knew that Tom had upset Bea before Christmas, although she didn't know the grisly details. She hovered in the hallway, grim-faced, as Bea put on her coat. Tom noticed her and waved.

'Evening, Mrs Jordan.'

'She's got work tomorrow, you know.'

'Don't worry, I'll have her back by midnight.'

'Mum, I'm twenty-one!' said Bea.

'I know. Have a good evening,' she said, grudgingly.

Goldie had pottered out to have a look, too, and Bea felt better leaving her mum, knowing she had Goldie for company.

'So, where are we going?' she asked as they walked down the path towards his car.

'Wagon and Horses. Nice little pub. Out of the way.'

Bea knew the pub. It was on a country road, about two miles out of Kingsleigh. 'Perfect.'

In the Lounge Bar, Tom helped her out of her fake fur jacket, easing it off her shoulders and draping it on the back of her chair. He looked approvingly at her outfit. She'd spent ages choosing what to wear. In the end she'd gone for a nice top and jeans, the top being a black cold shoulder one, with soft ruffles at the scooped neckline drawing attention to her rather magnificent cleavage.

'I'll get the drinks,' he said. 'What would you like?' His hand brushed her exposed shoulder as he turned to go to the bar, accidentally on purpose. Bea pretended not to notice.

While Tom was waiting to be served, she checked her make-up on her phone in selfie mode, and then looked around. There weren't many other customers, and she didn't recognise any of them. Good, there'd be no gossip getting back to Kingsleigh about her and Tom. A man in his thirties, sitting at a corner table, was in her direct eyeline. He had a checked shirt and khaki-coloured chinos, and his dark hair was thinning and a bit fuzzy on top. He kept checking the door, and then looking at his phone. He picked up his half-pint of lager and sipped at it. When he and Bea made eye contact, he quickly looked away.

Tom came back to the table bringing their drinks with him – Bea's white wine spritzer and his pint of ale. 'Here we are. Cheers.' They touched glasses.

'So what's happened about becoming a detective?' said Bea.

Tom sighed. 'I think that's a long way off. They've just got me doing all the shit work at the moment. Visiting all the shops and talking about cats. It's not exactly *Luther*, is it? I should be on the juicier cases, like the body on the bypass.'

'That was just a jumper, wasn't it?'

'Maybe. Maybe not. We're waiting for the post-mortem results.' He leaned forward and lowered his voice. 'Between you and me, it could be something else.'

'What do you mean?'

'Well, he was a long way from home. We haven't released this yet, but he wasn't from Kingsleigh. He was a young bloke from Henwood, other side of Bristol. Lived with his parents. They're in bits. They don't believe it, say it would be completely out of character. He was young, fit, looked after himself, down the gym all the time.'

'Well, anyone can get depression, can't they? You can't always tell what's going on in someone's head?'

'True. But there were marks on his hands and face, as if he'd been in a fight. Looks to me like a night out that went horribly wrong. Someone must know something.'

'Well, you're the community bobby, Tom. You know all the pubs in Kingsleigh. Are you going to ask around?'

Tom smiled. 'I've already started, Bea. I can smell something wrong and I'm going to find out what it is.'

'Unofficially?'

'Semi-officially. At least, my boss doesn't know I'm doing it. Not yet. I'll go to him when I've got something to report.'

'And in the meantime, you're officially on the missing cats.'

'Yeah, missing moggies.' He sighed.

'It's not nice, though, people's pets going missing. It matters to them.'

'Yeah, I know.'

'So, how much of a thing is it? How many pets are we talking about?'

'We're keeping it on the QT, but as far as we know, it's six cats – five missing and one dead, just in Kingsleigh. We're talking with other areas, seeing if it's a widespread thing or not. At the moment, it looks like it's just us. It's someone in the town.'

'Six? That's more than in the paper.'

'The *Bugle*'s only out once a week. Cats are going missing nearly every day.'

'So what are the theories?'

'I'm just a PC, Bea. They don't discuss it all with me, but I reckon it's a weirdo. Taking them and torturing them or whatever.'

Bea thought again about Dean and Tank. Should she tell him about them? At that moment the door opened and a man walked in. It took a while for Bea to remember where she'd seen him before, but the Barbour jacket reminded her. He was the customer that Jay had asked her about. Bea grabbed a Midweek Meals menu and held it up to her face. Squinting around it, she could see the man looking quickly around the room and then heading straight for the man at the corner table.

'It's sick, but it's surprisingly common. What are you doing, Bea?'

She tried to focus back on Tom. 'Sorry, what?'

'Are you hungry? I thought you'd eaten.'

'Oh, I have. I'm just . . .just a bit hot.' Bea started fanning herself with the menu.

Tom looked at her doubtfully, but carried on. 'Anyway, mistreating animals. There's a lot of it about. You should try googling it. No, don't. There's some horrible stuff out there.'

Barbour Jacket Man was reaching inside his coat now. He brought out a small brown paper envelope and handed it to the other man, under the table. He must have got something in return because his hand went back into his coat, as though it was reaching into an inside pocket. Bea's mouth had gone dry. It looked like a drugs deal, going on three metres behind Tom's back.

'Are you listening?'

'Yes. No. I mean, I am, but I'm, er, getting a headache. I've got some paracetamol somewhere.' She put the menu down and dumped her handbag on her lap, dug about inside, then pressed a couple of pills out of their packet and swallowed them down.

As she put her glass back down on the table, Barbour Jacket was leaving. He hadn't even taken off his coat. The man at the corner table took a deep draught of his half. He took a couple of breaths and then drained the glass, and he, too, left the pub.

Bea felt as if she'd missed her moment. By the time she'd explained what she saw to Tom, both men would be long gone. And, after all, had she seen enough to justify dobbing them in? All she had seen was an envelope. One side of the deal, if that's what it was.

'So, you think it's one person behind this?' she said.

'That's my guess, yeah. The thing is, where it's happened in other places, psychologists have said it can be a prelude to other sorts of violence. Attacks on vulnerable people.'

'Really?'

'Yeah. That's why we've got to take it seriously. If it's someone who enjoys violence, seeing animals suffer, they're a real risk to society.' Bea felt suddenly cold, as if a ghost had walked right through her. 'But let's not talk about work any more. How are things, Bea? What's going on with you?'

He leaned forward on the table, his hands resting only an inch or two away from hers. 'Ha, there's not much to say really. Same old same old.' His hands moved forward. The tips of his fingers brushed the back of her left hand, and a small charge of electricity shot from the point of contact up her arm, into her stomach and further below. 'I meant what I said earlier, Bea. I've got feelings for you, proper feelings. I can't help myself.'

She took up her drink and sat back in her chair. He was keen, no doubt about it, but she didn't need to rush into anything. For once, the ball was in her court.

They left the pub after two drinks. Tom had had an orange juice for his second one. It was only half past nine or so. There were no streetlights on these lanes and there was something comforting about the way the car's headlights created a tunnel in the darkness. It had been a good evening. Nothing had been decided, but Bea couldn't help liking Tom.

They were a mile or so from the pub when he put the left indicator on and pulled into a lay-by.

'What are you doing?' said Bea.

'Nice and quiet here. We can ...talk ...properly,' he said. He switched off the engine and they were plunged into darkness.

Bea didn't like it. 'Tom, I want to go home, please.'

'Come on, Bea. We've had a great evening. Let's finish it properly.'

She could hear him unclip his seatbelt and move towards her. The last time he'd done that they'd ended up on the back seat, but she didn't want that now.

'Tom, I've got a headache. I'm asking you to take me home.'

'Just a little kiss.' He leaned closer. She could smell the slightly beery breath, sense his body twisting towards her. Even in the dark, he was oozing confidence.

'Tom—'

'Bea,' he breathed, his face inches from hers.

'When exactly did you break up with your girlfriend?'

'What?'

'When did you break up with her?'

He gave a long sigh and shifted back into his seat. 'Between Christmas and New Year. We had an awful Christmas, made us realise we couldn't go on like that.'

'So, a week ago?'

'Yeah, something like that.'

Bea switched on the light above the rear-view mirror. 'Tom, it's a big deal, breaking up with the mother of your little boy. It's too soon for ...this.'

'Bea, it's been over for ages. We've been unhappy. It's not—'

'Take me home, please, Tom,' she said firmly.

'I really like you, Bea.'

'Of course you do, I'm bloody lovely, but I want to go home now.'

'Really?' He'd been staring straight ahead, but now he turned to look at her, and she could see he was using his best puppy-dog expression. But it was no good. She didn't want to be anyone's rebound shag.

'Really.' She reached up to the light and switched it off.

Tom did up his seatbelt and the car accelerated out of the lay-by, making the wheels spin in the slush. Bea was pressed backwards into her seat as Tom gunned it along the narrow lane. Not the time to tell him about his speed, thought Bea.

Within a few minutes the car pulled up outside her house. Tom hadn't said a word. Bea opened the door.

'Goodnight,' she said, stepping out of the car.

'Yup.' That was it. One word. Stony faced.

The engine roared before she'd even shut the door and the car raced off down the street. She tipped her head back and looked up at the sky. It was cloudy, a blank sheet, blotting out the stars. She puffed her cheeks out and blew her breath out strongly, trying to empty her lungs and her head at the same time, then walked up the path and let herself into the house. The lights were on and she could hear the telly playing in the lounge. She kicked off her shoes and walked across the kitchen to the lounge doorway. Queenie was asleep in her chair. Goldie was at her feet. On her feet, actually. She raised her head as Bea looked at her, and her tail made a gentle thump, thump, thump sound on the carpet.

'Mum,' Bea said quietly, leaning over the back of the chair and putting her hand on Queenie's shoulder. 'Nearly time for bed.'

Queenie's eyes flickered open. She wiped a little patch of drool from the side of her mouth on the back of her hand. 'Wha—? Oh. You back already? Did you have a nice evening?'

'It was okay,' said Bea. 'But it's good to be home.'

14

At six o'clock the next morning it was still dark, but Bea was wide awake and pretty miserable. In the days BG (Before Goldie) she would have got up, made a cup of tea and gone back to bed, but now she slung on some clothes and got ready to go out for a walk.

Outside, the sky was softly clouded, the air felt warmer, and it hadn't snowed again. Instead there was a layer of slush everywhere. As Bea stood near the launderette wondering which way to walk, a jogger went past, running in the road, following one of the clear tyre tracks in the half-melted snow. He was heading away from the allotments. Bea heard his hard, sharp breaths, saw them pluming in the air, like steam from a locomotive, and got a whiff of sweat and mud. She didn't see his face, hidden under his hood, but the size of him was a giveaway. It had to be Tank, even though she wouldn't have had him down as a fitness freak. She felt a little tightening in her stomach. She whipped out her phone, selected the camera and held it up. She clicked a couple of times, but when she looked at the screen, it was just a dark, indistinct mess. Her phone wasn't up to the low light. Damn.

She watched Tank disappear into the distance, heading towards the square. The sky was clearing and there were hints of light in its eastern edge. Bea changed her mind and led Goldie towards the path to the allotments and the fields beyond. Once over the stile, they followed the path over the brow of the hill and then down to the hedge. It was getting lighter every minute – a soft, dull grey light that comes before the sun breaks the horizon.

The dark bulk of the farm buildings sent a shiver down Bea's spine, so she chose the other path, the one that ran alongside the river. She let Goldie off her lead and enjoyed watching her snuffle about in the reeds and bushes, falling behind sometimes and then gently trotting to catch up. She never strayed far from Bea.

It was a pleasant, flat walk. The light was seeping through the treeline now, highlighting the surface of the river. Swollen by melted snow, the water was brown and thick.

Ahead of her, Bea saw a lone figure standing near the edge of the riverbank. She hesitated, wondering whether to go back before they noticed her. There was no denying it was isolated here. She felt a familiar pang of anxiety and then an answering surge of anger. She had every right to be here. She shouldn't feel worried about being on her own. Anyway, if there was trouble, she had a dog to defend her. She looked at Goldie, pottering quietly by her side, her golden fur catching the light and giving her a halo. Hmm, maybe not attack dog material. Still, Bea kept walking.

As Bea got closer she could see it was the man she'd seen in the path before, the one with the camouflage jacket. He was staring at something intently through binoculars. He didn't turn round or acknowledge her in any way. It seemed unlikely that he hadn't heard her, so Bea supposed he was more interested in whatever it was he was watching, and somehow she felt reassured.

As she drew level, he lowered his binoculars and raised a camera with a long lens. Now Bea was really curious. What was it?

She stopped walking and stood a couple of metres away from him. He seemed to be pressing a button on the camera, but there was no noise. After about a minute he lowered the camera and briefly glanced at Bea. She raised her eyebrows.

'Kingfisher,' he said, quietly, almost in a whisper.

'Really?' Bea had seen them on nature programmes on the telly, but never in real life.

'There's a pair. The female's on that hazel. The male's just downriver.'

Bea squinted across the river. She couldn't see anything apart from bushes and reeds.

'Do you see the red stems? Just to the right of that, about a foot above the surface.'

Bea looked and looked and then she thought she saw a hint of colour, a spot of turquoise in amongst the branches opposite.

'Here.' The guy had taken off his binoculars and was holding them out to Bea. He looped the strap over her head. Bea scanned the bushes but couldn't see the bird.

'Find the red stems and pan right slowly,' he said patiently.

She tried again, and suddenly there it was – a beautiful little thing, with colours like a jewel, and a sharp, cruel-looking beak.

'I've got it!' Bea squeaked. Then, more quietly, 'I've never seen anything so beautiful.'

The bird bobbed its head and sent a bright yellow jet out of its rear end. And then it was gone. Bea moved the binoculars away again and saw a flash of turquoise disappearing round the bend in the river.

'I only live fifteen minutes away. I never knew they were here.'

He smiled. 'Most people don't. You have to be looking to see them, although you'll often hear them first. They give themselves away with that call.'

'That peeping noise?'

'That's it.'

'I'll be listening out for it now. Honestly, that was brilliant.'

'New, is she? The dog. Haven't seen you out and about before.'

'Yeah. She's not mine. I'm just looking after her for a while. I quite like this, though, being out in the morning. Never thought I'd say that. Not in a million years. Do you come here often?' Bea winced internally at the corny question, no flirtation intended, but it seemed to have passed unnoticed.

'This is my patch. I'm here four or five days a week. I record the species I see.'

'Birds?'

'Birds, mostly. Insects, mammals as well. Foxes. Badgers. I've seen otters here.'

'No way.'

'Only a couple of times.'

Bea's mind was reeling. Otters? Badgers? Then she had another thought. 'People?'

'Sorry?'

'Do you see many people out here?'

'Not many out and about this early. Just a few dog-walkers like you.'

'Do you ever see people at that farm?'

'There was a lad this morning, big fella. Every now and again there are a lot of people there in the evenings, Saturdays mostly. The last time was New Year's Eve. I wondered if it was some sort of rave, but there was nothing in the news.'

'Hmm, not my idea of a fun place for an evening out,' said Bea.

'Me neither.' He smiled, but there was a wintriness in his face. She sensed he'd rather be on his own.

'Well,' said Bea. 'Nice to meet you. I'm Bea, by the way.'

'Cliff,' he said in return.

'Thanks again, for the kingfisher.'

She checked her watch. She should be getting back really, but she was tempted to walk a little further, maybe catch sight of the kingfisher again. She followed the path for another five minutes or so. It wound pleasantly through the valley. She got to a place where she had a good view back to the farm buildings. A lot of people? What was that all about?

Another path lead away from the river here. It was shaded, north-facing, and the snow was still quite thick. She reckoned she could follow this one and then loop round the farm.

'Come on, Goldie. This way.'

About a hundred metres along, she realised Goldie wasn't keeping up with her. She stopped and turned round. The dog was snuffling around in the bushes some way behind.

'Goldie, come on!' Bea called.

Goldie was unusually animated. She seemed to be digging her nose into the ground, eating something.

'Oh, crap, what have you got?'

Bea started back along the path, shouting to the dog as she ran. Goldie ignored her. The ground she was standing on was churned up, mottled with red. She was licking and chomping at something.

'God! What have you done! Get away! Come here!'

Bea grabbed her collar and pulled. The dog dug her feet in. Bea leaned back and hauled at her, and eventually she managed to drag her back to the path, feet sliding on the mud and slush.

Bea bent down and looked at the dog's face. Her muzzle was stained red and she kept licking at the fur around her mouth.

'Oh my God.' Bea took her a few metres away and found a sturdy trunk to tie her to. 'Wait there,' she said, and walked back to the stirred up, bloody area at the bottom of the hedge.

Now that she looked, this whole section of path and its surroundings were disturbed, like it had been trampled by a crowd of people or animals. There was something at the centre of it, a few mangled remains. Scraps of dark wet fur clinging to bits of bone, but there wasn't enough there to tell what it was. There were only fragments left. Parts of a corpse.

Bea took some photographs on her phone. She checked them on her screen, and they were just an indistinct mess. You couldn't tell what they were showing. She was going to leave it and move on when she thought of Anna, how worried she had been when Joan had gone missing, how devastated when her body was found. Chances were, there was someone else worrying and waiting now. This time Bea couldn't return a body to them, but she could perhaps provide evidence that their pet was no more.

Steeling her nerve, she took a poop scoop bag out of her pocket and delicately picked up one of the fragments. Flesh, fur, bone. She quickly tied the handles of the bag and put it in her pocket.

She fetched Goldie and decided to walk back the way they had come, after all. Cliff had gone from his post by the river, and they plodded towards home. Halfway across the large field, Goldie lay down. This time Bea barked, 'No you don't!' and gave a firm tug on the lead, and something about her tone prompted the dog to stand up and start walking. When they were nearly back to the allotments, Bea's phone rang.

Nobody rang this early, unless someone had died. Her heart missed a beat, thinking Queenie must be in trouble, but when she fished the phone of her pocket, the display said 'Ant Home'. She answered,

'Ant? What's up?'

'I'm going to be late for work, Bea. Can you cover for me?'

She checked the time. 'It's only quarter to eight. You've got ages.'

'Something's happened. I've gotta sort it out.'

'What is it?'

'It's just a mess here, Bea. I'll be in when I've cleaned it up. Don't want my mum to see it. I've gotta go, Bea.'

'Mess, what sort of—?' But he'd cut the call.

Bea found the answer back home, when she was scrolling through Twitter as she ate her Coco Pops. Someone had posted a photo of the front of an ordinary 1970s terraced house on the Kingsleigh South estate. Scrawled across it in angry red paint, spanning brickwork and the ground-floor window, was one word, repeated over and over, 'SCUM'.

15

'Sorry about your house, Ant.'

'I needn't have bothered cleaning it up this morning,' Ant said, glumly. 'It's all over Facebook and Twitter and everywhere. Stupid to think I could keep it from Mum and the girls.'

'How is your mum?'

He sighed, and took another long draw from his cigarette. 'She's taking it hard. She's pretty tough, my mum. I've never seen her like this before. The fight's gone out of her.'

Bea had seen Ant's mum in fighting mode, when she'd had a go at Dot in Costsave at Halloween, and she was pretty scary. She was a small, wiry, scrappy sort of woman. It was difficult to imagine her without the fire.

'We've lived in that house for eleven years. It's gotta be someone local that did that, hasn't it? Not nice to think that's one of your neighbours.'

'They're just cowards, Ant. Lowlifes.'

'Yeah. Seems like my dad crossed a line this time. A lot of people kind of knew what he did before, but now they've all turned against us.'

He was inside today, manning the cleaning trolley. After the break Bea kept an eye on him. He drifted around, mopping up spills and picking up cardboard in a lacklustre way. In truth his work rate was not much different from normal, although to Bea's eyes he looked as if he was carrying the weight of the world on his shoulders. In between customers, she wondered what she could do to cheer him up. Perhaps the latest news on their investigation would take his mind off things. What with Barbour Jacket Man and the mysterious stranger in the pub, and the poor dead animal on this morning's walk, she had plenty to tell him.

The store was busier today. The snow had brought panic buyers out in numbers, but had undoubtedly put some of her regular customers off. Now the pavements were clear the very old and those with the very young were back to stock up their supplies.

While her customer was paying, Bea noticed a woman walking into the store. Her hair was scraped back as usual, but even at this distance Bea could tell it needed a wash. And although she was wearing a thick, padded jacket, her shoulders were hunched and she was scuttling more than walking.

From the fresh veg area where he was tidying up apple boxes, Ant had spotted her too. He left his trolley and hurried over to her. They met near the checkouts. 'Mum, what are you doing here?'

She didn't have any make-up on and there were dark circles under her eyes. 'I just came to tell you that I'm taking Dani and Britney to my Linzi's.'

'What? Cardiff? There's no need to go that far, Mum.'

'It's not the end of the earth. Just till it all settles down.'

'What about school?'

'I've rung the girls' school up. They threatened me too, bastards, told me I couldn't take them out, it was an unauthorised absence, but I told them – we're not safe. Family comes first. Steve's staying and Ken wanted to as well. So you'll be all right. You're flavour of the month anyway, local hero, nothing'll happen to you.'

'Mum, if you go, then they've won.'

She considered that for a while, blinking hard. 'I'll be back. I just need some time.'

'Mum, please don't.'

'What if it wasn't paint, love? What if it was a brick through the window? If something happened to the girls, I'd never forgive myself.' She wiped her hand wearily across her brow.

'Let's report it to the cops, then. Get some protection.'

She almost laughed. 'They won't do nothing. They hate us too. We're going on the bus to Bristol and then a megabus to Cardiff. We'll be fine. Linzi's expecting us. Will you keep an eye on Ken? Make sure he eats something and keeps going to school?'

'Oh crikey, Mum. Can't you take him with you?'

'Says he doesn't want to miss his studies. It is his GCSE year, after all.'

Ant wrinkled his nose. 'Are you sure he said that?'

'Yeah. Surprised me too. Perhaps he's turned over a new leaf. Anyway, keep him on the straight and narrow, won't you?'

'I suppose ... Well, keep in touch, yeah? Have a couple of days and then come home. I'll try and keep it nice for you.'

'You're a good boy, Anthony. Stephen's home too, so it'll be all boys together. I'll see you soon, yeah?'

Bea thought she caught a little wobble in Ant's mum's voice as she threaded her thin arms round his waist and gave him a big squeeze. Ant hugged her back.

He shambled over to Bea after his mum had peeled herself away, and they both watched her leave the store.

'Hounded out of her own home,' said Ant. 'Fucking disgrace.'

Bea pulled a sympathetic face. 'Do you still want to go and see Charles in hospital this afternoon?'

'Might as well. I've got nothing to get home for.'

'What about Ken?'

Ant snorted. 'Ha! I won't see him until at least ten. Lying little toerag. Didn't want to miss his studies, my arse.'

Charles was propped up in bed, looking out of the window, when Bea and Ant found him. He waved Bea towards the plastic chair by his bed, while Ant hovered in the background.

'I wanted to see how you were, tell you how Goldie's getting on,' said Bea.

Charles' eyes lit up. 'How is she?'

'She's fine. My mum's with her all day and I walk her in the morning and evening. She's a very good dog. I think she's missing you, though.'

'Well, I'm still here. My ticker is still ticking.' Charles tapped his chest with the hand that didn't have a drip attached. 'I had an operation, you know. Couple of stents.'

'That should help, then,' said Bea.

'Yes. I broke my collarbone when I fell too. I don't know when I'll be allowed home. Old bones take longer to heal. They're talking about a care home until I can cope.'

'Sounds like a good idea, just till you're strong enough to be at home. Goldie's fine with us, unless you'd rather she was with a neighbour.'

'Oh, my neighbours won't have her. Next door is very anti-pet, always has been. He's been acting a bit oddly recently too. I wondered if it was dementia. The lady next to him has a cat. No, she's best off with you and I feel better knowing she's all right.'

'She's happy. It's lovely having her around actually.'

'Ah,' he said, 'once you've had a dog, there's no going back. A home's not a home without one.'

'I don't know about that, but she's a good house guest.' Bea turned towards Ant, and stood up.

'Do you remember Ant, Charles? He's the one who helped you in Costsave, kept you going until the ambulance got there.'

'It was *you*. Come here, then,' Charles' eyes filled with tears as he beckoned Ant forward. 'Thank you, young man. Thank you.'

Ant's eyes were brimming too. He sat in the chair vacated by Bea. 'That's okay. It was just lucky. I'd been on the training two days before.'

'You saved my life.'

Ant couldn't speak for a while. Charles' hands were lying on top of the crisp white sheets. His right hand had a cannula in, and a tube snaking to a bag of fluid on a stand. The other one was nearer to Ant and he reached forward and gently put his hand on top. Charles, also silent now, turned his hand over so that their palms met and their fingers were able to clasp each other. Bea felt a surge of emotion, and she realised she was in danger of succumbing to some very ugly crying indeed.

'I'll just get a coffee,' she muttered and fled before either of them could see her making a show of herself. By the time she came back, with three coffees in a cardboard cup holder, Charles and Ant were chatting away about football and the chances of Kingsleigh Football Club making it into the league above.

Ant and Bea sat on the top deck of the bus home, but there wasn't much to see. It was dark. The roads were wet, car headlights and tail lights reflecting on the surface. Every now and again, roadside branches whipped at the windows.

'Do you feel any better for seeing him?' said Bea.

'Yeah. I reckon. He's a nice man, isn't he? Old school.'

'Yeah.'

'I feel . . . I dunno . . . I feel fucking knackered. Like if I shut

119

my eyes, I'd sleep until the weekend.' He rubbed at his eyes and Bea was worried he might start crying again. On close inspection, his hoodie was quite stained and more than a little pongy. The smell seemed to have been following them around since they left work. He yawned loudly, then leaned his head on her shoulder and pretended to snore.

'Give over,' said Bea, but when he didn't move, she softened. 'It's been a bit of a day for you, hasn't it? Well, all of us.'

'Why? What's up with you?' Ant said, his head still comfortably using her shoulder as a pillow, his eyes starting to close. 'Can't hack it at work? I thought you loved it.'

'Work's fine. I just ...I found something this morning when I was out with the dog.'

'Mm?'

She wasn't sure he was really listening now, but it would only be five or six minutes until they were back in Kingsleigh. If he fell asleep now, she'd have a hell of a job waking him up. 'There was something dead near the path. An animal.'

'Hh?' His eyes were closed now.

'Actually, I've just remembered. I picked some of it up, as, you know, evidence. I was going to leave it outside the back door, but it's still in my pocket.' She felt a flush of embarrassment. Maybe that explained the smell.

'What?' Ant's eyes were open again now. 'You've got what in your pocket?'

'A bit of dead animal.'

'Which pocket?'

'The one you're leaning on.'

'Eurgh!' He sat bolt upright and shuffled to the edge of the seat away from her. 'What are you like?'

'I just forgot.' She reached into her pocket and brought out the black plastic bag.

'No! Don't open it in here!'

But she was already undoing the handles. She flinched a bit as the ripe smell was released and hit her nose. Ant scooted over to the seat on the other side of the aisle, flapping at his nose and mouth. Bea put the bag on the seat beside her and peered in. She couldn't see a great deal, so she tentatively peeled the edges down to reveal the contents at the bottom. It was all a bit sticky and wet, but the top had started to dry out a bit.

She ran through the list of missing cats that she knew about – two tabbies, a ginger one and the white one she'd seen with Tank and Dean. 'Oh Jesus, Ant. Look at this.'

'No, you're all right,' he said, holding the neck of his hoodie up to cover his nose and mouth. 'I'll stay over here. Weirdo.'

'No, really. You need to see this.'

'What?'

'This fur, Ant. It was all dark and wet when I picked it up, but look now. Look at the colour.'

Holding his breath, he leaned over the aisle. 'Oh no. Is that...blood?'

'I don't think so. The bloody bit is underneath.'

They both stared into the bag and then looked at each other with horror. The fur attached to the scraps of tissue and bone was unmistakeably ginger.

16

'What are we going to do with it?'

The bus had reached the outskirts of town now. It was only a minute or two until they needed to get off.

'There's a bin near your bus stop, isn't there?' said Ant. 'Chuck it in there. It stinks.'

'It's evidence, Ant.'

'Okay, Miss Marple, take some pictures on your phone and then chuck it in the bin. You can't walk around with that in your pocket. Even if you get it home, what are you gonna do?'

'Take it to someone? Get it tested for DNA?'

Ant snorted. 'You've been watching too much telly. Who the hell is going to DNA test a bit of animal you found under a hedge?'

'The RSPCA? The police?'

'Actually, that's not a bad idea, give it to that tosser Tom. Put it in an envelope and post it to him. It'll be even riper by the time it reaches him.'

At the mention of Tom's name, Bea went quiet.

'What?' said Ant.

'Nothing.'

'Yeah, there's something.'

'I don't want to talk about it.'

He looked about to say something else, press her on what the matter was, but she was saved by the bell. Someone had pinged the 'bus stopping' button and it was slowing down as it approached the next stop.

'This is us. Tie that bloody bag up.'

They got off the bus in the High Street and started walking along the pavement.

'I'm getting some chips,' said Ant. 'Want some?'

'I should get home.' They were by the chip shop door now, and the smell of hot fat hung in the air. 'God, that smells so good. I'm starving. I'll give Queenie a ring.' She dialled home. 'You all right? I'm back in K-town now. I might get some chips with Ant, but I know it's Tuesday, pizza day.'

'That's fine, love. We're all right here. We're having our tea now.'

Good old Goldie. Bea should have thought of this years ago – getting a dog or cat for Queenie, so she had company. It took a lot of the pressure off. 'Great, okay. I won't bring you any home, then. See you in a bit.'

'Bye, love.'

She was about to enter the shop, when Ant stepped in front of her. 'Bea. No.'

'What?'

'You can't go in there with that stinking *thing*.'

'I don't want to put it in the bin, Ant. That's somebody's pet cat.'

'Do you think anybody would want a small bit of their cat back like that?'

'Hi, guys!' Jay was behind them. 'What's it gonna be?' he said, rubbing his hands together. 'Chips and curry sauce?'

'Do vegans even eat chips?' said Ant.

'Yeah, if they're cooked in vegetable oil, which these are.'

'Oh.'

'Are you two going in?'

'Yes, we're just ...' Bea tried to hide the bag behind her back, but it was too late.

Jay wrinkled his nose. 'What the hell are you doing with that poo bag?'

'It's not poo, it's ...' She hesitated, trying desperately to think of some way not to tell the boy she quite fancied that she was carrying animal remains about with her.

'It's a dead cat,' said Ant. 'A bit of one.'

Jay screwed up his face, as disbelief turned to disgust. 'You're the cat killers!' he hissed. 'You two? I don't believe it!'

'No, no! Shhh!' Without really thinking, Bea grabbed Jay's elbow and pulled him away from the doorway.

'No! Get off me!' He tried to shrug her off, but Ant caught the other arm and they bundled him along the street and into the lane that ran behind the shops. 'What are you doing? Stop it!'

'Shh,' Bea said again.

When they were away from the High Street, they let go of him.

'I'm not going to "shhh". You're a pair of psychos. I thought you were a bit odd, but—'

'Odd?' said Bea. 'What do you mean?'

'Never mind that,' said Ant. 'We're not cat killers. We're trying to *find out* who it is.'

Jay narrowed his eyes. 'Yeah, well, you would say that, wouldn't you?'

'It's true, Jay. We want to stop it, whatever it is that's going on. The police don't seem to have a clue.'

'And you do?'

'Yes. This,' Bea said, holding the bag out towards him. He flinched a bit and took a step backwards.

'So where did you get this exactly?'

'On the footpath just in from the river, heading towards Lower Leigh.'

'Yeah, I know it. I go running along there sometimes. Nice. Near Leigh Manor House, down that way.'

'I dunno about that. I think that's a bit further along. Anyway, I was walking down there this morning and the dog found it. An animal, all ripped to bits. This is one of the bits.'

'And you picked it up?'

'Yeah. The thing is, I saw someone with a cat in a carrier heading out in that direction a few days ago. And as far as we know, they don't have a cat. And the fur of the animal I found is ginger and one of the missing cats in the Bugle is ginger too, so . . .'

' . . . so we reckon we've found the cat killers,' said Ant. 'Deano and Tank.'

'Deano and Tank?' said Jay. 'Sounds like you just made those names up. Are they for real?'

'Yes,' said Ant, slightly offended.

'Are you sure you're not adding two and two together and making five?'

Ant drew himself up a little straighter and glared at Jay. 'I may not be at uni, but I know what two and two makes . . .'

Bea put her hand on Ant's arm. 'He doesn't mean that, Ant. He means we're jumping to conclusions.'

'You might be,' said Jay. 'Go on, then. Let's have a look in the bag.'

'Oh, man. Not again.' Ant held his nose and backed off several metres, while Bea undid the knot.

Jay peered in. Then he got his phone out, switched on the torch function and shone the bright white light into the bag. Ant's eyes grew wide with horror as he watched Jay reaching in and picking up the stuff. Jay looked at it intently, then rubbed some of the fur between his finger and thumb.

'You're worse than she is. Think I'm going to be sick,' said Ant. He turned away, trying to control the heaving inside.

'It *could* be cat,' said Jay, 'but I think it's a bit coarse for that. More likely to be fox.'

Ant turned back round.

'Do you reckon?' said Bea.

'Yeah. Not a hundred per cent sure.'

'Is that what you do? In your environmental wotsit course?' said Ant.

'No, it's a hobby. Wildlife. The thing is, if it *is* a fox, how did it die? You said there was a lot of blood?'

'Yeah, all round the place, staining the snow. And the ground had been all trampled.'

'I'll ask my mates. See if any of them have heard anything.'

Ant started laughing.

'What's up with you?'

'It's just like . . .who the hell is going to know about some random fox dying in a field? Unless you're Doctor Doolittle or something. "I'll ask my friend Mister Squirrel and Mister Badger." Oh, man, we're not the weird ones.'

Jay looked at him blank-faced, unimpressed, then he shook his head and started walking back towards the chip shop. 'I'll let you know if I find out anything, shall I?' he said to Bea.

'Yeah, I could show you where it was. We could walk there together, if you like,' she said, imagining them walking together by the river – the sun glistening on the water, her stopping to point out the kingfisher, him not seeing, so she puts her face close to his. 'There,' she says. 'Beautiful,' he says, but he's not looking at the bird . . .

'The bin, Bea.' Back in the real world, in a cold High Street near a chip shop, Ant was saying something. 'Put it in the bin now. Better wash your hands and all before you order your chips.'

When Bea got home, Queenie wasn't in the kitchen waiting for her and Bea could hear voices coming from the lounge.

'—turned out they'd never even been to Blackpool!'

Queenie's familiar squawking laugh was joined by a man's guffaw. What the—? Bea walked to the lounge doorway. Goldie was lying on the carpet by the coffee table. She noticed Bea, but didn't raise her head or even manage a little tail wag. Queenie wasn't in her usual chair. She was on the sofa and next to her, really quite close, was Bob.

17

'Oh,' said Bea. 'Hello, Bob.'

He got to his feet. 'Hello, Bea. I was just going.'

'You don't need to leave because of me.'

'No, no. It's late.' He checked his watch. 'Crikey, don't know where the evening's gone. Thanks for tea, Maggie.'

'You're welcome, Bob. Any time,' said Queenie.

'And keep an eye on Goldie.'

'Why?' said Bea, feeling the stirring of anxiety in the pit of her stomach. 'What's wrong with her?'

'She just seems a bit off, love,' said Queenie. 'Didn't eat her biscuits at dinner, and didn't want to walk very far when we took her out.'

There was almost too much in that sentence for Bea to digest. Firstly, the dog normally hoovered up anything edible within a matter of seconds. Secondly—

'You took her out?'

'Yes. Me and Bob. We just went over to the rec and back.' She said it casually, but she was watching for Bea's reaction, her approval.

'Oh. Right,' said Bea. 'Good. I mean, wow.'

'Might do it again sometime,' said Bob. 'I'd better be off now. Let me know if you need a lift to the vet or anything, if you think she needs checking out.'

'Thanks, Bob. I'll see you out,' said Queenie.

'No, it's all right. I know the way.'

The next morning, Bea came down to a rueful-looking Goldie and a pile of sick on the floor near the back door. She let the dog out into the garden while she cleaned up. Goldie disappeared for a minute or two and then wandered back inside. Bea didn't know whether to try her with any biscuits or not, but decided against it and just left her with a full water bowl and instructions to Queenie to text her if there were any developments. Dog ownership was proving to be a lot of work and quite a worry.

As she walked into work, she saw the man with the *Bugle* trolley, trundling it across the rec. Ah, *Bugle* day, thought Bea, and now she thought about it, she realised that the man was one of Kingsleigh's local celebs, or the closest they got to it, anyway – the oldest paper boy in the West Country. There'd been some coverage about him a year or so ago, even made the local TV on a slow news day. Although his spine was curved, he walked surprisingly briskly.

'Morning!' Bea trilled.

He looked up and grunted. The trolley rattled as they passed each other on the path, and Bea idly wondered how far the old chap had to walk on his rounds.

At Costsave, Bob was ushering Dot from his car to the staff door.

'Thank you, kind sir,' Dot said, as he held the door open.

'You're welcome, madam,' Bob replied. Bea noticed his hand lingering on Dot's lower back, almost on her bottom, as he ushered her through.

Neville nabbed Dot and Bea as they got to the top of the stairs. 'Beatrice, I'd like you to do the periodicals before you log on to your checkout.' Bea could feel a giggle bubbling up inside her. Some things just got her every time. 'They should have been put out before we opened but, as you may know, an unfortunate rash of sick leave means we're short of staff today.'

Bea rolled her eyes. 'Ooh, do I have to? I can't stand my periodicals, Neville. They seem to come round so quickly,' she said, her voice wobbling a little as she got the words out.

He tipped his head to one side, wondering if he was being teased, and clutched his clipboard a bit tighter, like a toddler hugging a comfort blanket. 'It's not something I normally ask, Beatrice. I'm not sure what your trouble is.'

'I don't mind doing them, Neville,' said Dot, winking at Bea. 'It's a long time since periodicals caused me any trouble.'

'Oh, that's very kind of you to offer, Dot—'

'I'm a martyr to these hot flushes, though.' Dot fanned herself with both hands.

'I don't see what . . . Oh. Really, I'd expect better than this childishness, Dot.'

'Sorry, Neville. I think I've regressed while I've been away.'

'I'll do the mags, Neville. No problem,' said Bea, and she and Dot linked arms and walked down the corridor to the locker room.

It took Bea a good forty-five minutes to sort through the magazines, removing the out-of-date ones and putting the new issues in their place, checking everything in and out on a stock-monitoring tablet. She did the daily newspapers too, and tidied up the old *Bugle*s. The heap of new ones would be in soon, she thought, then checked the date again. No, she was a day early. They didn't come in until Thursday.

Although she quite enjoyed doing something different, she was glad to log on to checkout number six and settle in next to Dot.

'Blimey, Dot, I swear if anyone actually says New Year, New You to me, I'll smash their face in.'

'January magazines are a bit samey, aren't they? Daytime telly's the same. Diets, detoxes, resolutions, blah, blah, blah.'

'Can't remember the last time I made a New Year's resolution.'

'Me neither. What would you change if you could?'

'Dunno,' said Bea, gently scraping an annoying tag of skin away from the side of one nail. 'That's a tricky question when you're perfect like me.'

Dot grinned. 'You are, babe. I wouldn't want you to change. Not one bit, but maybe you want to change your life, branch out a bit, find someone.'

Since Bea's disastrous fling with Tom, her love life had been a subject more or less off limits. Now Bea breathed out noisily. 'I dunno, Dot. I don't know if I can be bothered.'

'It's nice having someone around, though,' said Dot, and her eyes seemed to naturally gravitate to the meat counter, where Bob was busy with the bacon slicer. Bea thought about him and Queenie, how close they'd been sitting on the sofa, and wondered if she should say anything to Dot, but decided against it.

At lunchtime she got a text from Queenie. 'Dog very sick.' She rang home for the details. Goldie had carried on vomiting through the morning. Queenie hadn't managed to coax her to drink anything, and now she was lying on the floor, panting.

'I'll see if I can come home early. I'll try and get us a lift to the vet.'

'Trouble?' asked Dot, looking up from her magazine article 'New Year, New You – our Essential Guide to your Detox'.

'Yeah. I'm going to have to ask Neville for the afternoon off. The dog's really ill.'

Dot's face creased with concern. 'Ill ill?'

'Throwing up. Panting. Not drinking. Oh God, Dot, imagine if she died. What would I tell Charles?'

'Never mind about Neville, ask George. She's here, look.'

George had, indeed, walked into the staffroom and was heading for the kettle. Today's suit was a sharply tailored black one, and her bob gleamed under the staffroom strip lights. 'Bea, hello. You look worried.'

'Yes, I am. It's the dog I'm looking after, the one that belongs to Charles? Goldie's really ill. My mum just texted me. I think I need to take her to the vet. Any chance I could have the afternoon off?'

George frowned. 'We're short-staffed anyway today, Bea. I'll need to talk to Neville. Give me two minutes—'

'Oh, have your tea or whatever, first. Please don't—'

But George had shot out of the room in search of her deputy. Bea looked in the mug she had left behind. A spoonful of instant coffee sat in the bottom, so Bea added some boiling water. George was back while she was still stirring it round and wondering whether or not to add milk.

'Oh, thank you,' George said. 'Just a drop of skimmed, please. If you went home now, could you be back for four? Be there for the evening rush?'

'Yes, I think so. I can stay on later, too, so I do the same hours.'

'Perfect. See you later. Thanks for the coffee.'

Bea turned to Dot and gave her the thumbs up, then scooted out of the staffroom and into the locker room to fetch her coat. She left via the shop floor and called briefly at Fresh Meat. Bob leaned heavily on the counter as he listened to her.

'I'm so sorry, Bea,' he said. 'I can't leave at the moment. Cara's off sick, so it's only me on here today. Here . . .' He dug in his pocket and pulled out a grubby ten pound note. 'Have this. Get a taxi.'

'Bob, I can't take your money.'

'Yes, you can. I insist.' He leaned over and pressed it into her hand.

'Okay. I'll let you know how we get on.'

Bea had been expecting carnage and devastation at home, but Queenie was on top of things. The house gleamed and smelt strongly of lemon Flash. Goldie was slumped in one corner, and didn't even raise her head when Bea came in.

'I've rung for a taxi, Mum,' Bea said. 'Will you help me get her in?'

'Of course. I'm coming with you. Can't let you deal with this on your own.'

'Really?' Now Bea noticed that Queenie already had her coat and boots on.

Between them they managed to coax Goldie into the taxi. The driver was surprisingly tolerant of having a potentially messy dog in his car. It was only a five-minute drive anyway and soon they drew up on the gravel drive outside a very smart building. It was an Edwardian detached house, but with a massive modern extension on the front. It could easily have been a hotel or conference centre.

'Do you want me to wait?' the driver asked.

'I don't know how long we'll be,' said Bea.

'I haven't got anything else at the moment. I'll wait here. If I get called away, just ring the company number. I'll get back as soon as I can.'

They entered through the automatic doors and into the bright reception area. Once inside Queenie sat on the nearest chair and Goldie slumped down at her feet, while Bea talked to the receptionist. It wasn't long before the vet appeared, a woman in her thirties with dark hair tied back in a ponytail and kind eyes behind wire-framed glasses. When she saw Goldie, she came to them and crouched down next to the dog.

'Who have we got here, then?' she said, gently ruffling the fur on Goldie's shoulder.

'She's been really sick,' said Bea.

'Can you bring her into the consulting room?'

They all stood up and encouraged Goldie to her feet. She plodded reluctantly past the reception desk, through a doorway into the back office area. Bea was amazed how big it was. There were at least four consulting rooms off one side of the corridor and mysterious rooms the other side, clearly marked, 'Staff Only'. One of the doors opened briefly as a nurse bustled through, and she got a glimpse of various uniformed staff and a state of the art operating theatre. A man at the far side of the table looked familiar. He had surgical scrubs on. Bea couldn't place him – probably a customer.

The vet ushered them into Room 4 and shut the door. She introduced herself as Xiao and listened as they told her about Goldie's symptoms.

'Has she eaten anything unusual?'

'No,' said Bea. 'Just biscuits. Oh. Hang on, she had a good go at something dead she found under a hedge.'

'When was that?'

'Yesterday morning. I was too slow to stop her.'

'A lot of them scavenge. It's normal behaviour. Normal, but not sensible.' She pressed her stethoscope into several points in Goldie's chest, examined her eyes and gums, and took her temperature. 'She's very unwell,' she said, and Bea felt little knives of anxiety stabbing at her insides. 'Her heart rate is elevated, her temperature is high and her oxygen levels are low. She's showing signs of dehydration.'

'Can you do anything, doctor?' said Queenie.

A quick smile flashed onto Xiao's face, but she didn't correct her. 'We need to get her onto a drip quickly. Once she's rehydrated, we'll observe her and be able to respond, if she needs anything else.'

'Do you mean keep her here?' Bea's heart rate was elevated too, and she wasn't just worrying about Goldie. She was thinking about the cost.

'Yes,' said Xiao. 'Do you have insurance?'

Bea and Queenie looked at each other blankly. 'I don't know,' said Bea. 'She's not our dog. We're looking after her for someone.'

'We would normally need payment today, at least for this examination, but I'll let reception know that you need some time.'

'How much is it likely to be?'

'The examination is £80, and it will be £250 per night, plus any treatment costs on top of that.'

Queenie tapped Bea's arm. 'Bea, we haven't got—'

'Shh,' Bea said. 'I'll deal with it. Don't worry.' Although, in truth, she had no idea how she would pay the bill.

'Okay,' said Xiao. 'I'll take it from here. Make sure we have your number at reception. I'll try to keep you informed, but you can ring here at any time. There's someone on-site twenty-four hours a day.'

Bea and Queenie said goodbye to Goldie, and Xiao led her out of the room. Queenie seemed on the verge of tears.

'It's all right, Mum. She'll be okay,' said Bea, trying to convince herself as much as Queenie. 'Thought you didn't like dogs, anyway,' she added, trying to tease her better.

'I don't. But they somehow …get under your skin, don't they?' She blew her nose loudly.

'I know. Come on, let's go and check out, and see if that taxi's still there.'

They trailed down the corridor back to reception. One of the receptionists was sticking up what looked like a hand-made poster on the noticeboard. 'Urgent! Keep your pets safe. 1. Is your pet microchipped? 2. Report any suspicious behaviour to the police animal crime hotline.'

The door from the back area opened and the guy from the operating theatre came in. He'd taken his scrubs off now and was in standard country vet attire – checked shirt and cord trousers. He went quickly to the cupboard behind the receptionists, dug around for a minute, pulled out a printed form and then disappeared through the door again.

'Who was that?' Bea asked the receptionist.

'Simon? He's one of our partners. The newest one, joined us eighteen months ago. He's a very good surgeon. Hopefully, your Goldie won't be needing surgery. We'll take good care of her.'

Bea could see the taxi through the plate glass window. The driver had his eyes closed and looked fast asleep. Business was clearly slow in Kingsleigh on a Thursday afternoon. Bea tapped on the window to wake him up.

On the way home, Queenie said, 'Why were you asking about that vet? Do you know him?'

'No,' said Bea. 'I don't.'

Queenie narrowed her eyes. 'You're being mysterious again. I don't like it.'

'I don't know him, Mum, but I've seen him somewhere, with someone, doing something.'

'That's it, as soon as we get home, we'll have that kettle on and you can tell me all about it.'

'It'll have to be later, I've got to get back to work. Anyway, it might not be anything.'

They paid for the taxi and Bea saw her mum back into the kitchen, and then set off walking back to Costsave for the second part of her shift. She'd downplayed things to Queenie, but as she walked across the rec, she felt a little buzz of excitement, because now she knew that the man who'd met the Barbour Jacket guy in the Wagon and Horses was Simon the vet. Of course, it might not be anything, but she was ninety-nine per cent sure it was something. It was something very fishy indeed.

18

Although working late was a drag, there were compensations. In this case, two hours back to back with Jay. In between customers, they chatted easily. Bea told him about Goldie and he listened sympathetically.

'Dogs are the best,' he said. 'I miss my dog.'

'Oh, what have you got?'

'Collie,' he said. 'Black and white one. She's really smart.'

'Is she at home with your parents, then?'

'Yeah. Can't have pets where I am now. Not officially, anyway. Here, I've asked around, about that fox you found. We don't think there was any sort of hunt meeting in our area at the weekend. It could just have happened where they were exercising the hounds, though. Or they might have dug one out, just for fun.'

'I thought fox-hunting was illegal?'

'Yup. They're not meant to hunt and kill foxes. They're meant to follow a trail laid down by a runner, but sometimes they find a fox anyway and the hounds do what hounds will always do – they chase it and rip it to bits.'

'How do you know all this stuff?'

He leaned towards her and beckoned. She leaned towards him, so that their heads were close together. 'It's what I do,' he said, with the volume down low. 'It's my thing. Sabbing.'

'Sabbing?' said Bea.

'I'm a hunt sab. I go out with my mates at the weekends and try to protect the foxes.'

'Isn't it dangerous?'

'A bit. But it's worth it. If we stop one animal being killed, it's worth it.'

'Wow,' said Bea. 'I've never met anyone like you.'

'You probably have. Sabbing isn't something anyone shouts about. You learn to keep your head down. There are some nasty fuckers on the other side.'

'Do you think the missing cats thing could be anything to do with the hunt?'

'No. It's unlikely. They've got other ways of getting their kicks. It could be . . .no.'

'What?'

'I have heard of cats being used to train dogs.'

'Train them to do what?'

'Chase them – racing dogs. Or just kill. It's one of the ways they hype up fighting dogs.'

'Fighting dogs? Is that even a thing?'

'It is, sadly.'

Bea thought about Dean's dog, Tyson, the way it lurched towards her, whining and slathering at the mouth. 'It's illegal, right?'

'Yeah. Totally.' He sat up straight again and Bea mirrored him.

'Hmm, that's a new angle,' she said. 'I'll have to look into that.'

'The mystery of the missing cats,' said Jay, and Bea wondered if he was mocking her.

'There are more missing than people know about,' she said. 'It's seriously creepy. I told Anna I'd find out who it is, and I will.'

He looked at her with a new appreciation. 'Nice,' he said, and Bea felt a warm glow inside. 'If you need any help, just let me know.'

A large man in a sweatshirt, baggy joggers and work boots, all covered in paint, was loading his shopping onto Bea's conveyor belt; sausages, oven chips, a four-pack of beer and a family-size bar of fruit and nut chocolate.

'That's got the main food groups covered,' she said to him, as she beeped it through.

'You don't get a body like this eating salad,' he said, patting the comfortable swell of his stomach. He paid contactless and didn't take a bag, just gathered the shopping up into a kind of hug and left. There was another lull at Bea's till. She twiddled round in her chair. Jay was serving the man in the Barbour jacket again – couple of steaks, some mushrooms and a bag of spuds.

Jay took the man's money and watched him go.

'You all right, Jay?' said Bea.

'Yeah. There's something about that bloke. He was right down the end of the tills and walked all the way up to mine. Odd that, isn't it?'

'Nah,' said Bea. 'People have all sorts of random reasons for choosing their checkout. He probably thought you'd be quick, whereas my regulars like to stop for a chat. Do you feel weird selling people meat, you know, being a vegan and everything?'

'I don't like it, but it's their choice and I need the cash.'

'Don't we all? What's it like, then? Being vegan?'

'What sort of question's that?'

'I mean, what do you actually eat?'

'Tofu, Quorn, beans, nuts, vegan cheese, lots of veggies,

139

lots of salad – pretty much anything you can think of, there's a vegan alternative. You can buy most of it here.'

'You don't miss eating meat, then?'

'No. I couldn't eat it now. I don't think people would eat it if they knew what farming really involves.'

Bea was about to explain that she couldn't imagine life without bacon sandwiches, when she stopped herself. Jay took her silence for interest.

'I could link you to some videos, if you like,' he said. 'If you watch them, though, you'll never eat meat again.'

'Really?' she said. 'Go on, then.'

'Add me on WhatsApp or Messenger or something. Here . . .' He pulled his phone from his pocket.

'Not here! We're not meant to have our phones on the shop floor. Neville's very hot on that. You have to leave them in your locker.'

'I'll message you when I clock off. I'm only doing till eight today.'

'Oh, me too,' said Bea.

'Drink, maybe?' He winked at her, and Bea felt deliciously happy. Talking to Jay made her feel as if her world was expanding. He was different. He didn't think like anyone else she knew. Perhaps this was a turning point. Perhaps she was meant to be more like him.

Meanwhile, in a corner of the Nag's Head, Ant was watching Saggy tackle the second pint of cider Ant had stood him. Ant himself was on halves, for financial reasons. His fingers kept playing with the change in his pocket – he had about three pounds fifty left in coins and that was it until payday. Somehow he had to feed himself and Ken. He hoped that Stevo would cover that – he'd text him later.

'So what's the word on Tank?' he said. 'What's he up to at the moment?'

Saggy narrowed his eyes and sucked air in through his teeth. 'Why do you wanna know?'

'Reasons.'

Saggy grinned. 'He's not dealing, anyway. You remember he got done for it last year? That stopped him for a bit.'

'You sure?' said Ant. He looked around them, checking they couldn't be overheard. A girl in the opposite corner caught his eye. She seemed to be on her own, sipping a Coke. He had a feeling he'd seen her somewhere before.

Concentrate, Ant, he told himself. You're on a case. But Saggy had noticed her too.

'It's your lucky night, mate,' he said.

'Huh?'

'That girl. The one giving you the eye. Don't you remember her?'

'I do, but I can't—'

'New Year's Eve, man. She was the one in the Prospect.'

Now the penny dropped, or rather the fog of alcoholic amnesia dissolved, and Ant *did* remember. His New Year's Eve snog. How could he have forgotten?

He lowered his voice. 'Do you know who she is?'

'No. Looks way too classy for the Prospect, though, doesn't she?'

'Mm. I reckon I should go and talk to her. I just need to know about Tank first. Are you sure he's not still dealing?'

'Yeah, man,' said Saggy. 'He lives two doors down from me at his mum and dad's, and my brother's still into all that – he's getting it from someone else now. Tank *is* busy, though. He looks like he's on a bit of a health kick. In and out all the time in running gear.'

'Can you dig a bit further, mate?' said Ant.

'What's in it for me?'

'Excitement. Glory. I dunno. I'll owe you. I'll buy you another pint.'

Saggy drained his glass and held it out towards Ant. 'Cheers, mate. What do you think he's up to?'

'I'm not sure but it might be something to do with these missing cats.'

'Yeah?'

'How much of a nutter is he?' said Ant. 'Would he like hurting things?'

'He likes hurting me,' said Saggy. 'I stay out of his way these days, if I can. That's weird shit, though, isn't it? Taking pets. Killing them.'

'It is, mate.'

Ant went to the bar and spread the last remnants of his spending money on the counter top. He just had enough for Saggy's next pint. As he made his way back to their table, he noticed that the girl had gone. He felt a sharp stab of disappointment.

'What are you up to, anyway, at the moment?' he asked Saggy.

'Ah, I was going to talk to you about that. Need any socks?'

Ant looked down at his sockless feet in his trainers. 'Nah, man. Socks are for losers. You've gotta go for skins to be cool, didn't you know?'

'And stink the place out?' Saggy waved one of his hands in front of his nose. 'You want those little socks that can't be seen. That's what everyone's wearing. And I'm the man to sort you out.'

'Yeah? How many have you got?'

Saggy grinned again. ''Bout six hundred pairs. Here.' His hand sank deep into the pocket of the jacket draped on the back of his chair and he drew out a packet of three pairs of white socks. 'You can have these for free. Come back for more if you like them. Mates' rates.'

Ant took them, turned the packet over in his hands and nodded. 'Thanks, Saggy. I'll let you know,' he said. 'And you let me know about Tank, or Deano. If it's them taking people's pets, we need to stop them. It's not right.'

It was only on his way out of the pub that Ant remembered he hadn't eaten anything since lunchtime. It was only half past eight, but he was skint now. The night air was bitingly cold after the warm fug of the pub. He pulled his hood up and was about to set off for home when he noticed the girl again, sitting on the wall of the pub car park.

'I'll see ya, Saggy,' he said. Saggy winked at Ant and left him to it. Ant pulled his hood down, smoothed his hands over his hair and walked over to the girl.

She was wearing a big fake fur jacket with the hood pulled up. She had a small, heart-shaped face, dark brown eyes, long eyelashes, and long straight almost black hair spilling out of the hood. She was beautiful.

'Hi, there,' he said.

'Hello.'

'Do you mind if I join you? Are you waiting for someone?'

'No, I don't mind. And, yes, I was waiting for someone, but they're here now.'

Ant felt a surge of excitement. Get in, he thought. He perched on the wall next to her, the concrete icy cold through the denim of his jeans. He offered her a cigarette.

'No, thanks,' she said.

'Do you mind if I do?'

She shook her head. Ant was glad to have something to do while he thought of the next thing to say.

'So, New Year's Eve,' he said, finally. 'That was a crazy night.' He sneaked a sideways look at her, and caught her looking at him. His stomach flipped.

'It was a good night,' she said. 'Needed it after a lousy Christmas.'

'Yeah?' said Ant. 'Why was that?'

'Someone nicked all our presents. Broke in and took them from under the tree.'

Ant's stomach flipped again, but not in a good way. It lurched and tightened, and he felt suddenly sick. She was still looking at him steadily, gauging his reaction.

'What is this?' he said, glancing around the car park. 'Some sort of ambush?'

'No, it's just me. I'm not out for revenge. I was, but I changed my mind.'

She reached into her pocket and pulled out a phone. His phone.

'What the—? I don't get it,' said Ant.

'We were broken into before Christmas. It was just awful, like properly awful. We were all crying. We didn't feel safe in our own home.'

'I'm so sorry about that.'

'Yeah, well. Everyone knew it was your dad, even before he was arrested. So I thought I'd get my own back. Show you what it felt like. I followed you to the pub that evening and robbed you when you walked me home. Took all your money and your phone.'

'Ah, that explains it. I was so wasted, I just thought I'd spent all my money and lost my phone somewhere.'

'I was going to do some stuff. You know, send texts to all your contacts or post photos from your phone up on Facebook or wherever, but having spent some time with you, well, I kind of liked you. And then I saw you on the telly. You saved that old guy's life. Here, you'd better have this back. Two wrongs don't make a right, do they?'

She held out the phone. Their hands touched as Ant took it.

'I'd better go,' she said, standing up.

'Thanks for giving it back,' Ant said. 'That took guts. You could've just chucked it away.' If only he hadn't bought that

144

last pint for Saggy. Being skint sucked so badly. 'Listen, could I walk you home?'

She smiled. 'Yeah. Okay.'

'I can't remember where it was, mind. I really was wasted.'

'Yeah. You were. Kind of cute, though, even off your head. You were a gentleman too.'

Ant checked behind him again. 'Don't say that out loud,' he said in a stage whisper. 'I've got a reputation to protect.'

'A reputation?'

'I'm a bad boy, aren't I?' He puffed his chest out a little, trying to get a bit of his swagger back.

'Yeah?'

'Yeah.'

'That's a shame. I was thinking you were better than that.'

He was off balance again now. She had the upper hand in this conversation.

'I'm only messing,' he said. 'Trying to impress.'

'You don't need to. Just tell me about yourself.'

'I'd rather talk about you,' he said.

She threw her arms out wide. 'What do you want to know?'

Everything, thought Ant. I want to know everything about you – your family, the music you like, your favourite films, whether you like ketchup or mayo on your chips, if you're a good dancer, what your breath smells like first thing in the morning.

'Ant?' she said, and he realised he was just standing there, staring at her. 'What do you want to know?'

'Better start at the beginning,' he said. 'I'm really sorry, but I can't even remember your name.'

19

'I don't know about the pub,' Bea said. 'I should get home really. My mum's on her own.'

Jay looked like she'd just told a joke but he didn't understand the punchline. 'And your mum is how old?'

'Fifty-three, but she's . . .it's complicated.'

'You can tell me. Sit down, Bea.'

'It's a bit cold, isn't it?'

Jay grinned. 'So let's sit in a nice warm pub and you can tell me why you can't be there.'

Bea dithered before deciding, 'Twenty minutes can't hurt, can it?'

'We can go to one near yours, so we're nearly home anyway. Is it the Jubilee round your way?'

'Yeah, it's a bit of hole, though.'

'I can cope with twenty minutes in a hole. Come on.'

In fact, Bea found herself telling Jay about her mum, and her dad, on their walk to the pub, past the bungalows and across the rec. By the time they got there she'd pretty much told him her life story. He bought them both a half of cider and they found a corner to sit in.

'So what about you?' said Bea. 'Where do you call home?'

Jay pulled a face. 'Kingsleigh is home for now. But my

146

parents live in Hampshire. They've just moved there. They move every few years, so nowhere's really home.'

'I don't even know where Hampshire is.'

'It's kind of southish, below London.'

They were sitting on opposite sides of a small table, both leaning in on their elbows. It felt intimate.

'So do they live in a town?'

'Converted farmhouse in the middle of a field. It's quite nice. There's a tennis court and an outdoor swimming pool.'

Bea swallowed her mouthful of cider quickly to stop herself spitting it out. 'There's a what now?'

'A tennis court and a swimming pool. Crazy, right? None of us even play tennis.'

Bea looked him up and down – his jeans and trainers were muddy. His hoodie had seen better days. She'd assumed that he was a bit like her, scraping by, just coping, but he was practically landed gentry. For a brief moment, she pictured herself reclining on a sun lounger, drinking some sort of cocktail out of a slim-stemmed glass, watching Jay, in only the skimpiest of swimming trunks, dive into a crystal blue pool ...

'Bea?' She came to and found Jay looking at her intently. 'You all right? You seemed kind of absent.'

'Yeah, I'm fine. I just, um, you know ...a fucking swimming pool? 'Scuse my language.'

'It doesn't matter, though, does it? It's just stuff.'

'It matters if you haven't got it.'

A silence fell between them. It was almost physical, pushing them apart. Bea sat up and leaned back in her seat. Jay mirrored her.

'Sorry,' he said. 'I guess it was kind of thoughtless. It's my parents, it's not me. They're not me and I'm not them.'

'You don't have to apologise, Jay. It's just, I dunno ...we're just different. Coming from different places.'

'Yeah, but that's not a bad thing. Not if we meet in the middle.'

Another silence but this time it was a melting thing, dissolving the distance between them, pulling them together. They looked at each other. Bea could see little images of herself reflected in her eyes. She didn't know why someone like him would be interested in someone like her, but he was. Maybe it was a happy new year after all.

Her phone vibrated on the table between them. Bea hated herself for checking the screen. A text coming in from her mum, of course. What else would it be? She clocked the time. They'd been there far longer than she thought. The spell was broken.

'I'd better get back,' she said.

'Sure,' said Jay. 'Hang on, let me send you that link I told you about.' He whipped out his phone and tapped at the screen. Bea's phone buzzed again as the message came in.

'I'll walk you back, shall I?' Jay said. 'I'll just nip to the bog.'

Bea put her coat on as she waited. When he reappeared, they pocketed their phones and walked out into the night.

'You don't need to walk me home,' she said.

'I'd like to,' said Jay.

There were footsteps behind them. Bea glanced over her shoulder. Two men had followed them out of the pub. Now they were both sheltering a little way down from the doorway, lighting cigarettes.

Bea and Jay left the pub car park, walked along the row of shops and then turned into her estate. As they turned the corner a jogger the size of a small mountain passed them, going the other way. He had to step off the pavement into the road to avoid them.

'Sorry, mate,' Jay called out to him.

The guy just grunted and carried on running, hood up, head down.

'I think that was Tank,' said Bea.

'The guy you saw with the cat?'

'Yeah.'

'Bloody hell, he's fucking massive. Does he live round here?'

'No,' said Bea. 'He lives near Ant's mate Saggy. Other side of town. I've seen him jogging here before.'

'Hmm, glad I am walking with you now.'

'I can look after myself, you know,' said Bea, 'but, yeah, I'm glad too.' They'd reached her house now. 'This is me.'

They stood slightly awkwardly, in a weird sort of limbo. They hadn't exactly been on a date. Nothing had really been said. But, Bea thought, they had definitely had a moment.

'Night, then,' she said. 'See you tomorrow.'

'Yeah. See you, Bea.'

She started turning to open the garden gate, when Jay swooped in and kissed her. He got her smack on the mouth – a quick, soft, gone-before-you'd-felt-it sort of kiss.

'Oops, wasn't expecting you to move,' said Jay. 'I was aiming for your cheek.'

'Oh. Right,' said Bea, a bit nonplussed both by the kiss and the disclaimer coming straight afterwards. 'I'll stand still next time. If there is a next time.'

'Um, I'm not sure about that,' he said, then kind of bashed his hand against his forehead. 'The standing still, not the next time bit. I'd like there to be a next time.'

'Oh, so would I.'

'Okay, I'm going to go before one of us actually dies of embarrassment. Night, Bea.'

'Night, Jay.'

20

The next morning, Bea spotted Ant trundling a stock trolley through the store. It was piled high with all sorts of odds and ends. He clocked her and swung by her checkout.

'I've got so much to tell you!' she said, excitedly.

'Yeah? Is Goldie all right?'

'Yes, should be able to get her this evening. You look like you're meant to be somewhere.' Bea tipped her head towards the trolley.

'Got me helping Eileen,' he said, pulling a face. He and Eileen had never seen eye to eye.

'For the new Crazy Aisle? Blimey, George doesn't waste any time, does she?'

'Nah. But guess what she's really calling it.'

'I dunno. Crap corner? Desperate deals?'

'Last Chance to Buy.'

'Ooh, that's genius. They do that in clothes shops, don't they? Make it seem like you need to snap the things up, because they're selling so fast. She's got her head screwed on, that one. Here, let's have a look.'

Bea got up from her chair and walked round to inspect Ant's trolley. It was full of the sort of ephemera that comes and goes with the commercial tide – promotional goods tied to films, comics and kids' TV series.

'Is it wrong that I love all this?' said Bea. 'Ooh, I *really* love this.' She picked up a plush toy – a tiny girl in a mask and cape.

Ant sighed. 'That how you see yourself, is it? Mild-mannered checkout girl by day, crime-fighting superhero by night?'

'I didn't, but I do now! How much is she?' She examined the label. 'Was £6.99, now £3.00. Even less with my discount. Sold! Actually, I'll take two. I'll get Kirsty to put them through her till at the end of my shift.' She took the little figures and set them next to her screen. 'Let's meet up later,' she said to Ant.

'Yeah. I've got stuff to tell you too. My contact's come through.' He tapped the side of his nose and started trundling the trolley towards aisle fifteen, walking at a faster pace than usual. If she didn't know better, Bea would have said there was almost a spring in his step.

'You know I saw some sort of deal going on in the pub the other night?'

Ant grunted, too busy with the chips and beans that Bea had paid for, taking pity on his 'cashflow crisis'.

'Well, one of the guys involved was a customer at Costsave. Jay recognised him, and I found out who the other one is.'

'Yeah?'

'He's a vet. He works at that big practice in Livingstone Lane where we took Goldie. He's called Simon.'

'Hmm, I wonder who was dealing what to who,' said Ant. 'You picking Goldie up later? How's she doing, by the way? Any news?'

'Yeah,' said Bea. 'God knows how I'm going to pay the bill.'

'Ask George, maybe? Costsave to the rescue? Charles and Goldie could be our second Costsave charity.'

'Hmm. Maybe. I've got to do something. I haven't got that sort of money.'

Ant's fork hovered midway between his plate and his mouth, and Bea realised the awkwardness. 'I can afford to buy you some chips, mate. Eat up.'

'Cheers,' he said, a bit glumly. 'Bloody money. Shall we just rob a bank, Bea?'

She snorted. 'Yeah, maybe. You get tired of just scraping a living, don't you?'

There was condensation on the window next to them, as the warm, greasy air of the café met the cold glass. It blotted out the world outside, but there was no escaping reality, thought Bea. The day-to-day grind just went on and on.

Ant grunted his agreement. 'I need some spending money, Bea. I've . . .' He hesitated. 'I've met someone.'

'Yeah?'

'She's called Ayesha. She's really nice. I'd like to see her again, but how can I take her out with no spends at all?'

'Hmm, I could lend you a tenner, just until payday.'

'No. I can't keep taking your money. I'll have to work something out. Do a bit of buying or selling or something.'

This was straying onto dodgy territory. To distract him, Bea steered the conversation back to their case. 'The cat thing, did your informant have any information?'

'No, he just said that Dean and Tank are both busy. In and out of the street. They're up to something. I've asked him to keep tabs on them and report back.' He hoovered up the rest of the chips and grabbed a slice of bread to wipe up the bean juice.

'Who is your informant, Ant?' Bea raised her eyebrows.

'Saggy,' he said.

She groaned. 'Saggy? Can't you do better than that?'

'Give over. He's the man on the ground, Bea. He lives two doors down from Tank. He's the actual best spy we could have.'

'I saw Tank last night,' she said.

'Yeah?'

'He was jogging near where I live, up along the top of the rec.'

'That's a good mile from where he lives. Are you sure it was him?'

'Positive. Unless he's got a twin or a doppelgänger.' She registered the baffled look on Ant's face. 'Someone who looks the same. Spitting image. Me and Jay both saw him.'

'You and Jay?'

'We went for a drink in the Jubilee after work.'

'You and me both on dates. Nice.'

'It wasn't a date, it was just a drink.'

'Yeah?'

'Yeah.' She felt an unwelcome warmth spreading into her face.

'Anyway, do you think the next step is following him?'

'Jay?'

'Tank.' Ant sat back in his chair, seeming to savour the feeling of a full stomach.

'What, jogging?' said Bea. 'Don't think so. Anyway how you could tail someone in Kingsleigh? It's so quiet, you couldn't do it without being seen.'

'Good point. Maybe we don't follow him or Dean. Maybe we go back to that farm.'

At the thought of those sad buildings grouped around the cold, shady yard, Bea shivered. 'Maybe,' she said, 'but for now we'd better get back to good old Costsave, earn our crust.'

They scraped back their chairs.

'Bea,' said Ant, remembering the swag in his pocket, 'do you need any socks? I reckon I could do you a good deal on some.'

21

Before Bea had steeled her nerve to speak to George about the vet's bill, Bob stepped in.

'I've been texting your mum,' he told Bea as they walked onto the shop floor after lunch. 'I'm going to give her a lift to pick up Goldie, and I'll cover the bill.'

'Bob, it could be hundreds.'

''S all right. If Charles is a secret millionaire I'll get it back from him. If not, no worries. She's our dog now, isn't she?'

Bea had a weird rushing sensation inside her head. Our dog. Did Bob mean he was part of the family now – Bea, Queenie, Goldie and Bob? Oh my God, she thought, he's going to ask me to call him Dad next.

'It's like all those pets on *Blue Peter* – they sort of belong to everyone. Goldie belongs to all of us at Costsave.'

Relief flooded through her and she broke into a smile. 'Yeah. That's exactly it. The Costsave family.'

They caught each other's eye, both aware of the echoes from Gavin, the previous manager, but neither of them said anything about him.

'If you're clocking off at five, I'll give you a lift home, shall I?' said Bob. 'Then we can pick up your mum and go straight to the vet?'

'Yeah. Great,' said Bea. 'Bob?'

'What?'

What did she actually want to ask him? How did he feel about Queenie? Were his intentions honourable? What was going on with Dot? 'Nothing,' she said. 'Just thanks.'

Dot was doing a short afternoon shift today, and the time seemed to fly by as she and Bea worked side by side.

'I get to meet Jay today. Quite excited about it,' said Dot. 'He'll be clocking on as I'm clocking off.'

At about four o'clock, Bea glanced up, and her stomach contracted. The next customer, already loading his shopping onto her conveyor belt, was Tank. He had six trays of meat – two stacks of three – as well as two large boxes of eggs, two bags of spinach, some salad and three four-pinters of milk.

'Hi,' said Bea, beeping the packs of frying steak, 'these are good value, aren't they? Just gone on offer this morning.'

Tank looked at her and grunted.

'Plenty for the cat,' she said, holding a large carton of milk.

'Huh?'

'You've got some to spare for your cat. I met you the other morning, remember?'

'Oh, right. Not my cat, but, yeah.'

He piled the shopping into a couple of plastic bags. Bea noticed there were fresh scabs and scars all over his big sausagey fingers. The sorts of injuries a cat would cause, fighting for its life?

'Oh, right, not your cat,' she repeated. 'Whose was it?'

'Huh?'

Bea winced inside, but ploughed on. 'Whose cat was it?'

'My grandad's,' he said, glancing away from Bea and then back again. 'I was looking after it for him. What is this anyway, all these questions?'

Bea beeped the bags of salad and rang up the total. 'Nothing,' she said, trying to keep things casual. 'I just...I've got a dog, I'm looking after it, too, like you, and well, I've started noticing other cats and dogs. It's like you're part of a club, isn't it? Pet owners.'

He looked at her stolidly, then shook his head, dismissing her words as not worthy of a reply.

'That's twenty-eight pounds, thirty-five pence, please,' Bea said.

He loaded the rest of his shopping into the bags, then took a wedge of cash out of his pocket and peeled off a couple of notes. Bea gave him his change and turned to greet her next customers, a husband and wife in their sixties wearing matching green anoraks. She started putting their shopping through when she realised that Tank was back, his considerable frame blocking out some of the light from the window.

She swivelled to face him, thinking he'd left something behind, or maybe she'd made a mistake with his change.

'Dean's told me about you,' Tank said. 'You're the reason he lost his job.'

He was a big lad anyway, intimidating. Now he towered over Bea, oozing the threat of violence. She wondered if she should stand up, but really that wouldn't help.

She needed to keep her nerve. 'He lost that job all by himself.' She reached for the call button next to her till and kept her finger hovering over it. She wasn't confident that Neville would be able to move an intractable Tank, if it came to it, but perhaps some of the other staff would muck in.

'You're a stirrer. You need to keep this—' he tapped the end of his nose with a battered index finger '—out.'

They stared at each other.

He could kill a cat with one squeeze of his big hands, Bea thought. And maybe he has done. She tried to keep looking into his eyes, to face him off, but she couldn't do it. She was aware of movement to her left and looked away. Dot's number five was flashing – she must have pressed her call button. Now she was getting to her feet. She tapped Tank's ankle with the end of her walking stick.

'You're leaking,' she said.

Tank turned on her. 'What?'

'One of your eggs must have broken. It's coming out of your bag. Give me the box. I'll get someone to fetch you another one.'

Tank looked down and, sure enough, a clear string of egg white was trailing from a little hole in the corner of one of his bags onto the floor. 'Shit.'

'Language,' said Dot, calmly.

'Sorry,' said Tank, fishing in the bag for the offending egg box.

Neville approached Dot's checkout. 'Is there a problem?'

'Just a cracked egg, Neville. We need another box and a cleaner.'

Neville bustled back to the customer service desk and made an announcement on the tannoy system. Soon afterwards, Ant shambled into view.

'All right?' he said warily, seeing Tank and the mess.

'Put your triangle out, Ant,' said Dot, 'and then fetch another box of eggs, there's a love.'

'On it,' said Ant.

'I'll put all this in another bag, shall I?' said Dot to Tank. 'Give it here.'

She caught Bea's eye and winked at her. Bea smiled her gratitude and turned back to her customers.

'Sorry about that,' she said.

'That's okay,' they said, at the same time.

'I'll pack, you load,' Mr Anorak said to wife. They set about their work cheerfully, making Bea wonder if she would ever end up as one of a matching pair. Or if she wanted to.

All the time she was dealing with them, she was acutely aware of Tank standing behind her. She willed Ant to hurry up and fetch his eggs. He seemed to take forever, but eventually he shambled back with a new box and handed it over.

Tank grunted and left the store with the Anorak Twins trailing in his wake. Ant set about clearing up the mess.

'He was in a bit of a mood,' he said. 'Did you see his hands and all?'

'Yes,' said Bea. 'Covered in cuts. I just kept thinking about how he got them. He's obviously got a bit of a temper. Didn't like me asking questions anyway.' Then, to Dot, 'Thanks, babe. You saved my bacon.'

''S all right, love. I've got your back, you know that.'

'Yeah. And vicey versey. We need to talk. All three of us.'

Ant glanced at Dot, who smiled at him. 'Come on, Ant,' she said. 'I won't bite. Let's just be mates, forget about the other stuff.'

Ant hesitated, then smiled. 'Yeah. Yeah, I'd like that. So, what are we talking about?'

'Tell you later,' said Bea. She had another customer already loading up their shopping and she was pleased to see it was Julie with Tiffany and Mason. 'Hiya,' she said, 'Nice to see you guys.'

Julie smiled back, but there was a weariness in her face and the smile faded quickly. 'We're on a bit of a schedule today,' she said, keeping her voice low and checking over her shoulder. 'I was late with dinner yesterday. Dave wasn't happy. He's waiting in the car outside for us now.'

Bea scanned her face. At least there were no bruises today. 'You okay?' she asked as she scanned the shopping as quickly as she could.

'Yes. Yes, I'm fine. I'm trying to be more organised today. Was going to make a fish pie but that'll take too long, so it's going to be spag bol. That's nice and quick.'

When the shopping had gone through, Bea helped her pack it into bags. She tried not to look at the photo in Julie's purse when she got her cash out to pay, but couldn't help focusing on Dave's face for a moment. He was a good-looking guy. She'd fancied him the first time she'd seen him, shopping on his own at Costsave. But looks could be deceptive.

Julie was about to start pushing the trolley towards the exit, when Bea reached up to the little shelf by her screen and brought down one of her Teeny Weeny Superheroes and held it towards Tiffany.

'Here,' she said, 'I got this for you.'

Tiffany shied away from her, clutching her pink plastic duck.

'It's all right,' said Bea. 'You can have it.'

'Oh, Bea, you didn't need to do that,' said Julie.

'I want to,' said Bea. 'Girl power and all that. I've got one too.' She picked up her own little Superhero and held the two together for a moment, making them dance in the air.

Julie smiled and took one toy and showed it to Tiffany. 'Look, darling. This is for you.'

Tiffany squirmed in her seat, shook her head and held her duck up to her face. Julie grimaced. 'Sorry, Bea. I think she thinks it's instead of her duck.'

'That's all right,' said Bea. 'Pop it in your handbag. You can give it to her later, if you like.'

'*I* like it.' Mason was standing on his tiptoes, looking longingly at the brightly coloured plush toy in his mother's hands.

'Do you, darling?' said Julie.

'Can I have it? She can be friends with my Transformers.'

Julie looked at Bea. 'Is that all right?'

'Of course,' said Bea, smiling at Mason. 'Girl power is for boys too.'

'Yeaaah!' Mason raised his little hand in the air and Julie flew the toy down to meet it. Grabbing it eagerly, the boy spun away, zooming along by the other checkouts.

'Careful, Mason!' Julie called. 'Oh. Oh no.' Head down, Mason had cannoned into his dad.

'Daddy, Daddy, look at this. That lady gave it to me.' He held the toy up towards Dave's face. Dave scowled, then snatched the toy away, causing Mason to start crying.

'That's very kind,' he said, 'but he can't have this.' He held the toy out towards Bea.

'It's okay,' said Bea. 'It's a present. It's only little.'

'It's for girls,' he said and dropped it onto the packing area. He turned on Julie. 'Why were you taking so long, anyway? I've been sitting in that car park for ages.'

'I was just coming. Mason, come here.' She carefully peeled Mason away from Dave and wiped his face with a tissue. 'It's all right,' she said. 'Let's go home.'

Bea watched as the little family group made its way to the front entrance. She felt a shudder run down her spine as she imagined what might happen when Julie and Dave were behind closed doors tonight. The Teeny Weeny Superhero lay on its back on the grey plastic counter. Bea picked it up and looked at it sadly.

'Put it by your other one,' said Dot. 'They can keep each other company.'

Bea was fighting back tears now. 'I was just trying to do a good thing,' she said, voice wobbling.

'I know, babe. Don't let twassocks like him put you off. Keep doing good things. Keep being you.'

A tear squeezed its way out of Bea's right eye. She quickly dashed it away and took a deep breath. 'Stop being nice, you. I can't cope.'

Dot smiled. 'Sorry, babe. The thing is, you can't fix other people's lives. Not really. But little things can mean a lot.'

'You're still doing it,' said Bea, sniffing hard. 'Being nice. I warned you.'

'Okay. I'll stop.'

'You're right, though, Dot. It is the little things, isn't it? Like having you here every day. I proper missed you when you were away. That's a big thing, really.'

'A big thing? Are you saying I'm fat?' Dot pretended to take umbrage.

'Yeah,' said Bea. 'That's exactly what I'm saying.'

'I can't work you girls out,' said Ant. 'If I used the "F" word to either of you, you'd turn my giblets into soup.'

'You still here?' said Bea. 'How can wiping up a smear of egg take a quarter of an hour?'

'It's a skill,' said Ant, leaning on the top of his mop, grinning. 'Not everyone can do it. It's nearly knocking-off time now. Where are we meeting? Are we having some chips?'

'I've got to go and pick Goldie up,' said Bea. 'It'll have to be tomorrow, unless we can WhatsApp or something.'

'What's what?' said Dot.

'Never mind. Are you in tomorrow?'

'No. Only two days this week. I could meet you for lunch, though. Café on the corner?'

'It's a date,' said Bea.

'Girl power,' said Dot with a wink.

'Here, what about me?' said Ant.

'You can be an honorary member of the sisterhood.'

He appeared to wrestle with this for a moment. 'Cheers. I think.' Then, as he spotted Neville emerging from the customer service desk, he shook his head and shambled away.

Not long afterwards, Bea put out her 'checkout closing' sign, processed her last customer and started to log out of her terminal. She swivelled round in her chair, expecting to see Dot doing the same but she showed no signs of stopping.

'It's five o'clock, Dot.'

'I know, love, I'm just hanging on here for a minute or two . . .'

'Wow, you really do want to meet Jay, don't you?'

'Too right I do. Specially if he's your new beau.'

'Shh,' said Bea. 'Not so loud, and he isn't, anyway. We just had a drink. Oh, here he is.'

They both looked towards the back of the store, to see Jay walking slowly towards them. He stood by the side of checkout five. 'You must be Dot.'

'That's me,' Dot said and stood up. 'I've been keeping this seat warm for you.'

Jay grinned. 'Much obliged,' he said. They chatted for a minute or two, before a warning look from Neville sent Bea and Dot heading for the staffroom.

'Bit too hipstery for me, Bea, but I can see what you mean. Those eyes! David Bowie or what?'

'Yeah, I know. There's something about him, too, Dot. He's kind and principled, you know?'

'Nice. Kind is good.'

'And . . .no, I shouldn't say really.'

'What?'

Bea drew Dot closer to her. 'His parents are minted.'

Dot's eyes grew wide. 'Tell me more.'

'Tennis courts and swimming pool sort of minted.'

Dot gave a low whistle. She clutched at Bea's arm. 'Get in there, girl!'

22

Bea looked at the figure on the bottom of the sheet of paper. The numbers seemed to swim in front of her eyes. £345.36. 'That can't be right.'

'Would you like me to print out an itemised bill?' said the woman behind the counter.

'Yes, please.'

'No. No, it's fine,' said Bob. He gently took the paper from Bea and put his debit card into the payment machine. 'I said I'd take care of it and I will.'

'Bob, you can't. It's too much,' said Bea.

'We'll pay you back,' said Queenie.

'Yes,' said Bea. 'We will.'

Having typed in his code, Bob took the card out of the machine and back into his wallet. Then he put a hand on both their shoulders and gave them a little squeeze. 'Ladies, I've paid. It's done. Let's say no more about it. We need to get *this* lady home.'

They all looked down at Goldie, who was sitting by their feet grinning up at them, apparently better after her overnight stay. They headed for the door. As they were going out, Simon was coming in. His eyes briefly met Bea's and there was a flash of recognition. He had a nice, open face and Bea couldn't imagine what he and Tank had in common. But she had seen them together and there was some sort of transaction going on. She wondered if he realised where he'd seen her before.

She hurried after Bob and Queenie. Goldie obligingly hopped into the boot of Bob's car.

Bob stayed on for tea – they made two Costsave Italiano pizzas stretch to the three of them by cooking a few oven chips as well – and afterwards they sat in the lounge, watching telly. It almost felt like he'd moved in. Bea didn't exactly mind him being there, but it felt odd. She couldn't properly relax, didn't feel she could change into her onesie and slob about as she would normally do. At a quarter to eight, he looked at his watch. Bea breathed a little sigh of relief – he was clearly about to go.

'Footie kicks off soon,' said Bob. 'It's on the other channel.'

'Oh,' said Queenie. 'Change over, then. We don't mind a bit of football, do we, Bea?'

Bea struggled to find a polite reply. It was one of their 'things', hers and Queenie's, that they both hated sport. She was just about to splutter something when she realised what Queenie was doing now, and she actually gasped as Queenie handed the remote to Bob.

The remote.

The centre of their existence was in Bob's hands now.

It was too much.

'I...I'm going to have a bath,' Bea said, clambering to her feet.

'Right-oh, love,' said Queenie.

'Can you put the kettle on, while you're on your feet?' said Bob. 'Fancy a cuppa now. Unless,' he paused, 'unless there's a beer in the fridge.'

'Sorry, Bob,' said Queenie, 'we don't have any. I'll have to get some in.'

After her bath, Bea took refuge in her room. She sat on her bed and opened her laptop intending to look at the link Jay

164

had sent. She found his message and was about to click on the link when his words came back to her. *I could link you to some videos, if you like. If you watch them, though, you'll never eat meat again.*

Bea paused. Was she ready for this? What if Jay was right and she was so disgusted by what she saw that she couldn't face eating meat again? She *liked* eating meat – bacon, chicken, the odd burger. Mm, bacon. Her mouth filled with saliva at the thought of it. If she viewed the video now, she might never eat a bacon sandwich again. She might have eaten her last one.

Bea sat back against the pillows and looked up at the ceiling. If she was going to do this, it shouldn't, couldn't, just be a casual thing. She should at least eat the final bacon sandwich mindfully, savour its salty deliciousness. Say goodbye properly.

She found herself thinking about the peck on the cheek that had turned into something else. What would it be like being involved with someone like Jay? She exited Messenger and brought up Google instead, and typed the words, 'Kingsleigh Hunt Sabs'.

There was a website, Facebook groups, a Twitter feed and several YouTube videos. Bea clicked on YouTube and selected the first video. The caption explained the footage – scenes from a day's sabbing including lining up where the hunt gathered, trying to distract the hounds by spraying scent on hedges and imitating the huntsmen's calls, and finding the bloody results of an 'accidental' kill.

To start with the two sides seemed amorphous in their own way, two tribes of anonymous people. The sabs were all in dark clothes, with black balaclavas or woolly hats and scarves, and heavy boots. The huntsmen wore red jackets, pale jodhpurs and black riding hats. They had their own people on the ground, too, following them on quad bikes or in Land Rovers.

There was antagonism between the groups from the start, and Bea found herself feeling anxious as she played the footage. There was an undercurrent of violence, never far from the surface. The sabs were keen not to be identified, but as the camera panned past one group, Bea gasped. She paused the video, rewound it, played it again and froze the screen. Only the sabs' eyes were visible through the postbox slots of their balaclavas, but there was no doubting the person frozen on screen – one blue eye and one green. It was clearly Jay.

Bea watched to the end of the video and loaded the next one. Another meet. Another Saturday. She was looking out for Jay again, but didn't spot him this time. But there was someone she did recognise. A man in a Barbour jacket and flat cap talking to a group of riders, before heels were dug into sides, reins gathered, and the group trotted and then cantered away, along the edge of a field.

'Well I never,' Bea said to herself. For some reason, she had never imagined any of her Costsave clientele as part of the hunting, shooting and fishing brigade, but, then again why not? All the world passes through the aisles of a supermarket.

She'd seen enough for one evening. She closed the laptop and wondered whether to go and make a bedtime cuppa, perhaps even take in an old episode of *The Kardashians* or a *Come Dine With Me*. There were muffled shouts from downstairs as Bob made his opinions about the referee clear. The ninety minutes were clearly not yet up. Bea sighed and reached towards the bedside table and her current book. She'd gone back to the classics recently – she'd always liked English at school and even A-Level English Literature hadn't put her off reading – and was enjoying the wicked adventures of Becky Sharp in *Vanity Fair*. Not a million miles from the shenanigans on reality TV, and the clothes were better, she thought to herself, as she snuggled under the duvet and found her bookmarked place.

23

It was a beautiful morning. The January sun was reaching over the horizon, sending long shadows across the fields. After a good sleep, Goldie seemed to be back to her usual self, plodding along happily beside Ant and Bea as they headed towards the farm.

'You sure you shouldn't be at home on Mother Hen duties?' said Bea.

'Yeah, it's fine,' said Ant. 'I checked on the little bastard before I left and he was actually in his bed. His room smelt rank, mind. Gonna go in like a SWAT team when I get back. Wake him up, throw him in the shower, make him eat some breakfast and march him off to school.'

Bea pulled a face. 'Good luck with all that.'

'The thing is, I can get him there, but I can't make him stay. He could go AWOL any time during the day. Used to do it myself.'

'You can only do what you can do.'

'True dat. Bet you didn't.'

'What?'

'Bunk off when you were at school.'

Bea smiled. 'No, I was a good girl. I did miss a bit of school, when my dad was ill and then ...you know.'

Ant's mouth formed a thin line. They walked in silence

for a minute or so, following the path across the field, then Ant suddenly swore. 'Jesus Christ, Bea, there's someone over there. Look.' He half ducked down, although there was nowhere to hide.

'Where?' said Bea.

'The other side of that hedge. There's someone bloody there.'

Bea squinted over to where he was pointing. Ant was right. She could see a figure walking along the river path, his form clearly visible through the gaps in the sparse hedge. She recognised the outline, a bulky jacket, a folded up tripod carried on one shoulder with a strap.

'Oh, that's all right,' she said. 'He's the guy who showed me the kingfisher the other day. His name's Cliff.'

'He's okay, is he?'

'Yeah. Knows so much stuff about nature, and he's the one who told me about people being at the farm.'

'Hmm. Okay.'

'Jumpy, aren't you?' said Bea. 'You sure you want to do this?'

Ant bridled. 'I'm fine.'

They carried on walking, getting closer to the farm all the time. After a little while Ant said, 'What was he like, Bea? Your dad?'

Bea's felt her face flush, and Ant suddenly looked mortified.

'I'm sorry, mate,' he said quickly. 'I shouldn't have asked.'

'No, it's fine. Hardly anyone ever talks about him.' Her face softened as she thought about him. 'He was great. He wasn't a noisy sort of person, but he was really funny. Just the things he said. He'd always find the bright side of things. He worked in the factory, on maintenance. Just an ordinary sort of job, but he always had something to tell us at the end of the day. He liked his job, but he lived for the holidays. When the factory was closed, we had to go away – the beach; buckets and spades, ice cream, fish and chips. Sitting on a pier somewhere eating chips out of the wrapper. "Proper job", that's what he called it. I suppose he was just ordinary, but . . .'

'What?'

'He was extraordinary to me. He was my hero, Ant. Still is.'

Ant seemed to be blinking rapidly. Now it was Bea's turn to worry.

'Sorry,' she said, 'It's not easy for you, is it? With your dad and everything.'

Ant wiped his sleeve across both his eyes and sniffed hard. 'The thing is, Bea, my dad's great,' he said quietly. 'He always has been.'

'That's very loyal, Ant, but, well, he does nick things from people.'

Ant shrugged. 'That's just his job. It's what he does. I know it's not nice, it's not right, yeah? But people have insurance, don't they?'

'God, Ant. That's not the point. Being broken into, it's more than "not nice", it's devastating. It's a violation of the place where people should feel safest.'

'Yeah, I get that now. It's what Ayesha said. Made me feel proper ashamed, even though it wasn't me that did it.'

'So you've never thought about it?'

'Listen.' Ant lowered his voice, even though there was no one around. 'He took me with him a couple of times, when I was younger, till my mum found out. Then she went mental and it stopped.'

'He took you with him?' Bea could hardly believe her ears. 'Yeah.'

'What was it . . .I mean, how did it . . .I mean, I don't know what I mean. I don't know where to start with that.'

'What was it like? Exciting. Scary. And I felt proud. Felt

169

like he didn't think I was a little kid any more, you know? I liked the quiet. Before you do anything, you look and you listen. That stillness, the moment before anything happens, it was a buzz.'

'He shouldn't have done that, Ant.'

'No, I know. But in a funny sort of way I'm glad he did.'

They were nearly at the farm now. Although the light was slanting through the trees surrounding the cluster of buildings, Bea felt a shiver run down her spine.

'I don't like this place,' she said.

'Shh,' said Ant. 'Tie Goldie up and let's go and look round properly.'

Bea tethered Goldie to the gatepost again and they climbed over. As she followed Ant along the side of the buildings and into the yard she noticed that he was treading softly, his feet making no sound at all, while she was managing to find every frosty, crackly leaf and scrapy bit of gravel going. His 'training' was kicking in.

They stood in the middle of the yard and looked around.

'What now?' said Bea.

'Shh.' Ant held his finger to his lips.

They both heard the sound at the same time. It was high-pitched, a whining, mournful sort of noise. Bea looked sharply at Ant.

'In there,' she whispered, and pointed at the long, low building to their right.

They tiptoed over. There was only one window in the wall facing the yard, and a tatty, but solid-looking door. Bea pressed her ear to the edge of the door and heard the noise again. Was somebody crying?

They skirted round the wall. There was another window at one end. The bottom edge was nearly five feet above ground level. Ant looked around and then took a thin card out of his pocket. The blue and yellow pattern told Bea it was his

Costsave Saver Card. He slid the card into the gap between the window and its frame and started moving it slowly and carefully along a section halfway up the window.

'Dammit,' he muttered, as the card seemed to stick. He tried again and Bea heard a metallic noise, something moving or giving. 'Yup,' said Ant. Now he used the plastic as a lever and the window started to open outwards.

With the window open, the sound was louder. They could hear that it wasn't a human cry.

It was unmistakeably a cat.

Ant stood on his tiptoes and peered in. 'I can't see it, but there's a load of, like, compartments, with little walls. I reckon it's in one of them. I'm going in.'

'It's quite high up,' said Bea, doubtfully.

But Ant meant business. He backed away from the wall, then took a curved, loping run up and leapt at the opening. Amazingly, his front half was through on his first attempt, leaving his bum and legs dangling in the fresh air.

'Wait a minute.' Bea grabbed his feet and pushed. 'Brace your legs,' she called. Ant straightened his knees, making his legs rigid, Bea shoved and he shot through the window and disappeared, leaving Bea standing outside listening to a crumpled sort of thud and a noise that sounded like, 'Oof!' as he hit the floor.

She stretched up and tried to see what was going on. 'You all right? Ant, mate, are you okay?'

There was a sort of scuffle and then she could see the top of Ant's head. 'Yeah. Hold on a minute.'

Bea started jumping on the spot, pogoing to get a better view. It was like an old-fashioned flickering film, or one of those flip-books where a series of pictures form a moving image. She saw Ant moving down the row of stalls, checking each one. Then he stopped, turned towards the window and gave her the thumbs up.

'What?' called Bea. She was breathless now, and her legs were complaining. She stopped jumping and waited, leaning her back against the wall. This part was in shadow, and she cooled down quickly after her exertions. She stared at the ground, concentrating on listening out for Ant. Then her eyes focused and she realised she was actually looking at something. A bit of rubbish, a receipt or something. She bent down and picked it up. There was handwriting on it, some numbers, but as she straightened up she heard Ant call her name. She stuffed the paper in her pocket, turned round and peered up at the window. A plastic box, with a wire door at one end was emerging through the window.

'Bea! Grab this, will you? Have you got it?'

She reached up and took hold of the sides of the box. 'Yup, got it.'

She felt the weight of it pass to her and she lifted it down carefully. The occupant was silent as the box was passed over, but when Bea looked through the wire door, it started to miaow pitifully and she could see two green eyes looking back at her, set in a dish-like face and a mass of pure white fur.

24

'Bea! This is nice.'

Even his voice on the end of a mobile phone caused mixed feelings with Bea, but there was no time to dwell on them. 'Sorry to ring so early, Tom.'

'It's fine. Just stepped out of the shower actually. Only wearing a towel.'

God, this is a mistake, thought Bea, trying to shove aside the not-entirely-unwelcome mental image of Tom's bare torso.

'Tom, I've found a cat,' she said. 'It's injured. Should I bring it into the station?'

'Hold on there, you found a cat. Where?'

'At some farm buildings.'

'So, why not knock on the door and tell them?'

'There's no farmhouse. No one lives there.'

'O-kay,' he said. 'How bad are its injuries?'

'Well, actually they look like they're healing up.'

'But it was in distress, right?'

'Yes. No. It was miaowing.'

There was a pause.

'You found a cat that's been hurt but is better now, and it was miaowing, so you brought it home.' He started laughing rather mirthlessly. 'Bea, you've basically stolen a cat. You'd better come down to the station and turn yourself in. I'll get the handcuffs ready.'

'I haven't stolen it. I think it's one of the missing ones.'

'Why would you think that?'

Should she drop Dean and Tank in it? She'd given Tom names before, including Dean's, and it hadn't ended well. Did she really have any evidence against them?

'I saw someone carrying it a few days ago.'

Tom sighed. 'It was probably their cat.'

'I don't think so.'

'Bea, stop. Okay? Stop it now. Take the cat back to where you found it and we'll say no more about it.'

'You don't understand—'

'No, and I don't want to, because it might mean you're in trouble.'

'Is there a white cat on your missing list?'

'I don't know. There's loads of the bloody things now, but I haven't worked on it for a couple of days. You'll never believe this, but I'm actually on the bypass body case.'

'Oh! Is it a case now? Have there been developments?'

'Yes. Hang on, my towel's going. Let me sort it out.' There was a clunk as Tom put his phone down somewhere, and a little gap and then he was back. 'That's better. Too cold in my bedsit to go starkers.'

He's in a bedsit, noted Bea. So he really has moved out.

'Yeah, guess what, Bea? You know I thought it was a night out gone wrong?'

'Yes.'

'They found drugs in his system.'

'Drugs?'

'Ketamine, to be precise. The amount he had in him, he would have been off his head, apparently. Now, I've just got to find out where he got it. So, the cats are on the back burner for the time being.'

174

'Oh. Okay, but can you at least check your list of the missing ones?'

Another sigh. 'The file's at work, Bea.'

'So, can you check it later and text me?'

'I guess so. And you'll take it back to where you found it, right?'

'No, I can't do that. I think I'd better get it checked out by the vet.' A little bit of her died as she thought about another vet's bill. She couldn't ask Bob to cover this one.

'Okay, you do that. If there even is a cat.'

'What?'

'I mean,' and she could hear the smile in his voice, imagine his freckly skin crinkling at the side of his mouth, 'you don't have to come up with excuses to ring me, Bea.'

'There *is* a cat, Tom, and I need you to check that list. You won't forget, will you?'

'I won't forget. And remember, you can ring me any time, Bea. Any time at all.'

'Okay,' she said. 'Thanks.'

'No, thank *you*,' he said. 'And Bea?'

'Yeah?'

'Look after that pussy.'

'Tom, you—' too late, he'd rung off '—sleazeball.' She looked at the cat in the carrier. 'He *is* a bit sleazy, but I kind of like him. Is that wrong?'

The cat blinked at her but said nothing back.

Bea rang into the office to request a later start. She was expecting Anna to answer, but it was George herself. She listened as Bea explained her situation and Bea crossed her fingers as she waited for a response.

'Your home's turning into an animal refuge,' said George. Her tone was light, rather than critical.

'I know. And I don't know anything about them,' said Bea.

'We've never even had a pet before. I'm so sorry, George. I don't really know why this is happening to me – I'm just a magnet for waifs and strays at the moment. If I can start later, then I'm happy to work later too.'

She could hear the clicking of a keyboard in the background.

'I'm looking at the rota now. We should be fine for a couple of hours, if you can get here by eleven.'

'That's brilliant. Thank you so much.'

'No problem. I know what it's like,' said George. 'We've got two cats, a dog and a rabbit, as well as the kids. It gets pretty hectic.'

'Wow,' said Bea, and then, without really thinking blurted out, 'How do you do all that and work full-time?'

'I've got a very understanding wife,' said George.

'Ah,' said Bea. 'We could all do with one of them.' She winced as soon as the words were out of her mouth. Had she overstepped the mark?

George chuckled at the other end of the line. 'I'm very lucky. See you at eleven, Bea.'

It was a good twenty-minute walk to the vet's surgery. By the time Bea got there, the cat carrier seemed to be weighing twice as much as when she'd set out.

The cat had kept up a noisy commentary pretty much the whole way. Bea had rung the vet in advance and didn't have long to wait when she got there. Her heart gave a twitch in her chest when the vet came out into the waiting area to call her in. It was Simon.

'Miss Jordan?'

'Yes, that's me.'

He frowned. 'Do we know each other? I've seen you somewhere, haven't I?'

'Um, no, I don't think so,' said Bea. 'At least, I've been here this week with my dog – the dog I'm looking after. I expect you've seen me here.'

He seemed to accept her burbled explanation. 'And this is ...?' He looked towards the cat carrier, inviting an introduction.

'I don't know,' said Bea. 'That's the thing. It's not my cat. I found it.'

His eyebrows lifted towards his hairline. 'Come along in and let's have a look.'

The cat was somewhat grumpy. It refused to come out of the little door when Simon opened it, and gave his hand a good swipe when he reached in.

'Sorry,' said Bea, then wondered why she was apologising.

Simon undid some plastic fittings along the side of the box, and lifted the top away from the bottom. There was nowhere for the cat to hide. He scooped it up and placed it on the examination table, and gave it the once-over, feeling all over its body, listening to its heart through a stethoscope, looking at its eyes, teeth and gums.

'Well,' he said at last, 'it's a boy, fairly elderly by the look of the teeth. There are some injuries to his shoulder and back legs, difficult to say how they were caused but they're flesh wounds, several days old, I'd say, and healing up well. I'll give him a shot of antibiotic to be on the safe side and then you can take him home.'

'Oh,' said Bea. 'I don't want to keep him. Like I said, he's not mine.'

'Then, you'll need to contact the Cats and Dogs Home, see if they'll take him.'

'Right.'

He'd given the injection before Bea had a chance to ask him how much it would be. Perhaps she would save that conversation for the receptionist. Simon put the cat in the carrier and fixed the lid back on.

177

'Where did you say you found him?' he said.

'I...um...didn't.'

Simon looked at her. 'So, where...?'

She wasn't quick enough to think of a lie. 'At the farm across the fields from the Manor Road allotments.'

'Hmm, don't think I know it,' he said. Then, without missing a beat, 'You know, I don't like the look of the wound on his shoulder. Perhaps we'd better keep him here, after all.'

There was something about the way he said it. Suddenly Bea knew she very much didn't want to leave the cat there. She put her hand on the handle on the top of the case. 'It's okay. I won't hand him into the Home for the time being. I'll keep an eye on him at home.'

'No, I think he should stay here.' Simon's hand was next to hers now, also trying to grip the handle. This was turning into a rather bizarre tug of war.

'He's coming with me,' said Bea firmly, and yanked the carrier away from the vet. She headed swiftly for the door and was out and into the waiting area before he could stop her. Bea didn't stop to settle up at reception, but kept on walking, out of the main door and down the street.

Her heart was racing and she gathered the carrier into both arms and started to run. As she puffed her way towards home, she couldn't help seeing herself as others might – a catnapper in mid-flight – but she didn't care. She ran as far as she could, about two hundred metres as it turned out, and then slowed to a walk, gasping and wheezing.

She checked behind her to see if she was being followed, then stopped to get her breath back, putting the carrier down on the pavement and leaning forward, hands on knees.

'I don't know what's going on,' she said to the cat, who was peering out through the wire door, thoroughly disgruntled at the shaking up he'd just had, 'but I'm not letting go of you until I do.'

25

'You're joking, Bea, not another one!'

Queenie's accent became broader when she was agitated. Bea kind of wanted to imitate her, but perhaps now wasn't the time.

'Not for long, Mum. Just until we find out whose it is.'

'No, Bea. I'm just getting used to Goldie, but not a cat as well. I mean, cats and dogs, how's that going to work?'

'We'll just have to keep them in separate rooms.'

'But the poo, Bea. The poo!'

'I'll run down to the corner shop, see if they've got a litter tray and that.'

'I don't want a filthy litter tray in the house!'

'Just for today, Mum. I'll sort it out. I promise. He's a nice cat.' Bea crossed her fingers behind her back as she said this. From what she'd seen of him, he wasn't entirely sweetness and light. 'Look at his little, face, Mum. Just look.'

Bea had put the cat carrier on the kitchen table. Now Queenie leant over and peered through the wire door. The cat peered back and gave a little miaow.

'Ooh,' said Queenie. 'It's pure white. Like Arthur.'

'Like who?'

'You're too young to remember. He used to be on the

179

adverts years ago, eating his dinner right out of the tin. What was it now? Kattomeat!'

'Perhaps we should keep him in the carrier. Just for today. I've got to go in to work soon. What do you think?'

'Well, I don't know, Bea. Isn't that a bit cruel? It's only a small box, but then I don't want a cat wandering about, pooing everywhere. And I don't want any argy-bargy between the two of them. Oh. Oh no.'

While they were talking, the cat had pushed his nose against the door, which had swung open.

'Oh crikey,' said Bea. 'We can't have done up the catch properly. Quick, Mum, get Goldie in the other room!'

'Wait a minute, Bea. Look.'

'Arthur' had crept to the edge of the table and was peering over the edge. Goldie shambled over to investigate this latest development. She padded closer and closer until she was only a few inches from the table, then tipped her head up to have a good sniff. Arthur flashed out his paw and swiped Goldie's nose. He got two good hits in before a rather dazed Goldie backed away.

'Hey!' Bea shouted. 'That'll do!'

'No, it's all right, Bea,' said Queenie. 'That's a good thing. He's showed her who's boss. I reckon they might be all right together. Go and fetch a tray and some litter, like you said. And a tin or two of cat food. I wonder if they still make Kattomeat?'

When Bea finally made it into work, Ant was skulking around with a big black cloud over his head.

'What's up with you?'

He scowled. 'Gotta help Eileen put out the Valentine's stuff.'

'It's not the worst job in the world, mate.'

'Hmph. I'd rather do the trolleys out in the rain.'

'Really?'

'She hates me. She just treats me like I'm thick.'

'She's pretty good at displaying stock, though, Ant. Just watch what she does and try and learn something.'

'I don't want to learn how to make his 'n' hers champagne glasses look good on a shelf.'

'Flutes,' said Bea.

'What?'

'They're called flutes.'

'God, don't you start bloody educating me. Jeez ... Anyway, I wanted to ask you, can you look out for Ken later? I told him to come into the shop and find me, tell me how he got on at school.'

'You got him there all right?'

'Yup. He smelt nice. He was dressed right. He'd had some breakfast.' Ant listed his triumphs on his fingers. 'I've done my bit, now he has to do his. How'd you get on with the cat?'

'Oh, I need to tell you about that—'

'Oi!'

They both looked round to see Eileen glowering at them from the end of aisle seven. She jabbed at her watch with her stubby index finger, and jerked her head to one side to indicate that Ant was needed.

'Tell me later, okay?' He shambled off towards aisle seven like a condemned man approaching the gallows.

Tom and Shaz joined Bea's queue with their lunchtime meal deals – a pack of sandwiches, some crisps and a drink for £3.99.

'There's nothing on the list about a white cat, Bea,' said Tom as they reached the front of the queue. 'I've checked.'

'Oh, are you sure?'

'Just give it back to your mate, or whatever the story was.'

'He isn't my mate,' said Bea.

'If you don't know them, take it to the Dogs and Cats Home, then. If someone's looking for it, they'll check there.'

'Oh, okay. Here's your change.'

'We're on that other thing today, the one I told you about.' He gave her a wink. 'Much more like it.' He moved along and stood waiting by the window as Shaz took her turn.

'That's not strictly true. What Tom just told you,' said Shaz. She leaned a little closer and lowered her voice. 'A woman did come in to report a missing cat, but she was rather confused. I heard her talking to Damien, the desk sergeant. She seemed to be talking about a cat but then she was talking about her husband and some sort of rant about her neighbour. I don't think it even got recorded as a missing cat – it's not on our list anyway – but I'll ask Damien when I see him.' She gave Bea a wink.

'Thank you, Shaz. He must belong to someone and I don't want to give him back to the person I saw with him. I don't trust them.'

Shaz raised an eyebrow. 'Want to tell me about that?'

Behind her, Tom was getting impatient. 'Come on, Shaz. We've only got twenty minutes to eat this in now, then we've got some hot leads to follow.'

Shaz rolled her eyes. She put her loose change in her trouser pocket and gathered up her lunch things. 'Seriously, if you've got some information, let me know. In confidence.'

She handed Bea a business card, with an email and mobile number on it, before going to join Tom. Bea put the card in the pocket of her tabard. As she did so, she remembered the scrap of paper she'd picked up at the farm that morning. Where was it? In her coat pocket? That had had a number on it too, hadn't it?

At lunchtime, Bea caught up with Ant. 'How's it going?'

He puffed out his cheeks. 'It's done. That's the best I can

say. If you want an overpriced box of chocs, some socks that say "I love you" on the side, or a tea towel with little hearts all over it, they're ready and waiting for you on aisle fifteen.'

Bea grinned. 'Don't think I'll be wanting any of that.'

'Me neither. Not that stuff anyway. I'll need to get something for Ayesha. I'm so skint I might have to liberate some flowers from somewhere. Valentine's Day's a rip-off, isn't it?'

'Yeah, although—' She stopped herself. This was more of a topic for Dot, not Ant.

'What?' he said.

'Nothing. It is a rip-off, but it's also miserable if you haven't got anyone on Valentine's Day.'

'What are you talking about? You've got guys queuing up for you. That copper's still sniffing around, isn't he? And Jay's obviously got the hots for you.'

Bea pulled a face. 'Yeah, I suppose.'

'I know so. No need for you to be a lonely heart. Just go for it. And, hey, if those two let you down —' he opened his arms out wide '—I'm here for you, any time you need me.'

She scanned his face, checking he was joking. She reckoned he was. She took a sip of tea.

'Seriously, Bea. Obviously I'm okay in the romance department at the moment, but how about we make a pact? If we get really old, like thirty or something, and we're still not fixed up, how about you and me?'

Bea started to choke on her tea, not knowing whether to gulp it down or spit it out. She ended up with a disastrous volley of coughs and burps all mixed up together. Everyone in the staffroom stopped what they were doing and looked at her.

'You all right, Bea?' Kirsty shouted out.

'Slap her back, Ant, quickly!' said Bob.

Bea flapped her hands in the air to indicate that she didn't

183

need any help, and eventually she recovered a bit of compo-
sure.

'Sorry, everyone,' she said. 'Tea down the wrong way.'

Ant grinned. 'Bit of a shock to the system,' he said, then
tapped the side of his head, 'but think about it. You don't
have to give me an answer now.'

'Ant, I don't need to think,' she said. 'The answer's—'

But Ant's phone started to ring. He held his hand up to
shush her and answered. His expression darkened. 'Oh no.
Yeah. Yeah, I know. Okay, thanks for telling me.' He killed
the call.

'What is it, mate?' asked Bea.

'That was the school. Ken's gone AWOL again.'

26

After the teatime rush, the store became eerily empty.

Ant was on 'put-backs', returning items left at the check-outs to their rightful places on the shelves. His meanderings took him to where Bea and Jay were working alongside each other.

'Did you track down Ken?' Bea asked.

'Nah. I keep trying his mobile but he's not answering.'

'You could ask George to leave early.'

'She's gone already. It would have to be Neville,' he cast a glance towards the customer service desk, 'and I'm not sure he'd be very sympathetic. Anyway, what am I going to do – walk round the whole town on the off-chance that I'll find him swigging cider in the park or doing some hippy crack round the back of the garages?'

'Well, yeah, maybe. He's just running wild, isn't he?'

'I know, but is it all my fault? Stevo's just moved in with his girlfriend's family – her mum's a really good cook – and left me to it. It's not really fair, is it?' There was more than a hint of truculence in Ant's tone.

'No, mate. I didn't say that,' said Bea. 'But it seems like you're the only one who's around and who cares enough to do something about it.'

'Not sure I do. He's always been a little shit.'

'Ant,' Bea said, reproachfully.

'I don't mean it. Not really. I'd like to help sort him out, but I'm not sure where to start. If he's home when I get back, I'll try and have a chat with him. Can we talk about something else?'

'Oops, incoming,' said Bea, spotting a customer approaching. 'Catch you later.'

Kevin, the photographer with the tragic comb-over, put his shopping on Bea's conveyor belt – a couple of meat pies, a bag of oven chips, a plain Viennetta, and a family bag of mint humbugs. Bea smiled and just managed to stop herself saying, *Dinner at your mum's, is it?* After all, she was in the same boat.

'Bea,' said Kevin. 'You haven't paid me a visit yet.' He'd offered to take Bea's photo last year and given her his business card. 'I'd do it for free,' he said. 'Seeing as we're friends.'

Bea's wit was letting her down. She couldn't think of a suitable put-down. 'I'm happy with a selfie,' she said, and then regretted it as Kevin's mouth spread into a leer.

'I bet you are,' he said.

Bea swallowed down the little bit of sick that had risen to the back of her throat. 'Any progress on the missing cats case?' she said, changing the subject as quickly as possible.

'Nah. Happy with this week's front page, though.'

This week's *Bugle* featured a montage of various views of Costsave and photos of the missing cats. It was bad news for Costsave but it had at least knocked the story of Ant's dad into the middle pages.

'You must get an instinct for these things, though. What do you think's going on?'

Kevin put his shopping in a canvas bag. 'I don't know, Bea. There might be a sicko out there, taking them. Or perhaps there's a mad old woman luring them in and keeping them as pets.' He put the mint humbugs in his bag. 'I'd better check round at Mum's, hadn't I, see if the daft old bird's turned into a catnapper. She's got one cat, and that's one too many. Nasty old thing. She'd be better off without it. Can't stand cats myself.'

After he'd gone, Bea sprayed her conveyor belt with disinfectant and used some hand sanitiser. It was the best she could do at work, although really she wanted to take a shower. Kevin always made her feel like that.

'He's a bit of a creep, isn't he?' said Jay.

'Got it in one,' said Bea.

'Do you know him?'

'Photographer for the local rag.'

'Figures,' he said.

Ant, Bea and Jay walked down the High Street together. They stopped outside the chip shop.

'You can't live on chips, Ant,' said Bea.

'I'm skint, Bea. And besides, I can't cook. I found a fiver stuffed in one of the kitchen drawers. So it's toast for breakfast and lunch. Chips for tea.'

'I was going to cook tonight,' said Jay, 'but it's a bit late. I'll come and get some chips with you.'

'Well, I'd better head home and see how Queenie's got on with a cat and a dog for company. Before I go, though, I wanted to show you something. I found it this morning at the farm.' She fished in her pocket and drew out the bit of paper.

Ant stood back. It wasn't public knowledge yet that he couldn't read, and he obviously wasn't keen to share the information. Jay took the paper from Bea and looked at it.

'It's a bit dark out here,' he said. 'Let's go inside. Have a quick cuppa with us, Bea.'

Bea didn't need her arm twisting. 'Well, just a quick one.'

They trooped into the chippy and Bea gave Jay a couple of pounds for her tea and nabbed a table in the furthest corner for them all. She smoothed the scrap of paper out on the table top.

'That's got your fingerprints all over it now,' said Ant, swinging into the chair opposite her. 'If it's evidence.'

'Ha! You're starting to think like a detective,' said Bea.

'I'm not just a pretty face, you know,' said Ant. He pushed his polystyrene tray of chips into the middle of the table, next to the paper. 'Have some,' he said.

'No, it's all right,' said Bea.

'Go on. They're nice today.'

She took a chip, dipped it in the reservoir of sauce Ant had squeezed into the corner of the tray and bit half of it off. It was piping hot and the perfect combination of grease, potato, salt, vinegar and ketchup.

'Bloody hell,' she said. 'They *are* good.'

Jay sat down next to Ant.

'What were you going to cook?' said Ant.

'Veggie curry and flatbreads. I've got all the stuff at home.'

'Flatbreads?'

'Yeah, unleavened bread. It's easy, you make up a dough and then cook them on a griddle. They puff up a bit if you're lucky.'

'You make them from scratch?'

'Yeah, man,' said Jay. 'It's easy. Look, come round tomorrow. Bring that brother of yours if you can find him. I'll cook dinner.'

'Really?' said Ant.

'Yeah. Why not? Bea's right, man cannot live on chips alone. Right, Bea?' Bea, feeling rather left out, had been pretending to study the piece of paper. Now she looked across the table at Ant and Jay. 'Fancy a curry tomorrow, Bea? I'm cooking.'

'Oh. Yes. I'll ask Queenie, but yes, that'd be really nice. If you've got enough to go round.'

'Ah, that's the good thing about curries. You can just keep chucking things in. Feed an army. The more the merrier. So, are we ringing the number on that paper, then?'

Bea looked back at it. There was a star or an asterisk and a mobile phone number.

'I reckon we should,' she said.

'Go on, then,' said Jay. 'Give it a ring and see who answers.'

'And then what?'

'Say they dropped something at the farm. See what happens.'

'Hmm.'

'Go on. Do you want me to?'

'No, I'll do it.'

'Put it on the table, on speakerphone.'

Bea did so and then dialled the number. It rang briefly, then someone picked up.

'Hello?'

It was a man's voice. Bea froze. She just didn't know what to say. The others looked at her, but she shook her head. Ant stepped in.

'All right?' he said.

'Who is this?' said the man.

'I've been given your number. It's about the farm. I wanted to know when the next . . .gig is.'

'Gig?'

'Yeah. I can't spell it out, mate. I'm in the pub.'

'Right. Gig. Who gave you this number?'

'Just a mate.' Ant hesitated for a moment, then said, 'Dean.'

'Oh, okay. Well, I'll have a bloody word with him when I see him. He shouldn't be giving this number out. Delete it off your phone, right?'

'Yeah. Okay. No problem.'

'It's Saturday anyway. You can get all the details off him.

Bring some friends, if you like. As many as you like as long as they've got the cash. No freeloaders.'

'Right. Okay, see you Saturday, man.'

'Yeah, what was your name again?'

'It's—' Ant cancelled the call.

'That was brilliant, Ant,' said Bea. 'You're like a private eye or something. Nice one. So something's kicking off at the farm on Saturday. What are we going to do about it?'

She and Ant looked at Jay. He was sitting, staring into space, apparently lost in thought.

'Jay,' said Bea. 'You all right? What are we going to do about Saturday?'

He snapped out of it. 'I don't know,' he said. 'But I do know I recognise that voice.'

'Yeah? Who was it?'

'I can't place them. I'll get there in the end.' He seemed to shiver.

'You all right?'

'Yeah. It's just . . .I don't know where I've met them, but I've got a bad feeling about this.'

They turned back to their chips, and as they were finishing up, Jay slapped the table and said, 'Got it!'

Ant and Bea looked up at him.

'That voice, it's the same guy you saw in the pub, Bea. The one who's been in Costsave. Barbour Jacket Man.'

'He works for the local hunt, you know,' said Bea. 'I saw him in a video online.'

'Of course!' Jay said. 'He's one of their men. He's a right bastard. So, what's he doing at the farm?'

190

27

Jay's eyes were burning brightly. He had an intensity about him that Bea found exciting. 'Okay,' he said, 'this changes things. Something's kicking off on Saturday. It's gotta be dog-fighting, hasn't it? They've been using the cats out at the farm to bait the dogs with.'

'Dog-fighting?' said Bea.

'Yeah, you know I told you they practise ripping them apart, encourage them to bring out their aggression. Well, they need stuff from the vet – painkillers, antibiotics, all that stuff – to keep the dogs going when they get injured. It all adds up.'

Ant put his last chip back in the plastic tray. 'God, that's sick,' he said. 'Puts you off your food, doesn't it?'

'It *does* all add up, though,' said Bea. 'If it's true, we've got to stop it. I guess we *should* go to the police. Shall I do it? Shall I just call Tom or the other one, Shaz?'

'You could do,' said Jay, 'but we've only got circumstantial evidence so far. We need hard proof. We need to catch them at it.'

He was leaning on his forearms, against the edge of the table. His eyes were shining in the stark strip light. It was quite different to his normal laid-back style. Bea liked it. There was passion there.

'Sneak up on them?' said Ant. He was looking animated too.

'Yeah.'

'And then what? Break it up?'

'I don't know if we can break up a fight meeting,' said Jay. 'They're rough buggers that go to those things and there'll be loads of them there. I could get my sab mates to come, safety in numbers, but I don't know if they'd do it. After dark, lots of them, not so many of us. We could disrupt it, I guess.'

'It's risky,' said Bea. 'I reckon it should just be us. We could take pictures, or ring the police once we're there.'

'Yeah,' said Jay, 'that sounds like a plan.'

'Except—' said Ant.

'Except what?' said Bea.

'Well, are you sure you want to come? If it *is* dog-fighting, and if we get spotted, it could turn nasty.'

Bea sighed. 'Ant, mate. I may only be five foot five, but I'm pretty sure I could punch harder than you. And there is no way on earth you two are going without me.'

'Okay, okay,' said Ant. He formed a fist with his right hand and held it across the table, inviting Bea to bump it back, which she did. 'So, we'll meet up at Jay's tomorrow and agree the operation, shall we?'

'Yup,' said Jay. 'In the meantime, get some dark clothes ready, black or camo, a balaclava, or a dark hat and a torch. I've got some spare if you haven't got any.'

Bea felt a little thrill of excitement ripple up her spine. From sitting at a checkout at Costsave to direct action with camouflage and torches. Life was definitely taking an interesting turn.

Outside the shop, they prepared to go their separate ways. They were just saying goodnight when they heard someone shouting. 'Ant-o-ny! Hey! Look at me!'

'Sounds like Ken,' said Ant. 'Where is he?'

They all turned round towards the civic centre, the little precinct that contained the library and the local council offices.

'Oh, Ant. He's on the clock. Look!' There was a modern clock tower on the corner of the precinct, a metal-framed structure with artwork panels reflecting the history of Kingsleigh. Ken was about twenty feet off the ground, clinging to one of the metal corner struts.

Ant, Bea and Jay checked for traffic and then ran across the road to stand at the base of the clock.

'Jesus, Ken, come down!' Ant called up to him.

'Woohoo! It's fucking ace up here!'

'Okay, but it's time to come down now. Come on, mate. Can you climb down?'

'I don't need to climb, bro, I can flyyyyy!'

He let go of the support with one hand and stretched his arm out into the night air, flapping it like a wing.

'No!' The three watchers shouted together.

'Ken! You can't fly! You need to climb down,' shouted Ant. 'Turn round and face the clock and then feel below with your foot.'

Jay had peeled away from them. Now, Bea watched as he took a run up and launched himself at the tower. He was a very skilled climber and was within a few feet of Ken in seconds. He pulled himself up again and was next to him. He started talking quietly to Ken. Bea couldn't hear what either of them was saying, but soon Ken turned his back on them and started feeling his way down. Jay stayed level with him, coaching him all the way.

When he got within reach, Ant put his hand on Ken's waist, and helped him back onto terra firma.

'Jesus, Ken. I don't know whether to batter you or hug you.'

'What's the problem? It's all good, Ant. I was just admiring

the view.' Ken was unsteady on his feet. He reeled towards
Bea and she saw that his pupils were enormous.

'Ant,' she said. 'He's on something.'

Ant gripped Ken's shoulders. 'Ken, what've you taken?'

But he couldn't or wouldn't answer.

'I can't get any sense out of him. I'll take him home and
try and get him to sleep it off.' He turned to Jay and patted
him on the back. 'Thanks, man. I owe you.'

'It's cool. Do you need any more help?'

'Nah, we'll be all right.'

Bea and Jay watched the two of them lurch off towards
their estate.

'Blimey,' said Bea. 'Ant's got his hands full, hasn't he?'

'Yeah. No harm done this time, though. How old is Ken?'

'Fifteen? Sixteen? He's got GCSEs this year.'

Jay blew air out of his mouth. 'That's young. He needs
help now, doesn't he? Before it's too late.'

'Yeah, but who can help? It's all down to Ant, as far as I
can see.'

Bea and Queenie were pottering round the kitchen, as part of
their end of evening routine. Bea hadn't told Queenie about
Ken. Sometimes it felt better feeding her an edited view of
the world.

'How've you got on, Mum?' she said.

'Fine,' said Queenie. 'I wouldn't say Goldie and Arthur
are best friends, but they're okay with each other. And guess
what, Bea, I took Goldie out on my own this afternoon.'

'Yeah?'

'Just onto the rec and up to the shops.'

'That's brilliant. Did you feel all right?'

Queenie refilled Goldie's water bowl. 'Yes. I did actually.
I didn't feel like I was on my own, not with this one by my
side. There's a sign up at the launderette. They want someone

194

to do a few hours, a couple of days a week. I was thinking maybe I could give it a go. Since my benefits stopped, I've felt dreadful letting it all fall onto your shoulders.'

'A job?' said Bea. 'Really?'

'Well, it's not far. I know I can get there and back now, and if I panic or anything, I can always come home. I might go back tomorrow and ask about it.'

'Wow. That's amazing. I'm so proud of you, Mum. I really am.'

Queenie smiled. 'I'm proud of me too. But really I've got this old gal to thank for it.' She leaned down and gave Goldie a good shoulder rub. Goldie responded by rolling onto her back and squirming, legs in the air. To Bea's astonishment, Queenie knelt down on the floor and tickled Goldie's tummy, talking to her like she was a baby. 'Oh, you like that, don't you? You like that? Yes, you do. Yes, you do.'

Smiling to herself, Bea got on with making a pot of tea. 'I can't believe you two,' she said.

'I don't know why we didn't get a dog ages ago.'

Bea decided that it was most tactful to say nothing and certainly not to point out that for six long years Queenie had been unable to even talk about leaving the house without getting hysterical.

'Bob was right. A dog really makes a home. Did you see him today, Bea?'

'Who? Bob?'

'Mm.'

'Yeah. Not really to talk to. He was there, just like normal.'

'Oh. I texted him, inviting him for tea, but he didn't reply. Perhaps the text didn't go through.'

Or perhaps he was keeping his feet warm at Dot's fire this evening, thought Bea. Another thing best left unsaid. 'Why don't you ask him for tea tomorrow?' she said. 'I'm going out, if that's okay.'

'Oh, of course. Somewhere nice?'

'Just round to a friend's.'

Queenie raised her eyebrows, and Bea knew she wouldn't get away with such scant information.

'The new guy on the checkouts. He's called Jay.'

Queenie smiled. 'Date, is it?'

'No, Ant's going as well, and his little brother, if he can keep hold of him.'

Queenie got up from the floor and sat at the table. 'I worry about that young man,' she said.

'Who, Ken?'

'No, Ant. He's got a lot to cope with. Difficult home life.'

'Yeah. He came with me and Goldie on our walk this morning and he was talking about his dad. He still loves him, despite everything he's done. I hadn't the heart to tell him he shouldn't. What his dad did, breaking into people's houses, was disgusting.'

'Yes, but whatever he's done, his dad is still his dad and always will be.'

They were both cradling their mugs of tea now, sitting opposite each other at the table.

'I was lucky, wasn't I?' said Bea. 'Having Dad as my dad. Even though it was only for fourteen years. They were the best years and he was the best dad ever.'

Queenie reached across and put her hands around Bea's. 'He was. And husband. We were both lucky.' She gave Bea's hands a little squeeze. 'But don't think your best years are behind you, love. You've got your whole life ahead of you. You'll never forget him, I know that, but, for you, the best is yet to come.'

'And for you too, Mum. You've got years ahead.'

Queenie developed a wistful look. 'I wouldn't have agreed with you until recently, but, you know, I think you're right, love. Things can change. It only takes someone special to come into your life, doesn't it?' They both looked down at

Goldie, now resting her head on her front paws, eyes closed, but Bea felt a sharp pang at the thought of her mum's vulnerability as she wondered if it wasn't the dog that Queenie was talking about, but someone else altogether.

'Forgot to say, there's post for you,' said Queenie. 'I put it on the side there.'

Bea got up and fetched the envelope. It was a white, businesslike one with her name and address printed out on a label.

'There's no stamp,' she said, turning it over and starting to pick away at the flap to open it up.

'No, it came at a funny time of day too. Halfway through the afternoon. Goldie barked when it came through the door, but I didn't see who it was.'

Bea had the envelope open now and drew out the single sheet of paper inside. 'Oh, it's the vet's bill for Arthur. Jeez. Sixty-four quid.'

'Have you got the money?'

'Just about. In my savings.' Bea had been putting money aside when she could, a few pounds here and there. She badly needed some new hair straighteners. 'I'm never going to get those GHDs, am I?'

'If I get that job, you will. You can have my first wage, all of it. I'd love to treat you.'

Bea put the letter down. 'Don't be daft. That'll be your money.'

'Yes, and I'd like to spend it on you.'

'Okay,' she said, 'but we'll make a deal. We'll spend it together, you and me, girls' shopping trip to the High Street, or even get a bus into the city.'

'Oh,' said Queenie, and Bea thought she was going to retreat into her shell again, raise objections, think of reasons it couldn't happen. But she looked into Bea's eyes, and her gaze was steady and confident. 'Right. It's a deal.'

Bea smiled. 'Brilliant.'

They decided it was too risky shutting Arthur in with Goldie in the kitchen overnight, so left him free range in the rest of the house when they went up to bed. Bea had just switched off her bedside light and snuggled down under her duvet when the bedroom door was nudged open and a thin wedge of light came in from the landing.

Lying on her side, Bea watched as Arthur padded in. He strutted up to her bed and looked up.

'No,' said Bea firmly. 'No cats on beds.'

With a little miaow he dismissed her words with the contempt they deserved and jumped up by her feet. He circled round a couple of times and settled down. Bea turned onto her back and prepared to wiggle her feet around and unseat the beast, but at that moment Arthur started purring. The noise triggered something in her, a feeling of peace, warmth, relaxation. Why was this sound so soothing? She lay back and closed her eyes, and soon started to drift off to Arthur's lullaby. In the warm, confused moments before she slept she thought about Arthur, the vet and the bill.

The bill. Hand-delivered by someone who knew where she lived. She opened her eyes.

The bill led to the vet's. The vet's led to Arthur. Arthur led to the farm and to Deano and Tank. And something – *something* – was kicking off there on Saturday. If she could trace the thread one way, could they, whoever they were, trace it the other way? Had they done so already? Was the bill actually a threat – we know where you live?

There was another thread, too, but she couldn't catch hold of it. It was like a strand of spider silk, blowing away in the breeze. Something to do with Ken and this evening's antics. How did that fit in?

She chased her thoughts round and round, until they became even more muddled and she drifted into a fitful sleep.

28

Arthur had vacated her bed by the time Bea woke up. She opened her eyes and faced Friday not with the feeling of threat from the vet's bill, but with a sense of possibility at the evening's dinner date at Jay's house. Okay, not date exactly, because Ant would be there too, but it was a step in the right direction. But what do you wear to dinner at a student house? She wanted to look nice, but not too try-hard. Normally, she'd reach for her biggest megalashes, but Jay was more of a hand-knitted, crystal deodorant, natural fibres, kind of guy.

She was still pondering this as she went downstairs. Arthur wove in and out of her legs as she headed for the kitchen door. When she opened it, Goldie and Arthur looked mildly surprised to see each other, and then seemed to remember that neither was a threat and both got on with the business of shadowing the human who was likely to give them breakfast.

'Walk first,' said Bea, firmly, 'and *you* need to stay indoors.' She shut Arthur out of the kitchen so that he didn't escape through the back door, then put on her duvet coat and clipped Goldie's lead onto her collar.

When she opened the back door it wasn't a bright, frosty morning, but cold and grey and damp. She and Goldie walked round to the front of the house intending to head for the rec.

He was standing in the road opposite, feet apart, hands by his sides, staring at the house. A mountain of a man. Tracksuit and trainers. Hood up.

Tank.

He didn't move as Bea approached, just kept staring as she got nearer. She shortened Goldie's lead, keeping the dog close to her, and crossed the road.

'What are you doing here?' she said, trying to keep her voice low and steady.

'You've got something that belongs to me. I want it back.'

'The cat?'

'Yup. Go and fetch it now.'

He was at least a foot taller than her and standing on the kerb, while she was still in the road. He towered over her. Bea bit her lip, hard, and felt a metallic zing on her tongue as blood oozed out.

'No,' she said. 'No, I can't do that.'

He seemed to gather himself, growing taller, bigger. 'I wasn't asking you, Bea. I was telling you.'

Bea stood her ground. 'You said it wasn't your cat. Anyway, I think you'd hurt it.' His eyes flicked away and then flicked back, and Bea sensed weakness for the first time.

'You don't know anything about me.'

'I know more than you think. I've been asking around. You don't have any pets.'

'And that's your problem, isn't it?' he said. 'You ask too many questions. You poke your nose in. I warned you about that, didn't I?'

He dug into his pocket and Bea felt a bead of sweat trickle from her hairline down the side of her face.

'I know you've got a knife,' she said, 'and if you pull it out on me, I'm ringing the police. I'm not messing.'

Tank snorted. 'I don't carry a blade. I don't need to.' He

pulled his hand out of his pocket and blew his nose on a rather small tissue. Again, Bea noticed the cuts on his hands.

'Why don't you turn yourself in? It can all be done quietly and calmly. It'll go in your favour.'

'I don't know what you're talking about.'

It was there again, that flick of the eyes. And now he was jiggling one of his legs.

'Tank, why didn't you knock on my door?'

'I didn't want to wake your mum up.'

His leg was still jiggling and he was flexing and closing his hands.

Bea's face softened. 'You see, you're a not a bad person. But people get in a muddle sometimes. Things get out of hand. We can stop it. Together. You can get the help you need. You'll be safe.'

'Safe,' Tank echoed. For a moment, his movements stopped and Bea held her breath. 'Safe,' he repeated.

Then, something changed. He balled up his fists and stepped towards her. 'I'm not going to the cops, and I need you to keep quiet. About the cat. The farm. Everything.'

Bea stepped back, keeping an even distance between them, hopefully beyond the range of his long, powerful arms. 'I'll tell you what,' she said, 'I think you're a decent person, who's taken a wrong turn. I'm going to give you twenty-four hours to do the right thing.'

He stopped advancing, and Bea stopped too. They faced each other.

'You've got to keep it shut,' Tank said, and he ran his finger and thumb along his lips, zipping them up. His forehead was glistening with sweat. He was worked up, thought Bea . . .or maybe something else.

Then, suddenly, he turned on his heel and started jogging away, across the middle of the rec. She was hot and sticky under her arms and across her back, and her breathing was fast and uneven. It was only now that she realised how very scared she'd been. But she wasn't the only one. The edginess, the threats, it all added up somehow, in a way she didn't quite understand, but there was one thing she was sure of.

'What is it, Tank?' she said to herself. 'What are you scared of?'

She and Goldie set off around the edge of the park, but the back of Bea's neck was prickling, imagining someone following her and she kept turning around. Tank had reached the other side of the park now. He'd caught up with the old man with his trolley, who was out with the papers again. He stopped running and walked alongside him. They seemed to be chatting. Well, thought Bea, he's got more conversation out of the old chap than I managed. Perhaps he will do the right thing, after all. Let's wait and see.

Her ears picked up the now familiar whine of the milk float and, sure enough, she saw it disappearing down the road as she and Goldie headed for home after a quick circuit of the rec. As they approached number twenty-three again, Goldie started pulling on her lead. Now Bea could see there was something on her front step. The dog liked the look of it, or maybe the smell. 'Oh no you don't,' Bea said, reining her in.

As they got nearer, Bea's stomach lurched. It was unmistakeably a severed head. A tabby cat's head, lying on a bit of paper.

She was sure it hadn't been there when she set off. Goldie had trotted past without a reaction on the way out. She looked around again, but there was no one in the street, or at any of the windows in the neighbouring houses.

She didn't want to touch the head, wanted nothing to do with it, but she couldn't leave it there. She hurried Goldie round the side of the house, let her into the kitchen and emptied some biscuits into her bowl. Then she shut her in and returned to the front step.

She bent down and took a couple of photographs, then steeled her nerve and got out a clean poo bag, putting her hand inside, and gently moved the head so she could see the paper underneath. There was a message scrawled on it: KEEP YOUR MOUTH SHUT.

It was a crude attempt to scare her, but it was working. She remembered what Tom had said. *It can be a prelude to other sorts of violence.* The hand that wielded this knife could do the same to her. The sick person behind all this knew where she lived. Had been there only minutes ago.

She wondered what to do. This was a clue. It might be the thing that led the police to the culprit, but if she called the police now, she'd have to tell Queenie. She'd only just started getting her confidence up. This would shatter it again. And whoever it was would see the car coming to the house. *They attack vulnerable people.* How could she leave Queenie open to this? How could she risk it?

She photographed the grisly item, then, using the bag, picked up the poor, sad head. She made herself look at it, cradled in her palm and sitting on black plastic. Its eyes were open a little, as was its mouth. It was caught, frozen forever, in a moment of fury. She started to retch, turning away from her hand, trying to breathe in some cold, calming air and get herself under control. When she looked back, the dry heaving started again. She drew up the sides of the bag and knotted the handles together. She put the bag inside the dustbin, resting on top of a bin bag, and shut the lid.

She went back into the house. Queenie was up now, padding about in her dressing gown.

'All right, love? I'm making porridge,' she said.

Bea thought of the hideous parcel in the bin and started to heave.

'Bea! What's up?' said Queenie.

'Nothing. I just . . . I don't want breakfast.'

Bea ran out of the kitchen and spent some time in the bathroom, kneeling in front of the loo, wondering if she was really going to be sick or not. Eventually, the feeling subsided and she went back downstairs.

'Have some tea, at least,' said Queenie. 'I've put an extra sugar in.'

Bea sat down and gingerly sipped at the tea, while her mother watched her like a hawk. Bea prayed she would have the sense to leave her in peace and, thankfully, she did.

'Are you still going out tonight?' she said, when Bea had got dressed in her work clothes and was about to set off.

'Yeah, planning to, but I'll come home first and change,' said Bea. 'What are you up to today?'

'Think I'll go and ask about that job.'

'Great. Tell me how you get on later, then.'

'I will.'

'And, Mum . . .'

'Yes?'

Bea wanted to warn her, but what would she warn her about exactly? To keep the door locked? To watch out of the window and report anyone suspicious? Queenie already thought the outside world was a dangerous place. If Bea said anything now she might stay inside for another six years.

'Nothing. Love you.'

Queenie put her hand up to Bea's face and cupped her cheek. 'Love you too, Bea. You take care today. Come home if you feel ill, or, you know, tired.'

'I'm fine, Mum. See you later.'

She tried not to think about the gruesome little parcel as she hurried past the bin. Once onto the rec, she spotted someone on the path ahead, walking away from her and recognised Dean with Tyson beside him. Dean. *Was it him, after all?*

She hurried to catch up, and shouted his name. He stopped

and turned round and Bea squealed as the dog lunged towards her. She backed off onto the grass and looked past the dog, straining and whining, to Dean. He seemed edgy, looking left and right and only glancing at her.

'What do you want?' he said.

For a moment, she couldn't think of anything to say. She pulled her coat more closely around her.

'Cat got your tongue?' he said, and Bea felt the nausea rising again. She was sick with the thought of the severed head. Sick with the certainty now that Dean was behind it. Sick at the thought of his hands holding a knife. Scared, too, but she wasn't going to try not to show it.

'That your idea of a joke, Dean? Leaving bits of animals on people's doorsteps?'

'I don't know what you're talking about.' He stuck his spotty chin forward in a gesture of defiance.

'Yes, you do. I don't care about your and Tank's threats. I'm ringing the police. This has gone too far. You're dangerous, you are. You're sick.'

'You shouldn't accuse people of things, Bea. And you shouldn't poke your nose into other people's business. Haven't you learnt anything?'

They were facing each other with the dog in between them.

'If your business is stealing people's pets and torturing them,' said Bea, 'then I will poke my nose in and nothing you can do will stop me.'

Dean's eyes narrowed, making his face more weasely than ever.

'I haven't stolen anything – not like your mate, Ant, and his nasty, thieving family – and I don't do anything to animals, but I'm telling you something for your own good. Stop poking around and keep your mouth shut.'

'I'm not scared of you or your mate,' said Bea, but in truth, she was rattled now. Scared for herself and scared for her mum. Queenie had got the better of Dean once, but Bea sensed that the wound of that humiliation had been festering inside him. That boil was ready to burst.

'Don't come near me again and don't go near my house,' she said, and turned on her heel and stalked away as confidently as her wobbly legs would allow.

29

The front of the store was coned off when Bea got to Cost-save.

Of course, the sight of a line of yellow cones acted like a beacon, and staff were gathering there on their way in to have a look. Heart thumping in her chest, Bea joined the cluster.

There was blood streaked down the plate glass door. At the bottom, on the ground, something was covered by a couple of sheets of plastic. Neville was standing in front of it. Without his clipboard, he looked strangely naked. He clearly didn't know what to do with his hands. He had one tucked awkwardly inside his coat, like Admiral Nelson and the other was flapping oddly at his side.

'Carry on inside, everyone,' he was saying. 'We'll get this cleared up and open the store when the police have been. Until then, get your uniforms on and wait in the staffroom.'

People were reluctant to move.

'Go on. Go on. There's nothing to see here.' His Adam's apple was bobbing up and down in distress.

There clearly *was* something to see. Thankfully, the heap was too small to be human.

'What is it, Neville?' said Bea. 'Is it another—'

At that moment there was a volley of flashlights. Kevin,

the photographer from the *Bugle*, had squeezed in next to Bea and was taking pictures.

Neville held his hands up in front of his face and made a sort of yelp. 'Get him away!'

Bea turned to Kevin. On his other side, Eileen looked like she was about to do some damage with her handbag.

'You'd better go,' said Bea.

'I've got a perfect right to be here. It's in the public interest,' Kevin said.

'It's private property,' Neville squeaked. 'You have no right.'

'That's it,' said Eileen. 'Bea?' She grabbed one of Kevin's elbows and nodded to Bea to take the other one. Caught by surprise, they walked Kevin backwards through the car park. After a few yards he shrugged them off.

'All right, all right, I'm going. I've got my shot anyway.'

He hotfooted it towards his car, then stopped and started taking more pictures as a police patrol car cruised in and pulled up near the front door. Tom and Shaz got out and started talking to Neville.

One of them lifted the sheet of plastic and they both peered underneath. Bea craned round and got a glimpse of a little tawny-furred corpse, front legs stretched out. Even at that distance, Bea could see that there was something missing. It was a cat's body, all right, but there was a hole where the head should be.

'Oh no,' Bea murmured, under her breath.

'Jesus,' said Ant, joining the crowd next to Bea. 'Another cat?'

'Yeah, looks like it,' said Bea.

'Okay,' said Tom, 'we need a statement from the person who found this. The rest of you can clear the area.'

'Do you want me to clean the window in a minute, Nev?' Ant asked.

'Yes. When the police have finished.'

Bea tried to catch Tom's attention. 'I need to talk to you.'

'Not now, Bea. You can see I'm busy.'

'I know, it's just that, well, you've got a body without a head and I know where the head is.'

George joined everyone in the staffroom while they were waiting for the police to give them the all clear. She came into the room looking shaken, flanked, as usual, by Anna and Neville.

'Obviously, we've had a bad start to the day,' she said. 'I'm told it will only be a few minutes and then we can prepare to open the store as normal. And that's what I want you to try to be today. Normal. We can't let one sick individual spoil things for our customers or ourselves. I don't know why we're being targeted, but if any of you have any ideas or any information at all, you must come forward and speak to me or to the police. Make no mistake, we will catch the person responsible.' She looked around the room. 'Now, the notices,' she said, trying to brighten the tone of her voice. 'The Valentine's display is looking brilliant. Well done to Eileen and to all of you. As we get nearer the day, remember to plug the dinner for two deal, if you can. A main, a side, a dessert and a half-bottle of Prosecco for ten pounds. It's a good deal any time of the year, but we can really push it now.'

'Don't see Smelly Reg going for it,' said Eileen in a low voice, causing a little ripple of sniggering in those near enough to hear her. George looked across sharply at that part of the room. Eileen shrank down a little and looked at the carpet.

'The 'Last Chance to Buy' display is going very well. We need to make sure it's kept neat and tidy, but we've already shifted a good proportion of, let's face it, quite unlikely goods. It just shows what we can do when we work together.

'I'm going to be honest with you guys, takings are likely to take a hit over the next few days, so let's sharpen up. Let's be the best we can be. Come on, let's get some energy going!' She started jogging up and down on the spot, no mean feat in heels.

The Costsave crew looked at each other with bemusement.

'Come on, everyone. Let's get the blood flowing!'

She'd put her tablet down on the floor and was whirling her arms round now. People at the front were starting to join in, at first self-consciously, and then with some gusto. The movement spread to the back of the crowd. Bea bobbed up and down a bit on her toes, while Ant flung himself into it as much as the space would allow.

'Oh God, Ant, look at Neville,' said Bea.

Standing awkwardly immobile next to George, Neville was still clutching his clipboard and looking like a very frightened rabbit in the headlights.

'Come on, Nev. Join in!' Ant hollered.

Neville sent some daggers in Ant's direction, but managed a painful, agonised sort of jig for a few seconds before George put them out of their misery.

'Great!' she said. 'I think we could make this a thing.'

She started clapping, turning slowly and directing her applause around the room. The staff felt honour-bound to clap back, but the noise petered out quickly as Shaz appeared in the doorway and gave George the thumbs up. George then gave everyone a ten-minute warning and she and Neville bustled out of the room.

'What the hell was that?' said Bob to Bea, as they walked towards the top of the stairs. He was noticeably out of breath.

'New methods of management,' said Bea. 'You've got to give her credit for trying.'

Bob muttered darkly and Bea held back to wait for Ant, who was putting his padded Costsave jacket on, ready to go outside and clean up by the front door.

'How's Ken today?'

'I don't know. He was still asleep when I left this morning. I rang the school and said he was sick.'

'How was he last night?'

'Ha, he was awake until about three and then he crashed out. I rang Stevo when we got home and made him come round and help me. He's going to look in on him at dinner time too. About time he helped out a bit.'

'Do you know what Ken took or where he got it from?'

'He wouldn't tell us. He was blabbering all sorts of nonsense, but nothing that we wanted to know. If I find the bastard he got it from, whatever it was, they're in trouble.'

'Talking about trouble, I hope I've done the right thing, Ant,' Bea said. 'I told Tom about everything, my conversations with Dean and Tank – their threats.'

'Don't see that you had any choice, Bea. If the cat killer's one of them, they need stopping.'

'I'm scared, though.'

'Scared of Dean?'

'Scared of anyone with a knife and a grudge. I've seen what he's capable of.' She shuddered. 'Plus it's not just him, is it? Tank's in it as well. Got to be. He openly threatened me.'

'Yeah, you wouldn't really argue with him, would you?'

'I kind of did. Bloody hell,' said Bea. She stopped walking and pressed her fingers together at the bridge of her nose. 'I know Dean's an odious little squirt, but if we're right, he's a lot more than that. He's an actual psycho.'

''Scuse me,' said Eileen. 'You're blocking the way.'

As she elbowed her way between them, Ant and Bea stared at each other. Had Eileen heard what they were saying?

'I think we're all right, Bea. She'd have said something, wouldn't she?' Ant hissed when she'd gone past.

'Yeah, she doesn't hold back, does she?'

'Not so you'd notice. Look, you done the right thing, Bea. Let's leave the whole cat thing to the cops now.'

30

Just before lunchtime, Bea saw Ant talking to a young woman in the World Cuisine aisle (fajita kits, pizza bases and three sorts of soy sauce). She was dressed in an oversized parka with pink fur around the hood, and black leggings and trainers. It was difficult to tell at this distance, but Ant seemed to be blushing. Ah, thought Bea, it's the New Year's Eve girl, the mysterious Ayesha.

She was pleased for Ant, but felt a bit put out that he was nowhere to be seen when she went to the staffroom for her break. She found a seat next to Anna, and rang home to check up on Queenie.

'Hiya, love. How's it going?' Bea could hear the telly on in the background.

'Okay,' said Bea. 'Everything all right at home?'

'Yes, of course. Just going to watch *Doctors* and maybe today's *Father Brown*, then I'm off to the launderette in an hour or two.'

'Oh, right. That's good. I'll see you later, then.'

'All right, lovely. You still going out this evening?'

'Yeah.'

'Oh, Bea, I put the wheelie bin out. Can't believe you forgot that.'

Bea's stomach lurched. 'You did what?'

'I put the bin out. Myself.' There was an unmistakeable note of pride in Queenie's voice. 'You've been at sixes and sevens since the council changed bin day, but luckily I remembered.'

'Oh, Mum.'

Tom had told her that he would be round to collect the cat's head at the end of the day, when Bea could be there too.

'What?'

'Have they been?'

'Yes. They came mid-morning like usual.'

'Oh. Okay. Thanks, Mum. Well remembered. See you later.' Bea killed the call and started texting Tom to tell him not to bother coming round.

At the other side of the room, Eileen was eating a chicken tikka wrap. It was a messy business, requiring two hands and an exclusion zone for the fallout. When her phone rang, she looked around for somewhere to put the wrap and ended up balancing it on the cellophane wrapper on her lap.

'You what? Slow down. You don't have to let them in. You don't have to— Dean? Dean!'

She stood up and the wrap fell onto the stained, bald carpet. She ignored it and strode across the room towards Bea. If she'd had time, Bea might have run away and locked herself in the toilets, but Eileen was too quick. She was trapped.

'It was *you*,' Eileen spat at her. 'You're a vindictive cow, aren't you? He lost his job here. What more do you want?'

'Eileen, I—'

She didn't wait for Bea's answer, but stomped out of the room.

'What did you do?' said Anna, who had paused in the middle of her salad box to watch the show. Practically everyone else in the staffroom had done the same.

Bea shifted in her seat, turning her back to the others and

213

whispered. 'I told Tom that I thought Dean was the cat killer.'

Anna put her fork down. 'Dean,' she breathed. 'Really?'

'Yeah,' said Bea. 'Really. I don't want to believe it, but there's too much pointing to him to ignore.'

'Oh my God, Bea!' said Anna. 'I don't know what to say. I feel sick.'

'I know,' said Bea. 'I'm so sorry, Anna. But at least we've caught him now.'

'It'd explain why he targeted Joan, why the . . .the bodies keep turning up here,' said Anna.

'What do you mean?'

'Vendetta. He hates this place since he got the sack. Trying to destroy our reputation, put the customers off.'

'Blimey, I hadn't even thought of that,' said Bea. 'You're right, Anna. That's another piece of the jigsaw puzzle. It's gotta be him. Do you think they'll lock him up?'

'Hope so. They should've done that last time, when he went round to frighten your mum,' said Anna.

'Yeah, I know. I couldn't believe he only got a warning.' Bea shook her head.

'Nasty piece of work.' Anna looked down at the salad in the plastic box on her lap.

'What's that like?' said Bea. 'That kwinoa stuff?'

'Keenwa?' Anna pulled a face. 'Inoffensive, but full of protein and fibre. It's good for you. I don't think I can eat it now, though.'

Bea had brought in a sandwich from home – chopped up boiled egg and mayo in sticky white bread – but she couldn't eat either. She was rattled from her encounter with Eileen and was on tenterhooks now, waiting for the reports of an arrest.

Eileen's outburst had set the staffroom fizzing. No one asked Bea what was going on but there were looks and nudges and enough low gossiping to make her really uncomfortable. She put her sandwiches in the bin.

Ant was coming through the staff door as Bea was returning to the tills. There was a definite spring in his step.

'Hey, Bea,' he said.

'Hi.'

'Lovely day, isn't it?'

'Not so as you'd notice, no.'

Ant frowned. 'Whassup?'

'What's up, Ant? Oh nothing, except dead cats keep following me, I got threatened by a bloke the size of a small country, and I feel like I'm being stalked by a nutter with a knife.' She huffed her disgust at him. 'I've got to get back to work. I'll see you later, at Jay's, yeah?'

'Ah,' said Ant. 'I might not go.' He was trying to keep a serious expression on his face, but a grin broke through.

'What's going on, Ant? Got a better offer?'

The grin got broader. 'Yeah. You could say that.'

'I saw her in aisle ten. She looks nice.'

'Better than nice, Bea. She's beautiful.' He took his hands out of his pockets and rubbed them together vigorously.

George was coming down the stairs towards them. 'Ant,' she said, brightly. 'I understand Eileen has had to go home, so I'm going to need you on shelf-stacking this afternoon.'

Bea saw a flash of panic in Ant's eyes. His lack of literacy made some tasks more difficult than others.

'Yeah, right, boss,' he said to George.

'Good.' George brushed past them and Bea was about to follow her into the store, when Ant put his hand on her shoulder.

'I reckon I can work out what goes where. I'll look for the gaps, match the packets and that, but, Bea—'

'Yeah?'

'Can you just swing by now and again to check the labels are right?'

215

'I'll try, Ant. If I can dodge Neville.'

'Thanks, mate.'

She was settling into her station and had logged on, preparing for the afternoon's customers, when her phone started vibrating in her pocket. She'd forgotten to move it into her bag and stow it away in her locker. She surreptitiously slid it out and had a look at the screen. It was an incoming call from Tom.

Bea had a look along the line of checkouts towards the customer service desk. Neville was looking right back at her. Damn! She put the phone back in her pocket. It continued vibrating for a few more seconds, then stopped. It stayed there, burning a hole in the polyester until she could reasonably take a loo break.

On her way to the back of the shop, she passed Ant. He was putting cardboard trays of baked bean tins onto the shelves, and everything was in the right place.

'You're doing a grand job,' she said.

Neville was bearing down on them.

'I'm sorry, Neville,' she said. 'Call of nature.'

'Beatrice, did I see you with your phone earlier?'

'This really won't wait,' she said. 'Time of the month. Think I've come on.' She had the satisfaction of seeing Neville's look of horror before she hurried off to the staff toilets.

She shut herself in a cubicle, and checked her phone again. One missed call from Tom. She pressed 'call'.

'Bea!'

'Sorry I missed your call. I couldn't pick up. How are things going?'

'We had a chat with your friend Dean and an informal look round his house and the back yard.'

Bea waited.

'Yes,' she said. 'And?'

'And nothing. There's nothing to suggest he's involved in taking or hurting animals.'

'But I *saw* him with a cat.'

'He said that belonged to a friend's grandparent. They were looking after it for him.'

'So you're going to check that out, right?'

'Bea, I think you're barking up the wrong tree. I know you don't like him, and, fair enough, he's been a bit of a tosser in the past, but he's not the cat killer.'

'Because he says so.'

'Because there's no evidence that he is.'

'I can't accept this.' Her hackles were up now.

'Bea, it's starting to feel a bit like harassment.'

'Yes! He left a cat's head on my doorstep.'

'Bea, you're missing the point. It seems like you're harassing him, or at least getting us to do your dirty work. Just leave it, okay? I'm saying this as a friend. Some friendly advice.'

Bea's heart was racing. Her palms were sweaty and damp. She killed the call before she said something she regretted. That's it, then, she thought. I've tried telling the police and they won't listen. I'm on my own with this. She was shaking now and starting to feel faint. Sitting on the toilet, she planted her feet more firmly on the ground and leaned forward, with her head between her knees. She took some deep breaths.

You're not on your own, she told herself. There's Ant and Dot and Jay.

Jay.

Now that Ant had bailed on them, she would have him all to herself tonight. But could she really leave Queenie alone after dark, with a maniac on the loose? She sighed out loud. Amid all this madness, the thought of Jay felt like a little beacon of hope. She wouldn't cancel just yet. She'd hold onto the hope that she would be able to go, and perhaps if Bob was going round to Queenie's for tea, she could.

Her breathing had calmed down now. She sat up and decided to have a wee since she was there anyway. She was just flushing when her phone sprang into life again, vibrating as a text came in.

'TALKING TO THE FILTH. BAD MOVE, BITCH.'

Was it Dean? Was it Tank? Was there someone else out there, watching her?

She took a screenshot and sent it to Tom's email.

He rang her back straight away. 'Hey, Bea. Are you okay?'

'Yeah. Sort of.'

'Is the text from Dean's phone?'

'I don't know. It's not a number I recognise. It's him, though. It's got to be.'

'Just let it all cool down, Bea. There's no direct threat there. He's just pissed off with you. The whole thing needs some heat taking out of it.'

'But—'

'Leave it for now, Bea. I won't let anything bad happen to you. Trust me, we're handling things.'

He rang off, leaving Bea feeling so frustrated she banged her hand against the wall, just as Eileen walked in.

'Temper, temper,' she said. 'They didn't find anything, did they? So you can stop picking on him now.'

'All right. I'm sorry, Eileen. I was wrong.'

'You were, and I won't forget this.'

She pushed past Bea, barging her shoulder into Bea's arm. Bea groaned and set off back to the shop floor.

31

On her way back to the checkout, Bea took a detour to see how Ant was getting on. He was in the fresh fruit and veg area, and seemed happier there. She looked around. Neville's customer service desk was out of sight, and there weren't any other staff about.

'Ant, look.' Not thinking, she slid her phone out of her pocket and showed him the message, forgetting he wouldn't be able to read it.

'What does it say?'

'Sorry, mate.' She read the message to him. 'It's Dean, got to be. Tom rang me and they searched his and Eileen's house and found nothing, so Dean's still out and about.'

Ant gave a low whistle. 'This is nasty. We need to stop. Stop investigating. Stop asking questions. Just go about our business.'

'That's giving in to them, though.'

'Sometimes it's best to keep a low profile. There's some bad shit going on here and it's better not to get mixed up in it.'

'But we must be close to something if they're threatening me.'

'And you've told the cops everything, so let them do the

rest. Bea,' he said, putting his hands on both her shoulders. 'It's not worth you getting hurt over this. Let it go.'

'I don't know if I can.'

He ruffled the top of her head, causing her to squeal in protest.

'Oi! Mind my hair!'

'Sorry.'

'I'd better get back before Neville throws a hissy fit. You seem okay here, anyway.'

'Yeah, it's pretty obvious where this stuff goes. I can do this,' he said, bending down and then lugging a tray of cabbages into place.

'Ha! I haven't seen you eat a vegetable all week,' Bea said.

'I *do* eat veg.'

'No, you don't.'

'I do.'

Bea sighed. 'Oh God, Ant, today's been so shit and now we're arguing about vegetables. I'm going back to my checkout. I'll see you later.'

'Hey, watch this!'

Ant eyed the display next to them and then reached for the nearest thing and popped it in his mouth. Bea watched agog as he crunched his way through a Brussels sprout. At one point he started to look a bit distressed, but he rallied and kept chewing before swallowing it all down.

'There,' he said. He opened his mouth to show her that it was empty, which was only partly true. She recoiled, then turned back to high-five him.

'Fair play to you,' she said.

'Not bad,' he said, 'but I don't think I could ever be vegan.'

Despite Ant's efforts to cheer her up, things were getting to Bea. She found herself making mistakes at the till. When a customer came back to complain that she'd charged her twice for the same item, Bea could only apologise, but by now she was feeling wretched.

At around half past three, her phone started vibrating in her pocket.

Oh no, she thought, another text. But that was normally just one notification, and this time it kept going. Someone was trying to ring her. The phone stopped buzzing briefly and then started again. Reluctantly, she got it out and checked it. It wasn't Tom. It was Queenie. Bea sighed. What now? Against all Costsave rules, she accepted the call.

'Bea, something dreadful's happened.'

Her mum's voice was shot through with distress. Bea's stomach went into knots.

'What?'

'I can't even . . .I don't know how to . . .it's Goldie.'

The misery in her mum's voice could only mean one thing. She was dead. Bea knew it.

'What happened?' said Bea.

'I only left her for a couple of minutes,' said Queenie.

'Left her? Left her where?'

'Outside the launderette.'

'Mum, what's happened to her? What's going on?'

'She's . . .she's gone, Bea. She's disappeared.'

32

'Okay, okay. Calm down. Calm down. Tell me again what happened.'

'I tied her up outside the launderette, Bea. On one of the railings. I did a double knot, not really tight or anything, but done up all right. I went in to talk to Jill about the job and we were getting on really well and she was showing me the machines and telling me what it involved and then I just had a feeling, I don't know what it was, and I said to Jill, "I'll just check on the dog" and so I went to the door and . . .' There was a pause and in that moment Bea could feel the sense of horror, the awfulness of the moment. 'And she was gone.'

'Do you think the lead came undone?'

'I don't see how. I s'pose it's not impossible but . . .'

'Okay, where are you now?'

'I'm still at the launderette. I went into the car park and started going along the shops, but then I froze. Jill brought me back in. She's making me a cuppa.'

'Have you rung the police?'

'No. I've just rung you.'

'Okay. Stay there. I'll see if I can get off work. Ring the police, Mum. Do it now.'

Mind going ten to the dozen, Bea logged out of her till

222

and stumbled towards the back of the store, colliding with Neville in aisle eleven, next to the freezers.

'Oof! Mind where you're—' He steadied Bea and then held her at arm's length, like something slightly dangerous or unsavoury.

'Neville!' she said. 'I've got to go home.'

He let go of her shoulders and looked from Bea to the staff door and back again. He seemed at a loss for words. 'If you're not well enough for work, then of course.'

Bea doubled over a little and screwed up her face. 'Yeah, it's just really painful. Bit of a flood, I—'

He held his hands up in self-defence. Bea almost expected him to cover his ears.

'Bea,' he said firmly. 'Go home. I'll tell Anna in the office. Do you need me to call you a taxi?'

'It's okay. I'll walk. Sometimes the fresh air helps. Thanks, Neville.'

She ran up the stairs and grabbed her bag from her locker, put her coat on over her tabard and rushed out of the building. She was halfway across the car park when she heard a shout behind her.

'Bea! Bea, wait up!'

She looked over her shoulder. Ant was running to catch up with her. She turned around and walked backwards.

'I can't stop, Ant,' she called out. 'I've got to get home. Goldie's gone missing.'

There was a thought forming at the back of her mind, a thought she was trying to suppress: I need you to keep quiet.

'Wait!' shouted Ant. 'I'll come with you!' He was pulling at his sweatshirt, stretching it over his head.

'Ant, don't be silly. You'll lose your job. Look, I've gotta go. I'll call you.'

He stood, with his sweatshirt in his hand, and watched as Bea turned back and started running.

She jogged along the High Street, dodging the afternoon shoppers and looking ahead for a glimpse of tawny fur. The thought of Goldie crossing a road on her own made her blood run cold, even as it was coursing painfully through her veins and arteries. She just wouldn't wander off, would she? And if she did, she wouldn't go far.

Anxiety fuelled her legs. She turned out of the High Street and went by the old people's bungalows. The Oldest Paper Boy was in his little square of garden in front of one of them. He was bending down, tying some string to one of a series of sticks, in some sort of bird-scaring arrangement.

Bea stopped running. 'Excuse me,' she said, her voice coming in gasps. 'Have you seen a stray dog? A big golden retriever?'

He straightened up, as much as he could. Even cowed, with age, he was a big chap, almost completely bald, with ancient tattoos on his forearms, corrupted over time into a blue blurry mess. 'No dogs here,' he said, brusquely. 'Not in my garden.'

'Right. Thanks,' said Bea. She was going to ask him to keep an eye out, but he was already bending down again, fiddling with the string, shutting the conversation down.

She started running again and came to the edge of the rec. There were a couple walking their dog in the middle, so she ran up to them and asked them about Goldie. They hadn't seen anything, but were more solicitous than the man at the bungalows.

'We'll keep our eyes open. Hope you find her.'

Schools were starting to turn out, bringing a cluster of parents and little kids in the fenced-off play area. Bea veered over and called across the fence. No one had seen Goldie. Sweating profusely under her coat, Bea carried on to the far side of the grass and up to the shops.

Queenie was standing in the doorway of the launderette,

her face pale and drawn. 'Oh, Bea, it's all my fault. I'm so sorry.'

'There's no sign of her between here and work. Did you ring the police?' said Bea.

'Yes. They didn't sound very interested. Just said they'd log the call and tell their officers to keep a lookout.'

'Nothing else?'

'No, she said there used to be council dog wardens but they all got cut.'

'Okay, we'll have to do it, then. We'll have to find her.'

'We can tweet about it,' said Jill. 'Spread the word.'

'Oh, good idea,' said Bea. She got out her phone again and quickly posted an appeal with a photo of Goldie. Despite only having the dog for a few days, she already had dozens of photographs.

'I only thought I was going to be a couple of minutes, Bea. I should never have left her.'

No, thought Bea, you shouldn't have. But there was no point saying it out loud. 'Let's just concentrate on finding her, Mum. I'm going to go out looking again. Are you staying here?'

'If she has got loose,' said Jill, 'she might have gone home.'

'Yes,' said Bea. 'We should check there. Mum, can you get there by yourself?'

Queenie was ashen. She was scratching at her wrists, making deep red marks. 'I don't think so. I don't think I can.'

Bea bit her tongue. Shouting at her would make everything worse. 'Okay, let's get you home. Quickly.'

She thanked Jill and bundled Queenie out of the shop.

'I bet that's where she is,' said Queenie. 'She'll be waiting by the back door.'

'Let's hope so.'

Bea was looking across the rec again and scanning the street as they walked. Her heart lifted a little when they got close to number twenty-three, and she saw that the gate was open. They usually left it closed. Had Goldie nudged it with her nose? Could she really be waiting for them?

But no. Goldie wasn't in the front garden and when they went round to the back, that was empty too.

Bea unlocked the door. Arthur immediately started winding himself round their legs, miaowing, and Queenie dissolved.

'I'm sorry, Arthur,' she said through her tears. 'She's gone. Your friend's gone.'

'Mum, I'm going to text all my contacts, get them looking too, then I'm going out again.' Bea started jabbing at her phone. When the text had gone, she checked Twitter. Fifteen retweets already. She felt a flutter of optimism. If everyone helped, surely they'd find her soon.

'But where will you look?' said Queenie, sniffing hard.

'Round the streets, round the rec. If she's wandered, she won't have gone far.'

'Bea,' said Queenie, dabbing at her face with a tissue. 'I don't know how she could have got loose, I really don't. Do you think someone's taken her?'

Yes, thought Bea. Yes, I really think they have. 'I don't know. I hope not. But I've had a thought. You know Jill said she might have come home?'

'Yes?'

'I need to check the bungalows properly. See if she's gone back to Charles's. Maybe she's just missing him.'

Queenie's face lit up. 'I bet that's it, Bea. You go and look there. Ring me if there's any news.'

'I will.'

'Promise?'

'Of course.'

As Bea left the house, she felt convinced they were clutching at straws. Who were they kidding? Goldie couldn't undo knots. Besides, she was the sort of dog that would stay put even if she wasn't tied up. But Bea couldn't just sit and wait. She had to do something, and so she gathered her bag to her side and set off running across the rec again.

33

There was a group of boys in crumpled uniforms on scooters and bikes near the youth shelter. Bea recognised them as the little gang that had tried to frighten her at Halloween. She'd managed to shame them into walking her safely home that time. Now, she took a deep breath and crossed the grass to the little island of concrete.

'All right, boys?' she said.

They looked at her with studied lack of interest. 'All right.'

'Have you seen a golden retriever in the park? With someone or on its own.'

'Nope.'

'Okay, if you do, can you let me know? Or ring the police or something.' Bea set off across the grass towards the bungalows, then stopped and turned around. 'Isn't Ken Thompson with you? He's one of your mates, isn't he?'

Unmasking Ken and threatening to tell Ant about his behaviour had been the key to getting the boys to calm down when they'd been harassing her.

The boys shuffled their feet.

'Do you know where he is?' she asked.

'We don't hang out with him any more,' one of the boys piped up. 'He's scum, isn't he? Him and his family.'

'Well,' said Bea, 'that's a bit harsh ...'

'We don't want people like them round here.'

This sounded to Bea like the sort of thing directly repeated from a parent. Normally, she would have tried to reason with them, make them look at things from another angle, but today wasn't the day and now wasn't the time.

'No. Right,' she said. 'Do you know who he hangs around with now?'

'No. Sorry.'

Bea left them and headed towards the top end of the rec, looking left and right as she went, hoping for a glimpse of a sturdy body or a swishy tail.

Please, God, let her be at Charles' house.

When she got there the terrace of little houses all presented blank faces to the world. No signs of life, even at the house where she'd seen the man earlier. From a way off she could see that Charles' front garden was empty. She followed the edge of the property. There was a wide alley at the back of the terrace, giving access to the small, rectangular back gardens on one side, bordered by low wooden fences, and a row of garages on the other. Bea walked into the alley, examining the backs of the houses.

Some of the gardens were concreted over, just a place to keep the bins. Others were lovingly tended, even in January perfect oases of grass and shrub and pot plant.

Charles' garden was neat and functional. By the back wall, there was a bench seat covered with a green plastic sheet. A water bowl sat on the concrete next to it and Bea felt a sharp pang of guilt as she pictured Charles and Goldie together in sunnier times. How could she ever tell him that they'd lost his dog? It was unforgivable. It would break his heart. The guilt intensified as she wondered if Charles had a mobile phone with him. What if he was on social media right now, seeing photos of Goldie flash up? If Goldie didn't turn up soon, Bea would have to go and tell him. She couldn't risk him hearing from someone else.

The yard was plainly, gut-wrenchingly empty. Goldie had not found her way here. She wasn't waiting for Charles. With a heavy heart, Bea walked further along the row, not quite ready to give up.

She took a couple of paces and was aware of the camera on the next house along moving on its hinge. She shivered a little at the thought of that large man inside the house. Was he operating the camera, watching her? 'No dogs here. Not in my garden.'

She pulled the collar of her coat up a bit further and walked along the row. At the next house the curtains at the back windows were all closed. The garden was a paved yard, with a large brick-built shed in it. Even in daylight, the windows of the shed were dark, like they'd got blackout blinds up or were even painted out. Bea went closer, leaning over the fence. It gave her the creeps. Then she remembered, Kevin, the photographer, and his 'studio' behind his mum's bungalow. This must be it.

Bea shivered again. What a sad, strange terrace this was. She walked back to the front of the row and something caught her eye. A curtain was moving at one of the windows, and Bea could see a face looking out. It was partly obscured by the reflection of the darkening sky in the glass, but Bea caught a wisp of white hair before whoever it was drew back. It must be Kevin's mum, the woman she'd met before, looking lost outside her own house.

On impulse, Bea opened the little gate and walked up to the house. She knocked on the door and then bent down and shouted, 'Hello?' through the letterbox.

There was no response and Bea was about to leave when she heard a sort of scrabbling behind the front door. It opened inwards a few inches and the woman peered out across the chain which prevented the door opening further.

'Hello,' said Bea. 'Mrs McKey, is it? My name's Bea. I'm looking for a lost dog. You'll know her. It's Goldie. She normally lives two doors down with Charles, but I've been looking after her. Have you seen her?'

The woman's skin was almost as pale as her hair. She looked washed out, faded and frail. 'You're looking for a dog?'

'Goldie, a golden retriever.'

'Have you found my cat?'

The sands of the conversation seemed to be shifting beneath her feet.

'No,' she said, patiently. 'I'm looking for a dog.' Bea checked her watch. It was starting to get dark. She really needed to get on with her search while there was still a little light left.

'He doesn't normally miss his dinner. It's been days now. He must be very hungry.'

'It's a girl, the dog. Goldie, from down the road. I've got a photo, if that helps.' Bea showed the woman the picture of Goldie she used as her screensaver.

'No, not a dog, dear. And Mr McKey isn't a girl. He's a very naughty boy. And he's very late for his dinner.'

'Mr McKey? Do you mean your husband?'

'My cat. Mr McKey. I do miss him. Kevin said he's probably been run over. He's never liked animals. Pulled the legs off spiders when he was little.' Her lower lip wobbled a bit and her pale eyes became watery.

'I'm sorry about your cat,' said Bea, and in the back of her mind she could sense some cogs whirring. 'Have you reported him missing?'

'They didn't want to know,' she said.

'They?'

'The police, dear. They sent me away.'

It couldn't be, could it? thought Bea. 'Mrs McKey, what colour is your cat?'

The woman looked at her, eyes brimming with tears. 'He's white. Pure white,' she said. 'He's a very handsome chap.'

34

'Mrs McKey,' said Bea. 'I know where your cat is.'

'You've found him?'

'Yes. He's safe and sound. I've got to look for my dog right now, but I could bring him back to you in a couple of hours.'

'Oh no, dear, I don't open the door after dark. My Kevin's told me not to.'

Bea looked up at the sky. The colour was leaching out of it already. It would be dark in less than half an hour. Her chances of finding Goldie were slipping away.

'I'll bring him at the weekend, then. He's fine, though.'

'I do my shopping tomorrow. Kevin takes me to the big Asda. They do a nice coffee there.'

'Shall I leave it until Sunday, then?'

'Why have you got him?'

'I found him. He was . . .lost.'

Her face darkened. 'Did you take him?'

'No! I rescued him. Honestly, I'll bring him back to you as soon as I can.' Bea wanted to get away now, but she wasn't convinced Mrs McKey didn't think she was the catnapper. Whatever. She needed to use the last of the light to look for Goldie. 'I've got to go now, but I'll be back.'

Her phone was constantly buzzing with notifications –

retweets, texts, messages coming in all the time. It was running out of juice, though, so she quickly scrolled through everything to see if there was any concrete news on Goldie. There wasn't, but people were offering to help her search and soon she was joined by two of the Musketeers, Georgia and Beth, as well as Jay and Ant. Jay brought his housemate with him, another student called Grace, who looked like a supermodel.

'I'm so sorry, Bea. It's just awful,' said Beth.

'Do you think she's run off?' said Georgia.

'She may have done. It's worth looking around in case she's outside and lost.'

'Of course! Not how I thought I'd spend my last evening before going back to uni, but I don't mind at all,' said Beth.

'Me neither,' said Georgia.

'Which one do you go to?' said Grace.

'Oh, we're at different ones. I'm at Exeter and Beth is at Aberystwyth.'

'Oh, nice. What are you studying?' said Jay.

And they were off – courses, lecturers, placements, house-sharing, general larks, loans and debts. As they warmed to their subject, they formed a sort of circle, leaving Ant and Bea on the outside.

Bea looked at Ant. 'It's like Happy Hour in the students' union,' she said, miserably.

He pulled a sympathetic face and put an arm round her shoulder, 'Bloody students,' he whispered. 'Told you, didn't I?'

'Yeah, you did. It's nice of them to help, though.'

'The more the merrier. We'll find her, Bea,' said Ant. 'We'll find her.' Then he took his arm away and clapped his hands, causing the others to look round. 'Right! How are we gonna do this?'

They split up into pairs and searched in various directions, meeting up at the top end of the rec after forty-five minutes, as agreed.

'It's like looking for a needle in a haystack. All the gardens and alleys and that,' said Ant. 'It's chuffing freezing as well. I reckon we should stop.'

'But what if she's out there? She'll freeze.'

'If she is out here, she'll have found somewhere to curl up by now,' said Jay. 'Animals know what to do to protect themselves. Ant's right, Bea. Do you want to come back for that curry?'

'No, I can't leave Queenie on her own tonight.'

'All right.' They were across the road from the Jubilee. 'Might go for a little warm-up in there. What do you reckon, girls? You coming, Ant?'

Ant checked his watch. 'Nah, I've got a date,' he said. 'Keep in touch, yeah?'

'My phone's completely out,' said Bea. 'I'll go home and charge it.'

They went their separate ways.

Queenie was in the kitchen, sitting at the table, nursing a cold cup of tea. 'Any luck?' she said.

Bea shook her head sadly, and plugged in her phone. When it had gathered enough charge to switch on, she worked her way through her notifications and then scrolled back through the text that she thought had come from Dean. She typed a reply – HAVE YOU GOT MY DOG? – then sent it.

The reply didn't come through until after she'd had a bath.

KEEP QUIET OR YOU'LL NEVER SEE HER AGAIN.

Shit, she thought. Dean's got her, or someone has. She felt herself growing cold. The hope that Goldie had just wandered off and would be found by someone and returned had gone now. She rang Ant's number. It took him a while to pick up.

'Yeah? Bea?'

'I've had another text. They've got her. The people that have been threatening me. They've got Goldie.'

'Okay. Keep calm. Do they want money?'

'No, they're just saying keep quiet.'

'So that's it, Bea. Like we agreed. Keep your head down. If we don't cause any trouble, she'll be okay.'

'Do you reckon? Don't you think I should tell the police?'

'Bea, what are they going to do? We don't know who it is, do we? They don't want money or nothing, so just do as they say.'

In the background, Bea could hear a woman's voice. 'Who is it?' And Ant replying, 'Just a minute. I'm nearly done.'

Bea cringed. She'd interrupted his date with Ayesha. 'Sorry, mate, I'll let you . . .get on,' she said, awkwardly.

'It's all right. You in tomorrow?'

'No.'

'Ah, okay, just have a quiet day, then. Get some sleep. I bet you're—'

'Night, Ant.' She cut the call, embarrassed and a little bit humiliated. She thought of Ant and Ayesha snuggling up somewhere, and Jay and all his acolytes – *her* friends – having a laugh in the pub, and the ball of misery that had started when she heard that Goldie was missing grew until it felt like a physical thing inside her, pressing outwards.

She and Queenie tried watching TV but neither of their hearts were in it. Queenie seemed numb – almost beside herself with worry. Bea couldn't bring herself to tell her that Goldie was kidnapped. She knew it would make her mum feel worse. They both went upstairs before nine.

Arthur was curled up on Bea's bed.

'Budge over,' she said, as she wriggled under the duvet and tried to shift him across with her legs.

He gave her a bad-tempered look, but then uncurled and

236

padded up the bed towards her, gently butting her hand with his head.

This was the friendliest he'd ever been. She tickled him tentatively behind the ears and his head and her hands entered a sort of dance, and Arthur narrowed his eyes with pleasure. And then she remembered that he, too, was going. He had a home, after all, and an owner who missed him. The ball of misery was in her throat now, making it difficult to swallow. It was pressing at her tear ducts, and without any reason not to, she gave in to it, and let herself have a little cry.

Ant looked at his phone. 'Hmm, she's rung off.'

'She all right?' Ayesha shifted a little on the sofa and snuggled her face against Ant's hand which was resting on her shoulder. There was a loud beat thudding through the house from the bedroom above them.

'Nah, she sounded rattled. She's had a text message – someone's taken her dog and they're threatening to kill it, if Bea doesn't keep quiet.'

'That's awful! There's some sick people in the world, aren't there?'

'Yeah. Tell me about it.' Ant put his phone down, drew Ayesha closer and kissed the top of her head. 'Hope you don't mind staying in,' he said. 'It's just that I need to keep an eye on Ken. He gave me a proper fright yesterday.'

Ayesha raised her eyes to the ceiling, then looked up at Ant. 'I don't mind. This is nice. You and me. Well, it would be if it was a bit quieter.'

'I'll go and shout at him. Oh, talk of the devil.'

Ken was standing in the doorway. He looked strung out. 'Go on, then, shout at me,' he said. 'Who do you think you are, anyway? You're not my dad. You can't tell me what to do.' He flounced off towards the kitchen.

'Hey!' Ant called after him. 'God, he'd better not be going out again.'

But they heard the fridge door slamming and footsteps on the stairs, and then the thudding baseline turned up even higher.

'Right, that's it!'

'No, don't move,' said Ayesha, snuggling closer. 'He's all right. I don't mind the noise really. Do you know what he took yesterday?'

'Ketamine, he said. Wouldn't say where he got it from, though.'

'Special K? Silly boy. I'm glad he's okay.'

'Yeah, could've been a lot worse.'

There was a copy of the *Bugle* on the coffee table, underneath Ant's feet. Ant guessed Stevo had brought it home and left it there. Ayesha sat up and reached for it.

'Move your feet a minute,' she said. She settled back into Ant's arms and studied the front page. 'Have you seen this?'

Ant was wary. She didn't know he couldn't read and he wasn't keen to confess. 'What about it?'

'They've identified the guy found by the bypass and released a photo. I know him.'

Ant sat up now. 'You know him?'

'Well, not know. I've seen him. I saw him on New Year's Eve.'

He unwound his arm from her shoulders. 'This guy?' he said, pointing to the picture.

'Yes. It was when you were walking me home. Do you really not remember anything about it?'

'No. I wish I did. I'd give anything to remember our first date. Special, innit? Anyway, tell me what you remember.'

'Well, it wasn't really a date, was it? Anyway, I already have—'

'No, about this guy.'

'Well, they're making out it was a suicide, like he was on his own, but he wasn't that night. I saw him in a car, one of those four-by-fours, with two other blokes. He was on the back seat, completely out of it. Like, *out*. Asleep. Unconscious.'

'Where was that?'

'Just past the church, on the road that goes across the bypass to the factory.'

Ant frowned. 'That's odd. You should tell the police.'

'Do you think?'

'Deffo. It might be important. Did you see the reg plate or anything? Do you know what sort it was?'

'No, cars are just cars, aren't they? Oh, one thing, one of its back lights wasn't working. They braked to go round the corner and only the left one came on.'

'Ayesha, you really should tell someone.'

'Yeah, okay. Not tonight, though, not now we're so cosy.' She paused. 'I wish you *did* remember that night.'

'Yeah, me too.'

'Perhaps you need something to remind you, jolt your memory. Here.' She put her arms round his neck and drew his face towards hers. They kissed tenderly, then drew apart.

'I think it's working. I'm not sure,' said Ant. 'Better try a bit harder.'

35

Bea fell into a fitful sleep, but woke sharply at six, listening for the dog's whine. When she remembered why it wasn't going to come, she groaned and sat up, wide awake. After only a few days, Goldie had turned her into a morning person. She wouldn't be able to go back to sleep now. She got dressed quickly, went to the bathroom, then tiptoed downstairs, leaving Arthur still asleep on her bed.

The kitchen smelt like a kitchen. There were no puddles. There was no one wagging and smiling to greet her. What would have been normal a week ago now seemed achingly empty and awful.

Bea made a cup of tea, gulped it down, then grabbed her coat and went out.

It was still dark. The snow had melted away, and the air was damp and cold. Bea started to walk, not consciously choosing a route, just going where her feet took her. She crossed the rec, passing the old people's houses, and walked along the High Street, where the council cleaner was out getting rid of the debris from Friday night in Kingsleigh, emptying bins, scooping up chip wrappers and plastic trays from the kebab shop.

She skirted the Costsave car park and then took a long

loop back via the network of paths and alleys that she knew so well. As she came back to her estate, the milk float was leaving it. She raised her hand in greeting to the milkman, and he waved back.

When she got back, Queenie was up, pottering around the kitchen. She'd just put a saucer of food down for Arthur, who was eating enthusiastically and messily.

'I suppose you're going to take him back today, then,' she said, miserably.

'Tomorrow,' said Bea. 'His owner said she was going out today.'

'And then we'll have an empty house.'

Bea couldn't think of anything to say.

'Have you been out looking?'

'Yeah, but it was pointless.' Bea took a deep breath. 'The thing is, I had some messages last night, Mum. Someone's got her. Taken her.'

Queenie's eyes grew wide. 'Taken her? Why didn't you say? Do they want money?'

'No. They just want me shut up, stop poking my nose into their business.'

'What business is that, Bea? What's going on?'

'I've been looking into the missing cats. Ant and Jay have been helping. We think it's illegal dog-fighting. They use cats to train dogs on. Let them rip them apart.'

'Oh my God!' Queenie gasped. 'It could've been you, Arthur!' She swooped down and picked up the cat, who reacted by twisting his body and scrabbling furiously at her hands and arms. She put him down again quickly, then sat down at the kitchen table trying to process the news.

'Bea,' she said eventually. 'We should tell Charles. I should tell him. I lost her, after all.'

'Do you think we could hold off one more day?'

Queenie shook her head. 'No, love. I feel sick, but it's got

241

to be done.' She rang the hospital, but they wouldn't put her through because she wasn't his next of kin.

'Shall we go in? Visit him?'

'I don't know, Mum. Give me the phone a minute. I'll have a go.'

Bea rang the hospital switchboard. The woman who answered told her that he was no longer a patient there and wouldn't tell her anything until Bea explained about the dog, and she relented. 'He's gone to Orchard View, it's a care home in Kingsleigh.'

'Oh yeah, I know it,' said Bea. 'Thank you.' She rang the Home, and they put her through to Charles. 'I don't know how to say this, but Goldie's missing.'

'Missing?'

'My mum, I mean, *we* left her outside a shop and she wasn't there when we got back. I'm so sorry.'

She waited for his reaction.

'She'll turn up,' he said, brightly.

'It was yesterday, Charles. She's been out all night.'

'Bea, my dear. I know she's all right. I'd feel it if she wasn't.'

'Really?'

'Really. I've had her since she was a puppy. We understand each other. Always have. I'd know if she was upset or in pain.'

After she'd rung off, Bea told Queenie what he'd said.

'Blimey, is he psychic or something?'

'No,' Bea sighed. 'Just very, very fond of his dog. If he thinks that there's a connection, and if he believes she's okay, that'll do for me until we know otherwise.'

'People are daft about their pets, aren't they?'

'Yeah, but you can see why.'

The day passed slowly. It was almost like those terrible grey, flat days after Bea's dad had died, Bea thought. She wondered

242

if her mum was thinking the same, but didn't want to say anything in case it made it worse.

The light faded outside, the clock on the mantelpiece ticked slowly on and on, and Queenie switched on the fire in the lounge. 'Bob's coming round in a minute,' she said. 'Thought it might cheer us up.'

'Oh, Mum, really?'

'I thought you liked him. He's been ever so kind and helpful with the dog and everything.'

'I know he has and he's all right, but I see enough of him at work. I just like a bit of space at home.'

'You don't like change, that's your trouble.'

Bea spluttered on her tea. She was about to say something about pots and kettles when her phone started ringing. She saw that it was Ant and accepted the call.

'Bea,' he said, 'something's going on.'

'What?'

'It's all kicking off on my estate. Someone's lit fires all over the place. There's one round the back of the garages and another in a bin by the kids' playground. There's police cars and fire engines and everything all over the bloody shop. I reckon it could be Ken. He nipped out while I was having a kip on the sofa earlier.'

A little fire ignited in the back of Bea's mind – suspicion catching hold of her and then crackling into certainty. 'Ant, I reckon it's a diversion. The cops will be running around like blue-arsed flies in Kingsleigh now, won't they?'

'So they won't be able to watch the farm.'

'Got it in one.'

'So, we should go, after all,' said Ant. 'Shall I ring Jay?'

'Okay. Call round here in twenty minutes, then. I'll get ready.'

'Bea, mate, that's not a good idea, is it?'

'I can look after myself, Ant.'

'Yeah, I know. I wouldn't pick a fight with you, but I meant you should stay home for Goldie's sake.'

'If I keep out of the way, no one will know, though, will they?'

'I dunno. I s'pose not. See you in twenty, yeah?'

36

Ant and Jay came to the back door. Bea had seen them coming and opened the door before they had time to knock. They looked like a pair of SAS soldiers dressed in head to toe black. Bea hadn't got a balaclava but she was pleased with the rest of her gear – camouflage jacket, leggings under some black jeans, Ugg-type boots, black scarf and gloves.

'What the fuck is that?' said Ant, looking her up and down.

'What?' Bea looked down at herself but couldn't see anything wrong.

'That jacket. It's got sparkles on.'

It was true. There were a few clusters of crystal-like beads attached to the jacket which Bea had thought were rather a nice touch when she'd been shopping online. Rather eye-catching.

'Only a few down the front,' she said. 'The back hasn't got any.'

'Bea, we're meant to be trying to blend in, not blinding them as their torches bounce off the jewels on your frontage. You might as well have sewn bloody headlights onto it.'

She looked at Jay for guidance. He shrugged. 'It's maybe not the best.'

'Take it off, then!' Ant squawked.

'No! I'll freeze.'

'Turn it inside out,' said Jay.

'What?'

'Turn it inside out.'

'Seriously?'

'Yeah.'

Bea sighed but threaded her arms out of the jacket and, holding onto the cuffs, pulled the sleeves through. She put the jacket back on. 'Happy now, you two?'

'That's better.' Jay handed Bea a balaclava.

She took it and had a look. 'Not with my hair!'

'You've got to, Bea. If you get spotted, it could be nasty for Goldie. We're going to try not to get seen at all, but if we do this'll help.'

'I don't think a balaclava's going to help. Not with my eyeliner and megalashes.'

'What are you wearing the lashes for?' said Ant.

'I was nervous. They make me feel better.'

'You'd better take them off, Bea. And the make-up,' said Jay. 'So you look more like one of the lads.'

Bea's resolve faltered. This felt like a deal-breaker. She couldn't let them, especially Jay, see her without make-up, could she? Perhaps she should stay at home, after all. From the next room she heard Bob laughing at something on the telly, and her mum joining in. That's it. She was going.

'One minute,' she said. 'Come in.'

They stepped into the kitchen. Bea went through the lounge and clattered upstairs.

'Where are you going, love? Who's that?'

'It's Ant and Jay. I'm just nipping upstairs for a minute.'

'Come in, lads!' Bob shouted through to the kitchen.

Bea shuddered inside and left them to their Costsave reunion. She hurtled up the stairs and into the bathroom where she tugged gently at one set of lashes and then the other and put them safely in their little plastic box. She got some wipes out of the cabinet and removed the eyeliner, shadow and mascara, eyebrow pencil, and foundation. It took a couple of goes, and then there she was, in all her natural glory – eyes piggy and small, face round and bland. She looked about twelve.

'Jesus,' she said. 'Okay, I can do this.' She clattered down the stairs.

Queenie looked up and almost choked on her tea. 'Bea, where are you actually going?'

'Just out for a drink.'

'In The Jubilee? Dressed like that?'

'Yeah. Maybe. We'll see how it goes.'

Queenie frowned. 'I don't believe you. What are you up to?'

'Nothing. We're just going out.'

'Is something going on?' said Bob.

'No, no. Just a drink.'

Bea quickly ushered Ant and Jay into the kitchen and out of the back door. 'See you later, Mum!' she shouted, closing the door behind her.

They set off along the street towards the allotments. It was dark already and the sky was quite clear, the temperature dropping fast. They could hear the wail of sirens in the distance.

'All hell's breaking loose in town,' said Ant. 'I'd bet you fifty quid Ken's doing it.'

'Starting fires?'

'It's his sort of thing,' admitted Ant.

When they got to the path, away from the last houses, they stopped and put on their balaclavas. SAS or burglars, thought Bea, stopping herself from saying it just in time.

'Is this all right, then?' she asked Jay. 'Do I look like one of the boys?'

Jay adjusted her balaclava a little so that the pillar box slit wasn't at an angle. It felt quite an intimate thing to do, and

247

for a moment their eyes met. Bea was glad most of her face was behind a layer of wool as she felt herself blushing under his gaze.

'You'll do,' he said and patted the top of her woolly head, as you would pat a child or a dog. Disconcerted, Bea pretended to be pulling her gloves on more firmly.

'We look really scary now,' said Ant. 'If we meet a dog walker along here, they'll shit themselves.'

They walked in single file along the path by the allotments. Jay had a head torch on and he led the way to the stile. Once there, he switched the torch off. 'Better to manage without, if we can,' he said. 'There'll be more light in the open field. I reckon we'll be all right. Stick together. We'll find somewhere to stake it out.'

Bea felt a frisson of excitement now. Her eyes had adjusted to the dark, and Jay was right, there was enough light from the moon for them to pick their way across the field. An owl hooted in the distance and another answered closer by. Bea stopped walking and looked round, keen to see it. Her eyes couldn't pick it out and she realised she could only just see the dark shapes of Ant and Jay ahead of her. She was getting left behind.

She started to run, but the ground was uneven. After nearly turning her ankle, she slowed to a fast walk. She was a bit out of breath and pleased to find they'd stopped to wait for her at the next stile.

'Okay?' Jay said.

'Yeah.'

They pressed on. When they got to the brow of the hill, they could see the farm. There was a soft glow of light from the yard and a couple of sets of headlights showing the bumpy progress of cars in the lane leading up to it.

'Shit, it's already under way. We'll have to be careful,' Jay whispered. 'We'll go down to the gate, maybe work along the hedge.'

They filed down the hill and leaned on the gate. The lower building, where they'd found Arthur, was obscuring their view of the yard and the other buildings, but there was a steady stream of vehicles approaching the farm.

'If we move further along, we might see them get out of their cars. Come on,' said Jay.

They crouched down and walked along the side of the field towards the top of the lane. The hedge was a fairly thin layer of stems and twigs, providing plenty of little viewpoints through. They stayed close to the ground at a point where they could see people parking up. The yard was full now and people were leaving their cars on the far side of the lane. Light was shining out from the large barn and there was a steady buzz of shouted greetings and blokeish banter.

'Bloody hell,' said Ant. 'I've never seen so many toffs and Range Rovers in one place before.'

'Not all toffs,' said Bea. 'There's all sorts.'

'That reminds me, Ayesha told me last night that she saw that lad that ended up on the bypass in a four-by-four on New Year's Eve.'

'Really?' said Bea. 'What, driving?'

'No, slumped in the back. Out of it. With two blokes in the front.'

'Blimey! Has she told the cops?'

'Dunno,' said Ant. 'She hadn't done when she left mine in the early hours.'

'Keep it down!' Jay whispered fiercely. 'Do you want to get caught and lynched by this lot?'

People walked towards the farm in twos and threes. Some were in the country uniform of waxed jackets and wellies, others in padded coats and beanie hats. Bea spotted one familiar figure scuttling up from his car.

'Oh God, not him,' she whispered.

'Who?' said Jay.

'Kevin, the photographer from the local rag. Might have known he'd be in on this.'

A car pulled up quite close to them.

'Shh,' Jay said.

The car doors opened and then slammed shut. Bea could see two pairs of feet crunching on the frosty gravel. She looked up and gasped. One of the men was Dave, Julie's bully of a husband.

She waited until they were safely into the yard, then whispered, 'They're all crawling out of the woodwork tonight.'

'Oh, shit,' said Ant.

'What?'

'In the opening to the yard. Fuckin' hell. What's he doing here?'

Bea changed position and peered through a different gap in the hedge. 'Oh.'

She could clearly see Ken, lurking near a group of men. Then one of them, a guy with a flat cap on and wearing a Barbour jacket, jeans and heavy boots, turned to him and seemed to be giving him instructions. Ken nodded and the man clapped him on the shoulder.

Jay nudged Bea. 'That's the bloke, Bea. The guy in the Barbour jacket.'

Bea felt a stab of anxiety in her stomach. Keep calm, she thought. Don't get the jitters now.

The influx of cars slowed down. The noise of the gathering crowd diminished too, as the men moved from the yard into the barn. And then suddenly the beam of light, which had been illuminating their view, disappeared. The doors to the barn were closed.

'It's starting,' said Jay.

'We can't see a thing now,' said Ant. 'Let's get closer.'

37

'Come on, let's get over by the gate.'

No need to crouch any longer, they walked swiftly back along the hedge and clambered over the gate. They crept along the wall of the low building and waited by the corner.

Jay peered round into the yard. He retreated and turned to the others. 'There's someone there, over on the other side,' he whispered. 'Looks like your lad.'

'Let me have a look,' said Ant. He squeezed past Jay and he, too, peered round. He moved back, flattening his back against the wall. 'It's Ken all right. Let me deal with him.'

'We all will,' said Jay. 'He's looking down the lane. Let's go round through the yard.'

They crept back along the wall and went round the other end into the yard. They were closer to the barn now and could hear a groundswell of shouting, cheering and jeering. The main event was under way.

Bea could see Ken at the far corner of the yard now. He had his back to them and was illuminated by the light from his phone. They were able to get right up to him without him noticing.

Ant tapped him on the shoulder. 'Oi, what are you doing here?'

Ken jumped out of his skin. He looked like a rabbit in the headlights. 'Nothing.'

He swiped his finger across the screen of his phone.

'Oh no you don't.' Ant wrestled it away from him and held it up in the air. Ken launched a counter-attack, kicking at his shins and grabbing his arm.

'Ant, here! Chuck it!' Jay hissed.

Ant drew back his wrist and flicked the phone through the air. Jay caught it, held it low with both hands and then booted it into the darkness.

'What the fuck did you do that for?' said Ken, facing Jay and flailing his arms around in frustration.

'To stop you phoning whoever it was you were phoning.'

'We could've found out who it was, though,' said Bea. 'Useful to get the numbers.'

Ken dived between his brother and Jay in the direction the phone went.

'Uh-uh,' said Ant, grabbing him on his way through. He got Ken in an armlock. 'So, what's going on? What are you doing here?'

'I'm not doing anything. Ow!' He clutched at Ant's arms as he jerked at his neck. 'I'm just the lookout,' he gasped.

'Lookout for what?'

'It's not illegal,' said Ken. 'What they're doing. It's not breaking any laws.'

'You're kidding,' said Bea. 'Dog-fighting?'

'It's an offence under the Animal Welfare Act 2006,' said Jay. 'Fifty-one weeks in prison.'

'Dog-fighting?' said Ken. 'It's not dog-fighting. I wouldn't get involved in that. It's disgusting.'

Ant loosened his grip a little. 'What is it, then?'

'Let me go and I'll show you. You can see in that window. They haven't covered it up properly.'

Ant relaxed his arms for a second and Ken ducked out

252

from under them. He sped off down the lane, feet kicking up a shower of mucky grit as he went.

'Ken! Ken, you little fucker. Come back.' Ant was incandescent. 'I'll swing for him later.'

Bea had a momentary twinge of sympathy for Ken. After all, his dad was in prison and his mum had left him. She hoped Ant wouldn't actually 'swing for him', but she couldn't think about that now.

'Shall we go and look in the window?' she said, then realised that Jay had already gone. She could see him now, a dark shape against the darker wall of the building. When he reached the building the top of his head was silhouetted in the light escaping from the uncurtained window.

She could hear a roar of noise from inside. The men, and it did sound an entirely male noise, were getting into a frenzy.

Ant and Bea crept up behind him.

'What is it?' said Bea.

There was another roar of excitement.

'Ken was right,' said Jay. He'd turned away from the window. 'It's not dogs, but it is animals.'

'What?'

'I don't know if you want to see it,' he said.

Ant nudged him aside and peered in. 'Fuck me.'

'I know,' said Jay.

'What?' said Bea.

'Bea, don't look,' said Ant. 'It's not very nice.'

Although the anxious knot in her stomach was twisting and turning now, Bea had to know. 'Move aside, boys,' she said. She had to stand on tiptoe to see over the ledge of the window. She put her hands on the cold, damp brick to steady herself and peered in.

It was difficult to see through a mass of heads and shoulders. The crowd was moving, little surges and waves of excitement. One movement created a gap and Bea could see to the centre of the room where two men, stripped to the waist, were slugging it out. Blood was dripping down their faces, from noses and mouths. The bandages wrapped round their fists were red with it.

'Oh. My. God.'

One of the men was Tank. His opponent was much older, a beast of a man, thickset, entirely hairless, shiny with sweat and blood. They were both panting, chests heaving. Tank had a haunted look in his eyes, like he was trapped in something and didn't know how to get out. His opponent clumped him on the side of his head and Tank reeled sideways. The man followed up with a series of sickening blows to his head, and Tank dropped to the floor. Bea couldn't see him any more as the crowd surrounded him, shouting at him to get up.

Bea turned back to the others. 'Tank's down.'

They all squeezed together at the window.

'What's happening?' said Ant.

'He's getting up,' said Jay.

'He's in a heck of a state,' said Bea. 'They should stop the fight.'

'It's not going to happen, Bea. Listen to them. They're literally baying for blood.'

It was true. There was a roar from the watching men as Tank staggered to his feet. The other guy prowled round while Tank took a few deep breaths with his hands on his thighs. Then, just as he straightened up, his opponent went for him, landing a volley of punches to his stomach. The crowd went wild. Tank doubled over and the bloke started in on his head. One blow caught him on the underside of his chin and he arched backwards and fell into the crowd. They caught him, keeping him on his feet, and then launched him back towards the bloody fists waiting for him. Another sickening blow to his head and he was down again, crumpling like he wasn't made of flesh and bone but something far more delicate. His legs folded up underneath him and he dropped to the floor. This time he didn't get up.

'I can't see him,' said Ant.

Through the crowd, Bea could see the big man being led away. People were slapping him on the back, but he was looking a bit shaken up now.

'Give us some space!' someone shouted. 'Get back!'

The crowd thinned out a little and Bea was able to see through to the ground, where Tank was lying. Simon, the vet, was kneeling next to him. He was pressing his fingers against Tank's neck and shaking his head. The man who had been instructing Ken earlier seemed to be arguing with him, and suddenly Simon stood up. He was shouting back. Then he gathered his things up and pushed his way through the crowd to the way out.

'Who's that guy?' said Ant.

'It's the bloody vet,' said Bea.

Now the Barbour Jacket Man was cupping his hands and shouting round the room. 'Is there a doctor here? Anyone got First Aid?'

'Shit!' said Ant.

'Ant, no!' said Bea, but he had already left their huddle by the window and was running round the side of the building, tearing off his balaclava. Bea ran after him and watched as he sprinted up to the barn door. He almost bumped into Simon on his way out.

'Mate,' said Ant, grabbing his sleeve. 'You can't leave. He needs help.'

Simon spun away from him and started running towards the parked cars.

Ant didn't hesitate. He dived through the doors. Bea stayed where she was, at the corner of the building, then darted back to the window.

'He's in there,' said Jay.

Bea strained up onto the tips of her toes. She could see Ant kneeling by Tank's prostrate form. Now he had his fingers resting against Tank's neck, checking for a pulse. Then he got out his phone.

Quick as a flash the Barbour man snatched it away. Ant shouted at him and they started a furious argument.

'We need an ambulance,' said Bea.

'They won't want any blue lights here,' said Jay.

'I don't care.' She got her phone out and dialled.

38

It only took twelve minutes for the ambulance to get there. Bea was timing it on her phone and they were the longest twelve minutes of her life. She and Jay stayed out of sight, while Ant tried his best to revive Tank. He took his coat off and made a pillow out of it for Tank's head, then leaned over and used his thumb to open one of his eyes. He shone his torch in.

'Is he dead, do you think?' said Bea. 'Should we go in there?'

'I dunno. You should keep clear anyway,' said Jay. 'They mustn't know you're here.'

Ant was shouting at Barbour Jacket Man, who wouldn't give his phone back. The crowd was getting restless and in opposite corners of the room, the next pair of fighters were getting ready for their bout.

Now Barbour Jacket seemed to be asking Ant something else. Ant was shaking his head. Some others, including Dean and Dave moved forward. They bent down and took hold of Tank's shoulders and legs and started to half lift, half drag him away from the centre of the room.

Ant was on his feet now, screaming at them, his words reaching Bea and Jay. 'You can't move him. You can't do that! You've got to get an ambulance!'

But move him they did, his head flopping worryingly

backwards. Ant dived in and tried to support it. Tank was deposited at the far side of the room. Ant seemed to be remonstrating with Dean now, who looked, frankly, numb. He just stood there, with his hands at his sides. He was staring down at Tank, like a zombie.

The next fight didn't start, though. As more of the crowd became aware of Ant's fight to save Tank, an air of unease spread through the men. Bea saw a few of them make their way out of the barn. The rest hovered about, looking tense.

And now Bea thought she could hear the faint sound of a siren.

'Do you hear that?' she said to Jay.

Jay moved back from the window and tilted his head. 'Yeah. It's all going to kick off in a minute, Bea. Do you want to go back over the gate, get down behind the hedge?'

'No. I'm staying right here.'

'Okay, but don't go into the yard. I think it's going to get messy, but don't worry. If Ant's in trouble, I've got his back.'

It wasn't just one siren. There were two or three sending their warbling notes of alarm into the night air. Now Bea could see blue-white lights pulsating in the distance, getting closer.

Bea spotted someone peeling away from the crowd and walking towards the door. He stood there for a moment, listening and looking, and then he turned and shouted, 'Police!'

Only those nearest to him heard him, but the news started spreading through to the middle of the room. The barn doors were wide open now and there was the start of a stampede. The air was full of the sounds of engines being started, wheels skidding on the icy surface of the lane. Drivers were shouting at each other as they tried to extricate and turn their cars. And all the time the sirens and blue lights were getting closer and closer.

Bea looked back into the window. Tank was still on the

ground, with Ant next to him, pressing on his chest. Dean was hopping from foot to foot, a look of panic on his face. Then he saw the open door and started running. Now Barbour Jacket was striding towards Ant, his hand balled into fists at his side.

'Jay,' said Bea.

'Got it,' said Jay. 'Stay here.' He jogged round the side of the building and into the barn, just as Barbour Jacket was about to take a swing at Ant.

Jay shouted at him and he looked round giving Ant time to move. The man turned and squared up to Jay, who got his phone out and took his photograph, face on, close up. This was a red rag to a bull and the guy made a grab for his phone. Jay ducked away, but not too far. To Bea it looked like he was teasing him, drawing him away from Ant.

The sirens were very close now, but Bea could see that the lights weren't moving. The lane was clogged up. Horns were sounded, people were shouting. She checked back in the barn. Tank was still out cold. Ant had got up and was looking anxiously out of the doorway.

Bea broke cover and started running down the lane. It was crammed with cars and no one was going anywhere. She squeezed through and reached the ambulance which was only fifty metres away now. She ran up to the driver's door. The driver saw her coming and wound down the window. She looked warily at Bea, who was still wearing her balaclava. Bea pulled the hat off to look more human.

'Can you come on foot?' she said. 'It's not far. I don't know if he's still breathing.'

The paramedic nodded. 'We're not getting anywhere here, are we?' she said. Her partner, in the passenger seat, opened his door.

'I'll go and assess. I'll radio back.' He grabbed a couple of bags. 'Where is he?'

'In the big building. My friend's with him, but he's only got First Aid.'

'Okay.' He set off up the lane with Bea trotting in his wake. Bea saw Jay shoot out of the barn, followed by Barbour Jacket Man. When the man saw the lights and the ambulance guy running towards him, he stopped chasing Jay, who jogged up to Bea.

'Bea, what are you doing?'

'I had to fetch help,' she said. 'I couldn't just stand there.'

The lane was still choked with cars. Bea looked back and caught sight of Tom and Shaz further down, behind the ambulance. Someone had opened a gate nearby and cars were starting to drive into a field, bumping and careering in their efforts to get away.

'It's madness, isn't it?' said Jay.

'Yeah. Let's find Ant.'

They walked up to the barn. On the way in, they passed Barbour Man. He looked at Jay with open contempt. Then he turned his attention to Bea and his eyes glittered. 'I would have thought you'd know better.'

'Do I know you?' said Bea.

'No. But I know you.'

Jay put a hand on her arm. 'Come on.'

They were past him and into the barn when Bea heard him whisper, 'Shame about the dog.'

Goldie. Her stomach clenched with a sickening lurch. In the heat of the moment, Bea had forgotten about her. She spun round. 'Where is she? Tell me where she is. Is she here?'

The man smiled. 'I don't know what you're talking about.'

Bea stormed up to him, her fury overriding everything else. He was only a few inches taller than her. She looked up into his cruel, cool face. 'Where is she?'

He smiled again, sneering and nasty, and said nothing.

'Where *is* she?' Bea shoved both hands into his chest,

making him step backwards. He was surprised, but the smile stayed. He caught hold of both Bea's wrists and she started to feel panicky and powerless.

'That's enough, mate,' said Jay. 'Let her go.'

Bea was girding herself to slam her knee into his groin, but at that moment he let go of her, laughing in her face. She rubbed her wrists which were sore where he'd held them. Her mind was reeling. With Tank and Ant. And with Goldie – God knows where, maybe alive, maybe not.

It was his laughter that did it. The sound of it in her ears. Even now, with the chaos all around him, he still felt he held all the cards. He was still taunting them.

She brought her knee up as hard as she could.

At last the smile was gone He doubled over, making a high-pitched whining noise.

'Oi! I saw that. Break it up!' Tom came running up to her.

'Tom, thank God you're here,' she said. 'He assaulted me. I had to do it to get away from him.'

Tom looked at the figure of Barbour Man, still hunched over and breathing hard. 'What's been going on here, then?' said Tom, as the man straightened up. 'It's Eddie, isn't it?'

Bea's heart sank. Were this bloke and Tom friends?

'Nothing illegal, mate,' said Eddie. 'It's all above board, except for this woman here assaulting me, which you witnessed. Someone should teach her how to behave.'

39

'Okay, let's calm it all down. Do you need medical attention?'
Eddie shook his head. 'Right. There's a man down over there.
Let's get him sorted and then we'll take some statements.
None of you leave, okay? I'm going to need to talk to all of
you.'

Bea, Jay and Eddie looked at each other stonily.

'Come on, Bea,' said Jay. 'Come over here.' He drew her
away from Eddie and they walked towards the cluster of
people gathered round Tank. Ant was one of them. He was
still crouching next to him. The other ambulance worker
was there now. Bea leaned down and put her hand on Ant's
shoulder. He glanced round. His face was pasty, etched with
concern.

'Ant,' said Bea. 'Give them a bit of space.' She helped him
up and they walked towards the door.

'He had a pulse and he was breathing, but he was out
cold,' said Ant.

'You did everything you could. It's their job now.'

'Did one of you ring them?'

'Yeah. I did.'

Ant shook his head. 'It was crazy. He wouldn't let me ring.
He's still got my phone. Here—' He went over to Eddie.
'Give me my fucking phone back.'

Eddie fished it out of his pocket and threw it towards Ant.

'He needed an ambulance.' said Ant.

Eddie shrugged. 'He'll be fine.'

'You don't know that.' Ant was getting agitated again, ready to boil over.

'Leave it, Ant. Leave him. Get some fresh air,' said Bea.

'Yeah, okay. I can't stand the smell in here anyway,' said Ant.

The chaos in the lane was subsiding. There were only a couple of cars left parked up, and the ambulance and police car had made it into the yard. They watched as Tank was loaded onto a stretcher and transferred to the ambulance. The doors were closed and the vehicle started making its way out of the yard and down the lane.

'There was another phone, wasn't there?' said Jay. He darted across the yard and Bea could see the beam of his light playing on the hedge at one side of the lane.

'Ken,' said Ant. 'I need to go and find him.'

'What are you going to do to him?' said Bea.

'I want him to tell me how he got mixed up in all this. I want him to tell me the truth.'

'You said you'd give him a pasting.'

Ant looked suddenly very sad. 'I said it, but I never meant it. Even less now . . .' His voice trailed off, and Bea realised he was close to tears.

'Ant, you did your best. I was so bloody proud of you going in there like that. You didn't think about your own safety.'

He clamped his lips together, struggling with his emotions.

'I'll second that. And you were right to make that call, Bea.' They looked around. Shaz had come up behind them. 'He's not in a good way at all.'

'What's going to happen now?' said Bea.

'We'll need to take statements from you, but I'm not sure there's been an offence committed here.'

'You're kidding?' said Ant. 'There were two blokes trying to kill each other, and a load of other blokes cheering them on. You can't tell me that's legal.'

'Well, the participants were all willing and the organiser's claiming it's covered by the Dangerous Exhibitions Act. We might be able to treat it as a public order matter, though. That's why we need your statements, and any photos you took.'

'Shaz, there has been an offence. That man, Eddie, he's the one who kidnapped my dog. He admitted it to us just now.'

Shaz sighed, perhaps anticipating a long night of form filling ahead of her. 'We'd better go to the station, hadn't we?'

'Can you make him open up the other buildings, please?'

Shaz raised her eyebrows.

Bea lowered her voice. 'Shaz, this is where we found the white cat. It was inside the long, low building over there. It could be where they're holding Goldie.'

Shaz held her hand up. 'Whoa, whoa, whoa. One thing at a time, Bea. I don't think my notebook's big enough for all this. Let's pack up here, go to the station and put the kettle on.'

'At least let us search the buildings,' Bea pleaded. 'I need to find my dog. I think they're going to kill her.'

'Bea, why would anyone kill your dog?' said Tom.

'They threatened to kill her to keep me quiet, but now that we're here and I called the police and everyone saw me . . .he said I'd never see her again.'

'Who did?'

Bea tipped her head towards Barbour Jacket Man.

'Eddie?' said Tom. 'Doubt it. He looks after dogs, Bea. That's his job. He's one of the hunt workers.'

'He just said it. Jay heard him too.' Jay nodded vigorously. 'And I've got a text. Let me show you.'

Bea scrolled through her messages until she found it. Tom and Shaz looked at her phone.

'Same number as the one you sent me before. This is from Eddie, is it? I thought it was from Dean?'

'I don't know who it's from, but he knows about it. Trust me, Tom, he knows.' She looked at Tom, who returned her gaze steadily, then walked over to Eddie.

After a short exchange, Eddie got out a big bunch of keys and unlocked a padlock at the door. He flicked the light switch on, and he and Tom disappeared inside.

'Can I look?' said Bea.

'Don't push it, Bea,' said Shaz. 'Tom's there.'

After a few minutes, the two men emerged from the building and Eddie secured the padlock. They met the others in the middle of the yard.

'Nothing there,' said Tom.

'Am I all right to lock the barn up now?' said Eddie.

'Yes, sure. Do you want to do your statement now or in the morning?'

'Aren't you going to arrest him?' said Bea.

Eddie flung his arms out wide. 'What for? I've done nothing wrong. *You* assaulted *me*. I'm the injured party, and that'll be in my statement.'

'You've got my dog!' Bea shouted. She lunged towards him, and Ant and Jay restrained her.

'Okay, okay, let's keep it calm,' said Tom. 'Eddie, have you got Bea's dog?'

'No.'

'Liar! You *told* me—'

'Bea, shush. Eddie, you lock up here and get off home. Can you call into the station tomorrow morning? Eleven?' Eddie gave him the thumbs up. 'The rest of you, have you got a vehicle here? No? Let's get you back, then. We can take statements now, or we can drop you back home.'

'Can we do it tomorrow?' said Ant. 'I need to get home.'

'I've got to find Goldie,' said Bea. 'But if she's not here, I honestly don't know where to look.'

'Come home with me. Let's have a beer,' said Ant. 'Jay? You up for it?'

'Yeah. Why not?'

'Right,' said Tom. 'Get in the back, then.'

They piled into the back of the squad car, with Bea squashed in the middle between Ant and Jay. Ant had retreated inside himself. He gazed out of the side window, away from Bea. As they bumped down the track, Bea was overcome by a wave of exhaustion. Through the gap between the seats, she watched the tail lights of Eddie's Land Rover, bucking and lurching as it hit the potholes in the lane.

'We could do him for that missing brake light,' said Shaz.

'That's the least of our troubles, Shaz. It's gonna take bloody days to sort this lot out,' said Tom. Bea shut her eyes. She must have drifted off, because when she opened them again, her head was leaning on Jay's shoulder and there was a little stream of dribble seeping out of the corner of her mouth. She sat up. There wasn't enough room to dig into her pocket for a tissue so she surreptitiously wiped the drool away on her hand and wiped that in turn on her trouser leg.

They were back in the sulphur yellow streets of Kingsleigh's estates and it wasn't long before they drew up outside Ant's house. Ant, Bea and Jay bundled wearily out of the car.

'Check in with us at two tomorrow afternoon, yeah?' said Tom, out of his wound-down window.

'Okay.'

The car pulled away and the three of them trooped towards Ant's front door.

'Doesn't look like anyone's here,' said Ant. The house was in darkness, the curtains open. 'I wonder where the little fucker's got to?'

He unlocked the door which opened directly into the living room and flicked on the light. Bea and Jay followed him in.

'Stevo usually keeps a secret stash of cans in his room. Hang on.' Ant trotted upstairs.

'I think I fancy a cuppa anyway,' said Bea, going through to the kitchen and filling up the kettle. She was just looking for clean mugs among the rather unsavoury debris that littered every surface, when she heard a yelp. She and Jay looked at each other.

'You all right?' Bea called out.

There was no answer, so she and Jay headed towards the stairs.

Ant and a rather crumpled-looking Ken were standing at the top.

'Found him,' said Ant.

'Did you wake him up?' said Bea.

'No, he was huddled in a corner on the floor, sitting in the dark.'

'Turn the lights out,' said Ken, his voice a low whine. 'They'll know we're here.'

'I'm not turning the lights out. Of course, I'm bloody here. I live here,' said Ant. 'Get downstairs.' He bumped Ken's shoulder with his.

'Careful, Ant,' said Bea. 'Ken, do you want a cuppa?'

'I'd rather have a beer,' he said, eyeing the four-pack in his brother's hand.

'You're not having a sodding beer. You're fifteen,' said Ant. 'Get down those stairs.'

They gathered in the front room.

'At least close the curtains, can't you?' said Ken. He was huddled at one end of the sofa. He'd pulled his sleeves right down over his hands and was hugging himself. Bea realised that he was very, very scared.

She drew the curtains and went and sat next to him. 'There

we go,' she said. 'No one can see in now. Who are you scared of?'

'I heard all the sirens. I didn't warn them, did I? They're going to crucify me.'

'They've got other things to think about.'

He shook his head. His bottom lip was trembling. 'No. You don't know them. They won't forget.'

'Well, we're here anyway now. No one's going to hurt you.'

'He might,' Ken said, looking at Ant, who was handing out the beers.

Ant's shoulders seemed to sag. 'I'm not going to hurt you. It's just...I just...I don't know what's going on with you.'

Bea got up and fetched two mugs of tea, one for her and one for Ken.

'Did you put sugar in?' he asked.

'Two and one for luck,' she said, with a wink, and was pleased to get half a smile in return. 'Why don't you tell us what's been going on?'

'I can't.'

'I think we know most of it anyway. But we need to know the rest. This is serious stuff, Ken. Tank's in hospital.'

'Is he? What's wrong?'

'Beaten unconscious.'

Ken's lip wobbled even more, and his eyes went pink as tears seeped out. He dashed his arm across to wipe them away. 'My mates don't want to know me,' he said. 'After what Dad did, they just said I can't hang out with them any more.'

'They're not really mates, then,' said Bea.

'Yeah, but who else have I got? School's fucking miserable enough. There's no point if everyone hates you as well.'

'Why didn't you tell me?' said Ant. He was sitting on the floor opposite Ken, with his back against an armchair and his can on the floor next to him.

'I dunno. We don't exactly get on, do we? I didn't think . . . I dunno . . .'

Ant lit a cigarette and blew a long trail of smoke up towards the ceiling.

'Can I have one?' said Ken.

'No! Listen, mate, I'm sorry you couldn't talk to me. Tell me now. I'm listening.'

'All right, if you give a smoke.'

'No, you're not having a fucking cigarette.'

'Just a drag, then.'

'Ant . . .' Bea said, as Ant handed the cigarette over to Ken.

Ken took it and inhaled. Bea was expecting a coughing fit, but Ken dealt with it like a pro. He took another cheeky drag before handing it back to Ant.

'So, I had no mates and I stopped going to school. I knew Dean from round and about and I just kind of fell in with him.'

Ant groaned. 'Dean. It all comes back to him.'

'Shh,' said Bea. 'Let him talk.'

'Tank was training up for the fight and Dean was sort of his manager. They used to go out to the farm to train. There was a punchbag and weights and stuff there, and some old tyres. Dean made Tank run round the yard dragging tyres behind him. It was a laugh, but the fight was serious. Tank was being paid big money to fight.'

'How much?' Jay asked.

'Six hundred quid. He was giving Dean two hundred.'

Ant whistled. 'Six hundred quid!'

'I know. And Dean talked to the organiser, a bloke called Eddie, and he fixed it that I'd be lookout and get fifty quid.'

'Nice,' said Ant.

'Yeah, but I've messed up, haven't I? I've screwed it up for them, they're going to come after me.'

'I don't think so, Ken,' said Bea. 'They've got bigger things to worry about. Tank's in a bad way.'

'Is he going to be all right?'

'No one knows yet. Anyway, we won't let anyone get at you, okay?'

Ken looked unconvinced.

'Is that everything? Have you told us everything?'

'Yeah. Sort of.' Ant glared at him. 'Eddie was giving Tank stuff, drugs, to help him get stronger. He had something before the fight, too, to pep him up.'

'The stuff I saw him get from Simon,' said Bea. 'Stuff meant for animals.'

'Is that who you got the ketamine from?' said Ant. 'That bloke Eddie?'

'Yeah,' said Ken. 'But don't tell anyone, okay? He'll kill me if anyone tells. He doesn't look like much, but he's a scary guy. And don't tell Mum.' He was looking back at Ant now, pleading.

'Don't tell her what – the sagging off school? The smoking? The drugs?'

'Any of it.'

'She already knows about school,' said Ant, ''cos they rang her up.'

'The rest, then.'

'I've gotta tell her, Ken.'

'If you promise not to, I'll tell you where the dog is.'

Bea sat up now, spilling her tea. She clutched Ken's arm. 'Do you know? Really?'

'Yeah.'

'Where? Tell me!' Bea was almost squeaking now. The butterflies in her stomach were beating their little wings so hard it almost hurt.

'If he promises not to tell Mum.'

Bea gave Ant one of her most ferocious stares.

He visibly quailed. 'All right, all right.'

'And you've got to promise not to tell the cops, about the dog.'

'I've already told them she's missing,' said Bea.

'So, just say she turned up. Please. Keep me out of it.'

'Yes. Yes. All right. Just *tell* me.'

'And you'll give me a cigarette, and one of those cans,' he said to Ant.

'You're just pushing it now, you little—'

'Please, Ken,' Bea urged. 'If you really know, please tell me where she is. I've been going out of my mind.' She was gripping his arm quite strongly now, and he moved to shrug her off.

'She's right here,' said Ken.

'What?'

'She's in the garage.'

40

They tore out of the house and round to the row of garages behind. Bea had been here before and knew it was where the Thompson family kept an unlikely number of bicycles. Her heart was in her throat as she raced behind Ant.

Ant undid the padlock and heaved at the heavy metal door. He pulled it up and over. The fug that hit them confirmed that an animal of some sort was in there. Bea's eyes were still adjusting to the relative darkness, the only lighting spilling from nearby houses. But there – yes! – was a pale shape at the front of the garage and – yes! – the familiar thump, thump sound of a tail wagging against the floor.

'Goldie?' she said, and the shape changed, as Goldie lumbered to her feet and padded towards her. Bea met her halfway, kneeling on the concrete and hugging the dog tightly, burying her face in the top of her head. A sob exploded out of her, the dam of the last twenty-four hours' anxiety finally bursting.

'Is she all right?' said Ant.

Bea peeled herself away and Goldie took the opportunity to lick the side of her face all the way up from jawline to forehead.

'Yeah, she's fine.'

*

'That's it, then,' said Jay. He was walking Bea and Goldie home. Ken hadn't wanted to be left alone, so Ant had stayed with him. 'All over. Goldie's back. Case closed.'

'Yeah, I suppose so. I don't feel like it is over,' said Bea. 'We'll have to be careful what we say at the cop shop, so we don't drop Ken in it.'

'I don't know if we can keep him out of it, but we can try.'

They walked through the familiar streets. Little groups of people were straggling home from the pub. Bea found it difficult to believe that for them this was just a normal Saturday night. *She* felt she'd been put through the wringer.

'I still feel hepped up,' said Jay. 'Wish this town didn't close down at half past ten.'

'Ah, that's one of Kingsleigh's charms,' said Bea. 'No nightlife after closing time, dead on Sundays and even half-day closing on Wednesdays for the old-school shops.'

'Half-day closing? Is that a thing?'

'It is in Kingsleigh.'

It didn't take long to get back to Bea's road.

'Bea—'

'What?'

'Nothing.'

'No, go on. What?'

'It's just that, when it was all going crazy at the farm, and people were running everywhere, and it looked like Tank was dead . . .'

'Yeah?'

'In that crowd, in that craziness, I was looking for you. I was worried about you.'

'Were you?'

'Yeah.'

Bea was glad it was dark, so he couldn't see her expression.

'Bea?'

273

'Yeah?'

As she turned her face his mouth met hers, and just for a moment she forgot how cold and tired she was. She forgot everything until, by her side, Goldie gave a little whine and when Bea broke away from Jay and looked down she could see that she was shaking.

'I'd better get her indoors. She's been in that bloody garage for twenty-four hours, need to get her into the warm and give her some biscuits.'

'Yeah,' said Jay. 'Sure.'

'It's been a long day, Jay. Thanks for ...well, everything.' She followed the path round to the back of the house. As she did so, she glanced over her shoulder. Jay had already turned away and crossed the road.

'Here she is!' Queenie rushed over to Goldie. Bob stood in the lounge doorway behind her. 'Oh my goodness, we were so worried about you!' She ruffled the dog's neck and ears. 'What's this on her? Look at these marks.'

In the light of the kitchen, Bea could see dark patches on Goldie's legs and side.

'She's been kept in a garage, Mum. I reckon it's oil.'

'We'll have to give someone a bath, won't we?' said Queenie. 'But not tonight. She looks shattered.'

Bea thought she looked pretty normal, standing in the kitchen wagging her tail gently, but she wasn't going to argue. She herself was definitely shattered and couldn't imagine wrestling a dog into the bath and out again in this state.

'Just give her legs a little rub with a soapy flannel for now, Bea,' said Queenie.

Bea thought of her nice, soft bed, a microwaved beanbag owl and an extra blanket on top of her duvet. She sighed. 'What did your last slave die of?'

'Bea!' Bob barked. 'That's enough cheek.'

Bea's jaw dropped open and she stared at him with disbelief. 'What?'

Bob looked quickly at Queenie, who also appeared gobsmacked. If she doesn't back me up, thought Bea, I'm out of here. I'd rather sleep under a bloody hedge than be bossed around by Bob-on-Meat in my own home.

'Bob,' Queenie said, firmly, 'it's getting late. Bea and Goldie are home now. I think it's time to say goodnight.'

Little bright spots appeared in Bob's rosy cheeks. He knew he'd overstepped the mark. 'Right. Right.' He put his coat on. 'I'll be off. I'm glad you're both okay. Are you in tomorrow?'

'No,' said Bea. 'I'm off until Monday now.'

'Okay. See you then.' The door stuck a bit as he was closing it, so he gave it a tug and it slammed.

'Ouch,' said Queenie.

'It's just the door, Mum. I don't think he was angry.'

'He didn't mean anything, you know, Bea.'

'Didn't he? He's getting very cosy here. Is that what you really want?'

Queenie blinked rapidly. 'I don't know,' she said eventually. 'I don't know what I want.'

'It's too late for all this,' said Bea. 'I'll put some biccies in her bowl, and let's all go to bed.'

'Mm. Bea—'

'Yeah?'

'Come here.' Queenie opened her arms, inviting Bea in. Tired as she was, Bea couldn't refuse. They had a hug and as they stood together, Bea felt exhaustion overcoming her. Her head sank onto her mum's shoulder.

'I've got to go to bed, Mum, or I'll fall asleep standing up.'

She was hoping for a deep and dreamless sleep, but she'd gone past that point. Even Arthur's gentle purring couldn't lull her off. Wide-eyed and awake, she told herself, 'It's over.' She repeated the words, like a mantra, and felt herself starting to drift off again. And then she heard the noise.

The rattle of metal against metal, somewhere outside. A slight sighing sound. The side gate, she thought. Someone's let themselves into the back. Her senses were working overtime now, straining to pick up any other sound, but all was quiet. Had she imagined it?

But then, a muffled woof from the kitchen. And again.

Goldie knew there was someone outside too.

41

Bea sat up. Should she wake up Queenie? Ring the police?

She slid her legs out of bed and into her Disney princess slippers, then wrapped her dressing gown round her and tied the belt.

Downstairs, the dog barked again.

Bea walked onto the landing. There was another sound – the rhythmic grumble of Queenie snoring. Let her sleep, thought Bea. I'll sort this out.

She tiptoed down the stairs, carrying her phone. I need a weapon, she thought, and went upstairs again. She couldn't think of anything to grab and ended up brandishing the loo brush. It wouldn't do any damage, but she'd have the element of surprise.

She crept downstairs and opened the kitchen door. The usual doggish fug hit her nose. She'd missed it when Goldie was away. The dog was already on her feet and padded towards her. She bent down and whispered, 'Is there someone there, Goldie?'

There was a curtain across the window of the kitchen door, and Bea was grateful for it, queasy at the thought of someone being able to see in. She and Goldie stood in the dark room together, and waited. Bea couldn't hear anything except for Goldie's panting, and the thudding of her own blood in her ears – her heart was racing.

This is stupid, Bea thought. She flicked on the light and then her whole body jerked as someone tapped gently on the kitchen door. She went and stood near.

'Who is it?' she said. There was no answer, just another series of taps. Bea felt anxiety stabbing at her insides. 'Who is it? I'm not opening up if you don't say.'

There was a pause. Then, 'It's me. Ant.' The voice was muffled. It didn't sound like Ant, and why would he be so weird?

'What are you doing here?'

'Open up. I'll tell ya.'

She could slide the curtain back, but the glass in the window was frosted – all she would be able to see would be a shape. She started to move the bolt across, then stopped. She rang his number on her mobile and listened. The screen showed that it was ringing but she couldn't hear it. It wasn't Ant outside. It was someone else.

'It's too late,' she said to the door. 'I'm not opening up. Come back in the morning.'

'I just want to talk to you.'

She moved away from the door and that's when there was another noise, an insistent scratching or scraping sound, like fingernails on a chalkboard. 'What the—?'

The sound seemed to be working its way around the window in the door. And then suddenly, it stopped. The curtain moved as someone lifted the glass away and a hand came through, under the curtain and reached for the bolt. Above the hand was the end of the sleeve of a Barbour jacket.

Bea swore, and at that moment she heard Ant's voice. 'Bea? Is that you?' He'd finally picked up the phone. 'Eddie's here,' she squealed. 'He's breaking in.'

'Shit. I'm on my way. Call the cops.'

278

The door was opening. Bea dropped her phone and grabbed a knife from the kitchen drawer.

'Out!' she yelled at Goldie and ushered the dog into the hall, aware of someone entering the kitchen. She followed Goldie and tried to slam the hall door shut, but it wouldn't close; the intruder had put his foot in the way, and Bea could feel his weight pressing against the other side. She grunted with the effort of holding her ground.

'Bea? What's going on?' Bea couldn't look over her shoulder, but could picture Queenie leaning over the banister.

'Call the police, Mum!'

'No!' shouted the man on the other side of the door. 'If you call the police, I'll kill you.'

He seemed to find a surge of energy as he shouldered the gap wider. Bea yelped again and Goldie barked louder.

'Mum! Call them! He's going to kill us anyway!'

Her slippers slid on the parquet as the intruder rammed his shoulder into the door. She tried to recover her position, but it was too late. He was through. The force of the door knocked her over. As she tried to slither back onto her feet she got a proper view of him. It was Eddie, all right, and there was a cold, grey steeliness in his eyes that made her throat constrict.

He dived at her and squeezed the wrist of the hand that held the knife. His thumb dug into soft flesh. It was excruciating. Bea dropped the knife and watched in despair as it clattered onto the floor.

Now Eddie caught her under her arms and hauled her onto her feet. She felt something against her throat. The 'something' dug in, the blade of a knife pressing into her skin.

'I've got one too,' he said, his mouth close to her ear. 'Shouldn't carry one if you're not prepared to use it. Where's your mum?'

'Upstairs.'

'Tell her to put the phone down.'

'Mum!' Bea shouted, hoping desperately that Queenie had already made the call. She looked up. Queenie emerged from the bedroom with the cordless phone in her hand, held up to her ear. 'Put the phone down, Mum.'

Queenie gasped when she saw Bea and her attacker.

'Throw it down here!' Eddie shouted. 'Do it!'

Queenie reached over the banister and dropped the receiver. Part of its plastic cover broke off as it landed on the floor and skittered across the parquet.

Bea couldn't bear to look at her mum's terrified face. 'It's all right, Mum,' she said. 'Everything's going to be all right.'

'Get in your room, close the door and stay there!' Eddie barked.

'No. I'm not leaving Bea,' Queenie said.

'I just want a word with her,' said Eddie. 'Do what I say and no one will get hurt.'

'Mum, it's okay. I'll come and find you when it's all over.'

'Bea—?'

Eddie jabbed the knife into Bea's throat. She winced. 'Do it, Mum. Please.'

Reluctantly, Queenie backed away into her room. She closed the door but Bea could see there was a little gap left open. Whatever happened next, Queenie would be able to hear. Illogically, this bothered Bea more than the thought of whatever violence was to come. She couldn't bear the thought of Queenie listening to her being beaten or stabbed or raped. I can't let this happen, she thought. I can't let this man ruin our lives.

'What do you want?' she said, her words rasping against the pressure at her neck.

'I want to know that you will keep quiet,' he said.

They were still in the hall, locked together in a bizarre, horribly intimate way.

'Okay,' said Bea, 'let's just sit down and talk about it.'

He relaxed his grip a little and pushed her into the lounge, walking close behind, like a ghastly three-legged race, except they were linked not by a scarf round their legs, but the knife at her throat.

'Sit down,' he said. Bea felt the pressure release from her neck. She sank onto the sofa, while Eddie sat opposite her, the knife now pointed at her, no longer touching.

'You think you're so clever, don't you? Investigating. Poking your nose into other people's business.'

'I'm sorry. This is all a mistake,' said Bea. 'It was the cats. That's what I was investigating. I had no idea it was fighting.'

'Perfectly *legal* fighting.'

'Yes. Okay. Perfectly legal fighting. I only rang 999 because I thought Tank was dying. I still don't know how he is.'

'We had that under control. Besides, he knew what he was getting into.'

'Did he? When I saw him in the ring, he looked terrified.'

'It was a fight. People get hurt. It comes with the territory.'

'Well, he's in hospital now, so that's all right, isn't it? There's no need for you to be here.'

'Now you've got the dog back, I need to you to promise, swear to me, that you'll keep quiet.'

'What about? The police know about the fight. I won't say anything about the dog – I just wanted her back, that's all.'

What else? Bea thought. What was he really worried about? And then the penny started to drop. 'The pub,' she said. 'The Wagon and Horses. I didn't think you'd seen me, but you had.'

There was a flicker behind his eyes, and she knew she'd hit a bullseye. But even so, she thought, supplying drugs was bad, but was it enough to threaten her like this? There was something...something else. Think, she urged herself. Think harder. Think quicker.

'Yes,' said Eddie. 'The pub. I need you to tell me that that never happened, that you never saw me, that I wasn't there.'

'Okay,' she said. 'I promise. I didn't see you. You weren't there.' She was running through the chain of events in her head. Eddie had supplied drugs to Tank and Ken. Ketamine. Where had she heard about ketamine recently? Ketamine. The body on the bypass. Oh my God. It still wasn't crystal clear, but she had a horrible, sickening feeling she was sitting opposite a murderer, and that no words, no promises from her, would keep her safe.

Maybe she could keep him talking long enough for Ant to get here. Maybe, if she couldn't, she could at least make him face the truth.

'The stuff you bought in the pub, you gave it to Ant's little brother. You gave it to Tank. And you gave it to that poor lad by the bypass too.'

Eddie shifted in his seat. He was gripping the knife, but he was listening too.

'He was another fighter, wasn't he? Someone else you were "helping". Except that he overdosed and to cover it up, you tipped him off the bridge to make it look like suicide.'

He was clutching the handle of the knife so tightly, his knuckles were white, and he was staring at the ground.

'I'm right, aren't I?' Bea said, and now he looked at her, and there was a coldness in his eyes, a chilling blankness. And she knew that it was all over. There was no more time to be bought. He was going to kill her.

She started to stand up, to make a run for the door. Eddie lunged forward, thrusting the knife towards her. Bea screamed at the same time as Goldie issued a throaty growl that was almost a roar. The noise made Eddie look down and as the dog sprang up towards his face, he slashed at her throat.

'Nooo!'

In a blind rage, Bea grabbed the nearest object – a large china dog, one of a pair on the mantelpiece – and launched herself across the room. She smashed the ornament onto the back of Eddie's head. He tipped forward and fell on top of the dog.

'Get *off* her, you fucker!' Bea shouted and hauled him over to one side. He didn't react – no sound, no movement, his body limp in her hands. Confident he wasn't about to attack her, Bea turned her attention to Goldie. Blood was seeping through her fur from the wound at her neck. She was grizzling quietly.

'It's all right,' Bea soothed. 'It's going to be all right.' But she wasn't at all sure it was. There was a lot of blood. It was all over her hands now and leaking onto their beige carpet.

'Is he dead?' Queenie was standing in the doorway.

'I don't know. I don't care. He stabbed Goldie, slit her throat.'

'Oh my God, no! Bea, what are we going to do?'

'Ring the vet. We need to get her seen as soon as we can.'

Bea held her hands to Goldie's neck, not knowing if she should try and press the wound in some way to stop the bleeding or if that would just hurt the dog more. She shifted a little where she was kneeling, eased Goldie's head onto her lap and gently stroked her body.

'It's all right,' she said. 'There's a good girl.'

'I'll ring the vet and get some towels,' said Queenie, but her hands were shaking and she could barely dial.

Eddie was still out cold on the carpet next to Bea. He seemed to be breathing, but to be honest, Bea didn't care if he was or not. Shards of pottery littered the floor around him.

'Mum?' she said. 'I'm sorry about the pot dog.' Tears welled up now as she struggled to speak. 'I know it was special...'

'Don't worry about it now.' She left the room and when she came back, she put a folded towel under Goldie's head on Bea's lap. 'How's she doing?'

They both looked at Goldie. She was quiet now. Her eyes were closing. Bea could feel where the dog's blood had soaked through her dressing gown and pyjamas.

There was a sound outside, someone hammering on the front door, then the side gate banging against the wall of the house. Moments later, Ant burst into the room.

'Bea! Are you all right? Jesus, you're covered in blood! What the fuck happened here? Have you killed him?' He was wild-eyed and hyperventilating. Bea reckoned he was about to keel over.

'It's all right, Ant. Sit down for a minute. We're all right, but the dog's not.'

Ant was clutching onto the back of the sofa, chest heaving. 'He was round ours, looking for her. Broke the lock on the garage. What a lowlife. Have you . . . did you . . . kill him?'

At that moment, Eddie groaned a little and moved his head from side to side.

'He's alive,' said Bea. 'But he doesn't deserve to be. Ant, don't let him get up. Sit on him or something.'

'Got it. Should I look at Goldie, though?'

Bea shook her head. 'I don't think there's much you can do. We just need to get her to a vet. We need someone with a car.'

Ant sank down onto Eddie's legs.

'I've rung Bob,' said Queenie. 'But the vet should be here soon.'

The sirens were getting louder now. Soon the house was full of people in uniform; paramedics, Tom and Shaz, and the on-call vet, who happened to be Xiao. Bob turned up too, with Dot in tow.

'Dot? What are you doing here?' said Bea.

'I had to come,' she said. 'I was so worried about you all.'

'Coming through!' They all looked towards the door to the lounge now. Xiao, grim-faced, was carrying one end of Goldie, wrapped up in a blanket. Shaz held the other end. They all gasped.

'Is she going to be all right?' said Bea.

Xiao carried on walking. 'She needs stitching up, but she was lucky. He didn't manage to cut a main blood vessel, just a lot of superficial ones in the skin. I'll take her up to the hospital and stitch her up tonight. She'll probably be able to come home tomorrow.'

The next one to be carted out was Eddie, carried on a stretcher by the paramedics, with Tom trailing in their wake.

'I'm going to need quick statements from you all in a minute,' said Tom. He had grey rings under his eyes.

'I'll make some tea,' said Queenie.

'So, Dot,' said Bea, 'how did you get here so quickly?' As she said it, the penny dropped. Bob had obviously gone straight round to Dot's after he'd been kicked out by Queenie. Jeez, the cheek of the man! Bea hoped her mum wouldn't put two and two together, but, of course, she did.

'It was nice of you to come,' she said, managing to imply the exact opposite with her icy tone.

'Thanks, Maggie. I'm glad you're okay. I nearly had kittens when Bob got your call. What a nightmare. We had to come and help, didn't we, Bob?'

Bea winced at the word 'we'. Not now, she thought. I can't bear any more blood on the floor.

'Um, yes,' said Bob. He at least had the grace to look uneasy. They were all crammed into the kitchen, Bob sand-wiched between Dot and Queenie.

'I'm surprised you were over at Dot's,' said Queenie. 'Don't you have a home to go to any more?'

285

'Oh, he sometimes stays over,' said Dot. 'Don't you, Bob?'

'Um, yes,' he said again. He looked like he wanted to disappear, but he was a large man and in this small space, caught in a pincer action by the two women in his life, there was nowhere to go.

'He stays over, does he?' said Queenie. 'Interesting. He was after a "sleepover" here tonight, as it happens, but I said no.'

Bea wanted to hold her hands to her ears and sing loudly, but what she'd heard could never be unheard.

Dot's face seemed to sag. 'Was he?' The lines at the side of her mouth became more pronounced and she screwed up her eyes. 'So I was second best? Is that right, Bob? Am I your Plan B?'

He opened his mouth and shut it again.

'Well?' said Dot.

'Well?' said Queenie.

They both looked at him. Ant was staring, too, open-mouthed. Bea didn't know where to look or what to do with herself.

'I think we should get out of the way, Dot,' said Bob. 'Shall I give you a lift home?'

The tension in the room twitched up a notch or two, as Dot and Queenie exchanged looks.

'No, that's all right, Bob,' said Dot. 'I'll stay here for a while, help with the teas and that, then get a taxi home. If that's all right, Maggie?'

'Yes,' said Queenie. 'I'd like you to stay.'

In fact, they both made tea and sandwiches, while Bea spoke with Tom at the kitchen table. She refused to go into the lounge, couldn't face seeing the patch of blood where Goldie had been. She wearily answered his questions, keeping half an ear on her mum and Dot as they pottered about.

'Reckon I'll need a new carpet after all this,' said Queenie.

'You could ask Bob to help pick a colour scheme,' said Dot.

Queenie laughed. 'Not in a million years, Dot. Honestly, I didn't realise you were a couple. I'm sorry if I got in the way.'

'Oh, we weren't. We're not. I thought that maybe . . .but I can see now. We're just friends.' Bea looked up and caught Dot winking at Queenie. 'Friends with benefits.'

They both started giggling. Ant stood in the corner, wolfing down sandwiches as fast as they could make them, and saying nothing. It was his turn next with Tom. Bea got up from the table, making room for him to sit down.

'I'm going to have a shower and go to bed,' she said.

'All right,' said Ant. 'I'll get home to Ken when I've done this. I'll give you a ring tomorrow, yeah?'

'Yeah, okay.'

'I'd give you a hug, but you're a bit bloody.'

Bea looked down at her dressing gown. 'Oh God.' She started to feel faint.

'Bea?'

'I'm all right. I'm just . . .'

He put one arm round her, held her up. 'It's all right. You did really well.'

Bea had a strange urge to snuggle up close to him, let him wrap her up in his arms. I'm tired, she thought. Must go to bed. 'It's been the longest day ever,' she said.

'Go on. Up you go,' said Queenie.

'Do you need some help up the stairs?' said Ant.

'No, I'll be okay.'

He took his arm away and she stumbled out of the kitchen on wobbly legs.

Later, when everyone had gone home and Bea was tucked up in bed, Queenie looked in on her. She perched on the side of the bed and Bea felt herself tipping sideways as her body dented the mattress.

'I'm so sorry about the pot dog, Mum,' said Bea.

Queenie stroked Bea's forehead like she'd done when she was a little girl. 'It's all right.'

'It isn't, though, is it? Dad bought them, didn't he?'

'Yes. He bought them the first Christmas we were in this house. It was sort of ironic – they were old-fashioned even then. I remember my grandma having some on her mantelpiece. God knows what happened to them.'

'I'm so, so sorry.'

'No, darling, don't be. I've still got the other one and besides, I think it was Dad looking after us tonight. You stopped that bastard in his tracks – you and Dad together.'

Bea smiled. 'Yeah. We did.' She paused. 'What would you have done if I'd killed him?'

Queenie didn't need to think about it. 'I'd have helped you bury the body,' she said in a matter-of-fact sort of way.

Bea looked at her. 'I fucking love you, Mum.'

'Language, Bea.' She leaned forward and kissed her forehead. 'I love you too, baby girl.'

42

At six thirty the next morning, with Arthur curled up beside her on the bed, Bea was scrolling through her photos when her phone gave a shiver in her hand and started to ring. The screen showed that it was Ant.

'You awake?'

She was surprised how pleased she was to hear his voice. 'Yeah.'

'What's going on?' he said.

'Just thinking about everything. Worrying about the dog. Wondering what's happened to Tank. All that stuff. And the cats as well. I thought it was all over last night, but it isn't, is it?'

'Yeah, I've been thinking about that too. Unless Tank's the cat killer, which he might be.'

'In which case the moggies of Kingsleigh are safe again, but if he isn't, then there's still some sicko out there. Either way, I promised Anna I'd find out who it was, and I haven't done it.'

'Do you want to sort it out now, Bea?' he said, and despite her weariness, her spirits gave a little flutter.

'Yes. Yes, I do,' she said.

'I'll grab my bike and come up to yours. See you in ten, yeah?'

Bea walked quickly through the living room, trying hard not to look at the patch of blood on the carpet. She swigged some orange juice straight from the carton and grabbed a couple of digestive biscuits from the tin, then went to meet Ant.

Outside, she could see him pedalling across the rec towards her. She leaned against her front wall and ate one of the biscuits. The milk float whined its way along the road, and the milkman waved at her. She raised her hand in reply, as Ant bumped off the kerb and cycled over to her.

'Breakfast?' she said, holding out the second digestive. Ant's face brightened at once.

'Cheers,' he said. He crammed the biscuit in whole.

'So, the mystery of the missing cats,' Bea said. 'We haven't quite got to the bottom of it, but we know what to do, don't we?'

Ant nodded, still picking bits of biscuit out of his teeth with his tongue. 'We need to find Dean. I want a word with him anyway.'

'So, Eileen's?'

'Yeah. Don't think she'll be pleased to see us, but safety in numbers.'

They started walking through Bea's estate, following in the wake of the milk float.

'So, are you okay after last night?' said Ant.

'I think so. I'll be better when I've rung the vet, and I know that Goldie's okay.'

'It was proper carnage when I got there, Bea. Bloody hell.'

'Your Ken was right. Eddie is a nasty piece of work.'

'Yeah. The thing is, I worked out it was him, what he'd done, as I was heading over to yours after you'd rung. Ayesha had seen him, seen his car, it had a rear brake light missing. And when we were following him away from the farm last night, there it was, or, rather, wasn't. It should've clicked then. If it had, you and your mum wouldn't have had to go through that. Goldie wouldn't—'

'It's all right, Ant. It was all right in the end, wasn't it?'

'Mm.'

They were nearly at Eileen's house now.

'How are we going to play this?' said Ant.

'I don't know. Whatever we do, it'll be wrong. We'll just have to go for it.'

Eileen's house was bigger than Bea expected, semi-detached and on a corner plot with garden on three sides. 'Okay, here goes.'

They walked up to the front door and knocked, setting off a volley of barking from inside.

'Oh God, I'd forgotten about the dog,' said Bea.

There was no human response, so Bea tried knocking again. This time she clearly heard Eileen's dulcet tones coming from upstairs.

'For fuck's sake, Tyson. Shut the fuck up!'

'She's awake, then,' said Ant, with a nervous grin.

A window opened above them and Eileen peered down. She didn't seem pleased to see them, although, to be honest, the screwed-up eyes within her crumpled face seemed to be having trouble making much sense of anything.

'What the hell do you two want?' she said when she finally focused on them.

'Morning, Eileen!' Bea called as brightly as she could manage. 'Is Dean in?'

'What's it got to do with you? I have to be polite to you at work, but this is my home. Go on, clear off.'

'Eileen, we think he's in trouble. We want to help him.'

'Trouble? Ach, this is no good. I'm coming down.' She slammed the window shut, and a minute or two later the front door opened. Eileen was there, in a shiny dressing gown, stooping down and holding onto Tyson's studded collar. The dog was straining to get away, lunging towards Ant and Bea. A string of drool stretched out of his mouth, detached itself and landed on Eileen's doormat.

'Is he here, Eileen? Can we talk to him?' said Bea.

'No, he's not.'

'Can you tell us where he is? We want to help.'

'You've had my house searched twice, Bea. I don't need your sort of help. Just go, or I'll set the dog on you.'

Bea looked at Ant nervously.

'Eileen,' Ant said, 'I know we don't see eye to eye, but this is important. We know that Dean got mixed up in all sorts of stuff, and we need to talk to him.'

'All right,' Eileen said, 'you asked for this.'

She let go of Tyson's collar. The dog shot forward, like he'd been fired from a cannon. Bea squealed and recoiled backwards. She put her hands up to her face and half-closed her eyes, like she did when she was watching a scary movie – she'd seen enough blood yesterday to last a lifetime.

The dog made a beeline for Ant, who was trying not to flinch. He stood apparently calm and relaxed, his hands by his sides. The dog launched itself at him and put its two front paws on his legs reaching up towards him, tail wagging ten to the dozen.

'Hello, there,' said Ant. He slowly moved one hand and gently stroked the dog's shoulder. The tail wagged even faster. Ant moved his other hand and gave the dog a gentle ear rub. The dog twisted its head and licked Ant's hand, covering it, very efficiently, in a layer of drool.

'Nice doggie, aren't you?' said Ant. He crouched down and the dog started licking his face. 'Eileen, just tell us where Dean is. We'll try and make things better.'

Eileen sighed. 'He's at the hospital. He's been there all night, waiting for news about Tank.'

'He's still there now?'

Eileen nodded.

'Okay, thanks.'

'Don't go pestering him, though. He's very upset. He's sensitive, is my Dean.' She stepped forward and grabbed Tyson's collar. 'Come in, you silly dog. Come inside.' She hauled the dog in and closed the door.

'What time's the first bus?' said Ant.

'God knows. It's Sunday, so it's anyone's guess. Hang on.' Bea searched on her phone. 'There is one, but it's not for forty-five minutes.'

'Taxi?'

'Did you rob that bank after all?'

'Nope. How about Bob? He'll have some time on his hands this morning, won't he?'

Bea looked at Ant doubtfully. 'It's a bit early.'

'Worth a try. Give him a ring.'

They found Dean in the Intensive Care waiting room. It was a surprisingly small, dilapidated area, with wipe-clean chairs lining opposite walls and a TV set at one end that looked like it had never actually worked. Dean was sitting on his own, leaning forward, resting his head on his knees. He was a weaselly kind of guy anyway, but now he looked smaller, pathetic somehow.

'Dean,' Bea said, and at the sound of his name he jerked awake and sat up quickly. He looked at them, framed in the doorway, but it took a while for him to register who they were.

'What are you doing here?' he said.

Ant and Bea walked into the room and sat down opposite him.

'We came to find out how Tank is,' said Ant, which was half-true.

'They won't let me in. I'm not family, see. His mum and

293

dad are in there. They only let you in out of visiting hours if things are really bad.'

'I'm so sorry, Dean.' Bea reached forward and put one of her hands on top of his. He twitched a little, surprised at the contact, but he didn't move his hands away.

Bea could still remember the things he'd done to her in the past – spitting at her, trying to frighten her mum, threatening her – and they mattered, they really did. But right now, at this moment, he seemed broken.

'Dean,' she said gently, 'Eddie's been arrested. He attacked me at home, hurt Goldie too.'

'He's a nutter, that one. Tank and me, we didn't realise what we're were getting involved in.'

'He killed the lad that was found by the bypass. Did you know about that?'

Dean hung his head a bit lower. 'I didn't know. I thought something had gone on, though. He – Stan – was meant to be Tank's opponent last night. That old bloke they brought in at the last minute, he was a fucking animal. Didn't stop when Tank was obviously in trouble.'

'Well, it's all over now. And Tank's getting the best possible care.'

The words seemed to wash over Dean. He derived no comfort from them.

'There's one thing, though, Dean,' Bea said. 'One thing I've got to know.' He didn't respond, but Bea ploughed on anyway. 'Did you hurt the cats?'

Dean glanced quickly up at her and then back down again. He licked his lips. 'No,' he said, but there was something about the way he said it.

'But you know who did,' she said.

Dean hung his head lower. 'Yes,' he said. 'I know who killed the cats.'

43

'Dean, you've gotta tell us. Tell us what you know, and we'll try and help.'

'I promised that I wouldn't.'

Ant and Bea exchanged glances.

'Promised who?' said Ant.

'I can't tell you or that'd be telling.'

'What if the person you promised is in hospital,' said Bea, and Dean's eyes flicked up to meet hers and then flicked away again, and she knew she scored a bullseye.

'It's Tank, isn't it? I saw you, remember? With the white cat.'

'You've got it wrong.' It was almost refreshing to hear a flash of his trademark antagonism back again. 'We weren't hurting that cat. We were saving it. We got it antibiotics and everything, painkillers. We saved as many as we could.'

This made sense to Bea. Arthur, as she still liked to think of him, had been healing up nicely when she and Ant rescued him.

'Saved them from who?'

Dean looked down at the ground. He seemed to be wrestling with his conscience, which was a surprise to Bea, as she didn't think he had one.

'Saved them from who, Dean?' she repeated.

'Tank told you it was his grandad's cat. It wasn't. His grandad had stolen it. Sometimes he kills them. Sometimes he just hurts them.'

'Holy crap,' Ant said under his breath.

Bea shivered. 'Why?'

'He's always hated 'em on his garden. Used to get Tank to sit there and chase them away with water pistols, even air rifles. He tried all sorts, apparently. He got this electronic scarer. He even bought some lion poo on the internet. Mind you, Tank said he thought it was just any old poo. Someone was ripping him off.'

'It's a bit of jump from scaring them away to killing them,' said Ant. 'That's twisted stuff.'

'I know. He just flipped about three weeks ago. He's been like weird, too, shouting in the house and talking to himself. Tank's mum's been trying to get him to the doctor's but he won't go. He's been so odd, they haven't even told him about Tank yet. Didn't think he'd understand.'

'Blimey,' said Bea.

'He's definitely not right in the head. He's obsessed. His house is like Fort Knox. He's got cameras everywhere and bits of string all over the place outside.'

'String? Oh,' said Bea, 'I know where he lives. He's next door to Mrs McKey, isn't he?'

'The lady with the white cat? Yeah. He nabbed any cat that came into his garden, but he also …collected them on his rounds.'

'The West Country's oldest paper boy,' said Bea. 'God, I feel sick. I've seen him out and about, not just on a Thursday when the *Bugle* comes out.'

'Everyone has,' said Dean. 'He can walk anywhere he likes with that trolley and people don't take any notice. Or they wave at him.'

'The trolley,' said Bea.

'That's where we found the two dead ones. The grey one and the tabby. He'd killed them and stuffed them in his *Bugle* bag.'

'But, Dean, this is horrific,' said Bea. 'If you knew, why didn't you tell someone? You could have done it anonymously.'

'Tank was trying to keep a lid on it. It's his grandad, after all. He'd go there every day and check up on him. Rescue any cats that were still alive. Get rid of the bodies of the ones that weren't.'

'So it was Tank that kept dumping dead cats at Costsave? Who put the head on my front doorstep?'

Dean looked down at the floor again. 'No,' he said, quietly. 'That was me.'

'You absolute bellend,' said Ant.

'I know. I'm sorry. I liked my job at Costsave, though. I was gutted to lose it.'

'You can't keep blaming me,' said Bea. 'You lost that job all on your own. Anyway, your *mum* works there.'

'So?'

'All right, all right,' said Ant. 'Let's not go over all that again. What are we going to do now? We can't just let the old guy carry on.'

'They'll lock him up, won't they?' said Dean.

'Yes, if there's any justice,' said Bea. 'Or maybe they'll give him some help, if that's what he needs. If he's really ill.'

'Yeah. Yeah, that'd be good. To be honest, I don't think we could have kept covering for him any longer. It's too much.' He sagged a little further in his chair. 'Do you think they'll lock me up too?'

'I don't know, Dean.'

'I get that you'll have to tell someone about Mr Sherman, but can we keep me and Tank out of it?'

Ant looked at Bea. This was their chance to get revenge on

Dean, for all the shit he'd put them through. Revenge could be sweet, thought Bea, and yet it would also fuel the fire. This feud could go on and on for years, making things uncomfortable for everyone. She wanted to feel at ease at home with Queenie and walking about Kingsleigh. She didn't want to be looking over her shoulder. She didn't want enemies.

'If you swear you didn't hurt any of those animals . . .' she said.

'Oh, come on, Bea!' Ant howled.

'On my life, I swear I didn't . . .' Dean pleaded.

' . . .then perhaps we can just tip them off about Tank's grandad and leave it at that.'

'Really, Bea?' said Ant.

Bea looked at him steadily. 'Really, the important thing, the thing that matters, is stopping the killing. We all make mistakes, right? But we all need a chance to start again. Do things better this time.'

Ant sighed heavily. Bea had given him a second chance on his very first day at Costsave, the opportunity to do the right thing. She wondered if he was remembering that right now, if he was big enough to give someone else that chance.

Dean was staring at her, his mouth half-open. Bea tried to read his face, but it was difficult to tell if it was incredulity or respect. Maybe it was both.

'Thanks, Bea,' Dean said. 'I really appreciate that. I'll owe you one.'

'No,' said Bea firmly. 'Clean slate, Dean. I won't owe you. You won't owe me. Let's just start again.'

'Sounds good to me. And I'm sorry. Sorry for the stuff I've done in the past. Your mum and everything. I would never have hurt her.'

Bea held her hands up. 'Let's just forget about it. New Year, new start.' She got to her feet. Ant followed suit.

'Are you going to stay here?' Bea asked Dean.

'Yeah. I need to know how he is. I'll stay as long as ...oh.'

There were footsteps in the corridor. They all looked towards the door, as a very weary-looking couple walked in, a tall, stringy man with a bald head and an untidy beard, and a woman, much shorter than him, but stocky and muscular. When she looked into the room towards Dean, Bea could see the family resemblance instantly – she was definitely Tank's mum and the Newspaper Boy's daughter.

'We'll go,' said Bea. 'Leave you to it.'

But the couple were blocking the doorway and it seemed too rude to ask them to move.

'How is he?' said Dean, standing up now.

Bea tried to read their faces but all she could see was exhaustion.

'He's on a ventilator, but he's stable,' said the woman. 'The doctor just said we should go home and rest.'

'Is he going to be okay?'

'It's too early to say, Dean, but he'll be all right for a few hours. Do you want a lift back to Kingsleigh?'

They all shambled out of the waiting room and headed for the car park. Bob-on-Meat was waiting for Ant and Bea in his estate car. He'd told them he could hang on for twenty minutes and Ant and Bea were both pleased to see him still there.

'All right?' he said, as they climbed in.

'Well, yes and no. Tank's still in intensive care, but we've found out who the cat killer is.'

'Really?'

'Yeah, trouble is it's Tank's grandad. As if his family aren't suffering enough.'

'Did you tell them?' said Bob, looking towards Dean and Tank's parents walking slowly across the car park.

'No. We'll have to tell the police, though. Let them deal with it. I'll do it from home. Are you heading into Costsave now, Bob?'

'Yup. No rest for the wicked.'

It was just one of those sayings, but Bea couldn't help thinking that she'd seen a slightly wicked side to Bob recently – or at least a mischievous one. You never knew with people, did you?

44

Bob dropped them both off outside Bea's house.

'I won't come in, for obvious reasons,' he said. 'Anyway, the sausage machine is calling me. See you tomorrow?'

'Yeah, see you, Bob. And thanks!'

'You putting the kettle on?' said Ant.

'Yes, okay. I'll just ring the police.'

She rang Tom's number. He picked up straight away and she put him on speakerphone.

'Bea! Thought you'd be having a lie-in. You deserve one.'

'I know who the cat killer is, Tom. I can't tell you how I know, but it's a man called Fraser Sherman. He lives in Victoria Terrace. I'm a hundred per cent certain it's him. You need to get round there. Sounds like he's a sick man, in every sense.'

'Whoa, whoa, whoa. Hang on a minute. Where've you got this from?'

'I can't tell you. This will have to be an anonymous tip-off.'

'Okay, let me write the name down. I'm up to my eyes in the bypass case today, Bea, but I'll put it in the duty log and we'll see if someone else can call round. Might be later in the week, though.'

'Tom, this is urgent. What if he kills more cats between now and then?'

'Bea, calm down, okay? Seriously, you've been through a lot. Let us deal with this. Really. Put your feet up. Watch a nice film or something. Chill out, okay?'

When she'd rung off, she looked at Ant and raised her eyebrows. He held both his hands up. 'I know what you're thinking, Bea, but shouldn't we just do what he says? Leave it to them?'

'I promised Anna.'

'Yes, and you've kept that promise.'

'I don't know what I'd do if another cat was killed, though. He's not gonna stop unless someone stops him, is he?'

Ant sighed. 'We'd better do this, then, hadn't we?'

They walked across the rec and were soon at the little row of houses.

'Should we just, like, knock on the door?' said Bea.

''S'pose so.'

As they walked up to the front of the house, Bea was aware of the CCTV camera moving on its hinge. They were observed. There was no obvious door knocker or bell, so she rattled the letter box. After a short while, the door opened. Close to, it was obvious where Tank got his genes from. Bea mentally kicked herself for not seeing the resemblance earlier. He was only wearing a vest and jogging bottoms, and Bea could see his blurry tattoos spreading up both arms and across his chest.

'Yes?' he said, in a voice so rough it could have grated cheese.

'Excuse me, um, hello. We're, um, friends of your grandson and he asked us to . . .help him. With the cats.'

Mr Sherman stared at her, waiting for her to stop talking. There was an awkward silence, then he said, 'Where is he? Where's Finlay?'

Shit, thought Bea. 'He can't be here this morning, so he wanted us to just check in with you.'

'I'm fine. I don't need any help.' He shoved the door closed, and Bea could hear the sound of a bolt being slid into place.

'Great,' said Ant. 'Now what?'

'I think we should look round the back,' said Bea. 'That's where he parks his trolley.'

'Honestly? Do you think we should maybe just leave it?'

'No, come on, Ant. We're here now.'

They walked along the row of houses and followed the path round to the back, then stood looking into Mr Sherman's backyard. Sure enough, the trolley was parked by the tool store, leaning against the back wall of the house. Bea's stomach lurched uncomfortably at the thought of what it might contain, but she knew she had to look.

'Okay, I'm going in,' she said. She started to clamber over the waist-high fence when Ant grabbed her arm.

'Bea! Stop!'

'What is it?'

He was pointing towards the house. There was another camera, looking at the two of them, but that wasn't what was bothering Ant. One of the upstairs sash windows was open a fraction and there was something poking out of it. Bea gasped when she realised she was looking at the barrel of a gun – a gun that was aimed at her.

'Get down!' shouted Ant. He grabbed her shoulders and pushed her towards the ground. They both crouched down, wide-eyed, breathing fast.

'Not one of your better ideas,' said Ant. 'Ring the cops again. Do 999 this time.'

But as Bea reached into her pocket for her phone, they both heard the roar of a car engine and the squeal of brakes. Then, quite clearly, there was someone rapping on the front door and shouting, 'Police! Open up!'

The gun was withdrawn from the window.

'It's Tom!' said Bea. 'He's gonna get himself shot!'

'Okay, stay here,' said Ant. He crawled along the fence line and then ran around the side of the end house. Bea could hear him shouting, 'Tom! Careful, he's got a gun!' and then a series of noises – pops, or cracks. They didn't sound loud enough to be gunshots, but Bea was pretty sure that's what they were.

'Oh my God,' she gasped, and she, too, scuttled around the building. 'Please let them be all right. Please—'

Ant was kneeling on the ground, peering around the corner of the fence.

'I think he winged him,' he said.

'What?'

'Stay back, Bea. I'm going round.'

Before Bea could remonstrate with him, Ant was crawling on his hands and knees along the pavement at the front of the row. There was another volley of fire, and then Ant reappeared with Tom crawling behind him. They both joined Bea, sitting on the ground, with their backs against the fence. Tom was clutching his shoulder.

'He got me!' Tom wailed. 'Am I bleeding? Am I going to die?'

'Let's have a look,' said Bea. She helped him out of his jacket. There was a tear in the material, but underneath there was no blood, just a little red mark on Tom's skin when she looked inside his shirt.

'Hang on,' said Bea. She dug a long, red nail into the hole in Tom's jacket and levered a small pellet out of the wadding inside.

'Air rifle,' said Ant. 'I used to have one of them. Proper laugh.'

'I'm not laughing,' said Tom, and got on his radio and called for help. 'They'll be here in a few minutes. They don't mess around when it's firearms.'

While they waited, Bea said, 'Why are you even here, Tom? Thought this was a low priority.'

'Yes, but I guessed that you'd be daft enough to come here. Thought you might need some help. I know you, Bea.'

'Looks like you do,' she said, and just for a moment, she thought there was a little charge of electricity in the air, a connection.

When a whole squad of vans turned up with heavily armed cops in flak jackets and head protectors, Bea wondered if she was about to be in the middle of a siege, but Mr Sherman simply opened the door and came out with his arms up when instructed to. He was searched, handcuffed and bundled away in a matter of minutes, and then the officers swarmed through the house.

'I think the cats, if there are any, are round the back, in his trolley,' said Bea to Tom.

'Let's have a look, then,' he said.

They went to the back of the house. Tom put gloves on and then opened the vinyl flap at the top of the trolley. He pulled a face and Bea held her breath. 'Doesn't smell very nice, but there's nothing in here.'

Bea breathed again, but now there was a noise, high-pitched and unmistakeably feline coming from somewhere close.

'The tool store,' said Bea. 'Can you open it?'

It was padlocked, but Tom found an iron bar nearby and bashed the lock away. He opened one of the doors and there, peering out, was a large ginger cat. Beside it cowered a smaller, black one, and there were two more when the second door was opened.

Bea felt a wave of relief wash over her.

'Well done, Bea,' Tom said, as he handed her a cat to hold. 'Well done.'

'It *is* over now, isn't it?' she said, her bottom lip starting to tremble.

'Hope so,' said Ant. 'Being mates with you is fucking exhausting.'

Tom gave a sharp laugh and handed him another cat.

Tears were trickling down Bea's face now, and she snuggled her cat closer and nuzzled the top of its head with her chin. 'It's all right now,' she murmured. 'Everything's all right.'

45

'I've gone into the import-export business,' said Ant, later that afternoon. He and Bea were watching Goldie potter round Bea's back garden. She was still a bit too woozy to go for a proper walk.

'Socks, is it? Like Saggy?' said Bea.

Ant grinned. 'Nah. Anti-social boys. I put Ken on the bus to Cardiff half an hour ago. I'm exporting him to Wales.'

'Shouldn't you have gone with him to make sure he gets there?'

'Yeah, I should really, but I just wanted some time off, chill out a bit. If we hear reports on the news of a load of broken windows in Bristol, or moped thefts in Newport, we'll know he got off the bus early.' He leaned against the back wall of the house and lit a cigarette.

'So, are you going to be following him?' said Bea. 'Are you moving to Cardiff too?'

He tipped his head back and blew a long stream of smoke out of his pursed lips. 'No. Mum wants us to all start again over there, but I told her this morning. I've made up my mind. Whatever she does, I'm staying here.'

Bea felt a little surge of pleasure. She hadn't realised how much she wanted him to stay. 'That's great, Ant. What made you decide?'

'It's just, you know, I've got a job, I've got mates, I've got—'

Bea had a strong inkling that he was going to say 'you', but at that moment his phone rang. He turned away slightly, and Bea discreetly walked up the garden path to where Goldie was sniffing about the empty flowerbeds. Even so, she could hear his half of the conversation.

'Yeah, I know ...I'm sorry, Ayesha ... It all got a bit hairy ... I'll see you later, though. Yeah? ... Shall I come and meet you there? ... Yeah, me too.' He caught Bea up.

'So, you've got a job, mates and ...Ayesha. How's that going?' said Bea.

'Yeah. Good. She's great.'

Not quite the ringing endorsement Bea would have expected at the start of a relationship.

'She's not very impressed at spending Saturday night on her own, but I'll explain it all to her when I see her later. She's going down to the cop shop to make a statement about what she saw on New Year's Eve. I'll meet her when she's done,' he said, rubbing his hands together, 'I'm a lucky boy. So what about you and Jay?'

Bea screwed up her face. 'I dunno. I can't even think about it. I just feel washed out today. He rang up today, wanted to come round, but I was too tired to explain about everything.'

'Not surprised, mate. But you like him, don't you? You should go for it, when you're feeling better.'

'Maybe. I do like him. He's different.'

Ant laughed. 'You can say that again. He's gotta be better than Robocop, hasn't he? Bea?'

'Anyway, I took Arthur back to Mrs McKey this morning,' said Bea, happy to change the subject. 'She was very pleased to see him. He'll be able to prowl about in safety now.'

'If I was him,' said Ant, 'I'd take a long crap on next door's lawn.'

'He probably will. If she ever lets him out of the house again.'

'And you fetched this doggo back.' Ant looked at Goldie, who was inspecting a patch of grass near the garden shed.

'Yeah. Bob took us in his lunch hour. He brought Mum a bunch of Costsave tulips, too, but I don't think it'll do him much good. Things were definitely frosty in the car.'

'Ouch. Who knew he was such a player, though? Gotta give him a bit of respect for that.'

'You can give some respect, if you like. Not me. He was playing a dangerous game, and he got found out.'

Ant chuckled. 'Bob the babe magnet.'

'Ugh. Don't. Anyway, there was a bit of a hoo-hah at the vet's. Simon, the one who was supplying meds to Eddie, has done a runner. He was meant to be on duty today – he's left them high and dry.'

'Can vets get struck off?'

'I don't know,' said Bea. 'Wouldn't be surprised. He'll get arrested anyway if the police catch up with him. Tom reckoned it took two people to tip that poor lad off the bypass bridge. Could well have been Simon. Any word on Tank?'

'Oh yeah, I was going to say. I heard from Saggy, who heard from his brother, who heard from Tank's cousin, that Tank's out of danger. They're still talking about life-changing injuries, whatever that means.'

Bea pulled a face. 'Sounds pretty grim to me.'

'Yeah.' Ant dropped the remains of his cigarette on the path and ground it out beneath his trainer.

'You did a good thing there, Ant. Looking after him until the ambulance came. You're ace at that First Aid stuff, really ace.'

'I like it. I seem to know what to do. It's cool.'

'Maybe you could do some more training,' said Bea.

'I don't think Costsave would stretch to any more.'

'No, I meant proper training. Whatever you have to do to be a paramedic.'

'Jeez, Bea. I'm way too thick for that. Don't you remember?'

'Ant, you're not thick. You just haven't learnt to read yet. Once you do, it'll all open up for you. Trust me.'

'Like you, on the checkouts at Costsave.'

'Ouch.' She sent him a reproachful look.

'Sorry,' he said. 'It's just a big jump from here to there. Where I am now to becoming a paramedic.'

'So? Someone told me you jumped from the school library window to the roof of the science block, back in the day.'

He grinned. 'Oh yeah. I did do that.'

'Took some balls, I should think. This is the same, only different. And you'll need to start at the beginning. There are adult literacy classes at the library.'

'Yeah?'

'Yeah. Think about it.'

'I will.'

As they'd been talking, they had watched Goldie delicately bobbing down and anointing the border. Now she padded back towards the house and Ant and Bea followed.

'I've got to go, Bea,' said Ant. 'I've got a date. You going to give Jay a call?'

'Not today. I've got a date with a guy with dark brooding looks and a fancy horse.' Ant's eyebrows approached his hairline. 'I'm going to get my PJs on, curl up with a dog at my feet and watch *Poldark* with Queenie.'

'Ha! I'll get off, then.'

Bea watched from the kitchen doorway as he walked along the back path towards the side of the house.

'Ant!' she called, before he disappeared.

He stopped and looked back. 'Yeah?'

'I'm glad you're not going,' said Bea.

'Are you?'

'Yeah. 'Cos if we'd lost touch, how would I have been able to find you when I turned thirty?'

A slow grin spread across his face. 'Yeah, man,' he said. 'Ten years' time, you and me, Bea. You and me.'

Acknowledgements

I'd like to thank everyone at Sandstone Press, especially Kay, my editor, for her insight and good sense, and Bob, Moira, Ceris and Sue. Thank you also to Keara and Taran who worked on *The Cost of Living*. I'm also very grateful to David Wardle, who designed the beautiful cover for this and the previous book, and, of course, to my brilliant agent Kirsty McLachlan, for believing in Ant and Bea (and me).

As ever, I'm indebted to my family for supporting me, reassuring me and taking the mickey when necessary – Ali and Pete, and, most of all, Ozzy, who demonstrates every day that keeping going is a sort of heroism.

Have you read the first in the series?

'Utterly fresh and real' Fleur Hitchcock

THE COST OF LIVING

AN ANT & BEA MYSTERY

RACHEL WARD

'Ant and Bea are fabulous' Sophia Bennett

After a young woman is brutally attacked on her way home from the local supermarket, checkout girl Bea and trainee Ant are determined to find out who's responsible. Customers and colleagues become suspects, secrets are uncovered, and while fear stalks the town, Bea risks losing the people she loves most.

www.sandstonepress.com

 facebook.com/SandstonePress/

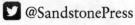 @SandstonePress